THE SHIPS OF EARTH

TOR BOOKS BY ORSON SCOTT CARD

The Folk of the Fringe
Future on Fire (editor)
Saints
Songmaster
The Worthing Saga
Wyrms

THE TALES OF ALVIN MAKER

Seventh Son
Red Prophet
Prentice Alvin

ENDER

Ender's Game
Speaker for the Dead
Xenocide

HOMECOMING

The Memory of Earth
The Call of Earth
The Ships of Earth

SHORT FICTION

Maps in a Mirror: The Short Fiction of Orson Scott Card (hardcover)
Maps in a Mirror, Volume 1: The Changed Man (paperback)
Maps in a Mirror, Volume 2: Flux (paperback)
Maps in a Mirror, Volume 3: Cruel Miracles (paperback)
Maps in a Mirror, Volume 4: Monkey Sonatas (paperback)

THE SHIPS OF EARTH

HOMECOMING
VOLUME 3

ORSON SCOTT CARD

A Tom Doherty Associates Book
New York

THE SHIPS OF EARTH

This book is printed on acid-free paper.

Map by Ellisa Mitchell

A Tor Book
Published by Tom Doherty Associates, Inc.
175 Fifth Avenue
New York, N.Y. 10010

Library of Congress Cataloging-in-Publication Data

Card, Orson Scott.
The ships of Earth / Orson Scott Card.
p. cm — (Homecoming ; v. 3)
"A Tom Doherty Associates Book."
ISBN 0-312-85659-8
1. Life on other planets–Fiction. I. Title. II. Series: Card, Orson Scott. Homecoming ; v. 3.
PS3553.A655S47 1994 93-42549
813′.54—dc20 CIP

First trade edition: February 1994

Printed in the United States of America

0 9 8 7 6 5 4 3 2 1

To Bill and Laraine Moon
with fond memories of temples and malls,
of copy machines and newsletters,
of great kids and good company;
of love freely given and honor unyielding.

ACKNOWLEDGMENTS

This was the novel that fate did not want me to write. I had set aside a good part of the summer to write it—even canceled a free trip to Australia because it would have come right in the middle of this project. Then, because that's how the world works, I suddenly found myself touring America signing copies of *Xenocide*, which for various excellent reasons had been released a couple of months early. Then, when I got home, we were caught up in the process of getting ready to move across town into a new house—we were going to be renters no more! Add to that the seductive details of remodeling the new house to contain not so much us as our computers, and I could see there was no way I'd be able to concentrate on writing *Ships of Earth* unless I went into hiding.

Which is precisely what I did. Poor Clark and Kathy Kidd! They must have thought that somehow, accidentally, back in the Pleistocene, they had spawned a child who now had come home to live with them! I descended on their house in Sterling, Virginia, took over their dining-room table, and then buried myself in writing. I surfaced only when two different computers failed on me and I had to whine and beg for Northgate to replace them. And when Clark and Kathy got a free weekend at Rehoboth Beach, there I was, tagging along—the first draft of Chapter 6 has Delaware sand in it. Yet through it all, the Kidds pretended they were having a wonderful time, and I'm grateful to them.

Much as I owe Clark and Kathy, though, I owe as much again to my wife, Kristine, and our assistant, Erin Absher, who kept our home running, our children alive, and the remodeling of the new house on track despite a plethora of disasters, major and minor. Kristine also managed to *read* this book and comment on it, making me take out the really icky parts—which greatly improved the novel, you may be sure! I can't write without peace of mind, and that was the gift that, among them, Kristine and Erin and Clark and Kathy gave to me, each in their own way.

I must also tip my hat to Shirley Strum, author of *Almost Human*, the book that gave me the baboons in *Ships of Earth*, which are some of my favorite characters; and to Beth Meacham, my editor, and Barbara Bova, my agent: Thank you for enduring all my whimpering, and helping me in so many ways that the public will never know about and that I will never forget.

CONTENTS

From Basilica to Dostatok
GREAT WESTERN DESERT
N
S
E
W
Gollod
Pravo Gollossa
– now called Gollossit
Gorayni
Sumasshedshyee
Ploshi
Khlam
Uslavat
Revis
Ulye
Nakayalnu
Basilica
Izmennik
Seggidugu
Cities of the Plain
Valley of Mebbeken
Lyudy Mts
Razoryat Mts
Potokgavan
Krutchni Valley
Earthbound Sea
Poras
Dorova Bay
Shazor
Scour Sea
Rivers Oykib and

Key
Route of Volemak's Company
Caravan route
Territorial boundaries
Rivers
Cities of Fire
Valley
Zheeyn River
Sea of Fire
Raspyutny
Dalatoi Mts.
Sea of Stars
Cities of the Stars
Caravan route
Caravan Route
Vusadka
Dostatok
1993
Ellisa Mitchell

NOTES ON PARENTAGE

Because of the marriage customs in the city of Basilica, family relationships can be somewhat complex. Perhaps these parentage charts can help keep things straight. Women's names are in italics.

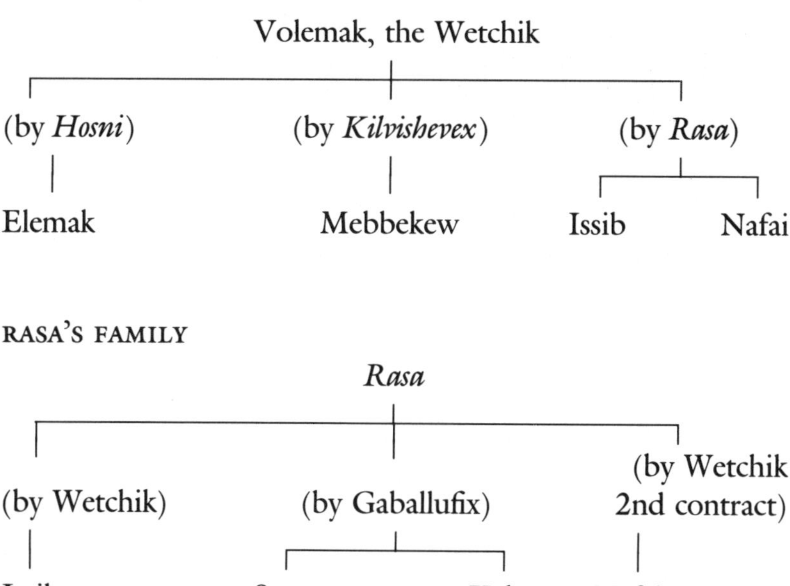

RASA'S NIECES

(her prize students, "adopted" into a permanent relationship of sponsorship)

Shedemei *Dol* *Eiadh* *Hushidh* and *Luet* (sisters)

HOSNI'S FAMILY

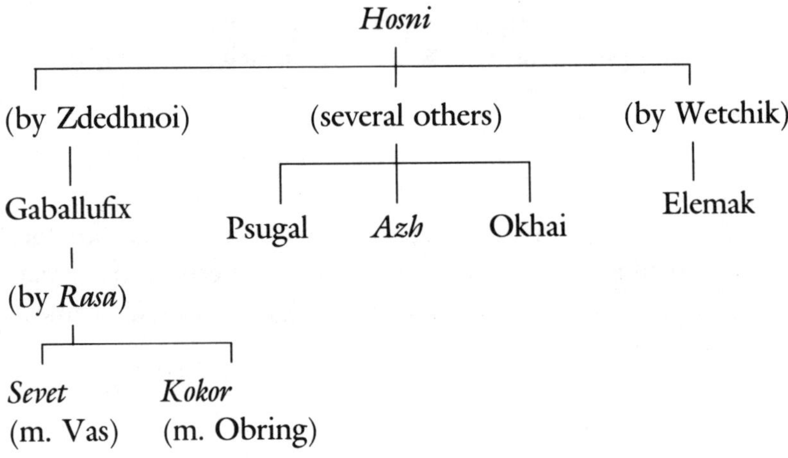

NICKNAMES

Most names have diminutive or familiar forms. Thus Gaballufix's near kin, close friends, current mate, and former mates could call him Gabya. Other nicknames are listed here. (Again, because these names are so unfamiliar, names of female characters are set off in italics.)

Basilikya—Syelsika—Skiya
Chveya—Veya
Dabrota—Dabya
Dol—Dolya
Dza—Dazya
Eiadh—Edhya
Elemak—Elya
Hushidh—Shuya
Issib—Issya
Izuchaya—Zuya
Kokor—Koya
Krasata—Krassya
Luet—Lutya
Mebbekew—Meb
Motiga—Motya
Nadezhny—Nadya
Nafai—Nyef
Obring—Briya
Oykib—Okya
Padarok—Rokya
Panimanya—Panya-Manya
Protchnu—Proya
Rasa—(no diminutive)
Serp—Sepya
Sevet—Sevya
Shedemei—Shedya
Spel—Spelya
Umene—Umya

Vas—Vasya
Vasnaminanya—Vasnya
Volemak—Volya
Yasai—Yaya
Zalatoya—Toya
Zaxodh—Xodhya
Zdorab—Zodya
Zhatva—Zhyat
Zhavaronok—Nokya

NOTES ON NAMES

For the purpose of reading this story, it hardly matters whether the reader pronounces the names of the characters correctly. But for those who might be interested, here is some information concerning the pronunciation of names.

The rules of vowel formation in the language of Basilica require that in most words, at least one vowel be pronounced with a leading *y* sound. With names, it can be almost any vowel, and it can legitimately be changed at the speaker's preference. Thus the name Gaballufix could be pronounced G*yah*-BAH-loo-fix or Gah-BAH-l*yoo*-fix; it happens that Gaballufix himself preferred to pronounce it Gah-BYAH-loo-fix, and of course most people followed that usage.

Basilikya [byah-see-lee-KEE-ya]
Chveya [shvey-YA]
Dabrota [dah-BROH-tyah]
Dol [DYOHL]
Dza [dzee-YAH]
Eiadh [A-yahth]
Elemak [EL-yeh-mahk]
Hushidh [HYOO-sheeth]
Issib [IS-yib]
Izuchaya [yee-zoo-CHA-yah]
Kokor [KYOH-kor]
Krasata [krah-SSYAH-tah]

Luet [LYOO-et]
Mebbekew [MEB-bek-kyoo]
Motiga [myoh-TEE-gah]
Nadezhny [nah-DYEZH-nee]
Nafai [NYAH-fie]
Oykib [OY-kyib]
Padarok [PYAH-dah-rohk]
Protchnu [PRYO-tchnu]
Rasa [RAHZ-yah]
Serp [SYAIRP]
Sevet [SEV-yet]
Shedemei [SHYED-eh-may]
Spel [SPYEHL]
Umene [ooh-MYEH-neh]
Vas [VYAHSS]
Vasnaminanya [vahss-nah-mee-NAH-nyah]
Volemak [VOHL-yeh-mak]
Yasai [YAH-sai]
Zalatoya [zah-lyah-TOH-yah]
Zaxodh [ZYAH-chothe]
Zdorab [ZDOR-yab]
Zhatva [ZHYAT-vah]
Zhavaronok [zhah-VYA-roh-nohk]

PROLOGUE

The master computer of the planet Harmony was full of hope at last. The chosen human beings had been drawn together and removed from the city of Basilica. Now they were embarked on the first of two journeys. This one would take them through the desert, through the Valley of Fires, to the southern tip of the island once called Vusadka, to a place where no human being had set foot for forty million years. The second journey would be from that place across a thousand lightyears to the home planet of the human species, Earth, abandoned forty million years ago and ready now for human beings to return.

Not just any human beings. *These* human beings. The ones born, after a million generations of guided evolution, with the strongest ability to communicate with the master computer, mind to mind, memory to memory. However, in encouraging people with this power to mate and therefore enhance it in their offspring, the master computer had not made any attempt to choose only the nicest or most obedient, or even the most intelligent or skillful. That was not within the purview of the computer's program. People could be more difficult or less difficult, more or less dangerous, more or less useful, but the master computer had not been programmed to show preference for decency or wit.

The master computer had been set in place by the first settlers on the planet Harmony for one purpose only—to preserve the human species by restraining it from the technologies that allowed wars and empires to spread so far that they could destroy a planet's ability to sustain human life, as had occurred on Earth. As long as men could fight only with hand weapons and could travel only on horseback, the world could endure, while the humans on it would remain free to be as good or evil as they chose.

Since that original programming, however, the master computer's hold on humanity had weakened. Some people were able to communicate with the master computer more clearly than anyone had ever imagined would be possible. Others, however, had only the weakest of connections. The result was that new weapons and new methods of transportation were beginning to enter the world, and while it might yet be thousands or tens of thousands of years before the end, the end would still come. And the master computer of Harmony had no idea of how to reverse the process.

This made it urgent enough for the master computer to attempt to return to Earth, where the Keeper of Earth could introduce new programming. But in recent months the master computer and some of its human allies discovered that the Keeper of Earth was already, somehow, introducing change. Different people had dreamed clear and powerful dreams of creatures that had never existed on Harmony, and the master computer itself discovered subtle alterations in its own programming. It should have been impossible for the Keeper of Earth to influence events so far away . . . and yet that entity which had dispatched the original refugee ships forty million years before was the only imaginable source of these changes.

How or why the Keeper of Earth was doing this, the master computer of the planet Harmony could not begin to guess. It only knew that forty million years had not been kind to its own systems, and it needed replenishment. It only knew that whatever the Keeper of Earth asked for, the master computer of Harmony would try to supply. It asked now for a group of human beings to recolonize the Earth.

So the master computer chose sixteen people from the population of Basilica. Many were kin to each other; all had unusual ability to communicate with the master computer. However, they were not all terribly bright, and not all were particularly trustworthy or kind. Many of them had strong dislikes or resentments toward others, and while some of them were committed to the master computer's cause, some were just as committed to thwarting it. The whole enterprise might fail at any time, if the darker impulses of the humans could not be curbed. Civilization was always fragile, even when strong social forces inhibited individual passions; now, cut off from the larger world, would they be able to forge a new, smaller, harmonious society? Or would the expedition be destroyed from the beginning?

The master computer had to plan and act as if the expedition would survive, would succeed. In a certain place the master computer triggered a sequence of events. Machinery that had long been silent began to hum. Robots that had long been in stasis were awakened and set to work, searching for machines that needed repair. They had waited a long, long time, and even in a stasis field they could not last forever.

It would take several years to determine just how much work would be needed, and how it should or even could be done. But there was no hurry. If the journey took time, then perhaps the people could use that time to make peace with each other. There was no hurry; or rather, no hurry that would be detectable to human beings. To the master computer, accomplishing a task within ten years was a breathless pace, while to humans it could seem unbearably long. For though the master computer could detect the passage of milliseconds, it had memories of forty million years of life on Harmony so far, and on that scale, compared to the normal human lifespan, ten years was as brief a span of time as five minutes.

The master computer would use those years well and productively, and hoped the people could manage to do the same. If they were wise, it would be a time in which they could create their families, bear and begin to raise many children, and develop into a community worthy to return to the Keeper of Earth. However, that would be no easy achievement, and at the moment all the master computer could really hope for was to keep them all alive.

ONE

THE LAW OF THE DESERT

Shedemei was a scientist, not a desert traveler. She had no great need for city comforts—she was as content sleeping on a floor or table as on a bed—but she resented having been dragged away from her laboratory, from her work, from all that gave her life meaning. She had never agreed to join this half-mad expedition. Yet here she was, atop a camel in the dry heat of the desert wind, rocking back and forth as she watched the backside of the camel in front of her sway in another rhythm. It made her faintly sick, the heat and the motion. It gave her a headache.

Several times she almost turned back. She could find the way well enough; all she had to do was get close enough to Basilica and her computer would link up with the city and show her the rest of the way home. Alone, she'd make much better time—perhaps she could even be back before nightfall. And they would surely let her into the city—she wasn't kin by blood or marriage to anyone else in this group. The only reason she had been exiled with them was because she had arranged for the dryboxes full of seeds and embryos that would reestablish some semblance of the old flora and fauna on Earth. She had done a favor for her old teacher, that's all—they could hardly force her into exile for *that*.

Yet that cargo was the reason she did not turn back. Who else would understand how to revive the myriad species carried on these camels? Who else would know which ones needed to go first, to establish themselves before later species came that would have to feed on them?

It's not fair, thought Shedemei for the thousandth time. I'm the only one in this party who can begin to do this task—but for me, it's not a challenge at all. It's not *science,* it's *agriculture.* I'm here, not because the task the Oversoul has chosen me for is so demanding, but because all the others are so deeply ignorant of it.

"You look angry and miserable."

Shedemei turned to see that it was Rasa who had brought her camel up beside Shedemei's on the wide stony path. Rasa, her teacher—almost her mother. But not *really* her mother, not by blood, not by *right*.

"Yes," said Shedemei.

"At me?" asked Rasa.

"Partly you," said Shedemei. "You maneuvered us all into this. I have no connection with any of these people, except through you."

"We all have the same connection," said Rasa. "The Oversoul sent you a dream, didn't she?"

"I didn't ask for it."

"Which of us did?" said Rasa. "No, I do understand what you mean, Shedya. The others all made choices that got them into this. Nafai and Luet and Hushidh and I have come willingly . . . more or less. And Elemak and Meb, not to mention my daughters, bless their nasty little hearts, are here because they made some stupid and vile decisions. The others are here because they have marriage contracts, though for some of them it's merely compounding the original mistake to come along.

But you, Shedemei, all that brings you here is your dream. And your loyalty to me."

The Oversoul had sent her a dream of floating through the air, scattering seeds and watching them grow, turning a desert land into forest and meadow, filled with greenery, abounding with animals. Shedemei looked around at the bleak desert landscape, seeing the few thorny plants that clung to life here and there, knowing that a few lizards lived on the few insects that found water enough to survive. "*This* is not my dream," said Shedemei.

"But you came," said Rasa. "Partly for the dream, and partly out of love for me."

"There's no hope of succeeding, you know," said Shedemei. "These aren't colonizers here. Only Elemak has the skill to survive."

"He's the one who's *most* experienced in desert travel. Nyef and Meb are doing well enough, for their part. And the rest of us will learn."

Shedemei fell silent, not wanting to argue.

"I hate it when you back away from a quarrel like that," said Rasa.

"I don't like conflict," said Shedemei.

"But you always back off at exactly the moment when you're about to tell the other person *exactly* what she needs to hear."

"I don't know what other people need to hear."

"Say what you had on your mind a moment ago," said Rasa. "Tell me why you think our expedition is doomed to failure."

"Basilica," said Shedemei.

"We've *left* the city. It can't possibly harm us now."

"Basilica will harm us in a thousand ways. It will always be our memory of a gentle, easier life. We'll always be torn with longing to go back."

"It's not homesickness that worries you, though, surely," said Rasa.

"We carry half the city with us," said Shedemei. "All the diseases of the city, but none of its strengths. We have the custom of leisure, but none of the wealth and property that made it possible. We have become used to indulging too many of our appetites, which can never be indulged in a tiny colony like ours will be."

"People have left the city and gone colonizing before."

"Those who want to adapt *will* adapt, I know," said Shedemei. "But how many want to? How many have the will to set aside their own desires, to sacrifice for the good of us all? *I* don't even have that degree of commitment. I'm more furious with every kilometer we move farther away from my work."

"Well, then, we're fortunate," said Rasa. "Nobody else here *had* any work worth mentioning. And those who did have lost everything so they couldn't go back anyway."

"Meb's work is waiting for him there," said Shedemei.

Rasa looked baffled for a moment. "I'm not aware that Meb *had* any work, unless you mean his sad little career as an actor."

"I meant his lifelong project of coupling with every female in Basilica who wasn't actually blood kin of his, or unspeakably ugly, or dead."

"Oh," said Rasa, smiling wanly. "*That* work."

"And he's not the only one," said Shedemei.

"Oh, I know," said Rasa. "You're too kind to say it, but my own daughters are no doubt longing to take up where they left off on their own versions of that project."

"I don't mean to offend you," said Shedemei.

"I'm not offended. I know my daughters far too well. They have too much of their father in them for me not to know what to expect from them. But tell me, Shedya, which of these men do you honestly expect them to find attractive?"

"After a few weeks or a few days, *all* the men will start looking good to them."

Rasa laughed lightly. "I daresay you're right, my dear. But all the men in our little party are married—and you can bet that their wives will be looking out to make sure no one intrudes in their territory."

Shedemei shook her head. "Rasa, you're making a false assumption. Just because *you* have chosen to stay married to the same man, renewing him year after year since—well, since you gave birth to Nafai—that doesn't mean that any of the *other* women here are going to feel that possessive and protective of their husbands."

"You think not?" said Rasa. "My darling daughter Kokor almost killed her sister Sevet because she was sleeping with Kokor's husband Obring."

"So . . . Obring won't try to sleep with Sevet again. That doesn't stop him from trying for Luet, for instance."

"Luet!" said Rasa. "She's a wonderful girl, Shedya, but she's not beautiful in the way that a man like Obring looks for, and she's also *very* young, and she's plainly in love with Nafai, and most important of all, she's the waterseer of Basilica and Obring would be scared to death to approach her."

Shedemei shook her head. Didn't Rasa see that *all* these arguments would fade to unimportance with the passage of time? Didn't she understand that people like Obring and Meb, Kokor and Sevet lived for the hunt, and cared very little who the quarry might be?

"And if you think Obring might try for Eiadh, I'd laugh out loud," said Rasa. "Oh, yes, he might *wish,* but Eiadh is a girl who loves and admires only strength in a man, and that is one virtue that Obring will never have. No, I think Obring will be quite faithful to Kokor."

"Rasa, my dear teacher and friend," said Shedemei, "before this month is out Obring will even have tried to seduce *me*."

Rasa looked at Shedemei with a startlement she could not conceal. "Oh, now," she said. "You're not his—"

"His type is whatever woman hasn't told him *no* recently," said Shedemei. "And I warn you—if there's one thing our group is too small to endure, it's sexual tension. If we were like baboons, and our females were only sexually attractive a few times between pregnancies, we could have the kind of improvised short-term matings that baboons have. We could endure the periodic conflicts between males because they would end very quickly and we'd have peace the rest of the year. But we're human, unfortunately, and we bond differently. Our children need stability and peace. And there are too few of us to take a few murders here and there in stride."

"Murders," said Rasa. "Shedemei, what's got into you?"

"Nafai has already killed one man," said Shedemei. "And he's probably the *nicest* of this group, except perhaps Vas."

"The Oversoul told him to."

"Yes, so Nafai's the one man in this group who obeys the Oversoul. The others are even more likely to obey *their* god."

"Which is?"

"It dangles between their legs," said Shedemei.

"You biologists have such a cynical view of human beings," said Rasa. "You'd think we were the lowest of animals."

"Oh, not the lowest. Our males don't try to eat their young."

"And our females don't devour their mates," said Rasa.

"Though some have tried."

They both laughed. They had been talking fairly quietly, and their camels were well separated from the others, but their laughter bridged the distance, and others turned to look at them.

"Don't mind us!" called Rasa. "We weren't laughing at you!"

But Elemak *did* mind them. He had been riding near the front of the caravan. Now he turned his animal and came back along the line until he reached them. His face was coldly angry.

"Try to have a little self-control, Lady Rasa," said Elemak.

"What," said Rasa, "my laughter was too loud?"

"Your laughter—and then your little jest. All at top volume. A woman's voice can be carried on this breeze for miles. This desert isn't thickly populated, but if anybody *does* hear you, you can find yourself raped, robbed, and killed in a remarkably short time."

Shedemei knew that Elemak was right, of course—he was the one who had led caravans through the desert. But she hated the condescension in his tone, the sarcasm. No man had a right to speak to Lady Rasa that way.

Yet Rasa herself seemed oblivious to the insult implied by Elya's attitude. "A group as large as ours?" asked Rasa innocently. "I thought robbers would stay away."

"They *pray* for groups like ours," said Elemak. "More women than men. Traveling slowly. Heavily burdened. Talking carelessly aloud. Two women drifting back and separating from the rest of the group."

Only then did Shedemei realize how vulnerable she and Rasa had been. It frightened her. She wasn't used to thinking this way—thinking about how to avoid getting attacked. In Basilica she had always been safe. *Women* had always been safe in Basilica.

"And you might take another look at the men of our caravan," said Elemak. "Which of them do you expect can fight for you and save you from a band of even three or four robbers, let alone a dozen?"

"*You* can," said Rasa.

Elemak regarded her steadily for a moment or two. "Here in the open, where they'd have to show themselves for some distance, I suppose I could. But I'd rather not have to. So keep up and shut up. Please."

The *please* at the end did little to ameliorate the sternness of his tone, but that did not keep Shedemei from deciding wholeheartedly to obey him. She did not have Rasa's confidence that Elemak could single-handedly protect them from even small numbers of marauders.

Elemak glanced briefly at Shedemei, but his expression carried no meaning that she could interpret. Then he wheeled his camel and it lurched on ahead toward the front of the little caravan.

"It'll be interesting to see whether it's your husband or Elemak who rules once we reach Wetchik's camp," said Shedemei.

"Pay no attention to Elya's bluster," said Rasa. "It will be my husband who rules."

"I wouldn't be too sure. Elemak takes to authority quite naturally."

"Oh, he likes the feel of it," said Rasa. "But he doesn't know how to maintain it except through fear. Doesn't he realize that the Oversoul is protecting this expedition? If any marauders so much as think of passing this way, the Oversoul will make them forget the idea. We're as safe as if we were home in bed."

Shedemei did not remind her that only a few days ago they had felt quite unsafe in their beds. Nor did she mention that Rasa had just proved Shedemei's own point—when Rasa thought of home and safety, it was Basilica she had in mind. The ghost of their old life in the city was going to haunt them for a long time to come.

Now it was Kokor's turn to stop her beast and wait for Rasa to catch up. "You were bad, weren't you, Mama?" she said. "Did nasty old Elemak have to come and tell you off?"

Shedemei was disgusted at Kokor's little-girl silliness—but then, Kokor usually disgusted her. Her attitude always seemed false and manipulative; to Shedemei the wonder of it was that these pathetically obvious ploys must work on people fairly often, or Kokor would have found new ones.

Well, whoever Kokor's little-girl act worked on, it *wasn't* her own mother. Rasa simply fixed Koya with an icy stare and said, "Shedya and I were having a private conversation, my dear. I'm sorry if you misunderstood and thought we had invited you to join us."

It took just a moment for Kokor to understand; when she did, her face darkened for a moment—with anger? Then she gave a prim little smile to Shedemei and said, "Mother is perpetually disappointed that I didn't turn out like *you* Shedya. But I'm afraid neither my brain nor my body had enough *inner* beauty." Then, awkwardly, Kokor got her camel moving faster and soon she was ahead of them again.

Shedemei knew that Kokor had meant to insult her by reminding her that the only kind of beauty she would ever have was the inner kind. But Shedemei had long since grown out of her adolescent jealousy of pulchritudinous girls.

Rasa must have been thinking the same thoughts. "Odd, isn't it, that physically plain people are perfectly able to see physical beauty in others, while people who are morally maimed are blind to goodness and decency. They honestly think it doesn't exist."

"Oh, they know it exists, all right," said Shedemei. "They just never know which people have it. Not that my feelings at this moment would prove me to be a moral beauty."

"Having thoughts of murder, were you?" said Rasa.

"Oh, nothing so direct or final," said Shedemei. "I was just wishing for her to develop truly awful saddle sores."

"And Elemak? Did you wish some uncomfortable curse on him?"

"Not at all," said Shedemei. "Perhaps, as you say, he didn't need to try to frighten us into obedience. But I think he was right. After all, the Oversoul hasn't had exactly a perfect record in keeping us out of danger. No, I harbor no resentment toward Elya."

"I wish I were as mature as you, then. I found myself resenting the way he spoke to me. So condescending. I know *why*, of course—he feels my status in the city is a threat to *his* authority out here, so he has to put me in my place. But he should realize that I'm wise enough to follow his leadership without his having to humiliate me first."

"It isn't a question of what *you* need," said Shedemei. "It never is. It's a question of what *he* needs. He needs to feel superior to you. For that matter, so do I, you silly old woman."

For a moment Rasa looked at her in horror. Then, just as Shedemei was about to explain that she was *joking*—why didn't anybody ever understand her humor?—Rasa grinned at her. "I'd rather be a silly old woman than a silly young one," she said. "Silly *old* women don't make such spectacular mistakes."

"Oh, I don't know about that," said Shedemei. "Coming on this expedition, for instance . . . "

"A mistake?"

"For me it certainly is. My life is genetics, but the closest I'm going to come to it for the rest of my life is if I manage to reproduce my *own* genes."

"You sound so despairing. Having children isn't all that awful. They aren't *all* Kokor, and even she may grow up to be human someday."

"Yes, but you *loved* your husbands," said Shedemei. "Whom will I end up with, Aunt Rasa? Your crippled son? Or Gaballufix's librarian?"

"I think Hushidh plans to marry Issib," said Rasa. Her voice was cold, but Shedemei didn't care.

"Oh, I know how you've got us sorted out. But tell me, Aunt Rasa, if Nafai hadn't happened to drag the librarian along with him when he was stealing the Index . . . would you have arranged to bring *me*?"

Rasa's face was positively stony. She didn't answer for a long time.

"Come now, Aunt Rasa. I'm not a fool, and I'd rather you not try to fool me."

"We needed your skills, Shedya. The Oversoul chose you, not me."

"You're sure it wasn't *you,* counting up males and females and making sure we came out even?"

"The Oversoul sent you that dream."

"The sad thing is," said Shedemei, "that except for you there's not a one of us that's a proven reproducer. For all you know, you've set up one of these men with a sterile wife. Or perhaps you've put one of us women with a sterile husband."

Rasa's anger was beginning to turn from cold to hot now. "I told you, it wasn't *my* choice . . . Luet had a vision, too, and—"

"*Are* you going to set the example? *Are* you going to have more children, Aunt Rasa?"

Rasa seemed completely nonplussed. "Me? At my age?"

"You've still got a few good eggs in you. I know you haven't reached menopause, because you're flowing now."

Rasa looked at her in consternation. "Why don't I just lie down under one of your microscopes?"

"You'd never fit. I'd have to slice you razor thin."

"Sometimes I feel as if you already had."

"Rasa, you make us stop several times a day. I *know* you have better bladder control than that. We *all* know you're shedding the tears of the moon."

Rasa raised her eyebrows briefly, a sort of facial shrug. "More children indeed."

"I think you must. To set an example for all of us," said Shedemei. "Don't you understand that we're not just taking a trip. We're a *colony*. The first priority of colonists is reproduction. Anyone who isn't having babies is next to worthless. And no matter how envious Elemak is of your authority, you *are* the leader of the women here. You must set the pattern for us all. If *you* are willing to get pregnant during this trip, the others will fall into line, particularly since their husbands will feel the need to demonstrate that they can get a woman just as pregnant as old Wetchik can."

"He's not Wetchik anymore," said Rasa irrelevantly. "He's Volemak."

"He can still perform, can't he?"

"Really, Shedemei, is there anything you won't ask? Would you like us to provide stool samples for you next?"

"Before this journey is over I imagine I'll be looking at samples of almost everything. I'm the closest thing to a physician we have."

Rasa suddenly chuckled. "I can just see Elemak bringing you a semen sample."

Shedemei had to laugh, too, at the very idea of asking him. Such an assault on his dignity as leader of the caravan!

They rode together in silence for a few minutes. Then Rasa spoke. "Will you do it?" she asked.

"Do what?"

"Marry Zdorab?"

"Who?"

"The librarian, Zdorab."

"Marry him," sighed Shedemei. "I never meant to marry anyone."

"Marry him and have his babies."

"Oh, I suppose I will," said Shedemei. "But *not* if we live under baboon law."

"Baboon law!"

"Like Basilica—with a competition for new mates every year. I'll take this middle-aged man that I've never seen, I'll let him bed me, I'll bear his children, I'll raise them with him—but not if I have to fight to keep him. Not if I have to watch him court Eiadh or Hushidh or Dolya or—or *Kokor*—every time our marriage contract is about to expire, and then come crawling back to me and ask me to renew his contract for another year *only* because none of the truly desirable women would have him."

Rasa nodded. "I see now what you were trying to say before. It wasn't about Kokor's infidelity, it was about the customs we all grew up with."

"Exactly," said Shedemei. "We're too small a group to keep the old marriage customs of Basilica."

"It's really just a matter of scale, isn't it," said Rasa. "In the city when a woman doesn't renew a man, or when he doesn't ask, you can avoid each other for a while until the pain wears off. You can find someone else, because there are so many thousands to choose from. But we'll have exactly sixteen people. Eight men, eight women. It would be unbearable."

"Some would want to kill, the way Kokor tried to do," said Shedemei. "And others would wish to die."

"You're right, you're right, you're right," murmured Rasa, thinking aloud now, it seemed. "But we can't tell them now. Some of them would turn back—desert or no desert, bandits or no bandits. Lifelong monogamy—why, I doubt that Sevet and Kokor have ever been faithful for a whole week. And Meb hadn't married till now for the good reason that he has no intention of being faithful but lacks my daughters' ability to behave with complete dishonesty. And now we're going to tell them that they *must* remain faithful. No one-year contracts, no chance to change."

"They're not going to like it."

"So we won't tell them until we're at Volemak's camp. When it's far too late for them to turn back."

Shedemei could hardly believe she had heard Rasa say such a thing. Still, she answered mildly. "Except it occurs to me," she said, "that if they want to turn back, perhaps we should let them. They're free people, aren't they?"

Rasa turned fiercely to her. "No, they aren't," she said. "They were free until they made the choices that brought them here, but now they're *not* free because our colony, our *journey* can't succeed without them."

"You're so certain you can hold people to their commitments," murmured Shedemei. "No one's ever made them do that before. Can you now?"

"It's not just for the sake of the expedition," said Rasa. "It's for their own good. The Oversoul has made it clear that Basilica is going to be destroyed—and them with it, if they're still there when the time comes. We're saving their lives. But the ones most likely to turn back are also the ones least likely to believe in the visions the Oversoul has shown us. So to save their lives we must—"

"Deceive them?"

"Withhold some explanations until later."

"Because you know so much better than they do what's good for them?"

"Yes," said Rasa. "Yes, I do."

It infuriated Shedemei. All that Rasa had said was true enough, but it didn't change Shedemei's conviction that people had the right to choose even their own destruction, if they wanted. Maybe that was another luxury of living in Basilica, having the right to destroy yourself through your own stupidity or shortsightedness, but if so it was a luxury that Shedemei was not yet ready to give up. It was one thing to tell people that faithful monogamy was one of the conditions of staying with the group. Then they could choose whether to stay and obey or leave and live by another rule. But to lie to them until it was too late to choose . . . it was *freedom* that was at stake here, and it was freedom that made survival worthwhile. "Aunt Rasa," said Shedemei, "*you* are not the Oversoul."

And with that remark, Shedemei urged her camel to move faster, leaving Rasa behind her. Not that Shedemei had nothing more she could have said. But she was too angry to stay there; the idea of quarreling with Aunt Rasa was unbearable. Shedemei hated to argue with anyone. It always set her to brooding for days. And she had enough to brood about as it was.

Zdorab. What kind of man becomes an archivist for a power-hungry killer like Gaballufix? What kind of man lets a boy like Nafai manipulate him into betraying his trust, giving up the precious Index, and then *follows* the thief right out of the city? What kind of man then lets Nafai wrestle him into submission and extract an oath from him to go out into the desert and never see Basilica again?

Shedemei knew *exactly* what kind of man: a tedious stupid weakling. A shy dull-witted coward who will formally ask my permission before each of his studious attempts to impregnate me. A man who will neither take nor give joy in our marriage. A man who will wish he had married any one of the other women here rather than me, but who will stay with me only because he knows that none of them would have him.

Zdorab, my husband-to-be. I can't wait to meet you.

The tents went up more smoothly their third night in the desert. Everyone knew well now which jobs they had to do—and which they could avoid. Rasa noticed with contempt that both Meb and Obring managed to spend more than half their time "helping" their wives do jobs that were already childishly easy—they *had* to be, or neither Dolya nor Kokor would have done them. Not that Dol wasn't willing to work sometimes, but as long as Kokor and Sevet weren't doing much that was worthwhile, she would not put herself beneath them. After all, Dol had been a starring actress when Kokor and Sevet were still chirping out their little children's songs. Rasa knew how Dol's mind worked. Status first, *then* human decency.

But at least decency was on her list! Who *are* these people I have raised and taught? The ones who are too selfish to endure threaten our peace, and yet some of the others are so compliant with the Oversoul that I fear even more for them.

I am not in charge of their lives now, Rasa reminded herself. I am in charge of getting the tent lines taut enough that it won't collapse in the first wind.

"It *will* collapse in a bad wind, no matter what you do," said Elemak. "So you don't have to make it strong enough to withstand a hurricane."

"Just a sandstorm?" Rasa felt a drop of sweat slip into her eye and sting, just as he spoke. She tried to wipe it away with her sleeve, but her arm was sweatier than her face, even under the light muslin.

"It's sweaty close work, no matter what the weather outside," said Elemak. "Let me."

He held the guyline tight while she cinched the knot into place. She well knew that he could just as easily have done the knot himself, without help holding the line. She saw at once what he was doing, making sure she learned her job, showing confidence in her, and letting her feel a sense of accomplishment when the tent held up. "You're good at this," she said.

"There's nothing hard about tying knots, once you learn them."

She smiled. "Ah, yes, knots. Is that what you're tying together here?"

He smiled back—and she could see that he *did* appreciate her praise. "Among other things, Lady Rasa."

"You are a leader of men," said Rasa. "I say this not as your stepmother, or even as your sister-in-law, but as a woman who has had some occasion of leadership myself. Even the lazy ones are ashamed to be too obvious about it." She did not mention that so far he had only succeeded in centering authority in himself—that no one had internalized anything yet, so that when he wasn't around, nothing happened. Perhaps that was all he had ever needed to learn about leadership during his years leading caravans. But if he meant to rule over this expedition (and Rasa was not such a fool as to think Elemak had any intention of allowing his father to have more than titular authority) he would have to learn how to do much more than make people dependent on him. The essence of leadership, my dear young ruler, is to make people *independent* and yet persuade them to follow you freely. Then they will obey the principles you've taught them even when your back is turned. But she could not say this to him aloud; he wasn't able yet to hear such counsel. So instead she continued to praise him, hoping to build his confidence until he *could* hear wise counsel. "And I've heard less argument and complaint from my daughters than I ever heard back when their lives were easy."

Elemak grimaced. "You know as well as I do that half of them would rather head back to Basilica this moment. I'm not sure that I'm not one of them."

"But we're not going back," said Rasa.

"I imagine it would be rather anticlimactic, returning to Moozh's city after he sent us away in such glory."

"Anticlimactic and dangerous," said Rasa.

"Well, Nafai *has* been cleared of the charge of killing my beloved half-brother Gaballufix."

"He's been cleared of nothing," said Rasa. "Nor, for that matter, have you, son of my husband."

"Me!" His face became hard and a little flushed. Not good, that he showed his emotion so easily. Not what a leader needed.

"I just want you to realize that returning to Basilica is out of the question."

"Be assured, Lady Rasa, that if I wanted to return to Basilica before seeing my father again, I would do so. And may *yet* do so after I see him."

She nodded slightly. "I'm glad that it cools off in the desert at night. So that we can bear the brutal heat of day, knowing the night will be gentle."

Elemak smiled. "I arranged it just for you, Lady Rasa."

"Shedemei and I were talking today," said Rasa.

"I know."

"About a very serious matter," said Rasa. "Something that could easily tear our colony apart. Sex, of course."

Elemak was instantly alert. "Yes?" he asked—but his voice was calm.

"In particular," said Rasa, "the matter of marriage."

"Everyone is paired up well enough for now," said Elemak. "None of the men are sleeping unsatisfied, which is better than the way it is with *most* of my caravans. As for you and Hushidh and Shedemei, you'll soon be with your husbands, or the men who will be their husbands."

"But for some it is not the coupling itself they desire, but rather the chase."

"I know," said Elemak. "But the choices are limited."

"And yet some are still choosing, even though their choice seems to be made."

She could see how he stiffened his back and his neck, pretending to be calm, refusing to lean toward her and ask her the question in his heart. He worries about Eiadh, his bride, his beloved. She had not realized he was so perceptive about her, that he would already worry.

"They must be held faithful to their spouses," said Rasa.

Elemak nodded. "I can't say that I've had the problem—on my caravans, the men are alone until we reach cities, and then it's whores for most of them."

"And for you?" said Rasa.

"I'm married now," said Elemak. "To a young wife. A good wife."

"A good wife for a young man," said Rasa.

A smile flickered at the corners of his mouth. "No one is young forever," he said.

"But will she be a good wife in five years? In ten?"

He looked at her strangely. "How should *I* know?"

"But you must think about it, Elya. What kind of wife will she be in fifty years?"

He looked dumbfounded. He had not thought ahead on this issue, and did not even know how to *pretend* he had thought ahead, it took him so much by surprise.

"Because what Shedemei was pointing out—confirming my own thoughts on the matter—is that there's no chance that we can continue the marriage customs of Basilica out here in the desert. Basilica was very large, and we will be but sixteen souls. Eight couples. When you abandon Eiadh for another, whom will she marry then?" Of course, Rasa knew—and knew that Elemak *also* knew—that it was far more likely that it would be Eiadh deciding not to renew her marriage contract with Elemak, and not the other way around. But the question was still the same—whom would Eiadh marry?

"And children," said Rasa. "There'll be children—but no schools to send them to. They'll stay with their mothers, and another man—other men—will rear them."

She could see that her account of the future was getting to him. She knew exactly what would worry him most, and Lady Rasa wasn't ashamed to use that knowledge. After all, the things she was warning him about were true.

"So you see, Elemak, that as long as we're just sixteen souls who must stay together in order to survive in the desert, marriage must be permanent."

Elemak did not look at her. But his thoughts were visible on his face as he sank down on the carpet that had been spread to make a floor for the tent, covering the sandy soil.

"We can't survive the quarreling," she said, "the hurt feelings—we'll be too close to each other all the time. They must be told. Your spouse now is your spouse forever."

Elemak lay back on the carpet. "Why would they listen to *me* on such a subject?" he said. "They'll think I'm saying that in order to try to keep Eiadh for myself. I happen to know that others have already looked with longing, expecting to court her when we've had our few years of marriage."

"So you must persuade them to accept the reasons for lifelong monogamous marriage—so they'll understand that it *isn't* a self-serving plan on your part."

"Persuade them?" Elemak hooted once, a single bitter laugh. "I doubt I could persuade Eiadh."

She could see that he regretted at once having said that last remark. It confessed too much. "Perhaps then persuasion isn't the term I want. They must be helped to understand that this is a law we must obey in order to keep this family from coming apart in an emotional and physical bloodbath, as surely as we must keep quiet during each traveling day."

Elemak sat up and leaned toward her, his eyes alight with—what, anger? Fear? Hurt? Is there something more to this than I understand? Rasa wondered.

"Lady Rasa," said Elemak, "is this law you want important enough to *kill* for?"

"Kill? Killing is the very thing that I most fear. It's what we must *avoid*."

"This is the desert, and when we reach Father's encampment it will still be the desert, and in the desert there is only one punishment for crime of any kind. Death."

"Don't be absurd," said Rasa.

"Whether you cut off his head or abandon him in the desert, it's all the same—out here exile *is* death."

"But I wouldn't dream of having a penalty so severe as *that*."

"Think about it, Lady Rasa. Where would we imprison somebody as we journey day to day? Who could spare the time to keep someone under guard? There's always flogging, of course, but then we would have to deal with an injured person and we couldn't travel safely anymore."

"What about withdrawing a privilege? Taking something away? Like a fine, the way they did it in Basilica."

"What do you take away, Lady Rasa? What privileges do any of us have? If we take away something the lawbreaker really *needs*—his shoes? his camel?—then we injure him anyway, and have to travel slower and put the whole group at risk. And if it isn't something he needs, but merely treasures, then you fill him with resentment and you have one more person you have to deal with but can't trust. No, Lady Rasa, if shame isn't strong enough to keep a man from breaking a law, then the only punishment that means anything is death. The lawbreaker will never break the law again, and everybody else knows you're serious. And any punishment short of death has the opposite result—the lawbreaker will simply do it again, and no one else will respect the law. That's why I say, before you decide that this should be the law during our travels, perhaps you ought to consider, is it worth killing for?"

"But no one will believe you'd kill anyway, would they?"

"You think not?" said Elemak. "I can tell you from experience that the hardest thing about punishing a man on a journey like that is telling his widow and his orphaned children why you didn't bring him home."

"Oh, Elemak, I never dreamed . . . "

"No one does. But the men of the desert know. And when you abandon a man instead of killing him outright, you don't give him any chance, either—no camel, no horse, not even any water. In fact, you tie him up so he can't even move, so the animals will get him quickly—because if he lives long enough, bandits might find him, and then he'll die far more cruelly, and in the process of dying he'll tell the bandits where you are, and how many you are, and how many you leave on watch, and where all your valuables are stored. He'll tell other things, too—the pet name he calls his woman, the nicknames of the guards, so the bandits'll know what to say in the darkness to confuse your party, to put them off their guard. He'll tell them—"

"Stop it!" cried Rasa. "You're doing this on purpose."

"You think that life in the desert is a matter of heat and cold, of camels and tents, of voiding your bowel in the sand and sleeping on rugs instead of on a bed. But I tell you that what

Father and you and Nafai, bless his heart, what you've all chosen for us—"

"What the *Oversoul* has chosen!"

"—is the hardest life imaginable, a dangerous and brutal world where death is breathing into the hair on the back of your head, and where you have to be ready to kill in order to maintain order."

"I'll think of something else," said Rasa. "Some other way of handling marriages . . . "

"But you won't," said Elemak. "You'll think and think, and in the end you'll come to the only conclusion. *If* this insane colony is to succeed, it must succeed in the desert and by desert law. That means that women will be faithful to their men, or they will die."

"And men, if *they're* unfaithful," said Rasa, sure that he couldn't possibly mean that only women would be punished.

"Oh, I see. If two people break this marriage law, you want them *both* to die, is that it? Who's the bloodthirsty one now? We can spare a woman more easily than a man. Unless you propose that I train Kokor and Sevet to fight. Unless you think Dol and Shedemei can really handle lifting the tents onto the camel's backs."

"So in your man-ruled world the woman bears the brunt of . . . "

"We're not in Basilica now, Lady Rasa. Women thrive where civilization is strong. Not here. No, if you think about it you'll see that punishing the woman alone is the surer way to keep the law. Because which man can whisper, 'I love you,' when they both know that what he really means is, 'I want to tup you so badly that I don't care if you die.' How much success will his seduction have then? And if he tries to force his way, she'll scream—because she'll know that it's her life at stake. And if he's taken for raping her, as she screams, why, then it *is* the man who dies. You see? It takes so much of the romance out of flirting."

* * *

Elemak almost laughed aloud at the stricken look on Rasa's face when he turned and left her tent. Oh, yes, she still fancied herself a leader, even out here in the desert where she knew less than nothing about survival, where she was a constant danger to everyone, with her chat, with her supposed wisdom that she was always *so* willing to share, with her air of command. She could bring off the illusion of power in Basilica, where women had men so fenced around with custom and manners that she could make decisions and people would comply. But here she would soon find—was already finding—that she lacked the true will to power. She wanted to rule, but didn't want to do the hard things that rule required.

Permanent marriage indeed. What woman could possibly satisfy a man of any strength for more than a year or two? He had never intended Eiadh to be anything more than a *first* wife. She would have been a great success at that role—she'd adorn him in his first Basilican household, bear him his firstborn, and then they'd both move on. Elemak even planned that Rasa herself would be his children's teacher—she did a fine job of schooling youngsters; Elemak knew what her true value was. But now to think that he would be willing to endure having Eiadh clinging to him when she was fat and old...

Except that in his heart he knew that he was lying to himself. He could pretend that he didn't want Eiadh forever, but in fact the only thing he felt for her was desire. A powerful, possessive desire that showed no signs of slackening. It was Eiadh, not Elemak, who was changeable. She was the one who had so admired Nafai when he stood against Moozh and refused the warlord's offer of the consulship. So pathetic, that she would admire Nyef more for refusing power than she admired her own new husband for having and using it. But Eiadh *was* a woman, after all, and had been raised with the same mystical dependence on the Oversoul, and since the Oversoul had so clearly "chosen" Nafai, it made him all the more attractive in her eyes.

As for Nafai... Elemak had known for many months that Nafai had his eye on Eiadh. That was part of what had made

Eiadh so attractive to Elemak from the start—that marrying her would put his snotty little brother in his place. Let him marry her later, when she had already had Elemak's first child or two. That would let Nafai know where he stood. But now Eiadh was casting an eye toward the boy—damn him for being the one who killed Gaballufix! That's what was seducing her! She loved the delusion that Nafai was strong. Well, Eiadh, my darling, Edhya my pet, *I* have killed before, and not a drunkard lying in the street, either. I killed a bandit who was charging my caravan, bent on murder and robbery. And I can kill again.

I can kill again, and Rasa has already consented to the justification. The law of the desert, yes, *that* is what will bring Nafai's interference to an end. Rasa is so sure that her dear sweet youngest boy would *never* break the law that she'll agree—they'll *all* agree—that the penalty for disobedience is death. And then Nafai will disobey. It will be so simple, so symmetrical, and I can then kill him on exactly the same pretext Nyef himself used for killing Gabya—I'm doing it for the good of all!

That night, when the cold supper was heavy in their bellies, when the chill night breeze had driven them all inside their tents, Elemak set Nafai to keep the first watch. He knew that Nafai, poor fellow, was keenly aware of who was waiting for Elemak inside his tent. He knew that Nafai was sitting there in the cold starlight imagining how Elya gathered Eiadh's naked body into his arms, how hot and humid they made their tent. He knew that Nafai heard, or imagined that he heard, the soft low cries that Eiadh made. And when Elemak emerged from his tent, the sweat and smell of love still on him, he knew that Nafai could taste the bitterness of going to his own tent, where the awkward shapeless body of Luet the waterseer was the only solace the poor boy would find. It was almost tempting to take Rasa's law and make it real, for then it would be Nafai who would grow old watching Eiadh always and knowing that she was Elemak's, and he could never, never, never have her for his own.

TWO

BINDING AND UNBINDING

Nafai stood his watch as he always did, by conversing with the Oversoul. It was easier now than it had been at first, back when he and Issib had practically forced the Oversoul to talk to them. Now he would form thoughts carefully in his mind, almost as if he were speaking them, and then, almost without trying, he could feel the Oversoul's answers come to him. They came as if they were Nafai's own thoughts, of course, so that at times he still had trouble distinguishing between the Oversoul's actual ideas and the ideas that came from his own mind; to be sure, he often asked the same question again, and the Oversoul, since it was a computer and therefore never felt a sense of hurry, willingly repeated as often as he liked.

Tonight, because he was on watch, he first asked the Oversoul if any danger was near.

⟨A coyote, tracking the scent of a hare.⟩

No, I meant danger to *us,* said Nafai silently.

⟨The same bandits I told you about before. But they keep

hearing noises in the night, and now they're hiding in a cave, trembling.⟩

You enjoy doing this to them, don't you? asked Nafai.

⟨No, but I sense *your* delight. This is what you call a game, isn't it?⟩

More like what we call a trick. Or a joke.

⟨And you love the fact that only you know that I am doing this.⟩

Luet knows.

⟨Of course.⟩

Any other danger?

⟨Elemak is plotting your death.⟩

What, a knife in the back?

⟨He is full of confidence. He believes he can do it openly, with the consent of all. Even your mother.⟩

And how will he do it? Blast me with his pulse and pretend it's an accident? Can he frighten my camel into throwing me from a cliff?

⟨His plan is more subtle than that. It has to do with marriage laws. Rasa and Shedemei realized today that marriages must be made permanent, and Rasa has now persuaded Elemak.⟩

Good. That will work much better than if the idea had come from Luet and me.

⟨But it *did* come from you and Luet.⟩

But only we and you are aware of that, and no one else will guess. They'll see the sensibleness of the law. And besides, I had to do something to stop Eiadh from trying to start something with me. I find it disgusting that it's only since I killed Gaballufix and refused to be Moozh's puppet that she finds me interesting. I think I was much nicer before . . . before all this started.

⟨You were a boy then.⟩

I'm still a boy.

⟨I know. That's one of our problems. Worse yet, you're a boy who's not very good at deception, Nafai.⟩

But you're a whiz at it.

⟨You can't lead these people by relying on me to plant your ideas in their minds. On the voyage from Harmony to Earth I won't have the same power to reach into their minds that I have here. You will have to learn how to speak with them directly. Teach them to look to you for decisions.⟩

Elya and Meb will *never* be willing to accept my lead.

⟨Then they are expendable.⟩

Like Gaballufix? I'll never do that again, Oversoul. You can be sure of that—I killed once for you, but never again, never, never, don't even make me think of it, *no!*

⟨I hear you. I understand you.⟩

No, you don't understand. You never felt the blood on your hands. You never felt the sword cut through the flesh and hack apart the cartilage between the vertebrae. You never heard his last gasping breaths through the bloody gap in his throat.

⟨Through your eyes I saw, through your arms I felt, through your ears I heard.⟩

You never felt the . . . that terrible irrevocability. That there's no turning back. That he's *gone,* and no matter how terrible a man he was, I had no right to cut him off like that . . .

⟨You had the right because I gave it to you, and I had the right because humankind built me in order to protect the entire species, and the death of that man was necessary for the preservation of humanity on this world.⟩

Yes, I know, again and again you tell me.

⟨Again and again you reject the truth and insist on remaining in this meaningless agony of guilt.⟩

I ended the life of a helpless drunken man. There was no glory in that act. There was no decency. There was no cleverness or wisdom. I was not a good man when I did that.

⟨You were my hands, Nafai. What I needed to do, you did for me.⟩

They were my own hands, Oversoul. I could have said no.

As I say no *now,* when you hint of my killing Elemak and Mebbekew. It will not happen. I will take no more lives for you.

⟨I'll keep that in mind as I make my plans for the future. But you *can* establish leadership. You *must.* Your father is too old and tired, and he relies on Elemak too much. He'll give in to your brother far too often, again and again he'll surrender to him, until he has no will left at all.⟩

So it's better that he surrenders to me?

⟨You won't make him surrender anything. You'll always lead *through* him, with great respect for him. If you lead, your father will remain a proud and powerful man. I've told you this. Now stand up and take your place.⟩

Not yet. This is not the time for me to challenge Elemak. We need him to lead us through the desert.

⟨And I tell you that he has no such qualms. At this very moment, even though he's making love to Eiadh, he is picturing you tied up and abandoned in the desert, where you'll soon discover, Nafai, that while I can influence bandits I can't do a thing about the beasts and birds of prey, the insects that think of anything that doesn't walk or fly or slither away as their next meal. They don't listen to *me,* they simply act out what their genes require them to do, and you *will* die, and what will I do then without you?⟩

Does he mean to act now, before we get to Father's camp?

⟨At last you're listening.⟩

What is his plan, then?

⟨I don't know. He never thinks of it plainly. I'm searching as best I can, but it's hard. I can't just ransack a human's memories, you know. He fears his own murderous heart so much that he won't let himself think of his whole plan openly.⟩

Perhaps when he's not distracted by lovemaking.

⟨Distracted? He's even doing *this* for your benefit. He thinks that you still want Eiadh, so he's hoping you notice the movement in the tent, and the noises she's making.⟩

It only makes me long for my watch to end, so I can go back to Luet.

⟨He can't conceive of a man not desiring the woman he desires.⟩

I did. I fancied that Eiadh was exactly what I needed and wanted. But I understood nothing then. Luet believes she's already pregnant. Luet and I can talk about everything. We've only been married for a few days, yet she understands my heart even better than you do, and I can speak her thoughts almost before she thinks them. Does Elemak imagine that I could desire a mere woman, when Luet is my *wife?*

⟨He knows that Eiadh is attracted to you. He remembers that you were once attracted to her. He also knows that I have chosen you to lead. He's mad with jealousy. He hungers for your death. It consumes him so that even the act of making love to her is a kind of murder in his heart.⟩

Don't you realize that this is the most terrible thing of all? If there's anything I want in my life, it's for Elemak to love me and respect me. What did I do, to turn him away!

⟨You refused to let him own your will.⟩

Love and respect have nothing to do with controlling what other people do.

⟨To Elemak, if he doesn't control you, you either don't exist or you're his enemy. For many years you didn't exist. Then he noticed you, and you weren't as easy to manipulate or intimidate as Mebbekew, and so you became a rival.⟩

Is it really that simple?

⟨I glossed over the hard parts.⟩

His tent isn't bouncing. Does that mean he's coming out soon?

⟨He's getting dressed. He's thinking of you. So is Eiadh.⟩

At least she doesn't want to kill me.

⟨If she ever got what she's wishing for, it would end the same, with you dead.⟩

Don't tell Luet that Elemak is planning to kill me.

⟨I'll tell Luet everything, exactly as I tell *you.* I don't lie to the humans who serve my cause.⟩

You lie to us whenever you think it's necessary. And I don't want you to lie to her, anyway—I just don't want her to worry.

⟨I *do* want her to worry, since you refuse to. I think sometimes you want to die.⟩

You can relieve your mind on that score. I like being alive and intend to continue.

⟨I think sometimes you look forward to death, because you think that you deserve to die for having killed Gaballufix.⟩

Here he comes.

⟨Notice how he makes sure you smell his hands.⟩

Nafai didn't appreciate the Oversoul's calling attention to that—he might not have noticed, otherwise. But, truth to tell, that was unlikely, because Elemak made a point of putting both hands on his shoulders, and even of brushing his fingers across Nafai's cheek as he said, "So you *did* stay awake. Maybe you'll amount to something in the desert after all."

"You didn't leave me on watch all that long," Nafai answered.

The womanly smell was plain enough. It was vaguely disgusting that Elemak would use his intimacy with his own wife this way. It was as if she had become nothing to him. A tool. Not a wife at all, but just a *thing* that he owned.

But if the Oversoul was right, then that was how Elemak experienced love—as ownership.

"Did you see anything?" asked Elemak.

"Darkness," said Nafai. He did not tell Elemak about the bandits only a few hundred meters away. First, it would only make him furious that Nafai was getting information from the Oversoul. And second, it would humiliate him that he chose as his campsite a place where bandits could conceal themselves so close. He would probably insist on searching for them, which would mean battle and bloodshed, or waking everybody up and moving on, which would be pointless, since the Oversoul was having no trouble keeping this spineless group of cutpurses under control.

"If you ever looked up, you'd notice there are stars," said Elemak.

Elemak was baiting him, of course, and Nafai knew that he should just ignore him, but he was filled with anger already, knowing that Elemak was plotting to kill him and yet still pretended to be his brother, knowing that Elemak had just made love to his wife in order to try to make Nafai suffer from jealousy. So Nafai could not contain himself. He flung a hand upward. "And that one is Sol, the Sun. Barely visible, but you can always find it if you know where to look. That's where we're going."

"Are we?" asked Elemak.

"It's the only reason the Oversoul brought us out of Basilica," said Nafai.

"Maybe the Oversoul won't necessarily get his way," said Elemak. "He's just a computer, after all—you said so yourself."

Nafai almost answered again, some snide comment to the effect that if the Oversoul was "just" a computer then Elemak himself was "just" a hairless baboon. Six months ago Nafai *would* have said it, and Elemak would have thrown him against a wall or knocked him down with a blow. But Nafai had learned a little since then, and so he held his tongue.

Luet was waiting for him in the tent. She had probably been dozing—she had worked hard since they started laying camp, and unlike the lazy ones she would be up early again in the morning. But she greeted him wordlessly with open eyes and a smile that warmed him in spite of the chill that Elemak had put in his heart.

Nafai undressed quickly and gathered her to him under the blankets. "You're warm," he said.

"I think the technical term is *hot,*" she answered.

"Elemak is planning to kill me," he whispered.

"I wish the Oversoul would just *stop* him," she whispered.

"I don't think it can. I think Elemak's will is too strong for the Oversoul to make him change his mind once he's set on doing something." He didn't tell her that the Oversoul had hinted that somewhere along the line Nafai might have to kill his brother. Since Nafai had no intention of ever doing it, there was no reason to put the idea in Luet's mind. He would be ashamed to say it anyway, for fear she would then think he might consider such a thing.

"Hushidh thinks she senses Elemak bonding more closely with the ones who want to turn back—Kokor and Sevet, Vas and Obring, Meb and Dol. They're forming a sort of community now, and separating almost completely from the rest of us."

"Shedemei?"

"She wants to turn back, but there's no bond between her and the others."

"So only you and I and Hushidh and Mother want to go on into the desert."

"And Eiadh. *She* wants to go wherever *you* go."

They both laughed, but Nafai understood that Luet needed reassurance that Eiadh's desire for him was not reciprocated. So he reassured her thoroughly, and then they slept.

In the morning, with the camels packed, Elemak called them together. "A couple of things," he said. "First, Rasa and Shedemei have proposed it and I agree with them completely. While we're living in the desert, we can't afford to have the kind of sexual freedom we had in Basilica. It would only cause rancor and disloyalty, and that's a death sentence for a caravan. So as long as we remain in the desert—and that includes at Father's camp, and anywhere else that our population consists of just us and the three who are waiting for us—this is the law: There'll be no sleeping with anyone except your own husband or wife, and all marriages as they presently stand are permanent."

Immediately there was a gasp of shock from several; Luet looked around and saw that it was the predictable ones—Kokor and Obring and Mebbekew—who were most upset.

"You have no right to make a decision like that," said Vas mildly. "We're all Basilicans, and we live under Basilican law."

"When we're in Basilica we live under Basilican law," said Elemak. "But when you're in the desert you live under desert law, and desert law has it that the word of the caravan leader is final. I'll listen to any ideas until I have to make a decision, but once the decision is made *any* resistance is mutiny, do you understand me?"

"No one tells me who I *must* sleep with and who I may *not,*" said Kokor.

Elemak walked up to her and faced her; she looked so frail compared to the sheer mass of Elemak's tall, well-muscled body. "And I tell you that in the desert, I won't have anyone creeping from tent to tent. It will lead to murder one way or another, and so instead of letting you improvise the dying, I'll let you know right now: If anyone is caught in a position that even *looks* like you're getting sexually involved with someone you aren't married to, I will personally kill the woman on the spot."

"The *woman!*" cried Kokor.

"We need the men to help load the camels," said Elemak. "Besides, the idea shouldn't seem strange to *you,* Koya, since you made exactly the same decision the last time *you* decided that somebody should die for the crime of adultery."

Luet could see how both Kokor and her sister Sevet immediately touched their throats—for it was in the throat that Kokor had struck Sevet, nearly killing her and leaving her almost voiceless ever since. While Kokor's husband, Obring, who had been bouncing away just as merrily when Kokor found the two of them, was unscathed. It was viciously unkind and exactly appropriate for Elemak to remind them all of that event, because it completely silenced any kind of opposition to the new law from three of the four people most likely to oppose it: Kokor, Sevet, and Obring had nothing to say at all.

"You don't have the right to decide this," said Mebbekew. He was, of course, the fourth—but Luet knew that Elemak would have no trouble bringing him into line. He never did, with Meb.

"I not only have the right," said Elemak, "I have the duty.

This is a law necessary for the survival of our little company in the desert, and so it will be obeyed or I will enforce the only penalty that I *can* enforce here, so many kilometers from civilization. If you can't grasp this idea, then I'm sure Lady Rasa can explain it to you."

He turned and faced Rasa, in a silent demand that she back him up. She did not disappoint him. "I tried and tried all night to think of another way to handle this," she said, "but we can't live without this law, and as Elya says, in the desert the only penalty that means anything at all is . . . what he said. But not killing outright!" she said, clearly hating the whole idea of it. "Only binding and leaving a person."

"Only?" said Elemak disdainfully. "It's by far the crueler death."

"It leaves her in the hands of the Oversoul," Rasa said. "Perhaps to be rescued."

"You should pray not," said Elemak. "The animals are kinder than any rescuers she'd find out here."

"A lawbreaker is to be bound and abandoned, *not* killed!" Rasa insisted.

Luet thought: She fears it will be a daughter of hers who will first break this law. As for Elemak's rule that having only the woman die will better restrain the man, he has it backward. Few men think of consequences when they're filled with desire, but a woman can put off her own desires if a man she loves would be at risk.

"As the lady wishes," said Elemak. "The law of the desert leaves the choice up to the leader of the caravan. I would normally choose a quick, clean death by pulse, but let us hope that no such choice ever has to be made." He looked around at the whole group, turning to include in his gaze the ones who were behind him. "I don't ask for your consent in this," he said. "I simply tell you that this is the way it will be. So now raise your hand if you understand the law we will live by."

They all raised their hands, though clearly some were furious.

No, not quite all. "Meb," said Elemak. "Raise your hand.

You're embarrassing your dear wife Dol. She's no doubt beginning to wonder who is the woman here whose love you consider so desirable that you would cause an imperfectly virtuous lady's certain death by pursuing it."

Now Meb raised his hand.

"Good," said Elemak. "And now for the other matter. We have a decision to make," he said.

The sun had not yet risen, so it was still bitterly cold—especially for the ones who had done very little of the work of striking the tents and loading the camels. So it might have been just the cold that made Mebbekew's voice tremble when he said, "I thought *you* were making all the decisions now."

"I make all the decisions that have to do with keeping us alive and moving," said Elemak. "But I don't fancy myself some kind of tyrant. The decisions that *don't* have to do with survival belong to the whole group, not to me. We can't survive unless we all stay together, so I'll tolerate *no* divisions among us. At the same time, I don't recall a point where anybody actually decided where it was we were going."

"We're going back to Father and Issib," said Nafai immediately. "You know they're counting on us to return."

"They have plenty of water as long as they stay put. They need someone to go and fetch them sometime in the next few months—they've got years of supplies, for that matter," said Elemak. "So let's not turn this into a life and death matter unless we have to. If the majority wants to go on until we reach Volemak in the desert, fine. That's where we'll *all* go."

"We can't go back to Basilica," said Luet. "My father made that very clear." Her father, of course, was Moozh, the great general of the Gorayni, though she had not known that until a few days ago. But by reminding the others of this newfound family connection, she hoped to make her words carry more weight. She wasn't skilled at persuasion; she had always simply told the truth, and because the women of Basilica knew her to be the waterseer, her words were taken seriously. It was a new thing, talking to a group that included men. But she knew that asserting one's family status was one of the ways people got their way in Basilica, and so she tried it now.

"Yes," said Kokor, "your tender loving father who tried to marry his own daughter and then threw us all out of the city when he couldn't."

"That's not the way it happened," said Luet.

Hushidh touched Luet's hand to still her. "Don't try," Hushidh whispered softly. "Koya's better at it than you are."

No one else heard Hushidh's words, but when Luet fell silent they understood the effect of what she said, and Kokor smirked.

"Luet is right enough that we probably can't go back to Basilica," said Elemak, "at least not right away—I think that was the message we were meant to understand from the fact that he sent an escort of soldiers to make sure we got safely away from the city."

"I'm so tired of hearing how *none* of us can get back to Basilica," said Mebbekew, "when it's only *those* who embarrassed him in front of everybody." He was pointing at Hushidh and Luet and Nafai.

"Do shut up, Meb," said Elemak with genial contempt. "I don't want us to be standing here talking when the sun comes up. We're in exactly the kind of country that bandits like to hole up in, and if there are some hiding from the darkness in caves nearby, they're bound to come out by daylight."

Luet wondered if in fact Elemak *had* picked up some intimation of the bandits that the Oversoul had been controlling. Perhaps Elemak knew all along that such men were only brave in the sunlight, and hid at night. Besides, it was possible that Elemak was receiving the Oversoul's messages subliminally, not realizing where the thoughts and ideas were coming from. After all, Elemak was as much a result of the Oversoul's secret breeding program as any of the rest of them were, and he *had* received a dream not long ago. If only Elemak would simply admit that he could communicate with the Oversoul and follow her plans willingly—it would uncomplicate everything. As it was, she and

Hushidh had been working on plans to try to thwart Elemak in whatever it was he was planning to do.

"Even though we really can't go back to Basilica immediately," Elemak went on, "that doesn't mean we have to go join Father at once. There are many other cities that would take in a caravan of strangers, if only because Shedemei has an extremely valuable cargo of embryos and seeds."

"They're not for sale," said Shedemei. Her voice was harsh enough, her answer abrupt enough, that everyone knew she had no intention of arguing about it.

"Not even to save our lives?" said Elemak sweetly. "But never mind—I don't propose selling them anyway. They're only valuable when they come along with the knowledge that Shedya has in her head. What matters is that they *will* let us in if they know that, far from being a band of penniless wanderers recently expelled from Basilica by General Moozh of the Gorayni, we are instead accompanying the famous geneticist Shedemei, who is moving her laboratory away from strife-torn Basilica to some peaceful city that will guarantee her a place to do her work without disturbance."

"Perfect," said Vas. "There's not a City of the Plain that would refuse us entry on those terms."

"They'd offer us money, in fact," said Obring.

"They'd offer *me* money, you mean," said Shedemei. But clearly she was flattered—she hadn't really thought of the fact that her presence would convey a certain amount of prestige on any city she settled in. Luet could see that Elemak's flattery was having its effect.

⟨He's going to put it to a vote.⟩ The Oversoul spoke in Luet's mind.

That much is obvious by now, said Luet. What is his *plan?*

⟨When Nafai opposes the decision to return to the city, it will be mutiny.⟩

Then he must not oppose.

⟨Then my work would be thwarted.⟩

Then control the vote.

⟨Whose vote should I change? Which of them would Elemak believe if he suddenly voted to go on?⟩

Then don't let the vote happen.

⟨I have no such influence with Elemak.⟩

Then tell Nafai not to oppose!

⟨He must oppose, or there will be no voyage to Earth.⟩

"No!" cried Luet.

Everyone looked at her. "No what?" asked Elemak.

"No vote," she said. "There will be *no* vote."

"Ah yes," said Elemak. "We have another freedom-lover here who realizes that she doesn't approve of democracy after all, when she thinks the vote will go against her."

"Who said anything about voting?" asked Dol, who was never terribly sharp about what was going on around her.

"I vote we go back to civilization," said Obring. "Otherwise we're slaves to marriage—and to Elemak, for that matter!"

"But I said nothing about putting things to a vote," said Elemak. "I said only that we must make a decision about where to go. A vote might be interesting, but I won't be bound by it. It's your counsel that I need, not your governance."

So they counseled him, eloquently—or tried to. But if anyone even began to advance an argument that someone else had already stated, Elemak would silence them at once. "I've already heard that. Anything new to add?" As a result, the discussion didn't last very long at all. Sooner than Luet would have thought possible, Elemak asked, "Anything else?" and no one answered.

He waited, looked around at them. The sun was coming over the tops of the distant mountains now, and his eyes and hair glowed with reflected light. This is his finest moment, thought Luet. This is what he has planned for—a whole community, including his father's wife, including his brother Nafai, including the waterseer and the raveler of Basilica, including his own bride, all waiting for the decision that will change their lives. Or end them.

"Thank you for your wise counsel," said Elemak gravely. "It

seems to me that we don't have to choose one way *or* another. Those who want to return to civilization may, and soon enough those who want to go on into the desert on this errand for the Oversoul may do so as well. We can call it a rescue of my father or we can call it the beginning of a voyage to Earth—that's not at issue now. What matters is that all can be satisfied. We'll go south a little way and then come over the mountains and down into the Cities of the Plain. There we can leave those who can't bear to live under the harsh law of the desert, and I can take the stronger ones with me."

"Thanks so much!" said Mebbekew.

"I don't care what he calls me, as long as I have my freedom," said Kokor.

"Fools," said Nafai. "Don't you see that he's only pretending?"

"What did you say?" said Elemak.

"He intended to take us back to civilization all along," said Nafai.

"Don't, Nafai," said Luet, for she knew what was coming next.

"Listen to your brideling, Brother," said Elemak. His voice was deceptively mild.

"I will listen to the Oversoul," said Nafai. "The only reason we're alive right now is because the Oversoul has been influencing a band of robbers to stay holed up in their cave not three hundred meters away. The Oversoul can lead us perfectly well across the desert, with or without Elemak and his stupid desert law. It's a game for boys that he's playing—who can make the boldest threats—"

"Not threats," said Elemak. "Laws that every desert traveler knows."

"If we trust in the Oversoul we will be perfectly safe on this journey. If we trust in Elemak we'll return to the Plain and be destroyed in the wars that are coming."

"Trust in the Oversoul," said Meb with a sneer. "What you mean is do whatever *you* say."

"Elemak knows that the Oversoul is real enough—he had a dream that led us back to the city to marry our wives, didn't he?"

Elemak only laughed. "Babble on, Nafai."

"It's as Elemak said. This isn't a matter for democracy. It's a matter for each of us to decide. Go on with the journey as the Oversoul has directed, and we'll take the greatest voyage in forty million years and inherit a world for us and our children. Or go back to the city where you can betray your spouse as some of you are already planning. As for me and Luet, we will never go back to the city."

"Enough," said Elemak. "Not another word or you're dead this instant." A pulse was in his hand. Luet had not noticed he was carrying it, but she knew what it meant. This was exactly what Elemak had been waiting for. He had set it up very carefully, and now he could kill Nafai and no one would dare condemn him for it. "I know the desert and you don't," said Elemak. "There are no bandits where you *claim* there are, or we'd already be dead. If that's what passes for wisdom in your fevered little brain, Brother, then anyone who stayed with you would surely be doomed. But no one *will* stay with you, because I'm not about to let this group split up. That would mean certain death for anyone who went with you."

"A lie," said Nafai.

"Please, speak again so I can kill you as the mutineer you are."

"Hold your tongue, Nafai, for my sake!" said Luet.

"You've all heard him, haven't you?" said Elemak. "He has proclaimed rebellion against my authority and attempted to lead a group away to their destruction. That's mutiny, which is far more serious than adultery, and the penalty is death. You are all witnesses. There's not one of you but would have to confess it in court, should it ever come to that."

"Please," said Luet. "Let him be, and he'll say no more."

"Is that true, Nafai?" asked Elemak.

"If you continue to head back to the city," said Nafai, "the

Oversoul will have no reason to restrain the bandits any further, and you will all be killed."

"You see?" said Elemak. "Even now he tries to frighten us with these fantasies of nonexistent bandits."

"That's what you've been doing all along," said Shedemei. "Making us do what you want for fear of bandits finding us."

Elemak turned to her. "I never claimed they were a few meters away, hiding in a cave, only that there was a chance that some would come upon us. I've said nothing but the truth to you—but this boy thinks you're such fools that you'll believe his obvious lies."

"Believe what you like," said Nafai. "You'll see the proof soon enough."

"Mutiny," said Elemak, "and all of you—even his own mother—will be my witnesses that I had no choice, because he would not desist in his rebellion. If he were not my own brother, I wouldn't have waited this long. He'd be dead already."

"And if you didn't carry genes that the Oversoul regards as precious ones," said Nafai, "Gaballufix would have killed you when you failed to lead Father into his trap."

"Accusing me does nothing but compound your crime," said Elemak. "Say good-bye to your mother and your wife—from where you are, and no nearer!"

"Elemak, you can't mean this," said Rasa.

"You yourself agreed with me, Rasa, that our survival depends on obedience to the law of the desert, and what the penalty had to be."

"I see that you maliciously—"

"Careful, Lady Rasa. I'll do what must be done, even if it includes leaving you to your death as well."

"Don't worry, Mother," said Nafai. "The Oversoul is with us, and Elemak is helpless."

Luet began to catch a glimmer of what Nafai was doing. He seemed quite calm—unbelievably calm. Therefore he must be quite sure that the Oversoul would be able to protect him after all. He must have a plan of his own, and so Luet would do best to be silent and let it unfold, no matter how frightened she was.

It would be nice if you would share the plan with me, though, she said to the Oversoul.

⟨Plan?⟩ answered the Oversoul.

Luet's hands began to tremble.

"We'll see how helpless you are," said Elemak. "Mebbekew, take a length of packing cord—the light line, and a good length, several meters—and tie his hands. Use the cinching knot, so it binds tight, and don't worry about cutting off the circulation in his hands."

"You see?" said Nafai. "He has to kill a bound man."

Don't! cried Luet in her heart. Don't provoke him into shooting you! If you let him tie you, then you have a chance.

Elemak glanced at Mebbekew, at which Meb took a few steps to one of the waiting camels and came back with a cord.

As he was tying Nafai's hands behind his back, twining the cords around and around his wrists, Hushidh stepped forward.

"Stay where you are," said Elemak. "I'm binding him and abandoning him out of respect for Lady Rasa, but I'll be just as happy to give him the pulse and have done with it."

Hushidh stayed where she was; she had what she wanted anyway, which was the group's attention. "Elemak planned this all along," said Hushidh to the others, "because he wanted to kill Nafai. He knew that if he decided to turn back, Nafai would have no choice but to oppose him. He set it up to provide him with a legal excuse for murder."

Elemak's eye twitched. Luet could see the rage building out of control in him. What are you doing, Hushidh, my sister! Don't talk him into killing my husband as we stand here!

"Why would Elya do that?" said Eiadh. "You're saying my Elemak is a murderer, and he's not!"

"Eiadh, you poor dear," said Hushidh. "Elemak wants Nafai dead because he knows that if you had the choice today, you'd leave him and choose Nafai."

"A lie!" cried Elemak. "Don't answer her, Eiadh! Say nothing!"

"Because he can't bear to hear the truth," said Hushidh. "He'll hear it in your voice."

Now Luet understood. Hushidh was using her talent from the Oversoul, just as she did when Rashgallivak stood in the foyer of Rasa's house, planning to use his soldiers to kidnap Rasa's daughters. Hushidh was saying the words that would destroy the loyalty of Elemak's followers, that would remove all support from him. She was unbinding them, and if she could just say a few more sentences, she would succeed.

Unfortunately, Luet wasn't the only one who realized this. "Silence her!" said Sevet. Her voice was harsh and husky, for she had not yet recovered well from the injury Kokor gave her. But she could speak well enough to be heard, and the very painfulness of her voice brought her all the more attention. "Don't let Hushidh speak. She's a raveler, and if she says enough she can turn everyone against everybody else. I saw her do it to Rashgallivak's men, and she can do it now, if you let her."

"Sevet is right," said Elemak. "Not another word from you, Hushidh, or I'll kill him."

Almost she opened her mouth to speak again, Luet could see it. But something—perhaps the Oversoul—restrained her. She turned and stepped back to where she had stood before, on the far side of Rasa and Shedemei. It was the last hope gone, as far as Luet could see. The Oversoul could make weak-willed people stupid or afraid for a short while, but she hadn't the strength to stop a man determined on murder. She hadn't the strength to make the bandits turn suddenly kind in their dealings with Nafai, should they find him. She certainly couldn't keep the animals of the desert from finding him and devouring him. Hushidh's ploy had been the last possibility, and it was gone.

No, I will *not* despair, thought Luet. Perhaps if we abandon him here I can slip away from the party and come back and untie him. Or perhaps I can kill Elemak in his sleep and . . .

No, no. She hadn't murder in her, and she knew it. Not even if the Oversoul commanded it, as she had commanded Nafai to kill Gaballufix. She couldn't do it even then. Nor would she be able to slip away and help Nafai in time. It was over. There was no hope.

"He's tied," said Mebbekew.

"Let me check the knot," said Elemak.

"Do you think I don't know how to tie it?" asked Mebbekew.

"This computer they worship supposedly has the power to make people stupider than usual," said Elemak. "Isn't that right, Nafai?"

Nafai said nothing. Luet was proud of him for that, but still frightened for him. For she knew that the Oversoul's power was very great over a long period of time, but very slight at any one moment.

Elemak was now standing close behind Nafai, with the pulse pointed at his back. "Kneel down, little brother."

Nafai didn't kneel, but as if by reflex Meb began to.

"Not you, fool. Nyef."

"The condemned man," said Nafai.

"Yes, you, little brother. Kneel."

"If you're going to use the pulse, I prefer to die standing up."

"Don't make such a show of this," said Elemak. "I want your hands tied to your ankles, so kneel down."

Slowly, carefully, Nafai sank to one knee, then to both.

"Sit on your heels," said Elemak. "Or near them. Yes. Now, Meb, pass the ends of the rope down between his ankles, bring them up and over his legs, and tie them together—in front of his wrists—yes, like that, where his fingers can't possibly reach them. Very good. Can you feel anything in your hands, Nafai?"

"Only the throbbing of my blood, trying to get past the ropes around my wrists."

"Strings, not ropes, Nafai, but they might as well be steel."

"You're not cutting off *my* blood, Elemak, you're cutting off your own," said Nafai. "For your blood will be unknown on Earth, while my blood will live on for a thousand generations."

"Enough," said Elemak.

"I'll say what I like now," said Nafai, "since you've already determined to kill me—what difference will it make now, for me to say the truth? Should I be afraid that you'll kick me or spit on me, when I already stare death in the face?"

"If you're trying to provoke me into shooting you, it won't work. I promised Lady Rasa, and I'll keep my word."

But Luet could see that Nafai's words *were* having an effect. The tension in the whole group was rising higher and higher, and it was clear that in everyone's eyes the showdown between them was yet to come, even when Elemak thought he had already won.

"We'll get on our camels now," said Elemak. "And no one will turn back to try to save this mutineer, or whoever tries will share his fate."

If Luet had not been sure that Nafai and the Oversoul must have some kind of plan, she would have insisted then on dying beside her husband. But she knew him well enough, even after only these few days, to know that Nafai felt no fear at all right now. And while he was a brave young man, she knew that if he truly believed he was going to die, *she* at least would be able to sense his fear. His mother must feel the same way, too, Luet realized, because she was not protesting, either. Instead they both waited and watched as the little play unfolded.

Elemak and Mebbekew started to walk away from Nafai. Then Mebbekew turned, put his foot on Nafai's shoulder, and pushed him over sideways to lie in the sand. With his hands tied to his ankles, he could do nothing to cushion his fall. But now Luet could see behind him, could see clearly that instead of being tied tightly, the strings were only loosely gathered.

So that was what the game was. The Oversoul was doing all she could to influence Mebbekew and Elemak to see tightly bound ropes where in fact the strands were only loops. She normally did not have the power to make them stupid—or at least not enough to make *Elemak* so unobservant. But between Hushidh and Nafai, with their dangerous, infuriating talk, they had managed to make Elemak so angry that the Oversoul had more power to confuse him. Indeed, there must be others who could see that Nafai was not firmly tied, though fortunately those in the best position to see were also those least likely to point it out—Lady Rasa, Hushidh, and Shedemei. As for the others, with the Oversoul's help they no doubt saw what they expected to see, what Elemak and Mebbekew had led them to *expect* to see.

"Yes," said Lady Rasa. "Let's go to the camels." She strode boldly toward the waiting animals. Luet and Hushidh followed her. The others also turned and moved.

All except Eiadh. She stood motionless, looking at Nafai. The others, standing beside their kneeling camels, could not help but turn and watch as Elemak walked up to her, put his hand on her back. "I know this hurts your tender heart, Edhya," said Elemak. "But a leader must sometimes act harshly, for the good of all."

She did not even glance at him. "I never thought a man could face death with such perfect calm," she said.

Wonderful, Luet said silently to the Oversoul. You're making her love Nafai all the more? How helpful of you, to guarantee that we'll never have peace, even if Nafai gets out of this alive.

⟨Have a little trust, will you? I can't do everything at once. Which would you rather have, Eiadh out of love with your husband, or your husband alive and the caravan headed toward Volemak?⟩

I trust you. I just wish you wouldn't cut it so close.

"Hear me!" cried Nafai.

"Pleading will get you nowhere now," said Elemak. "Or do you want to make one last speech of mutiny?"

"He wasn't speaking to us," said Eiadh. "He was speaking to her. To the Oversoul."

"Oversoul, because I have put my trust in you, deliver me

from the murdering hands of my brothers! Give me the strength to burst these cords that bind my hands!"

How did it look to the others? Luet could only guess. What *she* saw was Nafai easily pulling one hand, then the other out of the cords, then clambering without much grace to his feet. But the others surely saw what they feared most—Nafai tearing the cords apart with his hands, then springing to his feet with majesty and danger gathering about him. No doubt the Oversoul was focusing all her influence on the others, sparing none for those who already accepted her purpose. Luet, Hushidh, and Lady Rasa were seeing the facts of what happened. The others were no doubt seeing something, not factual, but filled with truth: that Nafai had the power of the Oversoul with him, that he was the chosen one, the true leader.

"You will not turn those camels toward any city known to humankind!" cried Nafai. His voice was tense and harsh-sounding as he strained to be heard across the broad expanse between him and the farthest camels, where Vas had been helping Sevet to mount. "This mutiny of yours against the Oversoul has ended, Elemak. Only the Oversoul is more merciful than you. The Oversoul will let you live—but only as long as you vow never again to lay one hand upon me. Only as long as you promise to fulfil the journey we began—to join with Father, and then to voyage onward to the world that the Oversoul has prepared for us!"

"What kind of trick is this!" cried Elemak.

"The only trick is the one you used to fool yourself," said Nafai. "You thought that by binding me with cords you could also bind the Oversoul, but you were wrong. You could have led this expedition if you had been obedient and wise, but you were filled with your own lust for power and your own envy, and so you have nothing left now but to obey the Oversoul or die."

"Don't threaten me!" cried Elemak. "I have the pulse, you fool, and I've passed a sentence of death on you!"

"Kill him!" shouted Mebbekew. "Kill him now, or you'll regret it forever!"

"So brave of you," said Hushidh, "to urge your brother to do what you would never have the heart for yourself, little Meb." Her voice had such sting to it that he stepped back as if he had been slapped.

But Elemak did not step back. Instead he strode forward, holding the pulse. Luet could see that he was terrified—he absolutely believed that Nafai had done something miraculous by breaking free so easily from his bonds—yet terrified or not, he was determined to kill his youngest brother, and the Oversoul could not possibly stop him. It hadn't the power to turn Elemak away from his firm purpose.

"Elya, no!" The cry was from Eiadh. She ran forward, clutched at him, plucked at the sleeve that held the pulse. "For my sake," she said. "If you touch him, Elya, the Oversoul will kill you, don't you know that? It's the law of the desert—what you yourself said. Mutiny is death! Don't rebel against the Oversoul."

"This isn't the Oversoul," Elemak said. His voice trembled with fear and uncertainty, though—and no doubt the Oversoul was seizing on every scrap of doubt in his heart, magnifying it as Eiadh pled with him. "This is my arrogant little brother."

"It should have been you," said Nafai. "You should have been the one who made the others go along with the Oversoul's plan. The Oversoul would never have chosen *me,* if you had only been willing to obey."

"Listen to *me,"* said Eiadh. "Not to *him*. You're the one who is the father of the child within me—how do you know I don't have a child within me? If you hurt him, if you disobey him, then you'll die, and my child will be fatherless!"

At first Luet feared that Elemak would interpret Eiadh's pleading for Nafai's life as yet another proof that his wife loved Nafai more than him. But no. Her pleading was that he must save his *own* life by not harming Nafai. Therefore he could only take it as proof that she loved *him,* for it was his life she was trying to save.

Vas had also come back to Elemak, and now laid a hand on

his other shoulder. "Elya, don't kill him. We won't go back to the city—none of us will, none of us!" He turned back to face the others. "Will we! We're all content to go on to join Volemak, aren't we!"

"We've seen the power of the Oversoul," said Eiadh. "None of us would have asked to return to the city if we had understood. Please, we all agree. Our purpose is one now, no division among us. Please, Elemak. Don't make me a widow over this. I'm your wife forever, if you turn away from killing him. But what am I if you rebel against the Oversoul and die?"

"You're still our travel leader," said Lady Rasa. "Nothing changes that. Only the destination, and you said yourself that the destination wasn't yours to choose alone. Now we see that the choice belongs to none of *us,* but only to the Oversoul."

Eiadh wept, and the tears were hot and real. "Oh, Elya, my husband, why do you hate me so much that you want to die!"

Luet could almost have predicted what would happen next. Dol, seeing how affecting Eiadh's tears were, could not bear to have her performance hold the center of everyone's attention. So she now clung to *her* husband, and wailed loudly—with very real-seeming tears indeed—that he, too, must refrain from harming Nafai. As if Mebbekew would ever have dared to act alone! As if her tears would ever have moved him! Luet would have laughed aloud, if she hadn't been so aware of the fact that Nafai's life depended now on how Elemak reacted to all the wailing.

She could almost see the change happening on his face. His determination to kill Nafai, which had not yielded to the influence of the Oversoul, now melted before the pleas of his wife. And as that will to murder faded, the Oversoul had more and more opportunity to seize upon and magnify his fears. So from being a dangerous killer, in only a few moments he turned into a trembling wreck of a man, appalled at what he had almost done. He looked down at the pulse in his hands and shuddered, then threw it away from him. It landed at Luet's feet.

"Oh, Nafai, my brother, what was I doing!" Elemak cried.

Mebbekew was even more abject. He flung himself belly-down on the ground. "Forgive me, Nafai! Forgive me for tying you up like an animal—don't let the Oversoul kill me!"

You're overdoing this, Luet said silently to the Oversoul. They're going to be deeply humiliated when they remember how they acted, no matter whether they figure out it was you making cowards of them or not.

⟨What, do you think I have some kind of fine control over this? I can shout fear at them, and they don't hear me and they don't hear me and then suddenly they hear me and collapse like this. I think I'm doing pretty well, for not having done this before.⟩

I'm just suggesting that you lighten up on them a little. The job is done.

"Elemak, Mebbekew, of course I forgive you," said Nafai. "What does it matter what happens to *me*? It's the Oversoul whose forgiveness matters, not mine."

"Kneel to the Oversoul," said Eiadh, urgently pulling Elemak downward. "Kneel and beg for forgiveness, please. Don't you see that your life is in danger?"

Elemak turned to her, and spoke almost calmly, despite the fear that Luet knew was gnawing at him. "And do you care so much whether I live or die?"

"You're my life," said Eiadh. "Haven't we all sworn an oath to stay married forever?"

As a matter of fact, they hadn't, thought Luet. All they had done was listen to Elemak's edict and raise their hands to show they *understood* it. But she prudently said nothing.

Elemak sank to his knees. "Oversoul," he said, his voice trembling. "I'll go where you want me to go."

"Me too," said Mebbekew. "Count me in." He didn't raise his head from the sand.

"As long as Eiadh is mine," said Elemak, "I'm content, whether I'm in the desert or the city, on Harmony or on Earth."

"Oh, Elya!" cried Eiadh. She flung her arms around him and wept into his shoulder.

Luet bent over and picked up the pulse from the sand at her

feet. It wouldn't do to risk losing a precious weapon. Who knew when they might need it for hunting?

Nafai walked over to her. It meant more than Luet could say, that he came first to her, his wife of only a few days, rather than to his mother. He embraced her, and she held him. She could feel his trembling. He *had* been afraid, despite his confidence in the Oversoul. And it had been a near thing, too.

"Did you know how it would all come out?" she whispered.

"The Oversoul wasn't sure it could bring off the rope thing," he murmured back to her. "Especially when he actually walked up to inspect the knot."

"He had to do that, if he was going to believe it was miraculous when you broke free."

"You know what I was thinking, when I was kneeling there with the pulse at my head, saying those things that were goading him to kill me? I was thinking—I'll never know what our baby looks like."

"And now you will."

He pulled away from her, then reached out and took the pulse out of her hand.

Hushidh stepped close and put her hand on the pulse. "Nyef," she said, "if you hold that, there's no hope of healing."

"What if I give it back to him?"

Hushidh nodded. "The best thing," she said.

No one understood better than Hushidh the Raveler what bound and unbound people. Nafai at once strode to Elemak and held out the pulse to him. "Please," he said. "I don't even know how to use this. We need you to lead us back to Father's camp."

Elemak paused just a moment before taking the pulse. Luet knew that he hated receiving it from Nafai's hand. But at the same time he also knew that Nafai didn't have to give it to him. That Nafai didn't have to give him back his place of leadership. And he needed that place, needed it so much that he would even take it from Nafai.

"Glad to," said Elemak. He took the pulse.

"Oh, thank you, Nafai," said Eiadh.

Luet felt a stab of fear through her heart. Does Elemak hear it in her voice? Can he see it in her face? How she looks with such awe at Nafai? She's a woman who loves only strength and courage and power—it is the alpha male in the tribe who attracts her. And in her eyes, Nafai is clearly that most desirable of men. She was the best actress of all today, thought Luet. She was the one who was able to convince Elemak of her love for him, in order to save the man she *really* loved. I can't help but admire her for that, thought Luet. She's really something.

Those thoughts of admiration were themselves lies, though, and Luet could not long fool herself. Beautiful Eiadh is still in love with my husband, and even though his love for me is strong right now, there'll come a day when the primate male in him overcomes the civilized man, and he'll look at Eiadh with desire, and she'll see it and in that moment I will surely lose him.

She shook the jealous thought from her, and walked with Lady Rasa, who was trembling with relief, in order to help her clamber onto her camel. "I thought he was dead," said Rasa softly, clinging to Luet's hand. "I thought I had lost him."

"So did I, for a few moments there," said Luet.

"I can tell you this," said Lady Rasa. "Elemak would have died before nightfall, if he had gone through with it."

"I was plotting his death in my own heart, too," said Luet.

"That's how close we are to animals. Did you ever dream of such a thing? That we would be ready to do murder all so suddenly?"

"Just like baboons, protecting the troop," said Luet.

"I think it's rather a grand discovery, don't you?"

Luet grinned at her and squeezed her hand. "Let's not tell anybody, though," she said. "It would make the men so nervous, to know how dangerous we really are."

"It doesn't matter now," said Rasa. "The Oversoul was stronger than I thought possible. It's all over and done with now."

But as Luet walked back to find her own camel, she knew it

was *not* finished. It had only been postponed. The day would come again when there would be a struggle for power. And next time there was no guarantee that the Oversoul would be able to bring off such a sweet little trick. If Elemak had once decided to fire off the pulse, it would have been over; next time he might realize that, and not let himself be sidetracked by something so foolish as Lady Rasa's plea that he only tie Nafai up and abandon him. It was *that* close, such a near thing. And at the end, Luet knew that Elemak's hatred for Nafai was stronger than ever, even though for a time at least he would deny it, would pretend even to himself that his hate was gone. You can fool the others, Elemak, but I'll be watching you. And if anything happens to my husband, you can be sure of it, you'd better kill me too. You'd better be sure I'm dead, and even then, if I can find a way, I'll come back and wreak some vengeance on you from the grave.

"You're trembling, Lutya," said Hushidh.

"Am I?" Perhaps that was why she was having so much trouble making certain of the cinch on her camel's saddle.

"Like a dragonfly's wing."

"It was a very emotional thing," said Luet. "I suppose that I'm still upset."

"Still jealous of Eiadh, that's what you are," said Hushidh.

"Not even a speck," said Luet. "He loves me absolutely and completely."

"Yes, he does," said Hushidh. "But still I see such rage in you toward Eiadh."

Luet knew that she *did,* yes, feel some jealousy toward Eiadh. But Hushidh had called it rage, and that was a far stronger feeling than she had been aware of in herself. "I'm not angry because she loves Nafai," said Luet, "truly I'm not."

"Oh, I know that," said Hushidh. "Or rather, I see that *now.* No, I think you're angry at her and jealous of her because she was able to save your husband's life, when you couldn't do it."

Yes, thought Luet. That was it. And now that Hushidh had named it, she could feel the agonizing frustration of it wash through her, and hot tears of rage and shame flooded out of her eyes and down her cheeks. "There," said Hushidh, holding her. "It's good to let it out. It's good."

"That's nice," said Luet. "Because apparently I'm going to cry like a ninny whether it's good to let it out or not, so it might as well be good."

She was still crying when Nafai came back to find her and help her on her beast. "You're the last one," said Nafai.

"I think I just needed to feel you touch me one more time," she said. "To be sure you were alive."

"Still breathing," he said. "Are you going to cry like that for long? Because all that moisture on your face is bound to attract flies."

"Whatever happened to those bandits?" she said, wiping her tears with her sleeve.

"The Oversoul managed to put them to sleep just before it started getting serious about influencing the others. They'll wake up in a couple of hours. Why did you think about *them?*"

"I was just thinking how stupid we would all have felt, if they had come running up and hacked us all to pieces while we stood there bickering about whether or not to kill you."

"Yes," said Nafai. "I know what you mean. To face death, that's nothing much. But to feel *really stupid* when you die, well, that would be insufferable."

She laughed and held his hand for just a moment. Just another moment, and then another long, long moment.

"They're waiting for us," said Nafai. "And the bandits *will* wake up eventually."

So she let go of him, and as soon as he headed toward his own camel, hers lurched to its feet and she rose high above the desert floor. It was like riding atop an unsteady tower in an earthquake, and she didn't usually like it. But today it felt as lovely as she had ever imagined it might be to sit upon a throne. For there, on the camel before her, sat Nafai, her husband. Even if it had not been Luet herself who saved him, what of it? It was enough that he was alive, and he was still in love with her.

THREE
HUNTING

They came down into Volemak's camp in the evening. They had traveled longer than usual that day, because they were close; yet still there was all the evening work to do, for Volemak had not known they were coming that night, and there were no extra tents pitched, and Zdorab had already washed up from the supper he prepared for himself and Volemak and Issib. The evening work went slower than usual, because they felt safer, and because, having arrived, it seemed so unfair to have as much work to do as during the journey.

Hushidh stayed as close to Luet and Nafai as she could. She caught glimpses of Issib now and then as he floated somewhere on his chair. There was nothing surprising to her about his appearance—she had known him for years, since he was Lady Rasa's oldest son and had studied at Rasa's house as long as Hushidh had been there herself. But she had always thought of him as the crippled one, and paid him little mind. Then, back in Basilica, as she came to realize that she was going out onto the desert with Nafai and Luet, it came clear to her—for she could always see the connections between people—that in the pairings of male and female in the Oversoul's expedition, she would end up with Issib. The Oversoul wanted his genes to go on, and hers as well, and for good or ill they would be making that effort together.

It had been a hard thing to accept. Especially on the wedding night, as Luet and Nafai, Elemak and Eiadh, Mebbekew and Dolya all were married by Lady Rasa and then went, two by two, to their bridal beds, Hushidh could hardly bear the rage and fear and bitter disappointment in her heart, that *she* could not have the kind of love that her sister Luet had.

In answer, the Oversoul—or so she had thought at first—sent her a dream that night. In it she saw herself linked with Issib; she saw him flying and flew with him; she understood from that that his body did not express his true nature, and that she would find that marriage with him was not something that would grind her down but rather would lift her up. And she saw herself bearing children with him, saw herself standing in the door of a desert tent with him, watching their children play, and she saw that in that future scene she would love him, would be bound with him by gold and silver threads tying them back through generations, and leading them also forward into the future, year by year, child by child, generation by generation. There were other parts of the dream, some of them terrifying, but she clung to the comfort of it all these days. As she had stood with General Moozh, forced to marry the conqueror of Basilica, she had thought about the dream and knew that she would not really end up with him, and sure enough, the Oversoul brought Hushidh's and Luet's mother, the woman named Thirsty, who named them as her daughters—with Moozh as their father. No marriage then, and within hours they were in the desert, on their way to join Volemak in the desert.

But since then she had had time to think—time to remember her fears. Of course she tried not to, tried instead to cling to the comfort of the dream, or to Nafai's reassurances, for he had told her that Issib was very bright and funny, a man of good company, which of course she had never had much chance to see at school.

Yet despite the dream, despite Nafai, her old impressions, the ones she had held for so many years, remained. All the way through the desert she kept seeing the almost macabre way his arms and legs used to move in the city, where he could wear lifts under his clothing, so that he always seemed to be bouncing through the air like gamboling ghost, or like a—what was it that Kokor had once called him?—like a rabbit under water. How they had laughed! And now, how disloyal she felt, although it had been Issib's own sister who made the joke. Hushidh could not have guessed that someday the cripple, the ghost, the underwater rabbit would be her husband. The old fear and strangeness remained as an undercurrent, despite all her attempts to reassure herself.

Until now, seeing him, she realized that she was not afraid of *him*. The dream had given her too much hope. No, she was afraid of what *he* would think of *her*—an even older and darker fear. Did Issib know yet what Aunt Rasa and the Oversoul had planned for him? Was he already eyeing her as she worked at tent-pitching, sizing her up? No doubt that if he was, he would be bitterly disappointed. She could imagine him thinking, Of course the *cripple* gets the plain one, the one too tall, the sour-faced one whose body has never caused a man to take a second glance. The studious one, who has no gift for causing anyone to laugh, except sometimes her younger sister Luet (ah, so bright! but *she* belongs to Nafai). He must be thinking: I'll have to make the best of it, because I'm a cripple and have no choice. Just as I'm thinking, I'll have to make do with the cripple, because no other man would have me.

How many marriages have begun with such feelings as these? Were any of them ever happy, in the end?

She delayed as long as she could, lingering over supper—which *was* better than anything they had eaten while traveling. Zdorab and Volemak had found wild greens and roots in this valley and simmered them down into a stew, so much better than handfuls of raisins and jerky, and the bread was fresh and leavened, instead of the crackers and hard biscuits they had made do with while traveling. Soon it would be better still, for Volemak had planted a garden here, and within a few weeks there would be melons and squashes, carrots and onions and radishes.

Everyone was tired and awkward with each other through supper. The memory of Nafai's near-execution still lingered in their minds, all the more embarrassing to them now that they had returned to Volemak and could see how easily he held command over all of them, being a man of *true* leadership, so much more powerful than Elemak's swaggering, bullying style. It made them all dread some kind of accounting with the old man, for how many of them, except perhaps Eiadh—and of course Nafai himself—were truly proud of how they acted? So, good as the food was, no one but Hushidh had much desire to stay and chat. There were no fond reminiscences of the journey, no amusing tales to recount to those who had waited here for them. As quickly as the supper was cleared away, the couples went to their tents.

They went so suddenly that despite her anxiousness to avoid exactly this moment, Hushidh returned from the stream with the last of the pots she had washed to find that only Shedemei remained of the women, and only Zdorab and Issib of the men. There was already a dreadful silence, for Shedemei had no gift of chat, and both Zdorab and Issib seemed painfully shy. How hard for all of us, thought Hushidh. We know we are the leftovers of the group, thrown together only because we weren't wanted by anyone but the Oversoul. And some of us not even by *her,* for poor Zdorab was here only because Nafai had extracted an oath from him instead of killing him at the gate of Basilica, on the night Nafai cut off Gaballufix's head.

"What a miserable group you are," said Volemak.

Hushidh looked over in relief to see Volemak and Rasa returning to the cookfire. They must have realized that something needed to be said—introductions needed to be made, at least, between Shedya and the librarian, who had never even met.

"I was entering my husband's tent," said Rasa, "thinking how good it was to be back with him, when suddenly I realized how much I missed my traveling companions, Shuya and Shedya, and *then* I remembered that I had failed in my duty as lady of this house."

"House?" said Issib.

"The walls may be stone and the roof may be sky, but this is my house, a place of refuge for my daughters and safety for my sons," said Rasa.

"*Our* house," said Volemak gently.

"Indeed—I spoke of it as *my* house only because of the old habits of Basilica, where the houses belonged only to women." Rasa lifted her husband's hand to her lips and kissed it and smiled at him.

"Out here," said Volemak, "the houses belong to the Oversoul, but he is renting this one to us at a very reasonable fee: When we leave here, the baboons downstream of us get to keep the garden."

"Hushidh, Shedemei, I believe you know my son Issib," said Rasa.

"*Our* son," said Volemak, as gently as before. "And this is Zdorab, who was once Gaballufix's archivist, but now serves our way station as gardener, librarian, and cook."

"Miserable at all three, I fear," said Zdorab.

Rasa smiled. "Volya tells me that both Issib and Zdorab have explored the Index while they've been waiting here. And I know both of my dear nieces, Shuya and Shedya, will have profound interest in what they've found there."

"The Index of the Oversoul is the pathway into all the memory of Earth," said Volemak. "And since Earth is where we are going, it's just as important for us to study in that great library as it is for us to do the work that keeps our bodies alive in this desert."

"You know we'll do our duty," said Shedemei.

Hushidh knew that she was not referring to studies alone.

"Oh, hang the courteous obliquities," said Lady Rasa. "You all know that you're the unmarried ones, and that everybody *has* to marry if this is going to work at all, and that leaves only the four of you. I know that there's no particular reason why you shouldn't at least have the freedom to sort things out among yourselves, but I'll tell you that because of age and experience I rather imagined that it would be Hushidh who ended up with Issib and Shedemei who ended up with Zdorab. It doesn't have to be that way, but I think it would be helpful if you at least explored the possibilities."

"The Lady Rasa speaks about experience," said Zdorab, "but I must point out that I am a man of no experience whatsoever when it comes to women, and I fear that I will offend with every word I say."

Shedemei gave one hoot of derisive laughter.

"What Shedemei meant, with her simple eloquence," said Rasa, "is that she cannot conceive of your having less experience of women than she has of men. She, too, is quite certain of her ability to offend *you* with every word, which is why she chose to respond to you without using any."

The absurdity of the whole situation combined with Shedemei's gracelessness and Zdorab's awkward courtesy was too much for Hushidh. She burst out laughing, and soon the others joined in.

"There's no hurry," said Volemak. "Take your time to become acquainted."

"I'd rather just get it over with," said Shedemei.

"Marriage is not something you get over with," said Rasa. "It's something you begin. So as Volemak was saying, take your time. When you're ready, come to either me or my husband, and we can arrange new tent assignments, along with the appropriate ceremonies."

"And if we're never ready?" asked Issib.

"None of us will live long enough to see never," said Volemak. "And for the present, it will be enough if you try to know and like each other."

That was it, except for a few pleasant words about the supper Zdorab had prepared. They quickly divided, and Hushidh followed Shedemei to the tent they would share for now.

"Well, *that* was reassuring," said Shedemei.

It took a moment for Hushidh to realize that Shedya was being ironic; it always did. "*I'm* not much reassured," Hushidh answered.

"Oh, you didn't think it was sweet of them to let us take our time about deciding whether to do the inevitable? Rather like giving a condemned murderer the lever of the gallows trap and telling him, 'Whenever you're ready.' "

It was a surprise to realize that Shedemei seemed far angrier about this than Hushidh was. But then, Shedemei was not a willing participant in the journey, the way Hushidh had been. Shedemei had not thought of herself as belonging to the Oversoul, not the way Hushidh had ever since she realized she was a raveler, or Luet, ever since she discovered she was a waterseer. So of course *everything* seemed out of kilter to her; all her plans were in disarray.

Hushidh thought to help her by saying, "Zdorab is as much a captive on this journey as you are—he never asked for this, and *you* at least had your dream." But she saw at once—for Hushidh *always* saw the connections between people—that her words, far from giving comfort, were driving a wedge between her and Shedemei, and so she fell silent.

Fell silent and suffered, for she well remembered that it was Issib who had asked, What if we're never ready? That was a terrible thing to hear your future husband say, a terrible thing, for it meant that he did not think he could ever love her.

Then a thought came abruptly into her mind: What if Issib said that, not because he thought *he* could never desire *her,* but because he was certain that *she* could never be ready to marry *him?* Now that she thought about it, she was certain that was what he meant, for she knew Issib to be a kind young man who was not likely to say something that he thought might hurt someone else. She suddenly found a floodgate of memory opened inside her mind, and saw all the images she had of Issib. He was quiet, and bore his infirmity without complaint. He had great courage, in his own way, and his mind was bright indeed—he had always been quick in class, the times they had been together, and his ideas were never the obvious ones, but always showed him thinking a step or two beyond the immediate question.

His body may be limited, she thought, but his mind is at least a match for mine. And plain as I am, I can't possibly be as worried about my own body as he is about his. Nafai may have assured me that Issib is physically capable of fathering children, but that doesn't mean he has any notion of lovemaking—indeed, he's probably terrified that I will be disgusted by him, or at least frustrated at how little he imagines he can give me in the way of pleasure. I am not the one who needs reassurance, *he* is, and it would only be destructive if I entered into our courtship with the idea that he must somehow reassure *my* self-doubting heart. No, I must make him confident of my acceptance of *him,* if we're to build a friendship and a marriage.

This insight filled Hushidh with such great relief that she almost wept with the joy of it. Only then did she realize that ideas that came to her so suddenly, with such great clarity, might not be her ideas at all. Indeed, she noticed now that she had been imagining a picture of Issib's body as it appeared to *him,* only it hadn't been imagination at all, had it? The Oversoul had shown her the thoughts and fears inside Issib's mind.

As so many times before, Hushidh wished she had the same easy communication with the Oversoul that Luet and Nafai had. Occasionally the Oversoul was able to put thoughts as words inside her mind, as always happened with them, but it was never a comfortable dialogue for her, never easy for her to sort out which were her own thoughts and which were the Oversoul's. So she had to make do with her gift of raveling, and then sometimes these clear insights that always felt like her own ideas when they came, and only afterward seemed to be too clear to be anything but visions from the Oversoul.

Still, she was certain that what she had seen was, not her imagination, but the truth: The Oversoul had shown her what she needed to see, if she was to get past her own fears.

Thank you, she thought, as clearly as she could, though she had no way of knowing if the Oversoul heard her thoughts, or was even listening at the moment. I needed to see through his eyes, at least for a moment.

Another thought came to her: Is he also seeing through *my* eyes at this moment? It disturbed her, to think that Issib might be seeing her body as she saw it, complete with her fears and dissatisfactions.

No, fair is fair. If he is to have confidence in himself, and if he is to be a kind husband to me, he must know that I am as fearful and uncertain as he is. So do, if you haven't already, *do* show him who I am, help him to see that even though I am no beauty, I'm still a woman, I still long to love, to be loved, to make a family with a man who is bound into my heart and I into his as tightly as Rasa and Volemak are woven through each other's souls. Show him who I am, so he will pity me instead of fearing me. And then we can turn pity into compassion, and compassion into understanding, and understanding into affection, and affection into love, and love into life, the life of our children, the life of the new self that we will become together.

To Hushidh's surprise, she was sleepy now—she had feared that she'd get no sleep at all tonight. And from Shedemei's slow and heavy breathing, she must already be asleep.

I hope you showed her what *she* needed to see, too, Oversoul. I only wonder how other men and women manage to love each other when they don't have your help to show them what is in the other's heart.

Rasa woke up angry, and it took her a while to figure out why. At first she thought it was because when Volemak had joined her in bed last night he offered her no more than an affectionate embrace, as if her long fast did not deserve to be broken with a feast of love. He was not blind; he knew that she was angry, and he explained, "You're wearier than you think, after such a journey. There'd be little pleasure in it for either of us." His very calmness had made her angry beyond reason, and she curled up to sleep apart from his arms; but this morning she knew that her pique last night had been clear proof that he was right. She had been too tired for anything but sleep, like a fussy little child.

Almost no light got into the tent from outside. It could be high noon or even later, and from the stiffness of her body and the lack of a wind outside the tent, she could well have slept late into the morning. Still, to lie abed was delicious; no need to rise in a hurry, eat a scant breakfast in the predawn light, strike the tents, pack the beasts and be underway by sunrise. The journey was over; she had come home to her husband.

With that thought she realized why she had come awake this morning with so much anger in her. Coming home was not supposed to be to a tent, even one with double walls that stayed fairly cool through the day. And it was not *she* who ought to come home to *him,* but rather her husband who should come home to *her*. That's how it had always been. The house had been hers, which she had kept ready for him, and offered to him as a gift of shade in the summer, shelter in the storm, refuge from the tumult of the city. Instead *he* was the one who had prepared this place, and the more comfortable it was the angrier it made her, for in this place she would have no idea how to prepare anything. She was helpless, a child, a student, and her husband would be her teacher and her guardian.

No one had directed her in her own affairs since she first came into her own house, which she had done young, using money she inherited from her mother to buy the house that her great-grandmother had made famous, then as a music conservatory; Rasa had made it still more famous as a school, and from that foundation she had risen to prominence in the City of Women, surrounded by students and admirers and envious competitors—and now here she was in the desert where she did not even know how to cook a meal or how toileting was handled in a semi-permanent encampment like this. No doubt it would be Elemak who explained it to her, in his oh-so-offhanded way, the elaborate pretense that he was telling you what you already knew—which *would* have been gracious except that there was always the undertone of studiedness that made it plain that both you and he knew that you did *not* already know and in fact you depended on him to teach you how to pee properly.

Elemak. She remembered that terrible morning when he stood there with a pulse pointed at Nafai's head and thought: I must tell Volemak. He must be warned about the murder in Elemak's heart.

Except that the Oversoul had clearly shown that murder would not be tolerated, and Elemak and Mebbekew both had begged forgiveness. The whole issue of going back to Basilica was closed now, surely. Why bring it up again? What would Volemak do about it now, anyway? Either he'd repudiate Elemak, which would make the young man useless through the rest of the journey, or Volemak would uphold him in his right to make such a vile decision, in which case there'd be no living with Elemak from then on, and Nafai would shrink to nothing in this company. Elemak would never let Nafai rise to his natural position of leadership. That would be unbearable, for Rasa knew that of her own children, only Nafai was suited to lead well, for only he of the men of his generation had both the wit to make wise decisions and the close communication with the Oversoul to make informed ones.

Of course, Luet was every bit as well qualified, but they were now in a primitive, nomadic setting, and it was almost inevitable that males would take the lead. Rasa hadn't needed Shedemei's instruction about primate community formation to know that in a wandering tribe, the males ruled. Soon enough the women would all be pregnant, and then they would turn inward; when the children were born, their circle would enlarge only enough to include the little ones. Food and safety and teaching would be their concern then, in such a fearful, hostile place as the desert. There would be neither reason nor possibility of challenging the leadership of men here.

Except that if the leader were a man like Nafai, he would be compassionate to the women and listen to good counsel. While Elemak would be what he had already shown himself to be—a jealous tyrant, slow to listen to advice and quick to twist things to his own advantage, unfair and conniving . . .

I can't let myself hate him. Elemak is a man of many fine gifts. Much like his half-brother, Gaballufix, who was once my husband. I loved Gabya for those gifts; but, alas, he passed few of them to our daughters, Sevet and Kokor. Instead they got his self-centeredness, his inability to bridle his hunger to possess everything that seemed even faintly desirable. And I see that in Elemak also, and so I hate and fear him as I came to hate and fear Gaballufix.

If only the Oversoul had been just the teeniest bit fussier about whom she brought along on this journey.

Then Rasa stopped in the middle of dressing herself and realized: I'm thinking of how selfish and controlling Elemak is, and yet I'm angry this morning because *I'm* not the one in charge here. Who is the controlling one! Perhaps if I had been deprived of real control as long as Elemak has, I'd be just as desperate to get it and keep it.

But she knew that she would not. Rasa had never undercut her mother as long as she lived, and Elemak had already acted to thwart his father several times—to the point of almost killing Volemak's youngest son.

I must tell Volya what Elemak did, so that Volemak can make his decisions based on complete information. I would be a bad wife indeed if I didn't give my husband good counsel, including telling him everything I know. He has always done the same for me.

Rasa pushed aside the flap and stepped into the air trap,

which was much hotter than the inside of the tent. Then, after closing the flap behind her, she parted the outer curtain and stepped out into the blazing sun. She felt herself immediately drenched in sweat.

"Lady Rasa!" cried Dol in delight.

"Dolya," said Rasa. What, had Dol been waiting for Rasa to emerge? There was *nothing* productive for her to do? Rasa could not resist giving her a little dig. "Working hard?"

"Oh, no, though I might as well be, with this hot sun."

Well, at least Dol wasn't a hypocrite...

"I volunteered to wait for you to come out of the tent, since Wetchik wouldn't let anybody waken you, not even for breakfast."

It occurred to Rasa that she was a little hungry.

"And Wetchik said that when you woke up you'd be starving, so I'm to take you to the kitchen tent. We keep everything locked up so the baboons don't ever find it, or Elemak says we'd have no peace. They can't ever learn to find food from us, or they'd probably follow us farther into the desert and then die."

So Dolya *did* absorb information from other people's conversation. It was so hard to remember sometimes that she was quite a bright girl. It was the cuteness thing she did that made it almost impossible to give her credit for having any wit.

"Well?" asked Dol.

"Well what?"

"You haven't said a thing. Do you want to eat now, or shall I call everyone together to hear Wetchik's dream?"

"Dream?" asked Rasa.

"He had a dream last night, from the Oversoul, and he wanted to tell us all together. But he didn't want to waken you, so we all started doing other things, and I was supposed to watch for you."

Now Rasa was deeply embarrassed. It was a bad precedent for Volya to set, making everyone else get up and work while Rasa slept. She did *not* want to be the pampered wife of the ruler, she wanted to be a full participant in the community. Surely Volemak understood that.

"Please, call everyone together. Point me to the kitchen tent first, of course. I'll bring a little bread to the gathering."

She heard Dol as she wandered off, calling out at the top of her lungs—with full theatrical training in projecting her voice— "Aunt Rasa's up now! Aunt Rasa's up!"

Rasa cringed inwardly. Why not announce to everybody *exactly* how late I slept in?

She found the kitchen tent easily enough—it was the one with a stone oven outside, where Zdorab was baking bread.

He looked up at her rather shamefacedly. "I must apologize, Lady Rasa. I never said I was a baker."

"But the bread smells wonderful," said Rasa.

"Smells, yes. I can do smells. You should catch a whiff of my favorite—I call it 'burning fish.' "

Rasa laughed. She liked this fellow. "You get fish from this stream?"

"Your husband thought of doing some shore fishing down there." He pointed toward where the stream flowed into the placid waters of the Scour Sea.

"So you had some luck?"

"Not really," said Zdorab. "We caught fish, but they weren't very good."

"Even the ones that didn't get turned into your favorite smell . . . "

"Even the ones we stewed. There just isn't enough life on the land here. The fish would gather at the stream mouth if there were more organic material in the sediment being deposited by the stream."

"You're a geologist?" asked Rasa, rather surprised.

"A librarian, so I'm a little bit of everything, I guess," said Zdorab. "I was trying to figure out why this place doesn't have a permanent human settlement, and the reason came from the Index, some old maps from the last time there was a major culture in this area. They always grow up on the big river just over that mountain range." He pointed east. "Right now there are still a couple of minor cities there. The reason they don't use this spot is because there isn't enough plantable land. And the river fails one year in five. That's too often to maintain a steady population."

"What do the baboons do?" asked Rasa.

"The Index doesn't really track baboons," said Zdorab.

"I guess not," said Rasa. "I guess the baboons will have to build their own Oversoul someday, eh?"

"I guess." He looked mildly puzzled. "It'd help if they'd just build their own latrine."

Rasa raised an eyebrow.

"We have to keep an eye on them, so one of them doesn't wander upstream of us and then foul our drinking water."

"Mm," said Rasa. "That reminds me. I'm thirsty."

"And hungry too, I'll bet," said Zdorab. "Well, help yourself. Cool water and yesterday's bread in the kitchen tent, locked up."

"Well, if it's locked up . . ."

"Locked to *baboons*. For humans, it should be easy enough."

When Rasa got into the kitchen tent she found he was right. The "lock" was nothing but a twist of wire holding the solar-powered cold chest closed. So why did they stress the fact that it was locked? Perhaps just to remind her to close it after her.

She opened the lid and found several dozen loaves of bread, as well as quite a few other cloth-wrapped parcels of food—frozen meat, perhaps? No, it couldn't be frozen, it wasn't cold enough inside. She reached down and opened one of the packages and found, of course, camel's milk cheese. Nasty stuff—she had eaten it once before, at Volemak's house, when she was visiting him once between the two times they were married. "See how much I loved you?" he had teased her. "The whole time we were married, and I never made you taste this!" But she knew now that she'd need the protein and the fat—they'd be on lean rations through most of the journey, and they had to eat everything that had nutritional value.

Taking a flat round bread, she tore off half, rewrapped the rest, and then stuffed the part she meant to eat with a few chunks from the cheese. The bread was dry and harsh enough to mask much of the taste of the cheese, so all in all it wasn't as nauseating a breakfast as it could have been. Welcome to the desert, Rasa.

She closed the lid and turned toward the door.

"Aaah!" she screeched, quite without meaning to. There in the doorway was a baboon on all fours, looking at her intently and sniffing.

"Shoo," she said. "Go away. This is *my* breakfast."

The baboon only studied her face a little longer. She remembered then that she had *not* locked the cold box. Shamefaced, she turned her back on the baboon and, hiding what she was doing with her body, she retwisted the wire. Supposedly the baboon's fingers weren't deft enough to undo the wire. But what if his teeth were strong enough to bite through it, what then? No point in letting him know that it was the wire keeping him out.

Of course, it was quite possible he could figure it out on his own. Didn't they say that baboons were the closest things to humans on Harmony? Perhaps that's why the original settlers of this planet brought them—for they were from Earth, not native to this place.

She turned back around and again let out a little screech, for the baboon was directly behind her now, standing up on his hind legs, regarding her with that same steady gaze.

"This is *my* breakfast," Rasa said mildly.

The baboon curled his lip as if in disgust, then dropped down to all fours and started out of the tent.

At that moment Zdorab entered the tent. "Ha," he said. "We call this one Yobar. He's a newcomer to the tribe, and so they don't really accept him yet. He doesn't mind because he thinks it makes him boss when they all run away from him. But the poor fellow's randy half the time and he can't ever get near the females."

"Which explains his name," said Rasa. *Yobar* was an ancient word for a man who is insatiable in lovemaking.

"We call him that to sort of encourage him," said Zdorab. "Get on out of here now, Yobar."

"He was already leaving, I think, after I declined to share my bread and cheese with him."

"The cheese is awful, isn't it?" said Zdorab. "But when you consider that the boons eat baby keeks alive when they can catch them, you can understand that to them, camel cheese is really good stuff."

"We humans *do* eat it, though, right?"

"Reluctantly and constantly," said Zdorab. "And you never get used to the aftertaste. It's the chief reason we drink so much water and then have to pee so much. Begging your pardon."

"I have a feeling that city rules of delicate speech won't be as practical out here," said Rasa.

"But I ought to try more, I think," said Zdorab. "Well, enjoy your meal, I'm trying not to create the aroma of burnt bread."

He backed on out of the kitchen tent.

Rasa took her first bite of bread and it was good. So she took her second and nearly gagged—this time there was cheese in it. She forced herself to chew it and swallow it. But it made her think with fondness of the recent past, when the only camel product she had to confront was manure and no one expected her to eat it.

The tent door opened again. Rasa half expected to see Yobar again, back for another try at begging. Instead it was Dol. "Wetchik says we won't gather until the shadows get long, so it won't be so miserably hot. Good idea, don't you think?"

"I'm only sorry you had to waste half the day waiting for me."

"Oh, that's all right," said Dol. "I didn't want to work anyway. I'm not much at gardening. I think I'd probably kill the flowers right along with the weeds."

"I don't think it's a flower garden," said Rasa.

"You know what I mean," said Dol.

Oh, yes, I understand exactly.

I also understand that I must find Volemak and insist that he put me to work at once. It will never do for me to get days of rest when everyone else is working hard. I may be the second oldest here, but that doesn't mean I'm *old*. Why, I can still have babies, and I certainly will, if I can get Volya to greet me as his long-lost wife, instead of treating me like an invalid child.

What she could not say to herself, though she knew it and hated it, was the fact that she would have to have babies to have any role at all here in the desert. For they were reverting to a primitive state of human life here, in which survival and reproduction were at the forefront, and the kind of civilized life that she had mastered in Basilica would never exist again for her. Instead she would be competing with younger women for position in this new tribe, and the coin of the competition would be babies. Those who had them would be somebody; those who didn't, wouldn't. And at Rasa's age, it was important to begin quickly, for she wouldn't have as long as the younger ones.

Angry again, though with no one but poor frivolous Dol to be angry *at,* Rasa left the kitchen tent, still eating her bread and cheese. She looked around the encampment. When they had come down the steep incline into the canyon, there had been only four tents. Now there were ten. Rasa recognized the traveling tents, and felt vaguely guilty that the others were still living in such cramped quarters, when she and Volya shared so much space—a large, double-walled tent. Now, though, she could see that the tents were laid out in a couple of concentric circles, but the tent she shared with Volemak was not the center; nor was the kitchen tent. Indeed, at the center was the smallest of the four original tents, and after a moment's thought Rasa realized that that was the tent where the Index was kept.

She had simply assumed that Volemak would keep the Index in his own tent, but of course that would not do—Zdorab and Issib would be using the Index all the time, and could hardly be expected to arrange their schedule around such inconveniences as an old woman whose husband let her sleep too late in the morning.

Rasa stood outside the door of the small tent and clapped twice.

"Come in."

From the voice she knew at once that it was Issya. She felt a stab of guilt, for last night she had hardly spoken to the boy—the man—that was her firstborn child. Only when she and Volya had spoken to the four unmarried ones all at once, really. And even now, knowing that he was inside the tent, she wanted to go away and come back another time.

Why was she avoiding him? Not because of his physical defects—she was used to *that* by now, having helped him through his infancy and early childhood, having fitted him for chairs and floats so he could move easily and have a nearly normal life—or at least a life of freedom. She knew his body almost more intimately than he knew it himself, since until he was well into puberty she had washed him head to toe, and massaged and moved his limbs to keep them flexible before he slowly, painfully learned to move them himself. During all those sessions together they had talked and talked—more than any of her other children, Issib was her friend. Yet she didn't want to face him.

So of course she parted the door and walked into the tent and faced him.

He was sitting in his chair which had linked itself to the solar panel atop the tent so he wasn't wasting battery power. The chair had picked up the Index and now held it in front of Issib, where it rested against his left hand. Rasa had never seen the Index but knew at once that this had to be it, if only because it was an object she had never seen.

"Does it speak to you?" she asked.

"Good afternoon, Mother," said Issib. "Was your morning restful?"

"Or does it have some kind of display, like a regular computer?" She refused to let him goad her by reminding her of how late she had arisen.

"Some of us didn't sleep at all," said Issib. "Some of us lay awake wondering how it happened that our wives-to-be were brought in and dumped on us with only the most cursory of introductions."

"Oh, Issya," said Rasa, "you know that this situation is the natural consequence of the way things are, and nobody planned it. You're feeling resentful? Well, so am I. So here's an idea—I won't take it out on you, and you don't take it out on me."

"Who else *can* I take it out on?" said Issib, smiling wanly.

"The Oversoul. Tell your chair to throw the Index across the room."

Issib shook his head. "The Oversoul would simply override my command. And besides, the Index isn't the Oversoul, it's simply our most powerful tool for accessing the Oversoul's memory."

"How much does it remember?"

Issib looked at her for a moment. "You know, I never thought you'd refer to the Oversoul as *it.*"

Rasa was startled to realize she had done so, but knew at once why she had done so. "I wasn't thinking of *her*—the Oversoul. I was thinking of *it*—the Index."

"It remembers everything," said Issib.

"How much of everything? The movements of every individual atom in the universe?"

Issib grinned at her. "Sometimes it seems like that. No, I meant everything about human history on Harmony."

"Forty million years," said Rasa. "Maybe two million generations of human beings. A world population of roughly a billion most of the time. Two quadrillion lives, with thousands of meaningful events in every life."

"That's right," said Issib. "And then add to those biographies the histories of every human community, starting with families and including those as large as nations and language groups and as small as childhood friends and casual sexual liaisons. And then include all natural events that impinged on human history. And then include every word that humans ever wrote and the map of every city we ever built and the plans for every building we ever constructed . . . "

"There wouldn't be room to contain all the information," said Rasa. "Not if the whole planet were devoted to nothing but storing it. We should be tripping over the Oversoul's data storage with every step."

"Not really," said Issib. "The Oversoul's memory isn't stored in the cheap and bulky memory we use for ordinary computers. Our computers are all binary, for one thing—every memory location can carry only two possible meanings."

"On or off," said Rasa. "Yes or no."

"It's read electrically," said Issib. "And we can only fit a few trillion bits of information into each computer before they start getting too bulky to carry around. And the *space* we waste inside our computers—just to represent simple numbers. For instance, in two bits we can only hold four numbers."

"A-1, B-1, A-2, and B-2," said Rasa. "I *did* teach the basic computer theory course in my little school, you know."

"But now imagine," said Issib, "that instead of only being able to represent two states at each location, on or off, you could represent *five* states. Then in two bits—"

"Twenty-five possible values," said Rasa. "A-1, B-1, V-1, G-1, D-1, and so on to D-5."

"Now imagine that each memory location can have thousands of possible states."

"That certainly does make the memory more efficient at containing meaning."

"Not really," said Issib. "Not yet anyway. The increase is only geometric, not exponential. And it would have a vicious limitation on it, in that each *single* location could only convey one state *at a time*. Even if there were a billion possible messages that a single location could deliver, each location could only deliver one of those at a time."

"But if they were paired, that problem disappears, since between them any two locations could deliver millions of possible meanings," said Rasa.

"But still only *one* meaning at any one time."

"Well, you can't very well use the same memory location to store contradictory information. Both G-9 *and* D-9."

"It depends on how the information is stored. For the Oversoul, each memory location is the interior edge of a circle—a very tiny, tiny circle—and that inside edge is fractally complex. That is, thousands of states can be represented by protrusions, like the points on a mechanical key, or the teeth on a comb—in each location it's either got a protrusion or it doesn't."

"But then the memory location is the tooth, and not the circle," said Rasa, "and we're back to binary."

"But it can stick out farther or not as far," said Issib. "The Oversoul's memory is capable of distinguishing hundreds of different degrees of protrusion at each location around the inside of the circle."

"Still a geometric increase, then," said Rasa.

"But now," said Issib, "you must include the fact that the Oversoul can also detect teeth *on* each protrusion—hundreds of different values from each of hundreds of teeth. And on each tooth, hundreds of barbs, each reporting hundreds of possible values. And on each barb, hundreds of thorns. And on each thorn, hundreds of hairs. And on each hair—"

"I get the idea," said Rasa.

"And then the meanings can change depending on *where* on the circle you start reading—at the north or the east or south-southeast. You see, Mother, at every memory location the Oversoul can store trillions of *different* pieces of information at once," said Issib. "We have nothing in our computers that can begin to compare to it."

"And yet it's not an infinite memory," said Rasa.

"No," said Issib. "Not infinite. Because eventually we get down to the minimum resolution—protrusions so small that the Oversoul can no longer detect protrusions *on* the protrusions. About twenty million years ago the Oversoul realized that it was running out of memory—or that it *would* run out in about ten million years. It began finding shorthand ways of recording things. It devoted a substantial area of memory to storing elaborate tables of *kinds* of stories. For instance, table entry ZH-5-SHCH might be, 'quarrels with parents over degree of personal freedom they permit and runs away from home city to another city.' So where a person's biography is stored, instead of explaining each event, the biographic listing simply refers you to the vast tables of possible events in a human life—it'll have the value ZH-5-SHCH and then the code for the city he ran away to."

"It makes our lives seem rather sterile, doesn't it. Unimaginative, I mean. We all keep doing the same things that others have done."

"The Oversoul explained to me that while ninety-nine percent of every life consists of events already present in the behavior tables, there's always the one percent that has to be spelled out because there's no pre-existing entry for it. No two lives have ever been duplicates yet."

"I suppose that's a comfort."

"You've got to believe that *ours* is following an unusual path. 'Called forth by the Oversoul to journey through the desert and eventually return to Earth'—I bet there's no table entry for *that*."

"Oh, but since it has happened now to sixteen of us, I'll bet the Oversoul *makes* a new entry."

Issib laughed. "It probably already has."

"It must have been a massive project, though, constructing those tables of possible human actions."

"If there's one thing the Oversoul has had plenty of, it's time," said Issib. "But even *with* all that, there's decay and loss."

"Memory locations can become unreadable," said Rasa.

"I don't know about that. I just know that the Oversoul is losing satellites. That makes it harder for it to keep an eye on us. So far there aren't any blind spots—but each satellite has to bring in far more information than it was originally meant to. There are bottlenecks in the system. Places where a satellite simply *can't* pass through all the information that it collects fast enough not to miss something going on among the humans it's observing. In short, there are events happening now that aren't getting remembered. The Oversoul is controlling the losses by guessing to fill in the gaps in its information, but it's only going to get worse and worse. There's still plenty of memory left, but soon there'll be millions of lives that are remembered only as vague sketches or outlines of a life. Someday, of course, enough satellites will fail that some lives will never be recorded at all."

"And eventually all the satellites will fall."

"Right. And, more to the point, when those blind spots occur, there will also be people who are not under the influence of the Oversoul in any way. At that point they'll begin to make the weapons again that can destroy the world."

"So—why not put up more satellites?"

"Who? What human society has the technology to build the ships to carry satellites out into space? Let alone building the satellites in the first place."

"We make computers, don't we?"

"The technology to put satellites into space is the same technology that can deliver weapons from one side of Harmony to the other. How can the Oversoul teach us how to replenish its satellites without also teaching us how to destroy each other? Not to mention the fact that we could probably then figure out how to reprogram the Oversoul and control it ourselves—or, failing that, we could build our own *little* Oversouls that key in on the part of our brain that the Oversoul communicates with, so that we'd have a weapon that could cause the enemy to panic or get stupid."

"I see the point," said Rasa.

"It's the quandary the Oversoul is in. It must get repaired or it will stop being able to protect humanity; yet the only way it can repair itself is to give human beings the very things that it's trying to prevent us from getting."

"How circular."

"So it's going home," said Issib. "Back to the Keeper of Earth. To find out what to do next."

"What if this Keeper of Earth doesn't know either?"

"Then we're up to our necks in kaka, aren't we?" Issib smiled. "But I think the Keeper knows. I think it has a plan."

"And why is that?"

"Because people keep getting dreams that aren't from the Oversoul."

"People have always had dreams that aren't from the Oversoul," said Rasa. "We had dreams long before there *was* an Oversoul."

"Yes, but we didn't have the *same* dreams, carrying clear messages about coming home to Earth, did we?"

"I just don't believe that some computer or whatever that's many lightyears from here could possibly send a *dream* into our minds."

"Who knows what's happened back on Earth?" said Issib. "Maybe the Keeper of Earth has learned things about the universe that we don't begin to understand. That wouldn't be a surprise, either, since *we've* had the Oversoul making us stupid whenever we tried to think about really advanced physics. For forty million years we've been slapped down whenever we used our brains too well, but in forty million years the Keeper of Earth, whoever or whatever it is, might well have thought of some really useful new stuff. Including how to send dreams to people lightyears away."

"And all this you learned from the Index."

"All this I dragged kicking and screaming from the Index, with Zdorab's and Father's help," said Issib. "The Oversoul doesn't like talking about itself, and it keeps trying to make us forget what we've learned about it."

"I thought the Oversoul was cooperating with us."

"No," said Issib. "We're cooperating with *it*. In the meantime, it's trying to keep us from learning even the tiniest bit of information that isn't directly pertinent to the tasks it has in mind for us."

"So how did you learn all that you just told me? About how the Oversoul's memory works?"

"Either we got around its defenses so well and so persistently that it finally gave up on trying to prevent us from knowing it, or it decided that this was harmless information after all."

"Or," said Rasa.

"Or?"

"Or the information is wrong and so it doesn't matter whether you know it or not."

Issib grinned at her. "But the Oversoul wouldn't *lie,* would it, Mother?"

Which brought back a conversation they had had when Issib was a child, asking about the Oversoul. What had the question been? Ah, yes—Why do men call the Oversoul *he* and women call the Oversoul *she?* And Rasa had answered that the Oversoul permitted men to think of her as if she were male, so they'd be more comfortable praying to her. And Issib had asked that same question: But the Oversoul wouldn't lie, would it, Mother?

As Rasa recalled it, she hadn't done very well answering that question the first time, and she wasn't about to embarrass herself by trying to answer it again now. "I interrupted your work, coming here like this," said Rasa.

"Not at all," said Issib. "Father said to explain anything you asked about."

"He knew I'd come here?"

"He said it was important that you understand our work with the Index."

"What *is* your work with the Index?"

"Trying to get it to tell us what *we* want to know instead of just what the Oversoul wants us to know."

"Are you getting anywhere?"

"Either yes or no."

"What do you mean?"

"We're finding out a lot of things, but whether that's just because the Oversoul wants us to know them or not is a moot point. Our experience is that the Index does different things for different people."

"Depending on what?"

"That's what we haven't figured out yet," said Issib. "I have days when the Index practically sings to me—it's like it lives inside my head, answering my questions before I even think of them. And then there are days when I think the Oversoul is trying to torture me, leading me on wild goose chases."

"Chasing after what?"

"The whole history of Harmony is wide open to me. I can give you the name of every person who ever came to this stream and drank from it. But I can't find out where the Oversoul is leading us, or how we're going to get to Earth, or even where the original human settlers of Harmony first landed, or where the central mind of the Oversoul is located."

"So she's keeping secrets from you," said Rasa.

"I think it *can't* tell us," said Issib. "I think it would like to tell, but it can't. A protective system built into it from the start, I assume, to prevent anybody from taking control of the Oversoul and using it to rule the world."

"So we have to follow it blindly, not even knowing where it's leading us?"

"That's about it," said Issib. "Just one of those times in life when things don't go your way but you still have to live with it."

Rasa looked at Issib, at the steady way he regarded her, and knew that he was reminding her that nothing the Oversoul was doing to her right now was even close to being as oppressive as Issib's life in a defective body.

I know that, foolish boy, she thought. I know perfectly well that your life is awful, and that you complain about it very little. But that was unpreventable and remains incurable. Perhaps the Oversoul's refusal to tell us what's going on is *also* unpreventable and incurable, in which case I'll try to bear it with at least as much patience as you. But if I *can* cure it, I will—and I won't let you shame me into accepting something that I may not have to accept.

"What the Oversoul can't tell us for the asking," said Rasa, "we might be able to find out on the sly."

"What do you think Zdorab and I have been working on?"

Ah. So Issib wasn't really being fatalistic about it, either. But then another thought occurred to her. "What does your *father* think you've been working on?"

Issib laughed. "Not *that,*" he said.

Of course not. Volemak wouldn't want to see the Index used to subvert the Oversoul. "Ah. So the Oversoul isn't the only one that doesn't tell others what she's doing."

"And what do *you* tell, Lady Mother?" asked Issib.

What an interesting question. Do I tell Volemak what Issib is doing and run the risk of Volya trying to ban his son from using the Index? And yet I have never kept secrets from Volemak.

Which brought her back to the decision she had made earlier that day, to tell Volemak about what happened in the desert—about Elemak passing a sentence of death on Nafai. That could also have awful consequences. Did she have the right to cause those consequences by telling? On the other hand, did she have the right to deprive Volemak of important information?

Issib didn't wait for her answer. "You know," he said, "the Oversoul already knows what we're trying to do, and hasn't done a thing to stop us."

"Or else has done it so well you don't know she's doing it," said Rasa.

"If the Oversoul felt no need to tell Father, then is it so urgent, really, for you to do so?"

Rasa thought about that for a moment. Issib thought he was asking only about his own secret, but she was deciding about both. This *was* the Oversoul's expedition, after all, and if anyone knew and understood human behavior, it was the Oversoul.

She knows what happened on the desert, just as she knows what Issib and Zdorab are doing with the Index. So why not leave it up to the Oversoul to decide what to tell?

Because that's exactly what Zdorab and Issib are trying to find a way to circumvent—the Oversoul's power to make all these decisions about telling or not telling. I don't want the Oversoul deciding what I can or cannot know—and yet here I am contemplating treating my husband exactly as the Oversoul treats me. And yet the Oversoul really *did* know better than Rasa whether Volemak should be informed about these things.

"I really hate dilemmas like this," said Rasa.

"So?"

"So I'll decide later," she said.

"That's a decision, too," said Issib.

"I know that, my clever firstborn," said Rasa. "But that doesn't mean it's a permanent one."

"You haven't finished your bread," said Issib.

"That's because there's camel cheese in it."

"Really vile stuff, isn't it," said Issib. "And you wouldn't believe how it constipates you."

"I can't wait."

"That's why none of the rest of us ever eat it," said Issib.

Rasa glared at him. "So why is there so much in the coldbox?"

"Because we share it with the baboons. They think it's candy."

Rasa looked at her half-eaten sandwich. "I've been eating baboon food." Then she laughed. "No wonder Yobar came into the kitchen tent! He thought I was preparing a treat for *him!*"

"Just wait till you actually *give* him a piece of cheese, and he tries to mate with your leg."

"I get goose bumps just thinking about it."

"Of course, I've only seen him do it with Father and Zdorab. He might be a zhop, in which case he'll just ignore you."

Rasa laughed, but Issib's crude little joke about the baboon being a homosexual made her think. What if the Oversoul had brought someone along in their company who wasn't going to be able to perform his siring duties? And then another thought—did the Oversoul send this idea to her? Was it a warning?

She shuddered and laid her hand on the Index. Tell me now, she said silently. Is one of our company unable to take part? Will one of the wives be disappointed?

But the Index answered her not at all.

It was late afternoon and the only one who had killed any game today was Nafai, which annoyed Mebbekew beyond endurance. So Nafai was better at climbing quietly on rocks than Mebbekew was—so what? So Nafai could aim a pulse like he'd been born with it in his hands—all that proved was that Elemak should have fired the thing when he had the chance out on the desert.

Out on the desert. As if they weren't *still* in the desert. Though in truth this place *was* lush compared to some of the country they had gone through. The green of the valley where they lived was like a drink of cool water for the eyes—he had caught a glimpse of the trees from a promontory a few minutes ago, and it was delicious to his eyes, such a *relief* after the bleak pale grey and yellow of the rocks and sand, the greyish green of the dryplants that Elemak persisted in naming whenever he saw them, as if anybody cared that he knew every plant that grew around here by its full name. Maybe Elemak really *did* have cousins among the desert plants. It would hardly have been surprising to know that some distant ancestor of Elemak's had mated with a prickly grey bush somewhere along the way. Maybe I peed on a cousin of Elya's today. That would be nice—to show exactly what I think of people who love the desert.

I didn't even *see* the hare, so how could I possibly aim at it? Of course Nafai shot it—he *saw* it. Of course, Meb had fired his pulse, because everybody else was, too. Only it turned out not to have been everybody else after all. Just Vas, who aimed too low and his pulse set on too diffuse a setting anyway, and Nafai, who actually hit the thing and burned a smoky little hole right in its head. And, of course, Mebbekew, aiming at nothing in particular, so that Elemak had said, "Nice shot, Nafai. You're aiming low and raggedly, Vas, and tighten the beam. And you, Mebbekew, were you trying to *draw* a hare on that rock with your pulse? This isn't an etchings class. Try to aim toward the same planet that the quarry is on."

Then Elemak and Nafai headed down to retrieve the hare.

"It's getting late," Mebbekew had said. "Can't the rest of us go home without waiting for you to find the bunny-body?"

Elemak had looked at him coldly then. "I thought that you'd want to know how to gut and clean a hare. But then, you'll probably never *need* to know how to do it."

Oh, very clever, Elemak. That's how to build up confidence in your poor struggling pupils. At least I *fired,* unlike Obring, who treats his pulse as if it were another man's hooy. But Meb said none of that, just glared back at Elya and said, "Then I can go?"

"Think you can find the way?" asked Elemak.

"Of course," said Mebbekew.

"I'm *sure* you can," said Elemak. "Go ahead, and take anybody with you who wants to go."

But nobody wanted to go with him. Elemak had made them afraid that Mebbekew would lose his way. Well, he *hadn't* lost his way. He had gone in just the right direction, retracing their path quite easily, and when he clambered up to the crest of that hill just to be sure, there was the valley, exactly where he had expected to see it. I'm not *completely* incompetent, O wise elder brother. Just because I didn't sweat my way across the desert a few dozen times like you, toting fancy plants on camelback from one city to another, doesn't mean that I have no sense of direction.

If only he could figure out exactly when and where he tore his tunic and split the crotch of his breeches. . . . He really hated it when his clothes weren't at their best, and these were now soaked with sweat and caked with dust. He'd never be clean again.

He came to the edge of the canyon and looked down, expecting to see the tents. But there wasn't a tent in sight.

For a moment he panicked. They've left without me, he thought. They hurried past me, struck the camp and left me behind, all because I couldn't see the stupid *hare*.

Then he realized that he was simply downstream from the camp. There were the tents, up there to the left. And of course he was much closer to the sea. If the Scour Sea had had any waves like the ones on the shore of the Earthbound Sea, he'd have been able to hear the surf from here. And there were the baboons, eking out their miserable supper from the roots and berries and plants and insects and warty little animals that lived near the river and the seashore.

How did I end up here? So much for my sense of direction.

Oh, yes. We did walk down this way this morning, when we left Daddy's lazy wife asleep in the camp and all the lazy women, *especially* my completely useless stupid lazy wife, lolling around the tents and the garden. That's the only part of the route that I missed, just that one turn, so big deal, I *still* have a good sense of direction.

But he had a really bad taste in his mouth, and he wanted to kick something, he wanted to break something, he wanted to *hurt* someone.

And there were the baboons, right down there, stupid doglike animals that thought they were human. One of the females was showing red right now, and so the males were cuffing each other and maneuvering to get a quick poke. Poor stupid males. That's how we live our lives.

Might as well go down the canyon wall here and walk up the valley to the camp. And on the way maybe I can get a clear shot at whichever male ends up plugging her siggle. He'll die happy, right? And Nafai won't be the only one going home with a dead animal to his credit.

About halfway down the rugged slope, after scuffing a knee and sliding a couple of times, Meb realized that the lower he got, the worse his line of sight would be toward the baboons. Already there were rocks and bushes blocking his view of some of them, including the ones who were busy trying to mate. However, a smallish one was in plain sight, considerably closer than the others had been. It would be an easier shot anyway.

Meb remembered what Elemak had taught them earlier in the day and braced his elbows on a boulder as he took aim. Even so, his hands kept trembling, and the more he tried to hold them steady, the worse the sight on the pulse seemed to bounce. And when he pressed his finger against the button to fire, it jostled the pulse again, so that a small jet of smoke erupted from a bush more than six meters from the baboon he had been aiming at. The baboon must have heard something, too, because it whipped around to look at the burning shrub and then backed away in fear.

But not for long. A moment later it moved in again, and watched the flame as if trying to learn some secret from it. The bush was dry, but not dead, and so it burned only slowly, and with a great deal of smoke. Meb aimed again, this time a little to the right to compensate for the movement that pushing the button would cause. He also found that his hands were a bit more steady this time, and now he remembered that Elemak had stressed the need to relax. So . . . now Mebbekew was doing it just as Elemak had said, and this boon would soon be history.

Just as he was about to pull the trigger, he was startled by a sharp cracking sound only a meter from his head. His own shot went wild as he turned sharply to look at the place the sound had come from. A small plant growing from a crack in the rock a couple of meters above his head had been burnt to nothing, and smoke was rising from the spot. Since he had just seen the same thing happen to the shrub near the baboon, Meb recognized immediately what had happened. Someone was firing a pulse at *him*. Bandits had come—the camp was in danger, and he was going to die, off by himself, because the bandits had no choice but to kill him to keep him from giving the alarm. But I won't give the alarm, he thought. Just let me live and I'll hide here and be very quiet until it's all over, just don't kill me . . .

"What were you doing, shooting at baboons!"

With a clatter of small stones, Nafai slid down the last slope to stand in on the stone where Meb was standing. Meb saw with some pleasure that Nafai had slipped down just as he had; but then realized that Nafai had somehow done it without losing control, and ended up on his feet instead of sitting on the stone.

Only then did Meb realize that it was Nafai who had shot at him, and missed him by only a couple of meters. "What were you trying to do, kill me?" demanded Meb. "You're not *that* good a shot that you should be shooting so close to humans!"

"We don't kill baboons," said Nafai. "They're like people—what are you thinking of!"

"Oh, since when do people sit around digging for grubs, looking for a chance to tup every woman with a red butt?"

"It pretty much describes your life, Meb," said Nafai. "Did you think we were going to *eat* baboon meat?"

"I didn't really care," said Meb. "I wasn't shooting for meat, I was going for the kill. You're not the only one who can shoot, you know."

With those words, it occurred to Meb that he and Nafai were alone now, with no one else watching, and Meb had a pulse. It could be an accident. I didn't mean to touch the button. I was just shooting at a target and Nafai came down out of nowhere. I didn't hear him, I was concentrating. Please, please forgive me, Father, I feel so terrible, my own brother, I deserve to die. Oh, you're forgiven, my son. Just let me grieve for my youngest boy, who just got his balls shot off in a terrible hunting accident and bled to death. Why don't you go get laid while I'm weeping here?

That'd be the day, Father actually wishing Mebbekew something he wanted!

"You don't waste pulsefire on nothing shots," said Nafai.

"Elemak said so—they don't last forever. And we don't eat baboon. Elemak said that, too."

"Elemak can fart into a flute and play it as a tune, it doesn't mean *I* have to do it *his* way." I have the pulse in my hand. Already sort of half-aimed at Nafai. I can show how I turned around, startled, and the pulse sort of fired and blew out Nafai's chest. At this range, it might blow him up entirely, spattering little Nafai bits all over. I'll come home with blood on my clothes no matter what.

Then he felt a pulse pressed against his head. "Hand me your pulse," said Elemak.

"Why!" demanded Meb. "I wasn't going to do it!"

Nafai piped up. "You already fired at the baboon once. If you were a better shot it would already be *done*." So Nafai, of course, misunderstood completely what Meb had meant that he wasn't going to do. But Elemak understood.

"I said give me your pulse, handle first."

Meb sighed dramatically and handed the pulse to Elemak. "Let's make a big deal about it, shall we. *I'm* forbidden to shoot at a baboon, but *you* can point your pulse at the head of whichever brother you feel like pointing at, and it's all *right* when you do it."

Elemak clearly didn't appreciate Meb's reminder about the supposed execution of Nafai for mutiny in the desert. But Elemak merely left his pulse pressed to Meb's temple as he spoke to Nafai. "Never let me see you aim your pulse at another human again," said Elemak.

"I wasn't aiming at him. I was aiming at the plant above his head and I hit it."

"Yes, you're a wonderful shot. But what if you sneeze? What if you stumble? It's quite possible for you to take your own brother's head off with one little slip. So you *never* aim at another person or anywhere near, do you understand me?"

"Yes," said Nafai.

Oh, yes, yes, Big Brother Elemak, I'll suck up to you just the way I've always sucked up to Papa. It made Meb want to puke.

"It *was* a good shot, though," said Elemak.

"Thanks."

"And Meb is lucky it was you who saw him, and not me, because I might have aimed for his foot and left him with a stump to help him remember that you don't shoot baboons."

This wasn't right, Elemak attacking him like this in front of Nafai of all people. Oh, and of course, here come Vas and Obring, they *have* to be here to see Elemak showing him such disdain as to rag him in front of Nafai. "So suddenly baboons are the sacred animal?" asked Meb.

"You don't kill them, you don't eat them," said Elemak.

"Why *not?*"

"Because they do no harm, and eating them would be like cannibalism."

"I get it," said Meb. "You're one of those people who believe that boons are magical. They've got a pot of gold hidden away somewhere, every tribe of them, and if you're really nice and feed them, then, after they've stripped your land bare of every edible thing and torn apart your house looking for more, they'll rush off to their hiding place and bring the pot of gold to *you*."

"More than one lost wanderer on the desert has been led to safety by baboons."

"Right," said Meb. "So that means we should let them all live forever? Let me tell you a secret, Elya. They'll all die eventually, so why not now, for target practice? I'm not saying we have to *eat* it or anything."

"And I'm saying you're through hunting. Give me your pulse."

"Oh, swell," said Meb. "I'm supposed to be the only man without a pulse?"

"The pulses are for hunting. Nafai's going to be a good hunter, and you're not."

"How do you know? It's only the first day of serious work on it."

"You're not because you're never going to have a pulse in your hands again as long as I live."

It stung Mebbekew to the heart. Elemak was stripping away all his dignity, and for what? Because of a stupid baboon. How could Elya do this to him? And in front of Nafai, no less. "Oh, I get it," said Meb. "This is how you show your *worship* for King Nafai."

There was a moment's pause in which Meb wondered if he might have goaded Elya just a speck too far and maybe this was the time Elemak was going to kill him or beat him to a pulp. Then Elemak spoke. "Head back to camp with the hare, Nafai," he said. "Zdorab will want to get it into the coldbox until he starts the stew in the morning."

"Yes," said Nafai. Immediately he scampered down the hill to the valley floor.

"You can follow him," Elemak said to Vas and Obring, who had just clattered down the slope, both of them landing on their butts.

Vas arose and dusted himself off. "Don't do anything stupid, Elya," said Vas. Then he turned and started down the nontrail that Nafai had used.

Since Meb figured these words from Vas were all the support he was going to get, he decided to make the most of it. "When you get back to camp, tell my father that the reason I'm dead is because Elya's little accident with his pulse wasn't an accident at all."

"Yes, tell Father that," said Elemak. "It'll prove to him what he's long suspected, that Meb is out of his dear little mind."

"I'll tell him nothing at all, for now—*unless* you two don't get back to camp right away," said Vas. "Come on, Obring."

"I'm not your puppy," said Obring.

"All right then, stay," said Vas.

"Stay and do *what?*" asked Obring.

"If you have to ask, you'd better come with me," said Vas. "We don't want to interfere in this little family quarrel."

Meb didn't want them to go. He wanted witnesses to whatever it was Elya was planning to do. "Elemak's just superstitious!" he called after them. "He believes those old stories about how if you kill a baboon, his whole troop comes and carries off your babies! Eiadh must be pregnant, that's all! Come on back, we can all walk to camp together!"

But they didn't come back.

"Listen, I'm sorry," said Meb. "You don't need to make such a fuss about it. It's not as if I hit the boon or anything."

Elemak leaned in close to him. "You'll never take a pulse in your hands again."

"Nafai was the one who shot at *me,*" said Meb. "You'll take away my pulse for shooting at a boon, and Nafai shoots at *me* and he gets to *keep* his?"

"You don't kill animals you don't plan to eat. That's a law of the desert, too. But you know why I'm taking your pulse, and it isn't the baboon."

"What, then?"

"Your fingers were itching," said Elemak. "To kill Nafai."

"Oh, you can read my mind now, is that it?"

"I can read your body, and Nafai's no fool, either, he knows what you were planning. Don't you realize that the second you started to move your pulse he would have blown your head off?"

"He doesn't have the spine for it."

"Maybe not," said Elemak. "And maybe neither do you. But you aren't going to get the chance."

This was the stupidest thing Meb had ever heard. "A couple of days ago on the desert you tried to tie him up and leave him for the animals!"

"A couple of days ago I thought I could get us back to civilization," said Elemak. "But that isn't going to happen now. We're stuck out here, together whether we like it or not, and if Eiadh isn't pregnant yet she will be soon."

"If you can just figure out how it's done."

He had pushed a bit too far, he discovered, for Elemak swung his left arm around and smacked him square on the nose with his palm.

"Gaah! Aah!" Mebbekew grabbed at his nose, and sure

enough his hands came away bloody. "You peedar! Hooy sauce!"

"Yeah, right," said Elemak. "I love how pain makes you eloquent."

"Now I've got blood all over my clothes."

"It'll only help you bring off the illusion of being manly," said Elemak. "Now listen to me, and listen close, because I mean this. I will *break* your nose next time, and I'll go on breaking it every day if I see you plotting anything against anybody. I tried one time to break free of this whole sickening thing, but I couldn't do it, and you know why."

"Yeah, the Oversoul is better with ropes than I am," said Meb.

"So we're stuck with it, and our wives are going to have babies, and they're going to grow up to be our children. Do you understand that? This company, these sixteen people we've got here, that's going to be the whole world that our children grow up in. And it's not going to be a world where a little ossly-ope like you goes around murdering people because they didn't let him shoot a baboon. Do you understand me?"

"Sure," said Meb. "It'll be a world where big tough he-men like *you* get their jollies by smacking people around."

"You won't get smacked again if you behave," said Elemak. "There'll be no killing, period. Because no matter how smart you think you are, I'll be there before you, waiting for you, and I'll tear you apart. Do you understand me, my little actor friend?"

"I understand that you're sucking up to Nafai for all you're worth," said Mebbekew. He half expected Elemak to hit him again. Instead Elya chuckled.

"Maybe so," said Elemak. "Maybe I am, for the moment. But then, Nafai is also sucking up to *me,* too, in case you didn't notice. Maybe we'll even make peace. What do you think of that?"

I think you've got camel kidneys where your brains should be, which is why your talk is nothing but hot piss in the dirt.

"Peace sounds just wonderful, my dear kind gentle older brother," said Meb.

"Just remember that," said Elemak, "and I'll try to make your loving words come true."

Rasa saw them come straggling home—Nafai first, with a hare in his poke, full of the triumph of making a kill, though of course, being Nafai, he tried vainly to conceal his pride; then Obring and Vas, looking tired and bored and sweaty and discouraged; and finally Elemak and Mebbekew, smug and jocular, as if *they* were the ones who had taken the hare, as if *they* were co-conspirators in the conquest of the universe. I'll never understand them, thought Rasa. No two men could be more different—Elemak so strong and competent and ambitious and brutal, Mebbekew so weak and flimsy and lustful and sly—and yet they always seemed to be in on the same jokes, sneering at everyone else from the same lofty pinnacle of private wisdom. Rasa could see how Nafai might annoy others, with his inability to conceal his own delight in his accomplishments, but at least he didn't make other people feel dirty and low just by being near them, the way Mebbekew and Elemak did.

No, I'm being unfair, Rasa told herself. I'm remembering that dawn on the desert. I'm remembering the pulse pointed at Nafai's head. I'll never forgive Elemak for that. I'll have to watch him every day of the journey, to make sure of the safety of my youngest son. That's one good thing about Mebbekew—he's cowardly enough that you don't really have to fear anything from him.

"I know you're hungry," said Volemak. "But it's early yet for supper, and the time will be well spent. Let me tell you the dream that came to me last night."

They had already gathered, of course, and now they sat on the flat stones that Zdorab and Volya had dragged into place days ago for just this purpose, so all would have a place to sit off the ground, for meals, for meetings.

"I don't know what it means," said Volemak, "and I don't know what it's for, but I know that it matters."

"If it matters so much," said Obring, "why doesn't the Oversoul just tell you what it means and have done?"

"Because, son-in-law of my wife," said Volemak, "the dream didn't come from the Oversoul, and he is just as puzzled by it as I am."

Rasa noted with interest that Volya still spoke of the Oversoul as *he;* so Nafai's and Issib's custom of calling her *it* had not yet overtaken him. She liked that. Perhaps it was just because he was getting old and unimaginative, but she liked it that Volemak still thought of the Oversoul in the old manly way, instead of thinking and speaking of her as a mere computer—even one with fractal-like memory that could hold the lives of every human who ever lived and still have room for more.

"So I'll begin, and tell the dream straight through," said Volemak. "And I'll warn you now, that because the dream didn't come from the Oversoul, it gives me more reason to rejoice—for Nafai and Issib, anyway—and yet also more reason to fear for my first sons, Elemak and Mebbekew, for you see, I thought I saw in my dream a dark and dreary wilderness."

"You can see *that* wide awake," murmured Mebbekew. Rasa could see that Meb's jest was nothing but a thin mask for anger—he didn't like having been singled out like that before the dream began. Elemak didn't like it either, of course—but Elemak knew how to hold his tongue.

Volemak gazed at Mebbekew placidly for a moment or two, to silence him, to let him know that he would brook no more interruption. Then he began again.

FOUR
THE TREE OF LIFE

"I thought I saw in my dream a dark and dreary wilderness," said Volemak, but he knew as he said it that they would not understand what his words meant to him. Not the hot desert that they knew so well by now, dreary as *that* wilderness was. Where he walked in his dream was dank, chill and dirty, with little light, barely enough to see each step he took. There might have been trees not far off, or he might have been underground for all he knew. He walked on and on, with no hope and yet unable to stop hoping that by moving he would eventually escape this desolate place.

"And then I saw a man, dressed in a white gown." Like a priest of Seggidugu, only those are ordinary men, sweating as they perform their rites. This man seemed so at ease with himself that I thought at once that he must be dead. I was in a place where dead men waited, and I thought perhaps that *I* was dead. "He up came to me, and stood there in front of me, and then he spoke to me. Told me to follow him."

Volemak could tell that the others were getting bored—or

at least the most childish of them. It was so frustrating, to have only words to tell them what the dream was like. If they could know how that voice sounded when the man spoke, how warm and kind he seemed, as if the very sound of him was the first light in this dark place, then they'd know why I followed him, and why it *mattered* that I followed him. Instead, to them, it's only a dream, and this is clearly the dull part. Yet to me it was not dull.

"I followed him for many hours in the darkness," said Volemak. "I spoke to him but he didn't answer. So, since by now I was convinced that this man was sent by the Oversoul, I began to speak to the Oversoul in my mind. I asked him how long this had to go on, and where I was going, and what it was all about. I got no answer. So I became impatient, and told him that if this was a dream it was time for me to wake up, and if there was going to be some point to this maybe he should get to it before dawn. And there was no answer. So I began to think that maybe it was real, that it would go on forever, that this is what happens to us after death, we go to a dreary wasteland and walk forever behind some man who won't tell us anything that's going on."

"Sounds like life, lately," murmured Mebbekew.

Volemak paused, not looking at Meb, waiting for the others to glare him into silence. Then he went on. "Thinking it might be real, I began to plead with the Oversoul or whoever was in charge of this place to have a little mercy and tell me something or let me see something, let me *understand* what was happening. It was only then, after I began to plead for relief, that the place lightened—not like sunrise or coming near a campfire, I couldn't see any source of the light, I could simply *see,* like bright daylight, and I came out of the stony place to a vast field of tall grass and flowers, bending slightly in the breeze. It was such a relief—to see *life*—that I can't describe it to you. And a little way off—perhaps three hundred meters or so—there was a tree. Even at that distance I could see that amid the bright green of the leaves there were spots of white—fruit, I knew at once. And suddenly I could smell the fruit, and I knew that whatever it was, it was delicious, the most perfect food that ever existed, and if I could only taste that fruit, I'd never be hungry again."

He paused for just a moment, waiting for Mebbekew's obligatory smart remark about how hungry they all were right now, waiting for this dream to end. But Meb had apparently been chastened, because he was silent.

"I walked—I *ran* to the tree—and the fruit was small and sweet. Yes, I tasted it, and I can tell you that no food I've ever had in life was as good."

"Yeah, like sex in dreams," said Obring, who apparently thought that he could fill in for Meb. Volemak bowed his head for a moment. He could hear a movement—yes, Elemak rising to his feet. Volemak knew the scene without looking, for Elemak had learned this technique from him. Elemak was standing, looking at Obring, saying nothing at all, until Obring withered before him. And yes, there it was, Obring's mumbled apology, "Sorry, go on, go on." Volemak waited a moment more, and there was the sound of Elemak sitting back down. Now he could go on, perhaps without another interruption.

But it had been spoiled. He had thought he might be on the verge of finding exactly the right words to explain how the taste of the fruit had been in his mouth, how it made him feel alive for the first time. "It *was* life, that fruit," he said, but now the words sounded empty and inadequate, and he knew the moment of lucidity had passed, and they would never understand. "The joy I felt when I tasted it—was so perfect—I wanted my family to have it. I couldn't bear the thought that I had this perfect fruit, this taste of life in my mouth, and my family didn't know about it, wasn't sharing it. So I turned to look for you, to see where I might find you. You weren't back in the direction *I* had come from, and as I turned around I saw that a river ran near the tree, and when I looked upriver, I saw Rasa and our two sons, Issib and Nafai, and they were looking around as if they didn't know where they were supposed to go. So I called to them, and waved, and finally they saw me and came to me, and I gave them the fruit and they ate it and felt what I had felt and I could see it in them, too, that when they ate the fruit it was as if life came into them for the first time. They had been alive all along, of course, but now they knew *why* they were alive, they were *glad* to be alive."

Volemak couldn't help the tears that flowed down his cheeks. The memory of the dream was so fresh and strong inside him that telling it was to relive it, and the joy he felt could not be contained even now, after a day of work in the garden, even with the sweat and dirt of the desert on him. He could still taste the fruit in his mouth, could still see the look on their faces. Could still feel the longing he felt then, for Elemak and Mebbekew to taste it, too.

"I thought then of Elemak and Mebbekew, my first two sons, and I looked for them, wanting them to come and taste the fruit as well. And there they were, too, toward the head of the river where Rasa and Issib and Nafai had been. And again I called to them, and beckoned, but they wouldn't come. I tried to tell them about the fruit, shouting to them, but they acted as if they couldn't hear me, though I thought at the time that perhaps they really could. Finally they turned away from me and wouldn't even pretend to listen. There I stood with that perfect fruit in my hand, that taste in my mouth, that scent in my nose, knowing that they would be as filled with joy as I was if only they would come and taste it, and yet I was powerless to bring them."

Before his tears had been of joy; now they flowed for Elemak and Mebbekew, and they tasted bitter to him. But there was nothing more to be said about their refusal—he went on with the dream.

"It was only then, after my two oldest sons had refused to come to the tree, that I realized we weren't the only people there in that huge meadow. You know how it is in dreams—there aren't any people, and now there are thousands of them. In fact, not just people, but others—some that flew, some that scurried along—but I knew that they were people too, if you know what I mean. A lot of them had seen the tree. I thought maybe they had heard me shouting to Elya and Meb about what the fruit was like, how it tasted and all, and now they were trying to get to the tree. Only the distance was much farther now than it had been before, and it was as if they couldn't actually see the tree itself, but only knew generally where it was. I thought, How are they going to find it if they can't see it?

"That was when I saw that there was a kind of railing along the bank of the river, and a narrow little path running right along the river's edge, and I could see that that was the only route they could follow to reach the tree. And the people who were trying to find the tree caught hold of the iron rail and began to follow the path, clinging to the rail whenever the ground was slippery, so they didn't fall into the water. They pressed forward, but then they came into a fog, a thick and heavy fog drifting up from the river, and those that didn't hold on to the rod got lost, and some of them fell into the river and drowned, and others wandered off into the mist and got lost in the field and never found the tree.

"But the ones who held on to the railing managed to find their way through the fog, and finally they came out into the light, near enough to the tree that now they could see it with their own eyes. They came on then, in a rush, and gathered around me and Rasa and Issib and Nafai, and they reached up and took the fruit, and those that couldn't reach high enough, we plucked fruit for them and handed it down, and when there weren't enough to reach from the ground, Nafai and Issib climbed the tree—"

"I climbed . . ." whispered Issib. All of them heard him, but no one said a thing about it, knowing or guessing what he must think, to imagine himself climbing a tree alongside Nafai.

"Climbed the tree and brought down more of the fruit to give to them," said Volemak. "And I saw in their faces that they all tasted what I had tasted, and felt what I had felt. Only then I noticed that after eating the fruit, many of them began to look around them furtively, as if they were ashamed of having eaten the fruit, and they were afraid to be seen. I couldn't believe that they could feel that way, but then I looked in the direction that many of them had looked and there on the other side of the river I could see a huge building, like the buildings of Basilica only larger, with a hundred windows, and in every window we could see rich people, extravagant people, stylish and beautiful people, laughing and drinking and singing, the way it is in Dolltown and Dauberville, only more so. Laughing and having a wonderful time. Only I knew that it wasn't real, that it was the wine making them think they were having fun—or rather, they *were* having fun, but the wine made them think it *mattered* to have fun, when here, just across the river, I had the fruit that would give them the kind of joy that they were pretending they already had. It was so sad, in a way. But then I realized that many of the people who were there with me, people who were actually *eating the fruit,* were looking at the people in that huge building and they were envious of them. They wanted to go *there,* give up the fruit of the tree and join the ones who were laughing so loudly and singing so merrily."

Volemak didn't tell them that for a moment he also felt a faint sting of envy, for seeing them laughing and playing across the river made him feel old, not to be at the party. Made him remember that when he was young, he had been with friends who laughed with him; he had loved women whose kisses were a game, and caressing them was like gamboling and rolling in soft grass and cool moss, and he had laughed, too, in those days, and sung songs with them, and had drunk the wine, and it was real enough, oh yes, it was real. Real, but also out of reach, because the first time was always the best time, and anything he repeated was never as good as it had been before, until finally it all slipped out of his reach, all became nothing but memory, and that was when he knew that he was old, when the joys of youth were completely unrecoverable. Some of his friends had kept trying, had pretended that it never faded for them—but those men and women faded themselves, became painted mannequins, badly made worn-out puppets made in a mockery of youth.

So Volemak envied the people in the building, and remembered having been one of them, or having tried at least to be one of them—was anyone every really a true part of this transient community of pleasure, which evaporated and re-formed itself over and over again in a single night, and a thousand times in a week? It never quite existed, this family of frolickers, it only seemed about to exist, always on the verge of becoming real, and then it retreated always just out of reach.

But here at this tree, Volemak realized, here is the real thing. Here with the taste of this fruit in our mouths, we are part of something that isn't just illusion. We're part of *life,* wives and husbands, parents and children, the vast onward passage of genes and dreams, bodies and memories, generation after generation, time without end. We are making something that will outlast us, that's what this fruit is, that's what *life* is, and what they have across the river, their mad pursuit of every sensation their bodies can experience, their frantic avoidance of anything painful or difficult, it all misses the point of being alive in the first place. Nothing that is new is ever new twice. While things that are true are still true the next time; truer, in fact, because they have been tested, they have been tasted, and they are always ripe, always ready . . .

Yet Volemak could explain none of this to the people gathered around him, because he knew that these feelings were his own. Not really part of the dream itself, but rather his own responses to the dream, and perhaps not even what the dream was supposed to mean.

"The people in the building looked out at us who were gathered by the tree, and they pointed and laughed, and I could hear them ridiculing us for having been duped into standing around eating fruit when we could really experience life if we would only come over the river and join them. Join the party."

"Yes," whispered Obring sharply.

"I saw a lot of the ones who had tasted the fruit drop what

was left of it onto the grass and head for the river, to cross it and get to the building, and many who had never tasted it or even come near the tree also headed for the endless party going on there. Some of them drowned in the river, were swept away downstream, but many of them made it across and went to the building, dripping wet, and went inside, and I saw them come to the windows and point at us and laugh. But I wasn't angry with them, because now I saw something I hadn't seen before. The river was filthy, you see. Raw sewage floating in it. All the garbage of an unfastidious city was flowing downstream, and when they got out of the water, that's what was dripping from their clothing, that's what they smelled like when they entered the party, and inside the building, everybody there was covered with the sludge from the river, and the smell was unspeakable. And when you looked into the building you could see that no one actually enjoyed being near anybody else, because of the filth and the stench. They'd come together for a short time, but then the vileness of the other person's clothing would drive them away. And yet nobody seemed to realize that—they all seemed so eager to cross the river and get into the party. They all seemed to be afraid that they'd be turned away if they didn't hurry and get there *now*."

Volemak sat straighter, leaned back on the rock he was sitting on. "That was all. Except that even at the end, I found myself looking for Elemak and Mebbekew, hoping they'd come join me at the tree. Because I still had that fruit in my hand, the taste of it in my mouth. And it was still delicious and perfect, and it didn't fade away; each bite of it was better than the one before, and I wanted all my family, all my *friends* to have it. To be part of the *life* of it. And then I knew that I was waking up—you know how it is in a dream—and I thought, I can still taste it. I can still feel the fruit in my hands. How wonderful—now I'll be able to bring it to Elya and Meb and they can taste it for themselves, because if they once taste it they'll join the rest of us at the tree. And then I really woke up and found that my hands were empty, and Rasa was asleep beside me having her own dream and so she hadn't tasted the fruit after all, and Nafai and Issib were still in their tents, and it hadn't happened."

Volemak leaned forward again. "But I could still taste it. I can taste it now. That's why I had to tell you. Even though the Oversoul denies that he sent the dream to me, it felt more real, more true than any dream I've ever had before. No, it felt—it *feels*—more real than reality, and while I ate the fruit I was more alive than I've ever been in life. Does this mean anything to you?"

"Yes, Volya," said Rasa. "More than you know."

There was a general murmur of assent, and Volemak could see, looking around the group, that most of them looked thoughtful, and many of them had been moved—perhaps more by Volemak's own emotions than by the tale of the dream itself, but at least something about it had touched them. He had done what he could to share his experience with them.

"In fact it's made me really hungry," said Dol. "All that talk about fruit and stuff."

"And the sewage in the river. Mm-mmmm," said Kokor. "What's for supper?"

They laughed. The seriousness of the mood was broken. Volemak couldn't be angry, though. He couldn't expect that they would spend the rest of their lives transformed by his dream.

But it *does* mean something. Even if it didn't come from the Oversoul, it's true, and it matters, and I'll never forget it. Or if I do, I'll be the poorer for it.

Those who had worked on supper got up to check on the food and begin to serve it. Rasa came and sat beside Volemak and put her arm around him. Volemak looked for Issib and saw that he had tearstains down his cheeks, and Nafai and Luet were walking arm-in-arm, thoughtful and tender with each other—so good, so right, the two of them. Most of the others Volemak barely knew. His gaze instinctively glided over and past them, searching for Mebbekew and Elemak. And when he saw them he was surprised, for they looked neither moved nor angry. In fact, if Volemak could have put a name on what he saw in their faces, he would have called it fear.

How could they hear this dream and be afraid?

"He's setting us up for later," whispered Mebbekew. "This whole dream thing, with us cut off from the family—he's going to disinherit us both."

"Oh, shut up," said Elemak. "He's just letting us know that he knows about what happened on the desert, and he isn't going to make a big fuss about it, but he *knows*. So this is probably the end of it—unless one of us does something really stupid."

Meb looked at him coldly. "As I recall, it was *you* who pointed the pulse at Nafai on the desert, not *me*. So let's not point the finger and call people stupid."

"I seem to remember a more recent incident," said Elemak.

"Of which you were the only witness. Even darling Nyef had no idea, and in fact it isn't even true, you made it all up, you sorry pizdook."

Elemak ignored the epithet. "I hope I never look as stupid as Father did, crying in front of everybody—about a dream."

"Yes, everybody's stupid except Elemak," said Mebbekew. "You're so smart you fart through your nose."

Elemak could not believe how disgustingly childish Meb could be. "Are we still twelve, Meb? Do we still think rhyming *smart* with *fart* is clever?"

"That was the irony of it, you poor thick-headed lummox," said Meb in his most charming voice. "Only you're so smart you never understand irony. No wonder you think everybody around you is dumb—you never understand what they're saying, so you think they must not be speaking intelligibly. Let me tell you the secret that everybody else in this camp knows, Elya, my pet brother. You may know how to get through the desert alive, but it's the only thing you *do* know. Even Eiadh jokes with the other women that you finish with her so quickly she doesn't even have time to notice you've started. You don't even know how to please a woman, and Elya, let me tell you, they're all *very* easy to please."

Elemak let the insults and the innuendos slide off him. He knew Meb when he was in these moods. When they were both boys, Elemak used to beat him up when he got this way—but then it finally dawned on him that this was exactly what Mebbekew wanted. As if he didn't mind the pain as long as he got to see Elemak so angry and red-faced, sweating, with sore hands from pounding on Mebbekew's bones. Because then Meb knew he was in control.

So Elemak didn't let himself be goaded. Instead he left Meb and joined the others getting their supper at the cookfire. Eiadh was serving from the stewpot—there hadn't been time to cook the hare, so the only meat in it was jerky, but Rasa had made sure to pack plenty of spices so at least there'd be some flavor to the soup tonight. And Eiadh looked so lovely ladling it out into the bowls that Elemak was filled with longing for her. He knew well that Meb was lying—Eiadh had nothing to complain about in their lovemaking—and if there wasn't a baby in her there would be soon. That knowledge tasted sweet indeed to Elemak. This is what I was searching for in all those journeys. And if that's what Father meant by his tree of life—taking part in the great enterprise of love and sex and birth and life and death—then Elemak had indeed tasted of the fruit of that tree, and it *was* delicious, more than anything else that life had to offer. So if Father thought that Elemak would be shamed because he didn't come to the tree in Father's dream, then he'd be disappointed, because Elemak was already at the tree and didn't need Father to show him the way.

After supper, Nafai and Luet headed for the Index tent. They would have gone before eating, they were that eager—but they knew that there'd be no stock of food for snacking later. They had to eat when meals were served. So now, as darkness fell, they parted the door and stepped inside—only to find Issib and Hushidh already there, their hands together on the Index.

"Sorry," said Luet.

"Join us," said Hushidh. "We're asking for an explanation of the dream."

Luet and Nafai laughed. "Even though it's perfectly clear what it means?"

"So Father told you that, too," said Issib. "Well, I suppose he's right—it's sort of a general moral lesson about taking care of your family and ignoring the fun life and all that—like the books they give to children to persuade them to be good."

"But," said Nafai.

"But why *now*? Why *us*?" said Issib. "That's what we're asking."

"Don't forget that he saw what the rest of us have seen," said Luet. "What General Moozh saw."

"What do you mean?" asked Issib.

"He wasn't there," Hushidh reminded them. "I haven't told him yet—about my dream."

"We saw dreams," said Luet. "And even though all our dreams were different, they all had something in common. We all saw these hairy flying creatures—I thought of them as angels, though they don't look particularly sweet. And the Oversoul told us that General Moozh saw them also—Hushidh's and my father. And our mother, too, the woman called Thirsty who stopped Hushidh from being married to General Moozh. And the ones on the ground, too . . ."

Hushidh spoke up. "I saw the ratlike ones eating—someone's children. Or trying to."

"And Father's dream is part of all that," said Luet, "because even though it's different from the others, it still has the rats and the angels in it. Remember that he said he saw some flying, and some scurrying along the ground? But he knew they were people, too."

"I remember that now," said Issib. "But he skipped right over it."

"Because he didn't realize that that was the sign," said Luet.

"Of what?"

"That the dream didn't come from the Oversoul," said Luet.

"But Father already said that," said Issib. "The Oversoul told him."

"Ah, but whom *did* it come from?" asked Nafai. "Did the Oversoul tell him *that?*"

"The Keeper of Earth," said Luet.

"Who is *that?*" asked Issib.

"That's the one that the Oversoul wants to go back to Earth to see," said Luet. "That's the one we're *all* going to go back there to see. Don't you understand? The Keeper of Earth is calling us all in our dreams, one by one, telling us things. And what happened in Father's dream *is* important because it really does come from the Keeper. If we could just put it together and understand it . . ."

"But something coming from Earth—it would have to travel faster than light," said Issib. "Nothing can do that."

"Or it sent these dreams a hundred years ago, at lightspeed," said Nafai.

"Sent dreams to people who aren't even born?" said Luet. "I thought you had dropped that idea."

"I still think that the dreams might be sort of—in the air," said Nafai. "And whichever of us is sleeping when the dream arrives, has the dream."

"Not possible," said Hushidh. "My dream was far too specific."

"Maybe you just worked the Keeper's stuff into your own dream," said Nafai. "It's possible."

"No it isn't," said Hushidh. "It was all of a piece, my dream. If any of it came from the Keeper of Earth, it all did. And the Keeper knew me. Do you understand what that means? The Keeper knew me and she knew . . . everything."

Silence fell over the group for a moment.

"Maybe the Keeper is only sending these dreams to the people it *wants* to have come back," said Issib.

"I hope you're wrong," said Nafai. "Because I haven't had one like that yet. I haven't seen these rats and angels."

"Neither have I," said Issib. "I was thinking that maybe—"

"But you were in *my* dream," said Hushidh, "and if the Keeper is calling to me, she wants you, too."

"And we were both in Father's dream," said Nafai. "Which is why we have to find out what it meant. It's obviously more than just telling us to be good. In fact, if that's what it was for it did a pretty lousy job, since it made Elemak and Mebbekew furious to be singled out in the dream because they refused to come to the tree."

"So join us," said Issib. "Touch the Index and ask."

The longer arm of Issib's chair held the Index so he could rest his hand on it; the others gathered near and touched it, too. Touched it and questioned it, asking over and over again, silently in their minds . . .

"No," said Issib, "nothing's happening. It doesn't work this way. We have to be clear."

"Then speak for us," said Hushidh. "Ask the question for all of us."

With their hands all on the Index, Issib put voice to their questions. He asked; they waited. He asked again. They waited again. Nothing.

"Come on," said Nafai. "We've done everything you asked. Even if all you can tell us is that you're as confused as we are, at least tell us *that*."

The voice of the Index came at once: "I'm as confused as you are."

"Well, why didn't you say so from the start?" asked Issib in disgust.

"Because you weren't asking me what *I* thought of it, you were asking what it means. I was trying to figure it out. I can't."

"You mean you haven't yet," said Nafai.

"I mean I can't," said the Index. "I don't have enough information. I can't intuit the way you humans do. My mind is too simple and direct. Don't ask me to do more than I'm capable of. I know everything that is knowable by observation, but I can't guess what the Keeper of Earth is trying to do, and you exhaust me when you demand that I try to do it."

"All right," said Luet. "We're sorry. But if you learn anything . . . "

"I'll tell you if I think it's appropriate for you to know."

"Tell us even if you don't," demanded Issib.

But the Index's voice did not come again.

"It can be so *infuriating* dealing with the Oversoul!" said Nafai.

"Speak of her with respect," said Hushidh, "and perhaps she'll be more cooperative with you."

"Show it *too* much respect and the computer starts thinking that it's really a god," said Issib. "Then it's *really* hard to deal with."

"Come to bed," said Luet to Nafai. "We'll talk of this again tomorrow, but tonight we need our sleep."

It took little persuasion to get Nafai to follow her to their tent, leaving Hushidh and Issib alone.

They sat in silence for a while. Issib felt the uncomfortableness as if it were smoke in the air; it made it hard to breathe. It was Father's dream that had brought them together here, to speak to the Oversoul through the Index. It was an easy thing to show Hushidh how comfortably he dealt with the Index; he was confident of himself, when it came to the Index, even when the Oversoul was itself confused and couldn't answer aright. But now there was no Index between them—it rested voiceless in its case, where Nafai had placed it, and now only Hushidh and Issib remained, and they were supposed to marry each other and yet Issib couldn't think of anything to say.

"I dreamed of you," said Hushidh.

Ah! She had spoken first! At once the pent-up need to speak brought words to Issib's lips. "And you woke screaming?" No, that was a stupid thing to say. But he had said it, and—yes, she was smiling. She knew it was a joke, so he didn't have to be embarrassed.

"I dreamed of you flying," she said.

"I do that a lot," he said. "But only in other people's dreams. I hope you didn't mind."

And she laughed.

He should have said something else then, something serious, because he knew she was doing all the hard part—she was saying serious things, and he was deflecting them with jokes. That was fine to make them comfortable with each other, but it also kept turning away from the hard things she was trying to say. So he knew he should help her say the hard things, and yet he couldn't think of what they were, not now, sitting here with her in the Index tent, alone. Except that he knew he was afraid, for she needed a husband and it was going to have to be him except he had no idea if he could do any of the husbandly things for her. He could talk, of course, and he knew Hushidh well enough to know that she was a talker, when she knew you—he'd heard her speak passionately in class, and also in private conversations that he'd overheard. So they'd probably be able to talk, except that for talking they wouldn't need to marry, would they? What kind of father will I be? Come here right now, son, or I'll mash you with my chair!

Not to mention the question of how he'd get to be a father in the first place. Oh, he had worked out the mechanics of it in his own mind, but he couldn't imagine any woman actually wanting to go through with her part of it. And so that was the hard question that he couldn't bring himself to ask. Here is the script for how we'll make babies—are you willing to consider taking the starring role? The only drawback is that you'll have to do everything, while I lie back and give you no pleasure whatsoever, and then you'll have the babies while I help you not at all, and finally when we get old you'll have to nurse me till I die except that it won't make much difference since you'll probably have been nursing me all along, since once I have a wife everybody will expect to leave off helping me, so it'll be you, performing personal services that will disgust you, and then you'll be expected to receive my seed and bear me babies after *that* and there's no words I can bring to my lips that could persuade you to do that.

Hushidh looked at him steadily in the silence. "You're breathing rather heavily," she said.

"Am I?" he asked.

"Is that passion or are you as scared of all this as I am?" she asked.

Yes. More scared. "Passion," he said.

It wasn't very light inside the tent, but it wasn't very dark, either. He could see her make a decision, then reach up under her blouse and do something or other, and when she brought out her hands again, he could see that her breasts now moved freely under the cloth. And because she did that, he was more scared than ever, but he also felt just a touch of desire, because no woman had ever done such a thing in front of him, and certainly not *for* him, for him to *see* on *purpose*. Only he was probably expected to do something now and he had no idea what to do.

"I'm not very experienced at this sort of thing," said Hushidh.

What sort of thing? he wanted to ask, but then decided not to, since he understood exactly what she meant and it wasn't a good moment to joke.

"But I thought we ought to perform a kind of experiment," she said. "Before we decide anything. To see if you could possibly be attracted to me."

"I could," he said.

"And to see if you can give anything to me," she said. "It'll be better if we can both enjoy it, don't you think?"

Her words were so matter-of-fact. He could hear, though, from the trembling in her voice, that it wasn't matter-of-fact to her. And for the first time it occurred to him that she probably didn't think of herself as a beautiful woman. She was never one that the young men in the school had drooled over behind her back; now it occurred to Issib that she might be perfectly aware of that, probably *was* aware, and that she might be as frightened about whether he would desire her as he was about whether he could please her. It put them on something closer to equal terms. And instead of worrying about whether she'd be disgusted, he could give some thought to what she might enjoy.

She moved closer to him. "I asked my sister Luet," she said. "What men do for women that she thought you might be able to do for me." Her hands now rested on the arms of the chair. And now her right hand dropped down and rested on his leg. His thin, thin leg; he wondered how it felt to her, this thigh that barely had muscle on it. Then she pressed closer to him and he realized that his hand was now touched by the cloth of her blouse. "She said that you could do buttons."

"Yes," he said. It was hard, but he had learned to button and unbutton clothing that fastened that way.

"And I assumed that meant you could also undo them."

Only then did he realize that he was being invited.

"An experiment," he said.

"A midterm exam," she said, "in unbuttoning and opening, with an extra credit question later."

He lifted his hand—it was such hard work—lifted it and took hold of her blouse's top button. It was a bad angle—backhanded.

"Not a good angle, is it," she said. Then she moved her right hand to his other thigh, and higher, and then leaned in front of him. Now he could use both hands, and unbuttoning her blouse was almost easy, even though he had never had to unbutton someone else's clothing before. It occurred to him that this would be a useful skill with children who hadn't learned to dress themselves yet.

"Perhaps you can improve your time on the next one," she said.

He did. And now as he worked the skin of his hands brushed against her breasts. He had dreamed, day and night, of touching a woman's breasts, but had always believed that it would never be more than a dream. And now, as he unbuttoned each button, she lifted herself higher, so the next lower button would be in reach, and this moved her breasts closer to his face, until finally, by turning his head just a little, he would be able to kiss her skin.

His fingers unbuttoned the last button, and now the two sides of her blouse swung free, too. I can't I can't, he said, and then he did anyway, turned his head and kissed her. The skin was a little sweaty, but also soft and smooth, not like skin that had been weathered—not like his own hands, smooth as *they* were, or even his mother's smooth cheek, which he had often kissed; this was such skin as had never touched his lips before, and he kissed her again.

"You only got an average mark for unbuttoning and opening," she said, "but your extra credit work seems promising. You don't always have to be *that* gentle."

"I'm actually being as rough and brutal and manly as I can," he said.

"Then it's fine," she said. "You can't do it wrong, you know. As long as I know you're doing it because you want to."

"I do," he said. And then, because he realized that she needed to hear it, he said, "I want to very much. You're so . . . perfect."

She seemed to wince a little.

"Like what I imagined," he said. "Like a dream."

Then *her* hand moved, and tested him as well, to see how he was responding, and though his first instinct was to hide, to shy away, for once he was glad that his body wouldn't allow him to move away that quickly, because she needed also to know that he had been aroused.

"I think the experiment was a success, don't you?" asked Hushidh.

"Yes," said Issib. "Does that mean you want me to stop now?"

"No," she said. "But someone might come into this tent at any moment." She drew away and rebuttoned her blouse. She was breathing rather heavily, though. He could hear her despite his own heavy breathing. "That was a lot of exercise, for me," he said.

"I hope to wear you out."

"Can't unless you marry me," he said.

"I thought you'd never ask."

"Will you?"

"Is tomorrow soon enough?"

"No," he said. "I don't think so."

"Then maybe I should go and get your parents." Her blouse was buttoned by now, and she got up and left the tent. Only then did he realize that whatever the underwear was that had bound her breasts before, it was lying in the middle of the carpet, a little white pile. He dropped his right hand to the controls of his chair and made the chair's long arm go out and pick it up, then bring it close to him. He could see how the undergarment was made, and thought it was rather ingenious, but at the same time resented the way the elasticized fabric must hold a woman's breasts close to her body all the time. Maybe the women wore such things only for riding camels. It would be sad if they were confined like that all the time. Especially for him, because he liked very much the way Hushidh's body moved under her blouse when this had been removed.

He told his chair to stow it in the small case under the chair; it complied. Only just in time—Hushidh came back in at once with Father and Mother. "I can't very well complain that it's too sudden," said Father. "We've been expecting this and hoping it would come sooner rather than later."

"Do you want us to call everyone together for the ceremony?" asked Mother.

And have them spend a half hour being alternately bored by the ceremony and curious about how Hushidh and Issib would handle sex? "No thanks," he said. "All the important people are here."

"Well, too bad," said Hushidh. "I asked Luet and Nafai to come in, too, as soon as they've notified Zdorab and Shedemei about the new sleeping arrangements."

Issib hadn't thought of that—Hushidh had been sharing a tent with Shedemei, just as Issib had with Zdorab. The two of them would be forced together before they were ready, and . . .

"Don't worry," said Father. "Zdorab will sleep here with the

Index, and Shedemei will stay where she is. Hushidh will move in with you, because your tent is already . . . equipped."

Equipped with his private latrine arrangements, the pans for his sponge baths, his bed with the mattress of air bubbles so he didn't get bedsores. And in the morning, he'd need to void his bladder and his bowels, and he'd say, Shuya, darling, would you mind bringing me my jar and my pan? And then wipe up after me, there's a dear . . .

"And Nafai and Zdorab will come in the morning, to help you get ready for the day," said Father.

"And to teach me," said Hushidh. "That's not going to be a barrier between us, Issib, if you're to be my husband. I refuse to let it bother me, and you must refuse to let it bother you."

Easier said than done, thought Issib, but he nodded his agreement, hoping that it would be true.

The ceremony took only a few moments, once Nafai and Luet got there. Nafai stood with Issib and Luet with Hushidh, while Mother and Father took turns saying the parts of the ceremony. It was really the women's marriage ceremony, which was the usual way in Basilica, and so Father had to be prompted now and then to say his part right, but that was just part of the ceremony, or so it felt, to have Father's voice repeating the words Mother had just spoken, so gently, to remind him. At last it was done, and Rasa joined their hands. Hushidh bent to him in his chair, and kissed him. It was the first time his lips had touched hers, and it surprised him. It also pleased him very much, and besides, during the kiss she knelt down beside the chair and as she did, her breasts came to press against his arm, and all he really wanted was for everyone else to leave them alone so he could see how the rest of the experiment would go.

It was another half hour, with some teasing and joking from Nafai and Luet, but at last they were alone in Issib's tent, and they took up the experiment where they left off. When Hushidh was naked, she lifted him out of the chair—he knew that she was surprised at how very light he was, though Nafai had no doubt assured her that she'd have no difficulty lifting him, tall as he was. She undressed him and then brought her body near him, so he could give to her as much as she would give to him. He thought that he could not bear how powerful the feelings were as he could see the pleasure he was giving her, and feel the pleasures she was giving him; his body spent itself almost the very moment she eased herself upon him. But that was all right, too, for she still held him, and moved upon him, and kissed him, and he kissed her cheek, her shoulder, her chest, her arm, whenever a part of her came near his lips; and when he could, he pulled his arms around her so that when she moved atop him she could feel his hands also on her back, her thighs; gently, weakly, capable of nothing, really—but there. Was that truly enough for her? Was it something she could enjoy, again and again, forever?

Then, instead of wondering, it occurred to him to ask.

"Yes," she said. "You're done, then?"

"The first time, anyway," he said. "I hope it didn't hurt you too much."

"A little," she said. "Luet told me that I shouldn't expect to be overwhelmed the first time anyway."

"How not-overwhelmed were you."

"I wasn't *over*whelmed," she said. "But it's not like I wasn't whelmed at all, either. In fact, I'd say that on my wedding night I was well and thoroughly whelmed, and I rather look forward to our next whelming, to see how much better it can get."

"How about first thing in the morning?" he asked.

"Perhaps," she said. "But don't be surprised if you wake up and find yourself being taken advantage of in the middle of the night."

"Are you just pretending, or do you really mean all this?" said Issib.

"Are *you* just pretending?" she asked.

"No," he said. "This is the most wonderful night of my life. Mostly because . . . "

She waited.

"Because I never thought it would happen."

"It did though," she said.

"I answered," he said. "Now you."

"I thought I might have to pretend, and I *would* have pretended if I'd had to, because I know our marriage can work in the long run—I know it because I saw it in my dream from the Keeper of Earth. So if it meant I had to pretend to make it work well at the start, then I would have done it."

"Oh."

"But I didn't have to pretend. I showed you what I really felt. It wasn't as good as it's going to be, but it was good. *You* were good to me. Very gentle. Very kind. Very . . . "

"Loving?"

"Was that what you meant to be?"

"Yes," he said. "I meant that part most of all."

"Ah," she said.

But then in a moment he realized that she hadn't said *ah* at all, but rather had let a sound escape her mouth without meaning to, and he saw in the dim light that she was crying, and it occurred to him that he had said exactly the right things to her, as she had said exactly the right things to him.

And as he drifted toward sleep, her body close to his, his arm resting lightly on her side, he thought: I have tasted of the fruit in Father's dream. Not when we coupled, not when my body first gave its seed into a woman's body, but rather when I let her see my fear, and my gratitude, and my love, and she let me also see hers. Then we both reached up and tasted just the first bite of that fruit, and now I know the secret from Father's dream, the thing that even he didn't understand—that you can never taste the fruit by reaching for it yourself. Rather you only taste it when you pick it from the tree for someone else, as Shuya gave the fruit to me, and I, though I never thought it possible, plucked and gave a taste of it to her.

FIVE

THE FACE OF THE KEEPER

Luet sat watching the baboons. The female that she thought of as Rubyet, because of a livid scar on her back, was in estrus, and it was interesting to watch the males compete for her. The most blustering male, Yobar, the one who spent so much time in camp with the humans, was the least effective at getting Rubyet's attention. In fact, the more aggressive he got, the less progress he made. He would display his rage, stamping and snarling, even snapping his teeth and taking swipes with his hands, to try to intimidate one of the males who was courting Rubyet. Every time, the one he was intimidating would give up very quickly and run away from him—but while Yobar was chasing his victim, other males would approach Rubyet. So when Yobar returned to Rubyet from his "victory," he would find other males there before him, and the whole play was enacted again.

Finally, Yobar got really angry and began to attack one of the males in earnest, biting and tearing at him. It was a male that Volemak had pointed out once with the name Salo, because he had once smeared grease all over his face while stealing food from the cookfire. Salo immediately became submissive, showing his backside to Yobar, but Yobar was too angry to accept the submission. The other males looked on, perhaps amused, as Yobar continued to pummel and nip at his victim.

Salo at last managed to break free, howling and whining as he ran away from Yobar, who, still raging, followed after him at a furious pace, knocking him this way and that whenever he got within reach.

Then Salo did the most extraordinary thing. He ran straight for a young mother called Ploxy, who had a nursing infant that Salo often played with, and tore the infant from Ploxy's arms. Ploxy hooted once in annoyance, but the baby immediately started to act happy and excited—until Yobar, still furious, came charging up and started pummeling Salo again.

This time, however, the infant Salo was holding started screeching in terror, and now, instead of watching complacently, the other males immediately became agitated. Ploxy began screaming, too, calling for help, and within a few moments the entire troop of baboons had assembled around Yobar and were beating him and screaming at him. Confused, frightened, Yobar tried to grab the infant out of Salo's hands, perhaps thinking that if *he* held the infant, everybody would be on *his* side, but Luet realized that it wouldn't work. Sure enough, the moment he grabbed for the baby, the others became downright brutal in their beating of him, finally ejecting him from the group and chasing him away. Several of the males chased him quite a distance and then stayed nearby to watch and make sure he didn't come near. Luet wondered if that would be the end of Yobar's attempt to be part of the troop.

Then she looked for Salo, trying to spot him somewhere near Ploxy and the baby—but he wasn't there, though most of the other baboons were still there, chattering and bobbing up and down and otherwise showing how agitated they were.

Salo, however, was off in the brush upstream of the main group. He had got Rubyet away from the rest and now was mounting her. She had the most comically resigned look on her face, which now and then gave way to a look of eyes-rolled-back pleasure—or exasperation. Luet wondered if human faces gave that same weirdly mixed signal under similar circumstances . . . a sort of distracted intensity that might mean pleasure or might mean perplexity.

In any event, Yobar, the aggressive one, had been completely defeated—might even have lost his place in the tribe. And Salo, who wasn't particularly large, had lost the skirmish but won the battle *and* the war.

All because Salo had grabbed a baby away from its mother.

"Lucky Salo," said Nafai. "I wondered who would win sweet Rubyet's heart."

"He did it with flowers," said Luet. "I didn't mean to be off here so long."

"I wasn't looking for you to *do* anything," said Nafai. "I was looking for you because I wanted to be with you. There isn't anything for me to do now anyway, till supper. I got my prey early this morning and brought the bloody thing home to lay at my mate's feet. Only she was busy throwing up and didn't give me my customary reward."

"Wouldn't you know that *I'd* be the one who'd get sick all the time," said Luet. "Hushidh burped once and that was it for her. And Kokor *tries* to throw up but she just can't bring it off, so she ends up *not* getting the sympathy she wants and I end up having it when I don't want it."

"Who would have thought that it would be a race between you and Hushidh and Kokor for the first baby in the colony."

"A good thing for you," said Luet. "It'll give you an infant to grab, in case there's trouble."

He hadn't seen Salo's strategem, so he didn't understand.

"Salo—he grabbed Ploxy's baby."

"Oh, yes, they do that," said Nafai. "Shedemei told me. The males who are fully accepted in the tribe make friends with an infant or two, so the infant likes them. Then, in combat, they grab the infant, who *doesn't* scream when his *friend* takes him.

The other male *isn't* his friend, so when he keeps attacking the baby gets scared and screams, which brings the whole tribe down on the poor pizdook's head."

"Oh," said Luet. "So it was routine."

"I've never seen it. I'm jealous that you did and I didn't."

"There's the prize," said Luet, pointing to Salo, who still hadn't finished with Rubyet.

"And where's the loser? I'll bet it's Yobar." Luet was already pointing, and sure enough, there was Yobar, looking forlorn off in the distance, watching the troop but not daring to come closer because of the two males who were browsing halfway between him and the rest of the troop.

"You'd better make friends with my baby, then," said Luet. "Or you won't ever get your way in this tribe we're forming."

Nafai put his hand on Luet's stomach. "No bigger yet."

"That's fine with me," said Luet. "Now, what did you really come out here for?"

He looked at her in consternation.

"You didn't know I was down here because nobody knew I was down here," said Luet, "so you didn't come looking for me, you came here to be alone."

He shrugged. "I'd rather be with you."

"You're so impatient," said Luet. "The Oversoul already said there's no hurry—she won't even be ready for us at Vusadka for years yet."

"This place can't sustain us—it's already getting harder to find game," said Nafai. "And we're too close to that settled valley over the mountains to the east."

"That isn't what you're anxious about, either," said Luet. "It's driving you crazy that the Keeper of Earth hasn't sent you a dream."

"*That* doesn't bother me at all," said Nafai. "What bothers me is the way you keep throwing it up to me. That you and Shuya and Father and Moozh and Thirsty all saw these angels and rats, and I didn't. What, does that mean that some computer orbiting a planet a hundred or so lightyears away somehow judged me a century before I was born and decided that I wasn't worthy to receive his neat little menagerie dreams?"

"You really *are* angry," said Luet.

"I want to *do* something, and if I can't then at least I want to *know* something!" cried Nafai. "I'm sick of waiting and waiting and *nothing* happens. It's no good for me to work with the Index because Zdorab and Issib are constantly using it and they're more familiar with how it works than I am—"

"But it still speaks more clearly to you than anybody."

"So while it tells me nothing it does it with greater clarity, how excellent."

"And you're a good hunter. Elemak even says so."

"Yes, that's about all anybody's found for me to do—kill things."

Luet could see the shadow of the memory of Gaballufix's death pass over Nafai's face. "Aren't you ever going to forgive yourself for that?"

"Yes. When Gaballufix comes down out of the baboons' sleeping caves and tells me he was just pretending to be dead."

"You just don't like waiting, that's all," said Luet. "But it's like my being pregnant. I'd like to have it over with. I'd like to have the baby. But it takes time, so I wait."

"You wait, but you can feel the change in you."

"As I vomit everything I eat."

"Not everything," said Nafai, "and you know what I mean. I don't feel any changes, I'm not needed for anything . . . "

"Except the food we eat."

"All right, you win. I'm vital, I'm necessary, I'm busy all the time, so I must be happy." He started to walk away from her.

She thought of calling after him, but she knew that it would do no good. He wanted to be miserable, and so all she would do by trying to cheer him up was thwart him in his mood of the day. Aunt Rasa had told her a few days ago that it wouldn't hurt for her to remember that Nafai was still just a boy, and that she shouldn't expect him to be a mature tower of strength for her. "You were both too young to marry," said Rasa then, "but events got away from us. You've come up to the challenge—in time, Nyef will too."

But Luet wasn't sure at all that she had come up to any challenge. She was terrified at the thought of giving birth out here in the wilderness, far from the physicians of the city. She had no idea whether they'd even have food in a few months—everything depended on their garden and the hunters, and it was really only Elemak and Nafai who were any good at *that,* though Obring and Vas sometimes went out with pulses, too. The food supply could fail at any time, and soon she'd have a baby and what if they suddenly decided they had to travel? Bad as her sickness was right now, what if she had to ride atop a swaying camel? She'd rather eat camel cheese.

Of course, the thought of camel cheese made the nausea come back in a wave, and she knew that this time it might well come out, so down she went on her knees again, sick of the pain of the acidy stuff that came up from her gut into her mouth. Her throat hurt, her head hurt, and she was tired of it all.

She felt hands touch her, gathering her hair away from her face, twisting it and holding it out of the way, so none of the flecks of vomitus would get in it. She wanted to say thank you, knowing it was Nafai; she also wanted him to go away, it was so humiliating and awful and painful to be like this and have somebody *watching*. But he was her husband. He was part of this, and she couldn't send him away. Didn't even *want* to send him away.

At last she was through puking.

"Not too effective," said Nafai, "if we judge these things by quantity."

"Please shut up," said Luet. "I don't want to be cheered up, I want my baby to be a ten-year-old child already so that I remember all of this as an amusing event from my childhood long ago."

"Your wish is granted," said Nafai. "The baby is here and aged ten. Of course, she's incredibly obnoxious and bratty, the way *you* were at ten."

"I wasn't."

"You were the waterseer already, and we all knew you bossed and sassed grownups all the time."

"I told them what I saw, that's all!" Then she realized that he was laughing. "Don't tease me, Nafai. I know I'd be sorry later, but I still may lose control and kill you now."

He gathered her into his arms and she had to twist away to keep him from kissing her. "Don't!" she said. "I've got the most awful taste in my mouth, it would probably kill you!"

So he held her and after a while she felt better.

"I think about Keeper of Earth all the time," said Nafai.

I would, too, if I weren't thinking about the baby, Luet said silently.

"I keep thinking that maybe it *isn't* just another computer," said Nafai. "That maybe it *isn't* calling us through hundred-year-old dreams, that maybe it knows us, and that it's just waiting for . . . for *something* before it speaks to me."

"It's waiting for the message that only you can receive."

"I don't care," said Nafai. "About it being only me. I'd take *Father's* dream, if only I could experience what it feels like inside my head. How the Keeper is different from what the Oversoul does inside me. I want to *know*."

I know you do. You keep coming back to it, day after day.

"I've been trying to talk to the Keeper of Earth. That's how crazy I'm getting, Luet. Show me what you showed Father! I say it over and over."

"And she ignores you."

"It's a hundred lightyears away!" said Nafai. "It doesn't know I exist!"

"Well if all you want is the same dream as Volemak, why not get the Oversoul to give it to you?"

"It isn't *from* the Oversoul."

"But she must have recorded the whole experience inside your father's mind, right? And she can retrieve it, and show it to you. And the way you get everything so much more clearly through the Index—"

"Just like experiencing it myself," said Nafai. "I can't believe I never thought of that. I can't believe the *Oversoul* never thought of that."

"She's not very creative, you know that."

"She's creatively *inert,*" said Nafai. "But *you're* not." He kissed her on the cheek, gave her one last hug, and bounded to his feet. "I have to go talk to the Oversoul."

"Give her my love," said Luet mildly.

"I—oh, I see. I can wait—let's walk back together."

"No, really—I wasn't hinting. I want to stay here a while longer. Maybe just to see if they let Yobar back."

"Don't miss supper," said Nafai. "You're eating for—"

"Two," said Luet.

"Maybe three!" said Nafai. "Who knows?"

She groaned theatrically, knowing that was what he wanted to hear. Then he ran off, back up the valley toward the camp.

He really is just a boy, as Aunt Rasa said. But what am I? His mother now? Not really—*She's* his mother. I shouldn't expect more of him—he works hard and well, and more than half the meat we eat is from his hunting. And he's kind and gentle with me—I don't know how Issib could be any sweeter and more tender than Nafai, no matter what Shuya says. And I'm his friend—he comes to me to talk about things that he says to no one else, and when I want to talk he listens and answers, unlike some of the other husbands, or so *their* wives say. By any standard I ever heard of, he's a fine husband, and mature beyond his years—but it isn't what I thought it was going to be. When I took him through the Lake of Women, I thought it meant that he and I were going to do great and majestic things together. I thought we would be like a king and a queen, or at least like a great priestess and her priest, doing powerful and majestic things to change the universe. Instead I throw up a lot and he bounds around like a fifteen-year-old who is really hurt because some computer from another planet won't send dreams to him . . .

Oh, I'm too tired to think. Too sick to care. Maybe someday

my image of our marriage will come true. Or maybe that'll be his second wife, after I puke to death and get buried in the sand.

Shedemei had spent her whole life knowing that people looked at her oddly. At first it was because she was so intelligent as a child, because she cared about things that children weren't supposed to care about. Adults would look at her strangely. So would other children, but sometimes the adults smiled and nodded their approval, while the children never did. Shedemei had thought this meant that when she was an adult, she would be fully accepted by everyone, but instead the opposite was true. When she became an adult it only meant that all the other adult were the same age now and treated her as the children had. Of course, now she was able to recognize what she was seeing. It was fear. It was resentment. It was envy.

Envy! Could she help it that she had been given a combination of genes that gave her an extraordinary memory, an enormous capacity for grasping and understanding ideas, and a mind that was able to make connections that no one else could see? It's not as if she *chose* to be able to do mental gymnastics beyond the reach of anyone she had ever met in person. (There were people just as intelligent as she, and some perhaps more intelligent, but they were in far cities, even on other continents, and she knew of them only through their published works, distributed by the Oversoul from city to city.) She had no malicious intent. She certainly didn't have the ability to share her ability with the envious ones—she could only share the products of her ability. They gladly took those, and then resented her for being able to produce them.

Most human beings, she concluded long ago, love to worship from afar people with extraordinary ability, but prefer to have their friends be genial incompetents. And, of course, most of them get their preference.

But now she was permanently attached to this little society of sixteen people, and unable to avoid meeting them day by day. She did her work—her time weeding in the garden, her water turn, her hours of baboon-watching during the day to make sure they didn't leave their area and get into the food. She gladly covered for Luet when she was throwing up, and uncomplainingly did the tasks that Sevet was too lazy and Kokor too pregnant and Dol just generally too precious a being to do. Yet still she did not fit, was not accepted, was not *part* of the group, and it only got worse, day by day.

It didn't help a bit that she understood exactly what was happening. The bonding between husband and wife triggers a need for others also to be bonded in the same pattern, she knew that, she had studied it. The old courtship patterns, the loose and easy friendships, those now make the married ones feel uneasy, because they don't want anything around them that threatens the stability of the monogamous marriage bond, while the essence of unmarried society is always to be off balance, always to be free and random and unconnected and playful.

Admittedly, that was precisely the way some of them still wished to behave—Shedemei could see how monogamy chafed at Mebbekew and Obring, Sevet and Kokor. But they were *acting* the role of spouse right now, perhaps even more aggressively than the ones who actually meant it. In any event, the result was that Shedemei was even more cut off from others around her than she had ever been before. Not that she was shunned. Hushidh and Luet were as warm to her as ever, and Eiadh in her way was decent, while Aunt Rasa was utterly unchanged—she would never change. However, the men were all universally . . . what, *civil?* And Dol's, Sevet's, and Kokor's attitudes ranged from ice to acid.

Worst of all, this little company of humans was taking a shape that systematically excluded her from any influence in it. Why had they stopped saying, "The men will do *this* while the women do *that*"? Now it was, "The *wives* can stay here while the men go off and" do whatever it was that the men wanted to do. It drove her crazy sometimes that the women were lumped together as *wives,* while the men never called themselves *hus-*

bands—they were still men. And, as if they were as stupid as baboons, the other women seemed not to know what Shedemei was talking about when she pointed it out.

Of course, they *did* notice, at least the brighter ones did, but they chose not to make an issue of it because . . . because they were all becoming so *wifelike*. All these years in Basilica, where women did *not* have to submerge their identity in order to have husbands, and now, six weeks into the journey, and they were acting like nomadic tribeswomen. The coding for getting along without making waves must be so deep in our genes that we can never get it out, thought Shedemei. I wish I could find it, though. I'd dig it out with a trowel, I'd burn it out with a hot coal held in my bare fingers. Never mind the absurdity of dealing with genes with such blunt instruments. Her rage at the unfairness of things went beyond reason.

I didn't plan to marry, not for years yet, and even when I did I expected it would only be for a year, long enough to conceive, and then I'd dismiss the husband except for his normal rights with the child. I had no place for bonding with a man in my life. And when I *did* marry it would *not* have been with a weak-kneed semi-vertebrate archivist who allowed himself to be turned into the only servant in a company of lords.

Shedemei had entered this camp determined to make the best of a bad situation, but the more she saw of Zdorab the less she liked him. She might have forgiven him the way he *came* to this company—tricked by Nafai into carrying the Index out of the city, and then bullied into taking an oath to go into the desert with them. A man could be forgiven for behaving in an unmanly fashion during a time of stress and uncertainty and surprise. But when she got here she found that Zdorab had taken a role that was so demeaning she was ashamed to belong to the same species as him. It wasn't that he took upon himself all the tasks that no one else would do—covering the latrines, digging new ones, carrying away Issib's bodily wastes, doing the baking, the washing up. She rather respected someone who was willing to help—she certainly preferred that to the laziness of Meb and Obring, Kokor and Sevet and Dol. No, what made her feel such contempt for Zdorab was his *attitude* toward doing all that work. He didn't *offer* to do it, as if he had a right *not* to offer; he simply acted as if it were his natural *place* to do the worst jobs in the camp, and then performed his work so silently, so invisibly that soon they all took it for granted that the repulsive or unbearably tedious jobs were all Zdorab's.

He's a natural-born servant, thought Shedemei. He was born to be a slave. I never thought there was such a human creature, but there is, and it's Zdorab, and the others have chosen *him* to be my husband!

Why the Oversoul permitted Zdorab to have such easy access to her memory through the Index was beyond Shedemei's comprehension. Unless the Oversoul, too, wanted a servant. Maybe that's what the Oversoul loves best—humans who act like servants. Isn't that why we're all out here, to serve the Oversoul? To be arms and legs for her, so she can make her journey back to Earth? Slaves, all of us . . . except *me*.

At least, that's what Shedemei had been telling herself for all these weeks, until at last she realized that she, too, was beginning to fall into the servant category. It came to her today, as she carried water up from the stream for Zdorab to cook and wash with. She used to do this job with Hushidh and Luet, but now Luet was too weak from all her vomiting—she had lost weight, and that was bad for the child—and Hushidh was nursing her, and so it fell to Shedemei. She kept waiting for Rasa to notice that she was hauling the water all alone, for Rasa to say, "Sevet, Dol, Eiadh, put a yoke on your shoulders and haul water! Do your fair share!" But Rasa saw Shedemei carrying the water every day now, saw her carry the water right past where Sevet and Kokor were gossiping as they pretended to card camel hair and twine it into string, and Aunt Rasa never said a thing.

Have you forgotten who I am! she wanted to shout. Don't you remember that I am the greatest woman of science in Basilica in a generation? In ten generations?

But she knew the answer, and so she did not shout. Aunt Rasa *had* forgotten, because this was a new world, this camp, and what one might have been in Basilica or any other place did not matter. In this camp you were either one of the wives or you were not, and if you were not, you were nothing.

Which is why, today, with her work done, she went looking for Zdorab. Servant or not, he was the only available male, and she was sick of second-class citizenship in this infinitesimal nation. Marriage would symbolize her bowing to the new order, it would be another kind of servitude, and her husband would be a man for whom she had nothing but contempt. But it would be better than *disappearing*.

Of course, when she thought of actually letting him do his business with her body, it made her skin crawl. All she could think of was Luet throwing up all the time—that's the result of letting men treat you like a bank in which to deposit their feeble little sperm.

No, I don't really feel that way, thought Shedemei. I'm just angry. The sharing of genetic material is elegant and beautiful; it's been my life. The grace of it when lizards mate, the male mounting and clinging, his long slender penis embracing the female and searching out the opening, as deft and prehensile as a baboon's tale; the dance of the octopuses, arms meeting tip to tip; the shuddering of salmon as they drop eggs, then sperm, onto the bottom of the stream; it is all beautiful, all part of the ballet of life.

But the females always get to have some choice. The *strong* females, anyway, the *clever* ones. They get to give their ova to the male who will give them the best chance of survival—to the strong male, the dominant male, the aggressive male, the intelligent male—not to some cowering slave. I don't want my children to have slave genes. Better to have no children at all than to spend years watching them grow up acting more and more like Zdorab so that I'm ashamed of the very sight of them.

Which is why she found herself at the door of the Index tent, ready to walk in and propose a sort of semi-marriage to Zdorab.

Because she felt such contempt for him, she intended it to be a marriage without sex, without children. And because he was so contemptible, she expected him to agree.

He was sitting on the carpet, his legs crossed, the Index on his lap, his hands together on the ball, his eyes closed. He spent every free moment with the Index—though that wasn't really all that much time, since so few of his moments were free. Often Issib was with him, but in late afternoons Issib took his watch at the garden—the long arm of his chair was quite effective at discouraging baboons from exploring the melons, and had been known to bat birds out of the air. It was Zdorab's time alone with the Index, rarely more than an hour, and the one respect that the company paid to him was to leave him alone then—provided that dinner was already cooking and somebody else didn't want to use the Index, in which case Zdorab was casually shunted aside.

Looking at him there, his eyes closed, she could almost believe that he was communing with the great mind of the Oversoul. But of course he didn't have the brains for that. He was probably just memorizing the main entries in the Index, so he could help Wetchik or Nafai or Luet or Shedemei herself locate some bit of information they wanted. Even with the Index, Zdorab was the pure servant.

He looked up. "Did you want the Index?" he asked mildly.

"No," she said. "I came to talk to you."

Did he shudder? Was that the quick involuntary movement of his shoulders? No, he was *shrugging,* that's what it was.

"I expected that you would, eventually."

"Everyone expects it, which is why I *haven't* come till now."

"All right then," he said. "Why now?"

"Because it's plain that in this company the unmarried people are going to slip further and further into oblivion as time goes on. *You* may be content with that, but I am not."

"I haven't noticed you slipping into oblivion," said Zdorab. "Your voice is listened to in councils."

"Patiently they listen," said Shedemei. "But I have no real influence."

"No one does," said Zdorab. "This is the Oversoul's expedition."

"I didn't think you'd grasp it," said Shedemei. "Try to think of this company as a troop of baboons. You and I are getting thrust farther and farther to the edges of the troop. It's only a matter of time until we are nothing."

"But that only matters if you actually care about being *something.*"

Shedemei could hardly believe that he would put it into words that way. "I *know* that you have utterly no ambition, Zdorab, but I don't intend to disappear as a human being. And what I propose is simple enough. We just go through the ceremony with Aunt Rasa, we share a tent, and that's it. No one has to know what goes on between us. I don't want your babies, and I have no particular interest in your company. We simply sleep in the same tent, and we're no longer shunted to the edge of the troop. It's that simple. Agreed?"

"Fine," said Zdorab.

She had expected him to say that, to go along. But there was something else in the way he said it, something very subtle . . .

"You wanted it that way," she said.

He looked at her blankly.

"You wanted it this way all along."

And again, something in his eyes . . .

"And you're afraid."

Suddenly his eyes flashed with anger. "Now you think you're Hushidh, is that it? You think you know how everybody fits with everybody else."

She had never seen him show anger before—not even sullen anger, and certainly not a hot, flashing scorn like the one she was seeing now. It was a side of Zdorab that she hadn't guessed existed. But it didn't make her like him any better. It reminded her, in fact, of the snarling of a whipped dog.

"I really don't care," she said, "whether you wanted to have sex with me or not. I never cared to make myself attractive to men—that's what women do who have nothing *else* to offer the world than a pair of breasts and a uterus."

"I have always valued you for your work with genetics," said Zdorab. "Especially for your study of genetic drift in so-called stable species."

She had no answer. It had never occurred to her that anyone in this group had read, much less understood, any of her scientific publications. They all thought of her as someone who came up with valuable genetic alterations that could be sold in faraway places—that's what her relationship had been with Wetchik and his sons for years.

"Though I couldn't help but regret that you didn't have access to the genetic records in the Index. It would have clinched several of your points, having the exact genetic coding of the subject species as they came off the ships from Earth."

She was stunned. "The Index has information like *that?*"

"I found it a few years ago. The Index didn't want to tell me—I realize now because there are military applications of some of the genetic information in its memory—you can make plagues. But there are ways to get around some of its proscriptions. I found them. I've never been sure how the Oversoul felt about that."

"And you haven't told me till now?"

"You didn't tell me you were continuing your research," said Zdorab. "You did those papers years ago, when you were fresh out of school. It was your first serious project. I assumed you had gone on."

"This is the kind of thing you do with the Index? Genetics?"

Zdorab shook his head. "No."

"What, then? What were you studying just now, when I came in?"

"Probable patterns of continental drift on Earth."

"On *Earth!* The Oversoul has information that specific about Earth?"

to collect and test the memory in every part of the ships and bring good memory together until we have one perfect ship. I can't do this myself—I have no hands.⟩

"So I'm here to replace broken machines."

⟨And I need you to pilot the starship.⟩

"Don't tell me you can't do that yourself."

⟨Your ancestors did not let their starships pass completely under the control of computers like me, Nafai. There must be a starmaster on every ship, to give command. I will carry out those commands, but the ship will be yours. *I* will be yours.⟩

"Not me," said Nafai. "Father should do this."

⟨Volemak didn't come here. Volemak didn't open this place.⟩

"He would have, if he'd known."

⟨He knew what you knew. But you acted. These things are not accidental, Nafai. It isn't coincidence that you are here and no one else is. If Volemak had found this place and forced his way in, risking his own life for the sake of coming here, then he would wear the cloak. Or Elemak, or Zdorab—whoever came would have that responsibility. It was you. It is yours.⟩

Almost Nafai said, I don't want it. But that would be a lie. He wanted it with his whole heart. To be the one chosen by the Oversoul to pilot the starship, even though he knew nothing about piloting anything—that would be wonderful. More glory and accomplishment than he ever dreamed of in his childhood. "I'll do it then," said Nafai, "as long as you show me how it's done."

⟨You can't do it without tools. I can give you some of them, and teach you how to make the rest. And you can't do it without help.⟩

"Help?"

⟨There will be thousands of memory plates to move from one ship to another. You will grow old and die if you try to do it all yourself. Your whole village will need to work together, if we are to have a reliable starship that contains all of the memory that I will need to bring to the Keeper of Earth.⟩

At once Nafai tried to imagine Elemak doing any job under

his direction, and he laughed aloud. "If that's so, then you'd better put someone else in charge. They won't follow me."

⟨They will.⟩

"Then you don't understand human nature very well after all," said Nafai. "The only reason we've had peace among us these past few years is that I've stayed pretty much in my place, as far as Elya is concerned. If I suddenly come back and tell them that I'm the starmaster and they have to help me put together a starship . . . "

⟨Trust me.⟩

"Yeah, right. I always have, haven't I?"

⟨Open the door.⟩

Nafai opened the door and stepped into a dimly lighted room. The door closed behind him, shutting off much of what light there had been. Blinking, Nafai soon grew accustomed to the dimmer light and saw that in the middle of the room, hanging in the air with no obvious means of support, was a block of—what, ice?

⟨Much of it is water.⟩

Nafai approached it, reached out, touched it. His finger went in easily.

⟨As I said. Water.⟩

"How does it hold this shape, then?" asked Nafai. "How does it float in the air?"

⟨Why should I explain, when in a few moments the memory will be yours just for the thinking of it?⟩

"What do you mean?"

⟨Pass through the water and you will emerge wearing the cloak of the starmaster. When that is in place, linked to you, then all my memories will be yours, as if they had been yours all along.⟩

"A human mind could never hold such information," said Nafai. "Your memory includes forty million years of history."

⟨You will see.⟩

"Having Father's memory of his vision in my mind almost

drove me mad," said Nafai. "Won't that happen this time, having yours?"

⟨I will be with you as I have never been with you before.⟩

"Will I still be *myself?*"

⟨You will be more yourself than ever before.⟩

"Do I have a choice?"

⟨Yes. You can choose to refuse this. Then I will bring another, and she *will* pass through the water, and then *she* will be starmaster.⟩

"She? Luet?"

⟨Does it matter? Once you have chosen not to be starmaster, what right do you have to concern yourself with the person I then choose to take your place?⟩

Nafai stood there, looking at the miraculous block of water resting in the air, and thought: This is less dangerous than passing through the barrier, and I did *that.* He also thought: Could I bear to follow the starmaster, knowing for the rest of my life that I *could* have been starmaster, and refused? And then: I have trusted the Oversoul so far. I have killed for it; I have nearly died for it. Will I now refuse to take the leadership of this voyage?

"How do I do it?" asked Nafai.

⟨Don't you know? Don't you remember when Luet told you of her vision?⟩

Only now, with the Oversoul's reminder, did Nafai remember what Luet had said, of seeing him sink down into a block of ice and emerge from the bottom, glowing and sparkling with light. He had thought it had some metaphorical meaning. But here was the block of ice.

"I sink down from the top," said Nafai. "How do I get above this?"

Almost at once, a meter-wide platter skimmed across the floor toward him. Nafai understood that he was to stand on it. But when he did, nothing happened.

⟨Your clothing will interfere.⟩

So he removed his clothing for the second time that day. Doing so reminded him of all the scratches and bruises he had suffered from the buffeting of the wind. Naked, he stepped again on the disk. Almost at once it rose straight up into the air and carried him above the block.

⟨Step off onto the water. It will support you like a floor.⟩

Having just put his finger easily into the side of the block, Nafai had his doubts, but he did as he was told—he stepped onto the surface of the block. It was smooth, but not slippery; like the surface of the barrier, it seemed to be moving in every direction at once under his feet.

⟨Lie down on your back.⟩

Nafai lay down. Almost at once the surface under him changed, and he began to sink down into the water. Soon it would cover his face, he realized. He wouldn't be able to breathe. The memory of his recent suffocation was still fresh inside him—he began to struggle.

⟨Peace. Sleep. You'll not lack for air, or anything else. Sleep. Peace.⟩

And he slept as he sank down into the water.

Elemak was surprised to find that it was Shedemei at the door. All things were possible, of course—she might actually be coming here to join him. But he doubted it—it was far more likely that she was here to try to negotiate some settlement on Rasa's behalf. In which case she wasn't a bad choice as an emissary. He had nothing against her, and she had no awkward family connections. Besides, hadn't she and Zdorab stood up at the end of the meeting, accepting Elemak's authority to dismiss it? It was worth hearing what she had to say.

So he ushered her in and let her sit down at the table, along with Meb, Obring, and Vas. Then, when she was seated, Elemak sat across from her and waited. Let *her* speak first, and thus let him know what to expect from her.

"Everyone advised me against coming to you," she said. "But I think they underestimate you, Elemak."

"They have before," said Elemak.

Meb chuckled. That annoyed Elemak—he wasn't sure whether Meb was laughing at *them* for having underestimated Elemak, or laughing at Elemak for making such a claim. One was *never* sure, with Meb, whom he was mocking. Only that he was mocking *somebody*.

"There are some important things that you seem not to understand," said Shedemei. "And I think you need to know *everything* in order to make wise decisions."

Ah. So she was here to teach him about "reality." Well, it was worth listening, if only so he could better plan how to undercut her position at the next meeting. He nodded for her to continue.

"This isn't a conspiracy to take authority away from you."

Right, thought Elemak. You start out by denying it, and you've as good as confirmed to me that that's *exactly* what's going on.

"Most of us know that you're the natural leader of this group, and with some exceptions, we're content with it."

Oh, yes. "Some" exceptions indeed.

"And the exceptions are more among *your* followers than you imagine. Here at this table there is more hatred and jealousy of you than has ever been found among those who gather in the Index House."

"Enough of that," said Elemak. "If you came here to try to sow distrust among those of us who are trying to protect our families from the meddlers, then you can leave now."

Shedemei shrugged. "I've said it, you've heard it, I care little what you do with the information. But here's the fact: The only person you're fighting right now is the Oversoul."

Meb hooted once. Shedemei ignored him.

"The Oversoul has at last got access to the starships. It's going to take a massive effort by all of us to cannibalize five of the ships to make one ship ready to fly. But it's going to be done, whether you approve or not. The Oversoul is hardly going to let you block her now, when she's come so far."

Elemak heard with amusement the way Shedemei persisted in referring to the inanimate computer as if it were a woman.

"When Nafai returns, he's going to be wearing the starmaster's cloak. It's a device that links him almost perfectly to the memory of the Oversoul. He's going to know far more about you than you know about yourself, do you understand me? And there are other powers that come along with the cloak—a focus of energy, for one thing, that makes the pulse look like a toy."

"Is this a threat?" asked Elemak.

"I'm telling you the simple truth. The Oversoul chose Nafai because he has the intelligence to pilot the ship, the loyalty to serve the Oversoul's cause well, and the strength of will that broke down a supposedly impenetrable barrier and allowed the expedition to continue. *Not* because Nafai was conspiring against you. If you had ever shown a scrap of loyalty to the Oversoul's cause, she might have chosen *you.*"

"Do you think pathetic flattery like this will move me?"

"I'm not flattering you," said Shedemei. "I already said—we know you're the born leader of this company. But you've chosen *not* to be the leader of the Oversoul's expedition. That was your *own* choice, freely made. So when it comes down to it, when you realize that you have lost the leadership of this group forever, you can blame no one but yourself."

He felt anger growing within him.

"Nor would you have been the second choice," said Shedemei. "There was some doubt that Nafai would accept the cloak—for the very reason that he knew you would reject his leadership. At that point the Oversoul made her second choice. She asked *me* whether I would accept the burden of leadership. She explained to me more about what the cloak does and how it works than she even explained to Nafai, though by now he undoubtedly knows all. I accepted the offer. If it hadn't been Nafai, it would have been me. Not you, Elemak. You did not miss this great office narrowly. You were never in the running, because you rejected the Oversoul from the start."

"Perhaps you had better leave now," said Elemak softly.

"But this doesn't mean that you can't have a valued, important role in the community," she went on, seeming not to hear him, seeming not to notice that he boiled with rage. "Don't force the issue, don't force Nafai to humiliate you in front of the others. Instead work with him, and he will gladly let you take as much of the leadership as the Oversoul will let him surrender to you. I don't think you've ever realized how Nafai worships you. How he has always wished he could be like you. How he has longed for your love and respect more than that of any other person."

"Get out of my house," said Elemak.

"Very well," said Shedemei. "I see that you are a person who refuses to revise his view of the world. You can only bear to live in a world where all the bad things that happen to you are someone else's fault, where everyone must have conspired against you to deprive you of what is your due." She rose and walked to the door. "Unfortunately, that world happens not to be the *real* world. And so you four will sit here and conspire to take over the rule of Dostatok, and it will come to nothing, and you will be humiliated, and it will have been nobody's fault but your own. Yet even then, Elemak, you have our deep respect and honor for your considerable abilities. Good night."

She closed the door behind her.

Elemak could hardly control himself. He longed to leap after her, hit her again and again, beat the unbearable condescension out of her. But that would be a show of weakness; to maintain control of these others, he had to make it clear that he was unaffected by such nonsense. So he smiled wanly at them. "You see how they want to make us stupid by making us angry," said Elemak.

"Don't tell me you're *not* angry," said Meb.

"Of course I am," said Elemak. "But I refuse to let my anger make me stupid. And she also gave us some valuable information. Apparently Nafai's going to be coming back with some kind of magic cloak or something. Maybe it's nothing more

than an illusion, like those masks that Gaballufix dredged up to have his soldiers wear back in Basilica, so they all looked alike. Or maybe there's some real power in it. But far from making us back down, that will simply force us to act all the more quickly and cleanly—and permanently."

"Meaning?" asked Vas.

"Meaning that we will *not* permit *anyone* to leave here and go join Nafai, wherever he is. We will make him come to us. And when he does, unless he immediately backs down and accepts our decisions, we'll eliminate his ability to make further problems."

"Meaning?" insisted Vas.

"Meaning kill him, you dolt," said Obring. "How stupid do you have to be?"

"I knew he meant that," said Vas quietly. "I just wanted to hear him say it with his own mouth, so that he can't claim later that he never meant any such thing."

"Oh, I see," said Elemak. "You're worried about responsibility." Elemak couldn't help but compare Vas with Nafai—for all his other faults, Nyef had never shrunk from his responsibility for the death of Gaballufix. "Well, the responsibility is mine. Mine alone, if you insist on it. But that also means that after we've won, the authority is mine."

"I'm with you," said Meb. "To the hilt. Does that mean that when it's done, I share authority with you?"

"Yes, it does," said Elemak. If you even know what authority is, you poor simpering baboon. "It's as simple as that. But if you haven't got the heart to put in the knife along with us, that doesn't mean you're our enemy. Only keep silence about our plan, join with us in preventing others from joining Nafai, and stay out of the way when we kill him—if it comes to that."

"I'll agree to that," said Obring.

Vas also nodded.

"Then it's done."

* * *

Nafai awoke on the floor of the room. Above him hung the block of water. He didn't feel any different.

That is, until he started trying to think of things. Like when he tried to feel, from the inside, whether anything was different about his own body. All of a sudden a great gush of information flowed into his mind. He was conscious for a moment of all his bodily functions, and had a detailed status report on all of them. The output of his glands; his heartrate; the amount of fecal matter built up in his rectum; the current deficiency of fuel for his body's cells, and how his fat cells were being accessed to make up the shortfall. Also, the rate of healing of all his bruises and scrapes had been accelerated, and he felt much better.

Is this what the Oversoul has always known about me?

At once the answer came, and now it truly was a clear voice—even clearer than when the Oversoul spoke through the Index. ⟨I never knew this much about you before. The cloak has connected with every nerve in your body, and reports on your condition continuously. It also samples your blood in various places and interprets and acts to enhance your condition many times a second.⟩

Cloak?

At once an image flashed into his mind. He could see himself from the outside, as the Oversoul no doubt saw him through its sensors. He could see his body as he rolled out from under the block and rose to his feet. His skin sparkled with light. He realized that most of the light in the room came from him. He saw himself run his hands over his own skin, trying to feel the cloak. But he felt nothing at all that was different from his normal skin.

He wondered if he would always shine like this—if his house would always light up like this whenever he was inside.

The thought had no sooner come to him than the Oversoul's voice responded. ⟨The cloak responds to your will. If you wish it to go dark, it will. If you wish it to build up a powerful electrical charge, it will—and you can point your finger and

send an arc of energy in whatever direction you choose. Nothing can harm you while you wear this, and you can be deeply dangerous to others—yet if you have no wish to harm someone, the cloak will be passive. Your children can sleep in the dark, and you can hold your wife as you always have. Indeed, the more physical contact you have with others, the more your cloak will extend to include them, and even respond, in a small way, to your will.⟩

So Luet will also wear this cloak?

⟨Through you, yes. It will protect her; it will give her better access to my memory. But why do you ask me these things? Instead of thinking of questions, why not simply cast your mind back and try to remember, as if you had always known about the cloak. The memories will come to your mind easily and clearly, then. You'll know all there is to know.⟩

Nafai tried it, and suddenly he had no more questions about the cloak. He understood what it meant to be shipmaster. He even understood exactly what the Oversoul needed him to do to prepare a starship for departure.

"We don't have enough lifetimes among us, including our children, to do all of this," said Nafai.

⟨I told you that I'd give you the tools to work with. Some aspects of the robots are unsalvageable now, but other parts can be used. The machines themselves are perfectly workable—it's only my program to control them that is defective. Parts of it can be reactivated, and then you and the others can set the robots to doing the meaningless tasks under your direction. You'll see.⟩

And now Nafai "remembered" exactly what the Oversoul had determined was possible. It would take some serious work for several hours to get the robots working, but he could do it—he remembered how. "I'll get started at once," he said. "Is there anything to eat here?"

No sooner had he asked than he remembered that of course there was no food here. It made him impatient to think of having to leave this place and go hunt for food. "Can't you

bring the others here? Have them bring food, and . . . I don't see why we should have to take a day's journey every time someone comes here. We can rebuild our village here—there's plenty of water in the hills to the south, and plenty of lumber. We can spend a week doing that and save ourselves many days of travel each year until the ships are done."

⟨I'll pass the word. Or you can tell them yourself.⟩

"Tell them myself?" And then he remembered: Since the Oversoul's memory was now "his" memory, he could speak to the others through the Index. So he did.

"You're not going," said Elemak.

Zdorab and Volemak stood before him in bafflement. "What do you mean?" said Volemak. "Nafai needs food, and we need to mark out the new village. I assumed you'd want to come along."

"And I say you're not going. Nobody's going. We're not moving the village, and nobody is moving from here to go join Nafai. His attempt at seizing power here has failed. Give it up, Father. When Nyef gets hungry enough, he'll come home."

"I'm your father, Elya, not your child. You can decide not to go yourself, but you have no authority to stop *me*."

Elemak tapped his finger on the table.

"Unless you're threatening to use violence against your father," said Volemak.

"I have told you the law of this place," said Elemak. "Nobody leaves this town without my permission. And you don't have my permission."

"And if I disobey your presumptuous, illegal command?" said Volemak.

"Then you're no longer part of Dostatok," said Elemak. "If you're caught skulking around here, you'll be treated as a thief."

"Do you think the others will consent to this?" asked Volemak. "If you raise a hand against me, you'll earn only the disgust of the others."

"I'll earn their obedience," said Elemak. "I advise you... don't force the issue. No one takes food to Nafai. He comes home, and the charade about starships ends."

Volemak stood in silence, Zdorab beside him. Their faces were inscrutable.

"All right," said Volemak.

Elemak was surprised—could Father be giving in so easily?

"Nafai says he'll come home now. He has the first robots recommissioned and working. He'll be home in an hour."

"In an hour!" said Meb, who was standing nearby. "Well there it is. This Vusadka place was supposed to be a whole day's journey away."

"Nafai only just got the paritkas working. If they function well enough, we won't have to move the village."

"What's a paritka?" asked Meb.

Don't ask, you fool, Elemak said silently. It just plays into Father's hands.

"A flying wagon," said Volemak.

"And I suppose you're talking to Nafai right now?"

"When we don't have the Index with us," said Volemak, "his voice is as hard to distinguish from our normal thoughts as the Oversoul's voice normally is. But he's talking to us, yes. You could hear him yourself, if you only listened."

Elemak couldn't help laughing. "Oh, yes, I'm sure that I'm going to sit here and listen for the voice of my faraway brother, talking in my mind."

"Why not?" asked Zdorab. "He already sees everything that the Oversoul sees. Including what's going on in your mind. For instance, he knows that you and Meb plan to kill him as soon as he gets back here."

Elemak leapt to his feet. "That's a lie!" Out of the corner of his eye, he could see Meb getting a panicked look on his face. Just keep your mouth shut, Meb. Can't you recognize a wild guess when you hear one? Just don't do anything to *confirm* their guess. "Now get back to your house, Father. You too,

Zdorab. The only way Nafai will be in any danger is if he attacks *us* or tries to mutiny."

"This isn't the desert now," said Volemak. "And you're not in command."

"On the contrary," said Elemak. "Desert law still applies, and I am the leader of this expedition. I have been all along. I only deferred to you, old man, out of courtesy."

"Let's go," said Zdorab, drawing Volemak out of Elemak's house.

"And deprive Elemak of the chance of showing exactly how malicious he really is?"

"Not malicious, Father," said Elemak. "Just fed up. It's you and Nyef, Rasa and Luet and your group who started this. Nobody asked you to start this stupid business about traveling out among the stars. Everything was going fine—you're the ones who decided to change all the rules. Well, the rules *have* changed, and for once they don't favor you. Now take your medicine like a man."

"I grieve for you," said Volemak. Then Zdorab had him out the door and they were gone.

"They knew," said Mebbekew. "They knew what we were planning."

"Oh, shut up," said Elemak. "They *guessed,* and you nearly blurted out a confirmation of their guess."

"I didn't," said Meb. "I didn't say a thing."

"Get your bow and arrow. You're a good enough shot for *this.*"

"You mean we aren't going to wait and talk to him first?"

"I think Nafai will talk more reasonably if he has an arrow in him, don't you?"

Meb left the house. Elemak rose to his feet and reached for his bow over the fireplace.

"Don't do it."

He turned and saw Eiadh standing in the doorway to the bedroom, holding the baby on her hip.

"Did I hear you correctly, Edhya?" asked Elemak. "Are you telling me what to do?"

"You tried to kill him once before," said Eiadh. "The Oversoul won't let you. Don't you realize that? And this time you might get hurt."

"I appreciate your concern for me, Edhya, but I know what I'm doing."

"I know what you're doing, too," said Eiadh. "I've watched you with Nafai for all these years, and I thought, at last, Elya has learned to give Nafai his proper respect. Elya's stopped being jealous of his little brother. But now I see that you were just biding your time."

Elemak would have slapped her face for that, except that the baby's head was in the way, and he would never harm his own child. "You've said enough," he warned.

"I'd beg you to stop because you love me," said Eiadh, "but I know that would never work. So I'm begging you to stop for your children's sake."

"For their sake? It's for *their* sake that I'm doing this. I don't want their lives disrupted for the sake of Rasa's conspiracies to get control of Dostatok and turn this into a village of women like Basilica."

"For their sake," said Eiadh again. "Don't make them see their father humiliated in front of everyone. Or worse."

"I can see how much you love me," said Elemak. "Apparently your bets are on the other side."

"Don't shame them by letting them see that you're a murderer in your heart."

"Do you think I don't understand this?" said Elemak. "You've had a yen for Nafai ever since Basilica. I thought you'd outgrown it, but I was wrong."

"Fool," said Eiadh. "I admired his strength. I admired yours, too. But *his* strength has never wavered, and he's never used it to bully other people. The way you treated your father was shameful. Your sons were in the other room, listening to how you talked to your father. Don't you know that someday, when

you're old and frail, you may hear that same kind of disrespect from *them?* Go ahead, hit me. I'll set down the baby. Let your sons see how strong you are, that you can beat up a woman for no greater crime than telling you the truth."

Meb burst through the door. He had his bow and arrows. "Well?" he said. "Are you coming or not?"

"I'm coming," said Elemak. He turned to Eiadh. "I'll never forgive you for that."

She smirked at him. "In an hour you'll be asking for *my* forgiveness."

Nafai knew as he approached exactly what to expect. He had the memories of the Oversoul. He had heard the conversations between Elemak and his fellow plotters. He had listened as he ordered everyone to keep the children in their houses. He had felt the fear in everyone's hearts. He knew the damage Elemak was doing to his own family. He knew the fear and rage that filled his heart.

"Can't you make him forget this?" asked Nafai.

⟨No. That wasn't one of the powers I was given. Besides, he's very strong. My influence over him is oblique at best.⟩

"If he had chosen to follow you, he would have been better for your purposes than I am, wouldn't he?"

⟨Yes.⟩ It might as well speak plainly, since it could keep no secrets from Nafai now.

"So I'm second choice," said Nafai.

⟨First choice. Because Elemak doesn't have it in him to recognize a purpose higher than his own ambition. He's far more crippled than Issib.⟩

Nafai sped south, the paritka skimming over the ground, automatically finding a smooth route at a pace Nafai found unimaginable. He cared nothing for the miracle of this machine. It was all he could do to keep from weeping. For now, as he focused on the people of Dostatok instead of the labors of restoring a starship, he "remembered" things that he had never guessed. The struggles and sacrifices Zdorab and Shedemei had

made for each other. The cold hatred Vas felt for Obring and Sevet, and, ever since Shazer, for Elemak. Sevet's bitter self-loathing. Luet's and Hushidh's pain as their husbands treated them more and more like Elemak's idea of what wives should be, and less and less like the friends they were supposed to be.

Issib, who depends on Hushidh for everything in his life, how shameful for him to regard his wife as something less than a partner in all his work! And how *more* shameful for me, when my wife is the greatest of women, at least as wise as I am, that I have made her feel as she felt when I left her.

For he had seen all their hearts from the inside, and that is a vision that leaves no room for hate. Yes, he knew that Vas was a murderer in his heart—but he also "remembered" the agony that Vas went through when Sevet and Obring brought such shame on him. Never mind that Nafai himself had never thought that humiliation was an excuse for murder. He knew how the world looked from Vas's point of view, and it was impossible to hate him after that. He would *stop* him from getting his revenge, of course. But even as he did, he would understand.

Just as he understood Elemak. Understood how Nafai himself looked through Elemak's eyes. If only I'd known, thought Nafai. If only I'd seen the things I did that made him hate me.

⟨Don't be a fool. He hated your intelligence. He hated how you *loved* being intelligent. He hated your willing obedience to your father and mother. He hated even your hero-worship of Elemak himself. He hated you for being yourself, because you were so similar to him, and yet so different. The only way you could have kept him from hating you would have been to die young.⟩

Nafai understood this, but it changed nothing. Knowing all that he knew did not change the fact that he longed for things to be different. Oh, how he longed to have Elemak look at him and say, "Well done, Brother. I'm proud of you." More than those words from Father, Nafai needed to hear them from

Elemak. And he never would. The best he would get from Elemak today was his sullen compliance. The worst would be Elya's dead body.

"I don't want to kill him," whispered Nafai, over and over.

⟨If you don't want to, then you won't.⟩

And then, again and again, Nafai's thoughts came back to Luet. Ah, Luet, why did it take this cloak to make me understand what I was doing to you? You tried to tell me. Lovingly at first, and in anger lately, but the message was the same: You're hurting me. You're losing my trust. Please don't do it. And yet I didn't hear. I was so caught up in being the best of the hunters, in living the man's life among men, that I forgot that before I was really a man, you took my hand and led me down to the Lake of Women; you not only saved my life, you also gave me my place with the Oversoul. All that I am, all that I have, my self, my children, I received it all at your hands, Luet, and then rewarded you shamefully.

⟨You're nearly there. Get control of yourself.⟩

Nafai pulled himself together. He could feel how the cloak worked within him, healing the skin around his eyes from the reddening that had come with his tears. Instantly his face gave no sign of having been in tears.

Is this how it will be? My face a mask, because I have this cloak?

⟨Only if you want it to be.⟩

Nafai "remembered" where Elemak and Mebbekew had gone, to lay an ambush for him. Vas and Obring were back in the village, making sure everyone stayed indoors. Elya and Meb were waiting, bows in hand, to kill Nafai as he approached.

Nafai's first thought had been to simply go around them, where they couldn't see him. Then he thought of flying past them so quickly they couldn't shoot. But neither course would be useful. They had to commit themselves. They had to put the arrows in him, unprovoked. "Let them strike me," said

Nafai. "Help Meb with his aim—he'll never do it without your help—calming him, helping him concentrate. Let both arrows hit me."

⟨The cloak doesn't stop pain.⟩

"But it will heal me, once I pull the arrows out, right?"

⟨Well enough. But don't expect miracles.⟩

"All of this is a miracle," said Nafai. "Help Elemak miss my heart, if you're worried."

Elemak missed his heart, but not by much. Nafai slowed the paritka enough that they could get a clear aim. He could see, only an instant after the Oversoul itself saw, how the paritka frightened them both; how Meb almost lost his nerve, almost threw down his bow and ran. But Elemak never wavered, and his murmured command held Meb at his post, and then they aimed and fired.

Nafai felt the arrows enter his body, Elemak's buried deep in his chest, Meb's arrow through his neck. The latter arrow was more painful, the former more dangerous. The pain of both was exquisite. Nafai almost lost consciousness.

⟨Wake up. You've got too much to do to nap now.⟩

It hurts it hurts, Nafai cried out silently.

⟨It was *your* plan, not mine.⟩

But it was the right plan, so Nafai didn't pull the arrows out until the paritka brought him into the center of the village. As he had expected, Vas and Obring were terrified when they saw the paritka fly in and hover over the grass of the meetingplace, Nafai slumped in the seat, an arrow protruding from his chest, another stuck clear through his throat.

Luet, called Nafai silently. Come out and pull the arrows from me. Let everyone see how I was ambushed. That I carried no weapon. You must do your part.

He could see as if through Luet's own eyes; the kind of closeness that had almost driven him mad, back when he received his father's vision so long ago, was now much more easily borne, for the cloak protected him from the most distracting aspects of the Oversoul's recorded memories. He saw clearly what her eyes

saw, but only hints of her feelings, and almost none of that stream of consciousness that had maddened him before.

He saw how her heart leapt within her at the sight of him, and how she was stricken by the sight of the arrows in him. How she loves me! he thought. Will she ever know how I love *her?*

She cried out. "Come out, all of you, and see!"

Almost at once Elemak's voice came from the distance. "Stay in your houses!"

"Everybody!" cried Luet. "See how they tried to murder my husband!"

They were pouring out of the houses, adults and children alike. Many of them screamed and cried at the sight of Nafai, the arrows in him.

"Look—he didn't have even a bow with him," she said. "They shot at him with no provocation!"

"It's a lie!" cried Elemak, striding into the village. "I thought they'd try something like this! Nafai put the arrows in himself, to make it look like an attack."

Now Zdorab and Volemak were there with her, and they were the ones who reached up and pulled the arrows from him. The one in his neck had to be broken and pulled out from the arrowhead side. Elemak's arrow tore his chest badly coming out. He felt the blood rush out of both wounds, and speech was still impossible for him, but Nafai also could feel the cloak working within him, healing him, keeping the wounds from killing him.

"I refuse to let you blame us for this," said Elemak. "Nafai's an expert at playing the victim."

But Nafai could see that no one was buying Elemak's lies, except perhaps Kokor and Dol, who were never terribly bright and were easily deceived.

"No one believes you," said Father. "Nafai himself knew that you were planning this."

"Oh, really?" asked Elemak. "Well, if he's so wise now, why did he stroll right into this supposed ambush?"

Nafai put the answer in his father's mind.

"Because he wanted everyone to see your arrows in him," said Father. "He wanted everyone to see clearly who and what you are, so there's never any doubt about it."

"Most of us saw it all along," said Rasa. "We hardly needed Nafai to bear such wounds."

"It doesn't matter," said Luet. "Nafai wears the cloak of the Oversoul. He's the starmaster now. The cloak is healing him. There's nothing Elemak and Mebbekew can do to harm him now."

Am I ready yet? Nafai asked. The pain had subsided considerably.

⟨Almost.⟩

Elemak was keenly aware that no one was with him now, except Meb, who had no choice. Even Vas and Obring were averting their gaze from him—there'd be no support from *them*. But then, he had never expected any. "Whatever we did," said Elemak, "we did for the sake of our children, our wives—and *your* wives and children, too. Do you really want to leave here? Is there a one of you who wants to leave this place?"

"None of us *want* to go," said Luet. "But we all knew that this was the plan from the beginning—to take us to Earth. That was never a secret. No one lied to you."

And then—the crowning insult—Eiadh added her voice to Luet's. "I don't want to leave Dostatok," she said. "But I would rather wander in the desert forever than have a decent man killed to keep us here."

She spoke with fire, and Elemak felt it burn within him. My own wife, and she damns me with her accusations.

"Ah, you're all so brave *now!*" he cried. "But yesterday you agreed with me. Did any of you really think that our peace and happiness here would be preserved without bloodshed? You've all known it from the beginning—as long as Nafai was free to stir things up, there'd be mutiny and dissension among us. The only hope we have of peace is what I tried to do more than eight years ago."

⟨Now.⟩

He rose to his feet. To his surprise, he was unsteady, lightheaded. At once he "remembered" why—the cloak took energy from his own body when it had to, and the process of healing him so quickly was sucking strength from him faster than the cloak could replenish itself from the sunlight. However, he also knew that this temporary weakness would not stop him from doing all that he needed to do.

"Elemak," he said. "I've wept all the way here. It fills me with anguish, what you've tried to do. If only you'd bend enough to accept the Oversoul's plan—I would have followed you gladly if you had only done that. But all along, it's been you, your ambition to rule, that has torn us apart. If you hadn't plotted with them, *led* them, do you think these weak ones would ever have resisted the Oversoul? Elemak, don't you see that you've brought *yourself* to the edge of death? The Oversoul is acting for the good of all humanity, and it will *not* be stopped. Do you have to die before you'll believe that?"

"All I know is that whenever the Oversoul gets mentioned, it's you or your whiny wife or your mother the queen who's angling for control."

"None of us has sought to rule over you or anybody else," said Nafai. "Just because you live every waking moment with dreams of controlling other people doesn't mean that the rest of us do. Do you think that it's my *ambition* that created this paritka I'm standing on? Do you think it's Mother's *plotting* that holds it off the ground? Do you think it was Luet's—what did you call it, *whining*?—that brought me here, a day's journey in an hour?"

"It's an ancient machine, that's all," said Elemak. "An ancient machine, just like the Oversoul. Are we going to take our orders from *machines?*"

He looked around for support, but the blood on Nafai's throat and tunic was too fresh; no one met his gaze except Mebbekew.

"We're moving the village to the north, near Vusadka," said

Nafai. "And all of us, including the older children, will work with the Oversoul's machines to restore one starship. And when it's ready, then *all* of us will enter the starship and rise up into space. It will take us a hundred years to reach Earth, but to most of us it will seem like a single night, because they'll sleep through the whole voyage, while to the rest of us it will seem like a few months. And when the voyage ends, we will come out of the ship and stand on the soil of Earth, the first humans to do so in forty million years. Are you telling me that you mean to deprive us all of *that* adventure?"

Elemak was silent; so was Mebbekew. But Nafai knew what was passing through their minds. A grim resolve to back down now, but at the first opportunity knock him unconscious, slit his throat, and throw his body in the sea.

It would not do. They had to be convinced of the futility of resistance. They had to stop their plotting and concentrate their efforts on making the ship spaceworthy.

"Don't you see that you can't kill me, even though at this very moment, Elemak, you're imagining slitting my throat and throwing my body into the sea?"

Elemak's rage and fear redoubled within him. Nafai could feel it, striking at him in waves.

"Don't you see that already the Oversoul is healing the wounds in my throat, in my chest?"

"If they were real wounds at all!" cried Meb. Poor Meb, who still thought that Elemak's original lie might be revived.

In answer, Nafai plunged his finger into the wound in his own throat. Because the scar tissue was already forming, his finger had to tear its way in—but no one could miss the fact that Nafai's finger was into the wound nearly to the third knuckle. A couple of people gagged; the rest gasped or moaned or cried out in sympathetic pain. And, in truth, the pain *was* considerable—worse as he pulled his finger out than when he plunged it in. I must learn to avoid theatrical gestures like that, thought Nafai.

He held up his bloody finger. "I forgive you for this, Elemak,"

said Nafai. "I forgive you, Mebbekew. If I have your solemn oath to help me and the Oversoul as we build a good ship."

It was too much for Elemak. The humiliation was far worse now than it had been in the desert eight years before. It could not be contained. There was nothing in his heart but murderous rage. He cared not at all now what others thought—he knew he had already lost their good opinion anyway. He knew he had lost his wife and his children—what was left? The only thing that could heal any part of the agony he felt inside was to kill Nafai. to drag him to the sea and plunge him in until he stopped kicking and struggling. Then let the others do what they wanted—Elemak would be content, as long as Nafai was dead.

Elemak took a step toward Nafai. Then another.

"Stop him," said Luet. But no one got in his way. No one dared—the look on Elemak's face was too terrible.

Mebbekew smiled and fell in step beside Elemak.

"Don't touch me," said Nafai. "The power of the Oversoul is in me like fire. I'm weak right now, from the wounds you gave me—I may not have the strength to control the power I have. If you touch me, I think you'll die."

He spoke with such simplicity that his words had the plain force of truth. He could feel something crumble inside Elemak. Not that the rage had died; what broke in him was that part of him that could not bear to be afraid. And when that barrier was gone, all the rage turned back into what it had really been all along: fear. Fear that he would lose his place to his younger brother. Fear that people would look at him and see weakness instead of strength. Fear that people wouldn't love him. Above all, fear that he really had no control over anything or anybody in the world. And now, all those fears that he had long hidden from himself were turned loose within him—and they had all, all of them, come true. He had lost his place. He looked weak to everyone, even his children. No one here could love him now. And he had no control at all, not even enough control to kill this boy who had supplanted him.

With Elemak no longer moving forward, Meb, too, stopped—always the opportunist, he seemed to have no will of his own. But Nafai well knew that Meb was less broken in spirit than Elemak. He would go on plotting and sneaking, and with Elemak out of the picture, there would be nothing to restrain him.

It was clear to Nafai, therefore, that he had not yet won. He had to demonstrate clearly, unforgettably, to Meb and Elemak and to all the others, that this was not just a struggle between brothers, that in fact it was the Oversoul who had overcome Elemak and Meb, not Nafai at all. And in the back of his mind, Nafai clung to this hope: that if Elya and Meb could come to understand that it was the Oversoul who broke them today, they might eventually forgive Nafai himself, and be his true brothers again.

Enough power to shock them, said Nafai silently. Not to kill.

⟨As you intend, the cloak will act.⟩

Nafai held out his hand. He could see the sparking himself, but it was far more imposing when he saw through the eyes of others. By accessing the Oversoul he could see dozens of views of himself at once, his face a-dazzle with dancing light, growing brighter and brighter. And his hand, alive with light as if a thousand fireflies had swarmed around it. He pointed his finger at Elemak, and an arc of fire like lightning leapt from his fingertip, striking Elemak in the head.

Elya's body spasmed brutally and he was flung to the ground.

Have I killed him? cried Nafai in silent anguish.

⟨Just shocked him. Have a little trust in me, will you?⟩

Sure enough, Elemak was moving now, writhing and jerking on the ground. So Nafai extended his hand toward Meb.

"No!" cried Mebbekew. Having seen what happened to Elemak, he wanted no part of it. But Nafai could see that in his heart, he was still plotting and scheming. "I promise, I'll do whatever you want! I never wanted to help Elemak anyway, he just kept pushing me and pushing me."

"Meb, you're such a fool. Do you think I don't know that it was Elemak who stopped you from murdering me in the desert, when I stopped you from killing a baboon?"

Meb's face became a mask of guilty fear. For the first time in his life, Mebbekew had come face to face with one of his own secrets, one that he thought no one could know; there'd be no escaping from the consequences now. "I have children!" cried Mebbekew. "Don't kill me!"

The arc of lightning again crackled through the air, connecting with Meb's head and knocking him to the ground.

Nafai was exhausted. He could barely stand. Luet, help me, he said silently, urgently.

He felt her hands on his arm, holding him up. She must have climbed into the paritka beside him.

Ah, Luet, this is how it should always be. I can never stand without you beside me. If you're not part of this I can't do it at all.

In answer, all he could feel from her was her love for him, her vast relief that the danger was over, her pride at the strength he had shown.

How can you be so forgiving? he asked her silently.

I love you was the only message for him that he could find in her heart.

Nafai decided that the paritka should settle to the ground, and so it did. Luet helped him step from it, and with their children swarming around him, she led him back to the house. Over the next few minutes, all the others came to the house to see if they could help. But all he needed was to sleep. "Look after the others," he whispered. "I'm worried that the damage might be permanent."

When he awoke, it was near dusk. Zdorab was in their kitchen, cooking; Issib, Hushidh, Shedemei, and Luet were gathered around his bed. They weren't looking at him . . . they were talking among themselves. He listened.

They spoke of how sorry they felt for Eiadh and Dol, and

for their children. Especially Proya, who lived for the pride he felt in his father, Elemak. "He looked as if he had just seen his father die," said Luet.

"He did," said Hushidh. "At least, it was the death of the father that he knew."

"The damage from this day will be a long time healing," said Shedemei.

"Was it damage?" said Luet. "Or the beginning of the process of healing wounds that we had only ignored for the past eight years?"

Hushidh clucked her tongue. "Nafai would be the first to tell you that what happened today wasn't healing, it was war. The Oversoul got her way today—the starship will be outfitted, and Elemak and Mebbekew will work as hard as anyone, when they recover from this. But the damage was permanent. Elemak and Mebbekew will always see Nafai as their enemy. And anyone who serves Nafai."

"Nobody serves Nafai," said Luet. "We only serve the Oversoul, as Nafai himself does."

"Yes," Shedemei agreed quickly. "We all understand that, Luet. This wasn't Nafai's battle, it was the Oversoul's. It might have been any of us with the cloak."

Nafai noticed that, however close she might come to the edge, *this* time Shedemei wasn't telling that she was the one who would have had the cloak if Nafai had refused it. She would keep that now as private knowledge, between her and Zdorab. Elemak and Mebbekew, Vas and Obring—they weren't likely to tell anybody, if they had even understood what she told them last night. She would always know that she was the Oversoul's next choice for the leadership of the colony—that was enough for her, she was content.

"He's awake," said Luet.

"How do you know?" asked Issib.

"His breathing changed."

"I'm awake," said Nafai.

"How are you?" asked Luet.

"Still tired. But better. In fact, *good.* In fact, not even tired." He propped himself up onto one elbow, and at once felt a little light-headed. "On second thought, *definitely* still tired." He lay back down.

The others laughed.

"How are Elya and Meb?"

"Sleeping it off, same as you," said Shedemei.

"And who has *your* children?" Nafai asked them.

"Mother," said Issib.

"Lady Rasa," said Shedemei. "Zdorab decided you'd want *real* food when you woke up, so he came over and cooked."

"Nonsense," said Luet. "He just knew how worried I'd be and didn't want me to have to worry about cooking. You haven't asked about *our* children."

"Actually, I don't have to ask about anybody's children," he said. "I know where they are."

There was nothing they could say to that. Soon they brought food in to him, and they all ate together, gathered around the bed. Nafai explained to them what kind of work would be required at the starship, and they began to think through the division of labor. They didn't talk long, though, because Nafai was clearly exhausted—in body, if not in mind. Soon they were gone, even Luet; but Luet returned soon with the children, who came in and embraced their father. Chveya especially clung to him. "Papa," she said, "I heard your voice in my heart."

"Yes," he said. "But that's really the voice of the Oversoul."

"It was your voice, when you thought you were dying," she said. "You were standing on a hill, about to run down and throw yourself through an invisible wall. And you shouted to me, Veya, I love you."

"Yes," he said. "That was *my* voice, after all."

"I love you too, Papa," she said.

He slept again.

And woke in the middle of the night, hearing a breeze from the sea as it played through the thatch of the roof. He felt strong again, strong enough to rise up into the wind and fly.

Instead he reached out and touched Luet, gathered her to him. She woke sleepily, and did not protest. Rather she snuggled closer. She was willing to make love, if he had wanted to. But all he wanted tonight was to touch her, to hold her. To share the dancing light of the cloak with her, so she could also remember all the things that he remembered from the mind of the Oversoul. So she could see into his heart as clearly as he saw into hers, and know his love for her as surely as he knew her love for him.

The light from the cloak grew and brightened. He kissed her forehead, and when his lips came away, he could see that a faint light also sparked on her. It will grow, he knew. It will grow until there is no difference between us. Let there be no barrier between us, Luet, my love. I never want to be alone again.

"The Oversoul didn't *know* it had that information. I kind of had to coax it out. A lot of things are hidden from the Oversoul itself, you know. But the Index has the key. The Oversoul has been quite excited about some of the things I've found in its memory."

Shedemei was so surprised she had to laugh.

"I suppose it's amusing," said Zdorab, not amused.

"No, I was just . . . "

"Surprised to know that I was worth something besides baking breads and burying fecal matter."

He had struck so close to her previous attitude that it made her angry. "Surprised that *you* knew you were worth more than that."

"You have no idea what I know or think about myself or anything else. And you made no effort to find out, either," said Zdorab. "You came in here like the chief god of all pantheons and deigned to offer me marriage as long as I didn't actually *touch* you and expected me to accept gratefully. Well, I did. And you can go on treating me like I don't exist and it'll be fine with me."

She had never felt so ashamed of herself before in her life. Even as she had hated the way everybody else treated Zdorab as a nonentity, she had treated him that way herself, and in her own mind had given no thought for his feelings, as if they didn't matter. But now, having stabbed him with the contemptuousness of her proposal of marriage, she felt she had wronged him and had to make it right. "I'm sorry," she said.

"I'm not," said Zdorab. "Let's just forget everything about this conversation, get married tonight and then we don't have to talk again, agreed?"

"You really don't like me," said Shedemei.

"As if you have ever cared for one moment whether I or anyone else liked you, as long as we didn't interfere too much with your work."

Shedemei laughed. "You're right."

"It seems that we were both sizing each other up, but one of us did a better job of it than the other."

She nodded, accepting the chastening. "Of course we *will* have to talk again."

"Will we?"

"So you can show me how to get to that information from Earth."

"The genetic stuff?"

"And the continental drift. You forget that I'm carrying seeds to replenish lost species on Earth. I need to know the landforms. And a lot more."

He nodded. "I can show you that. As long as you realize that what I have are forty-million-year-old extrapolations of what *might* happen in another forty million years. It could be off by a lot—a little mistake early on would be hugely magnified by now."

"I *am* a scientist, you know," she said.

"And I'm a librarian," said Zdorab. "I'll be glad to show you how to get to the Earth information. It's sort of a back door—I found a path through the agricultural information, through pig breeding, if you can believe it. It helps to be interested in everything. Here, sit across from me and hold on to the Index. You *are* sensitive to it, I hope."

"Sensitive enough," said Shedemei. "Wetchik and Nafai both took me through sessions, and I've used it to look things up. Mostly I just use my own computer, though, because I thought I already knew everything that was on the Index in my field."

Now she was sitting across from him, and he set the Index between them and they both bowed forward to lean their elbows on their knees and rest their hands on the golden ball. Her hands touched his, but he did not move his hands out of the way, and there was no trembling; just cool, calm hands, as if he didn't even notice she was there.

She immediately caught the voice of the Index, answering Zdorab's inquiries, responding with names of paths and headings, subheads, and catalogs within the memory of the Oversoul. But as the names droned on she lost the thread of them, because of his fingers touching hers. Not that she felt anything for him herself; what bothered her was that he felt nothing at all for *her*. He had known for more than a month that she was going to be his wife, or at least that she was expected to; he had been watching her, certainly he had. And yet there was not even a glimmer of desire. He had accepted her proscription of sexual relations between them without a hint of regret. And he could endure her touch without showing the slightest sign of sexual tension.

Shedemei had never felt more ugly and undesirable than she did right now. It was absurd—until a few minutes ago she had had such contempt for this man that if he *had* expressed any sexual interest she would have been nauseated. But he was not the same man now, he was a much more interesting person, an intelligent person with a mind and a will, and while she didn't exactly feel a great flood of love or even sexual desire for him, she still felt enough new respect that his utter lack of desire for her was painful.

Another wound in the same old place, opening all the fragile scabs and scars, and she bled afresh at the shame of being a woman that no man wanted.

"You're not paying attention," said Zdorab.

"Sorry," she said.

He said nothing in reply. She opened her eyes. He was looking at her.

"Nothing," she said, brushing away the tear that clung to her lower eyelashes. "I didn't mean to distract you. Can we start again?"

But he didn't look back down to the Index. "It isn't that I don't desire you, Shedemei."

What, was her heart naked, that he could see right through her pretenses and see into the source of her pain?

"It's that I don't desire *any* woman."

It took her a moment for the idea to register. Then she laughed. "You're a zhop."

"That's really an old word for the human anus," said Zdorab quietly. "There are those who might be hurt at being called by such a name."

"But no one guessed," she said.

"I have made quite *sure* that no one would guess," said Zdorab, "and I'm putting my life in your hands telling *you*."

"Oh, it's not as dramatic as that," she said.

"Two of my friends were killed in Dog Town," he said.

Dog Town was where men who didn't have a woman in Basilica had to live, since it was illegal for an unattached male to live or even stay overnight inside the city walls.

"One was set upon by a mob because they heard a rumor he was a zhop, a peedar. They hung him by the feet from a second-story window, cut off his male organs, and then slashed him to death with knives. The other one was tricked by a man who pretended to be . . . one of us. He was arrested, but on the way to prison he had an accident. It was the oddest sort of accident, too. He was trying to escape, and somehow he tripped and in the act of falling, his testicles somehow came off and got jammed down his throat, probably with a broomhandle or the butt of a spear, and he suffocated on them before anybody could come to his aid."

"They do *that*?"

"Oh, I can understand it perfectly. Basilica was a very difficult place for male humans. We have an innate need to dominate, you see, but in Basilica we had to deal with the fact that we had no control except as we had influence with a woman. The men living outside the walls in Dog Town were, by the very fact they didn't live inside, branded as second-raters, men that women didn't want. There was the constant imputation that Dog Town men weren't real men at all, that they didn't have what it took to please a woman. Their very identity as males was in question. And so their fear and hatred of *zhops*"—he said the word with scorching contempt—"reached peaks I've never heard of anywhere else."

"These friends of yours . . . were they your lovers?"

"The one who was arrested—he had been my lover for several weeks, and he wanted to continue, but I wouldn't let him because if we went on any longer people would begin to suspect what we were. To save our lives I refused to see him again. He went straight from me into the trap. So you see, Nafai and Elemak aren't the only ones who have killed a man."

The pain and grief he was showing seemed deeper than anything Shedemei had ever felt. For the first time she realized how sheltered her scholarly life had been. She had never had such a close connection with someone that she would feel their death *this* strongly, so long after. If it *was* long after.

"How long ago?"

"I was twenty. Nine years ago. No, ten. I'm thirty now. I forgot."

"And the other one?"

"A couple of months before I—left the city."

"He was your lover, too?"

"Oh, no—he wasn't like me that way. He had a girl in the city, only she wanted it kept secret so he didn't talk about it—she was in a bad marriage and was marking time till it ended, and so he never spoke about her. That's why the rumor started that he was a zhop. He died without telling them."

"That's—gallant, I suppose."

"It was stupid beyond belief," said Zdorab. "He never believed me when I told him how terrifying it was in Basilica for people like me."

"You told him what you are?"

"I thought of him as a man who could keep a secret. He proved me right. I kind of think—that he died in my place. So that I could be alive when Nafai came to take the Index out of the city."

It was so far beyond anything she had experienced—beyond anything she had imagined. "Why did you keep on living there, then? Why didn't you go to someplace that isn't so—terrible?"

"In the first place, while there are places that aren't so bad, I don't know of any place that I could actually get to that is actually safe for someone like me. And in the second place, the Index was in Basilica. Now that the Index is out of there, I hope the city burns to the ground. I only wish that Moozh had killed every one of the strutting men of Dog Town."

"The Index was that important to you, to make you stay?"

"I learned of its existence when I was a young boy. Just a story, that there was a magic ball that if you held it, you could talk to God and he would have to tell you the answer to any question you asked. I thought, How wonderful. And then I saw a picture of the Index of the Palwashantu, and it looked exactly like the image in my mind of the magic ball."

"But that's not evidence at all," said Shedemei. "That's a childhood dream."

"I know it. I knew it then," said Zdorab. "But without even meaning to, I found myself preparing. For the day when I'd have the magic ball. I found myself trying to learn the questions that it would be worth asking God to answer. And, still without meaning to, I found myself making choices that took me closer and closer to Basilica, to the place where the Palwashantu kept their sacred Index. At the same time, being a studious young man helped me conceal my—defect. My father would say, 'You need to set down the books now and then, go and find some friends. Find a girl! How will you ever marry if you never meet any girls?' When I got to Basilica I used to write to him about my girlfriends, so he felt much better, though he would tell me that the way Basilicans marry, for just a year at a time, was awful and against nature. He really didn't like things that were against nature."

"That must have hurt," said Shedemei.

"Not really," said Zdorab. "It *is* against nature. I'm cut off from that tree of life that Volemak saw, I'm not part of the chain—I'm a genetic dead end. I think I read once, in an article by a genetics student, that it was not unreasonable to suppose that homosexuality might be a mechanism that nature used to weed out defective genes. The organism could detect some otherwise unnoticeable genetic flaw, and this started a mechanism that caused the hypothalamus to remain stunted, causing us to be highly sexual beings but with an inability to fixate on the opposite sex. A sort of self-closing wound in the gene pool. We were, I think the article said, the *culls* of humanity."

Shedemei blushed deeply—a feeling she rarely had and didn't like. "That was student work. I never published it outside the scholarly community. It was speculation."

"I know," he said.

"How did you even find it?"

"When I realized that I was expected to marry you, I read everything you wrote. I was trying to discover what I could and could not tell you."

"And what did you decide?"

"That I'd better keep my secrets to myself. That's why I never spoke to you, and why I was so relieved that you didn't want me."

"And now you *did* tell me."

"Because I could see that it hurt you, the fact that I didn't want you. I hadn't planned on that. You didn't come across as someone who would ever want the love of a contemptible crawling worm like me."

Worse and worse. "Was I so obvious in my attitude?"

"Not at all," he said. "I deliberately cultivated my wormhood. I have worked hard to become the most unnoticeable, despicable, spineless being that anyone in this company will ever know."

And now, thinking of what happened to his two friends, she understood. "Camouflage," she said. "For you to remain single and not be suspected of what you are, you had to be sexless."

"Spineless."

"But Zdorab, we're not in Basilica now."

"We carry Basilica with us. Look at the men here. Look at Obring, for instance, and Meb—doomed by their particular lack of gifts to be at the bottom of any pecking order you can imagine. Both of them aggressive and yet cowardly—they long to be on top, but haven't the gumption to take on the big men and take them down. That's why they're doomed to follow men like Elemak and Volemak and even Nafai, though he's the youngest, because they can't take risks. Imagine the rage built up inside them. And then imagine what they'd do if they learned that I was the monstrous thing, the crime against nature, the unmanly man, the perfect image of what they fear that they are."

"Volemak wouldn't let them touch you."

"Volemak won't live forever," said Zdorab. "And I don't trust my secret to those who won't keep it."

"Are you that sure of me?" said Shedemei.

"I have put my life into your hands," said Zdorab. "But no, I'm not that sure of you. Like it or not, though, we've been forced together. So I've taken a calculated risk. To tell you, so that I have one person here that I don't have to lie to. One person who knows that what I seem to be is only a pretense."

"I'll make them stop treating you so—so unregardingly."

"No!" cried Zdorab. "No, you mustn't. Things will be better when we're married, for both of us—you were right about that. But you must let me remain invisible, as much as possible. I know best how to deal with what I am, believe me—you've never even imagined it, you said so yourself, so don't bull your way into my survival strategy and start trying to fix things because you'll end up killing me if you do. Do you understand that? You're brilliant, one of the finest minds of our time, but you know absolutely nothing about this situation, you are hopelessly ignorant, you will destroy anything you touch, so keep your *hands off.*"

He spoke with unbelievable vehemence and power. She had not imagined him capable of talking this way. She loathed it—being put in her place so firmly. But when she thought about it, instead of reacting viscerally, she realized that he was right. That for now, at least, she really *was* ignorant and the best thing she could do was let him continue to handle things however he thought best.

"All right," she said. "I'll say nothing, I'll do nothing."

"Nobody expects you to be *proud* to be married to me," said Zdorab. "In fact, they'll all think of it as a noble sacrifice you're making. So you won't lose any status by being my wife. It'll make you sort of heroic to them."

She laughed bitterly. "Zdorab, that's how I thought of it myself."

"I know," he said. "But that's not how *I* thought of it. I even hoped—imagine, having the right to be alone in the same tent with the keenest scientific mind on the planet Harmony—every night—with nothing to do but talk!"

It was so sweetly flattering and yet, for reasons she couldn't quite grasp yet, it was also vaguely tragic.

"That's a marriage, after a fashion, don't you think? We won't have babies like the others, but we'll have *thoughts*. You can teach me, you can *talk* to me about your work and if I don't understand I can promise you that I'll educate myself through the Index until I do. And maybe I can tell you some of the things I've found."

"I'd love that."

"We can be friends, then," he said. "That'll make ours a better marriage than most of *theirs*. Can you imagine what Obring and Kokor talk about?"

She laughed. "Do you think they actually *do?*"

"And Mebbekew and Dol, both playacting and secretly loathing each other."

"No, I don't think Dol hates Mebbekew, I think she actually *believes* the part she's playing."

"You're probably right. But they're pretty awful, don't you think? And *they're* going to have children!"

"Terrifying."

They laughed, long and loud, till tears ran down both their faces.

The door parted. It was Nafai.

"I clapped," he said, "but you didn't hear me. Then I realized you were laughing and I thought I might come in."

Both of them immediately grew sober. "Of course," said Zdorab.

"We were just discussing our marriage," said Shedemei.

Shedemei could see the relief spread over Nafai's face as if the shadow of a cloud had just passed. "You're going ahead and doing it," he said.

"We were just stubborn enough to want to wait until it was our idea," said Zdorab.

"I believe it," said Nafai.

"In fact," said Zdorab, "we ought to go tell Rasa and Volemak, and besides, you wanted to use the Index."

"I did, but not if you're not done with it," said Nafai.

"It'll still be here," said Shedemei, "when we're ready for it again." And in moments they were outside the tent, heading for—where?

Zdorab took her by the hand and led her to the cookfire. "Dol was supposed to be watching here," he said, "but she usually runs off—she needs her little nap, you know. It doesn't matter—I let Yobar touch the cookpot once, and he must have spread the word about how it feels, because the boons don't come anywhere near here now, even when it smells as good as this."

It *did* smell good.

"How did you learn to cook?"

"My father was a cook," said Zdorab. "It was the family business. He was good enough that he was able to afford to send me to Basilica to study, and I learned a lot of what he knew. I think he'd be proud of what I've been able to do in these piss-poor conditions."

"Except the camel cheese."

"I think I've found an herb that will improve it," said Zdorab. He lifted the lid of the cookpot. "I'm trying it tonight—there's twice as much cheese in this as usual, but I don't think anybody will mind." He lifted the stirring spoon and she saw how cheesily the liquid strung and glopped off of it.

"Mmm," she said. "Can't wait."

He detected the irony in her voice. "Well, it's not as though you don't have ample reason to be suspicious of anything that looks like it might taste like the cheese, but I figure that we've all had years of loving cheese and only a couple of months of hating it, so I should be able to win you all back if I do it right. And we *will* need the cheese—it's too good a source of animal protein for all the nursing mothers we're going to have."

"You've got it all planned out," she said.

"I have plenty of time to myself, to think," he said.

"In a way," she said, "you're really the leader of this group."

"In a way," he said, "you'd best not say that in front of anyone else or they'll be sure you've lost your mind."

"You're the one who decides what we'll eat and when, where we'll void ourselves, what we'll plant in the garden, and you guide us around in the Index—"

"But if I do it right, no one ever notices," he said.

"You take responsibility for us all. Without ever waiting to be told."

"So do all good people," he said. "That's what it *means* to be a good person. And I *am* a good person, Shedya."

"I know that now," she said. "And I should have known it before. I interpreted all you did as weakness—but I should have known that it was wisdom and strength, freely shared with all of us, even the ones who don't deserve it."

And now at last it was time for tears to come to *his* eyes. Just a little shining, but she saw, and knew that he knew that she saw. It occurred to her that their marriage would be far more than the sham she had intended. It could be a real friendship, between the two people who had least expected to find friends and companions on this journey.

He stirred the pottage and then replaced the lid, leaving the spoon hooked over the side.

"I imagine this is the safest place we could come and talk, if we didn't want to be disturbed or overheard," she said. "Because I don't imagine anybody ever comes near the cookfire if they can help it, for fear of being asked to work."

Zdorab chuckled. "I'll always be glad for your company while I'm working here, as long as you understand that cooking is an art, and I *do* concentrate on it sometimes while I do it."

"I hope I can tell you things so stimulating and interesting that you ruin the soup sometimes."

"Do it too often and they'll be pleading with us to get a divorce."

They laughed, and then again their laughter trailed off into silence.

"Why don't I go and tell Aunt Rasa?" said Shedemei. "She'll want to do up a wedding for us tonight, I'm sure. She'll be even more relieved than Nafai was."

"And we want it as public as possible," said Zdorab.

She understood. "We'll make sure everybody sees that we are definitely man and wife." And the unspoken promise: I will never tell anyone that we are *not* man and wife at all.

Shedemei turned to leave, to look for Rasa, but Zdorab's voice detained her. "Shedya," he said.

"Yes?"

"Please call me Zodya."

"Of course," she said, though in fact she had never heard his familiar name. No one used it.

"And another thing," he said.

"Yes?"

"Your student article—you were wrong. About genetic culls."

"I said it was just speculation . . ."

"I mean, I *know* you were wrong because I know what we are. In the ancient science, the Earth science that I've been exploring through the Index: it's not some internal mechanism of the human body. It's not genetic. It's just the level of male hormones in the mother's bloodstream at the time the hypothalamus goes through its active differentiation and growth."

"But that's almost random," said Shedemei. "It wouldn't mean anything, it would just be an accident if the level happened to be low for those couple of days."

"Not really random," said Zdorab. "But an accident all the same. It means nothing, except that we're born crippled."

"Like Issib."

"I think when Issib sees me walking, sees what I can do with my hands, that he would gladly trade places with me," said Zdorab. "But when I see him with Hushidh, and see her pregnant as she is, and see how the others have given him real respect because of that, how they recognize him as being one of *them,* then there are moments—only moments, mind you—when I would gladly trade places with *him.*"

Shedemei impulsively squeezed his hand, though she was not one who was apt to make such affectionate gestures. It seemed appropriate, though. A friendly thing to do, and so she did it, and he squeezed back, so it was all right. Then she walked briskly away, looking for Lady Rasa.

And as she went, she thought: Who would have believed that finding out my husband-to-be is a zhop would come as such wonderful news, and that it would make me like him *more.* The world is truly standing on its head these days.

Alone in the Index tent after Shedemei and Zdorab left, Nafai did not hesitate. He took the Index—still warm from their hands—and held it close to him and spoke almost fiercely to the Oversoul. "All this time you've been telling me that Father's dream of the tree didn't come from you, but you never mentioned that you have his whole experience in your memory."

"Of course I do," said the Index. "It would be remiss of me not to record something as important as that."

"And you knew how much I wanted a dream from the Keeper of Earth. You *knew* that!"

"Yes," said the Index.

"Then why didn't you give me my father's dream!"

"Because it was your father's dream," said the Index.

"He told it—it isn't secret anymore! I want to *see* what he *saw!*"

"That's not a good idea."

"I'm tired of your deciding all the time what's a good idea and what isn't. You thought that killing Gaballufix was a *fine* idea."

"And it was."

"For *you*. You've got no blood on *your* hands."

"I have your memory of it. And I didn't do too badly by you out in the desert, when Elemak was plotting to kill you."

"So... you saved my life because you wanted my genes in our little gene pool."

"I'm a computer, Nafai. Do you expect me to save your life because I *like* you? My motives are a great deal more dependable than human emotions."

"I don't want any of that from you! I want a dream from the Keeper."

"Exactly. And having me put your father's dream into your mind is *not* the same thing as having a dream from the Keeper. It's merely having a memory report from me."

"I want to see those Earth creatures that the others have seen. The bats and angels."

"Which they *think* are Earth creatures."

"I want to have the taste of the fruit of the tree in my mouth!"

Even as he said it—as his lips silently formed the words, as the cry of anguish formed in his mind—Nafai knew that he was being childish. But he wanted it, wanted so badly to know what his father knew, to have seen what Luet saw, what Hushidh saw, what even General Moozh and Luet's strange mother, Thirsty, saw. He wanted to know, not what they told about it, but what it looked like, felt like, sounded like, smelled like, tasted like. And he wanted it enough that even if he was being childish, he had to have it, he *demanded* it.

And so the Oversoul, regarding it as undesirable to have the male it had earmarked as the eventual leader of the party be in such an anguished and therefore unpredictable state, gave him what he asked for.

It came on him all at once, as he held the Index. The darkness that Father had described, the man who invited him to follow, the endless walking. Only there was something more, something Father hadn't mentioned—a terrible disturbing feeling of wrongness, of unwanted, unthinkable thoughts going on in a powerful undercurrent. This wasn't just a wilderness, it was a mental hell, and he couldn't bear to stay in it.

"Skip past this part," he said to the Index. "Take me past here, get me out of here."

All at once the dream stopped.

"Not out of the *dream,*" said Nafai impatiently. "Just skip the dull part."

"The Keeper sent the dull part as much as it sent anything else," said the Index.

"Skip to the end of it where things start happening."

"That's cheating, but I'll do it." Nafai hated it when the Index talked like that. It had learned that humans interpreted resistance followed by compliance as teasing, and therefore it now teased them as a way of simulating natural behavior. Only because Nafai knew that it was only a computer doing the teasing, and not a person, it was merely tedious, not fun. Yet when he complained about it, the Index merely replied that everybody else liked it and Nafai shouldn't be such a killjoy.

The dream came back again, and immediately he was plunged into the darkness, the walking, the back of the man leading him, and that awful mental undercurrent that was so painful and distracting. But then he could hear his Father's voice pleading with the man to tell him something, to lead him out of the place. Only it was not his Father's voice. It was a strange voice that Nafai had never heard before, except that in his mind he kept perceiving it as his *own* voice, only it was Father's thought that this voice was his own, not Nafai's, because his own voice sounded nothing like this and neither did Father's. Until finally Nafai realized that this was how his Father's voice sounded *to his father*. In a dream, of course, Father wouldn't hear the voice everyone else hears. He'd hear the voice he thinks he hears when he's speaking. Only it's not even *that* voice, it's much younger, it's the voice he learned to think of as his own when he formed his identity as a man. Deeper than his real voice, more manly, and younger.

Except Nafai couldn't shake the powerful conviction that, no matter how he analyzed it, this *was* his *own* voice, not Father's at all, though it was also completely wrong for his voice. And then Nafai realized that of course, if the Index was playing back for him his memory of Volemak's experience of the dream, it would be filtered through Volemak's consciousness, and therefore would have all of Volemak's attitudes inextricably tied to it.

That's what that undercurrent was of distracting, meaningless, confusing, frightening thoughts. It was Father's stream of consciousness, constantly evaluating and understanding and interpreting and responding to the dream. Thoughts that Father wouldn't even have been particularly conscious of himself, because they hadn't surfaced yet—including scraps of ideas like This is a dream, and This is from the Oversoul, and I'm really dead, and This is not a dream, and all kinds of contradictory thoughts jumbled up and piled on top of each other. When *Father* was having these thoughts they arose out of his own unconscious mind and his own will sorted them out, and the thoughts responded to his will, terminated a thought as soon as he wanted to move on to another. But in Nafai's mind, with all of this replayed, the thoughts did *not* respond to his own will, and in fact were superimposed on his own stream of consciousness. Therefore he was having twice as many under-the-breath thoughts as he usually had, and half of them did not respond to his will in any way, so it was at once confusing and terrifying, for his mind was out of control.

Father had given up talking to the man and now was crying out to the Oversoul, pleading with him. It was humiliating to hear the fear, the anxiety, the *whining* in Father's voice. He had *said* that he was pleading, but Nafai had never actually heard his father take this self-abasing tone with anyone, and it was like seeing his father going to the toilet or something disgusting like that, he *hated* seeing his father this way. I'm spying on him. I'm seeing him as he sees himself at his worst moments, instead of seeing the man he presents to the world, to his sons. I'm stealing his self from him, and it's wrong, it's a terrible thing for me to do. But then maybe I should know this about my father, how *weak* he is. I can't rely on him, a man who whimpers like this to the Oversoul, begging for help like a baby...

And then he thought of how he himself had pleaded with the Index to show him Father's dream and realized that, in their own minds, even the bravest and strongest of men must have moments like these, only no one ever saw them because they never acted on them outside their dreams and nightmares. I only know this about Father because I'm spying on him.

At that moment, just as he was about to ask the Index to stop the dream, it changed, and suddenly he was in the field that Father had described. At once Nafai wanted to find the tree, but of course he could only look where Father looked in the dream, and could only see it when Father saw it.

Father saw now, and it *was* beautiful, and a great relief after all the darkness and bleakness. Only Nafai not only felt his own relief, but also had Father's relief superimposed on his, and therefore it wasn't relief at all, but more tension, and more distraction and disorientation and it didn't help that, instead of walking to the tree in an orderly way, Father sort of just *went* to it. He *thought* of it as walking but he really just got closer suddenly and there he was at the tree.

Nafai felt Father's desire for the fruit, his delight at the smell of it, but because he was faintly nauseated by the movement toward the tree and faintly headachy because of the constant undercurrent of Father's thoughts, the smell did *not* arouse any desire in Nafai. Rather it made him sick. Father reached up and picked a fruit and tasted it. Nafai could feel that Father found it delicious, and for a moment, as the taste came into Nafai's mind, it *was* delicious, powerfully, exquisitely delicious in a way Nafai could hardly have imagined. But almost immediately the experience was subverted by Father's own reaction to it, his own associations with the taste and the smell of it; his reactions were so powerful, Father had been so overwhelmed by the taste that his feelings were out of control, and Nafai could not contain them. It was physically painful. He was terrified. He screamed to the Index to stop the dream.

It stopped, and Nafai let himself fall sideways onto the carpet, gasping and sobbing, trying to get the madness out of his mind.

And in a little while he was all right again, because the madness *was* gone.

"You see the problem I have communicating clearly with humans?" said the voice inside his head. "I have to frame my ideas so clearly and loudly, and even then most of them think that they're hearing nothing but their own thoughts. Only the Index makes it possible for real clarity of communication with most people. Except you and Luet—I can talk to the two of you better than anybody." The voice of the Index was silent for a moment. "I thought you were going to go insane there for a while. It wasn't pretty, what was happening inside your head."

"You warned me."

"Well, I didn't warn you of all *that* because I didn't know it would happen. I've never put one person's dream inside somebody else's head before. I don't think I'll do it again, either, even if somebody gets very upset because I said no."

"I agree with your decision," said Nafai.

"And you were very unkind to judge your father that way. He's a very strong and courageous man."

"I know. If you were listening in, you know that I figured that all out."

"I wasn't sure if you'd remember that. Human memory is very unreliable."

"Leave me alone," said Nafai. "I don't want to talk to you or anybody right now."

"Then let go of the Index. You can always walk away."

Nafai removed his hand from the Index, then rolled over,

got to his knees, to his feet. His head reeled. He was dizzy and felt sick.

He staggered outside the tent. Issib and Mebbekew were there. "We're on our way to dinner," said Issib. "Did you have a good session with the Index?"

"I'm not hungry," said Nafai. "I don't feel well."

Mebbekew hooted. It sounded to Nafai very much like the pant-hoots of the baboons. "Don't tell me *Nafai's* going to try to get out of work by claiming to be sick all the time. But I guess it's worked so well for Luet that he figures it's worth a try, right?"

Nafai didn't even bother to answer Meb. He just staggered away, looking for his tent. I've got to sleep, he thought. That's what I need, to sleep.

Only when he got there and lay down on the bed, he realized he couldn't possibly sleep. He was too agitated, too nauseated, his head was swimming and he couldn't think but he also couldn't *stop* thinking.

So I'll go hunting, thought Nafai. I'll go out and find some small helpless animal and I'll kill it and tear its skin off and rip its guts out and I'm sure I'll feel better because that's the kind of man I am. Or maybe when the smell of the guts hits me I'll throw up and *then* I'll feel better.

No one saw him on the way out of camp—if they had seen him, walking so unsteadily and carrying a pulse, they probably would have stopped him. He crossed the stream and went up the hills on the other side. They never hunted in that direction because that was the side where the baboons slept in the cliffs and because if you went too far in that direction you'd get close enough to the villages in the valley called Luzha that you might run into somebody. But Nafai wasn't thinking clearly. He only remembered that once before he had been on the other side of the stream and something wonderful had happened, and right now he very much wanted for something wonderful to happen. Or to die. Whatever.

I should have waited, he said to himself over and over again, when he could think well enough to know what he was thinking. If the Keeper of Earth wanted to send me a dream, it would have sent me a dream. And if it didn't, I should have waited. I'm sorry. I just wanted to know for myself, but I should have waited. I can stand the waiting now, only now you'll never send me a dream, will you, because I cheated, just as the Index said, I cheated, and so I'm not entitled . . . in fact I'm worthless now, I've ruined my own brain by what I insisted the Oversoul do for me, and now I'm going to be sick in the head forever and neither you nor the Oversoul nor Luet nor anybody else will have any use for me and I might as well drop off the edge of a cliff somewhere and die.

It was sundown when he realized that he had no idea of where he was, or how far he had wandered. He only knew that he was sitting on a rock on the crest of a hill—in plain sight, if there were some bandit looking for someone to rob, or a hunter looking for prey. And even though he had his head in his hands and was looking at the ground, he was aware that someone was sitting across from him. Someone who had not yet said anything, but who was watching him intently.

Say something, said Nafai silently. Or kill me and get it over with.

"Oo. Oo-oo," said the stranger.

Nafai looked up then, for he knew the voice. "Yobar," he said.

Yobar wiggled a little and hooted a few more times, in delight, apparently, at having been recognized.

"I don't have anything for you to eat," said Nafai.

"Oo," said Yobar cheerfully. He was probably just grateful for someone to notice him, since he had been ostracized by the troop.

Nafai reached out a hand to him, and Yobar strode boldly forward and laid his forehand in Nafai's.

And in that moment, Yobar was not a baboon at all. Instead, Nafai saw him as a winged animal, with a face at once more fierce and more intelligent than a baboon's. The one wing flexed and stretched, but the other wing did not, for it was the hand that Nafai held in his own. The winged creature who had taken Yobar's place spoke to him, but Nafai couldn't understand his language. The creature—the angel, Nafai knew that's what it was—spoke again, only now Nafai understood, vaguely, that it was warning him of danger.

"What should I do?" asked Nafai.

But the angel looked around and became more agitated and then, seeming to be quite frightened, it let go of his hand and leapt skyward and flew, circling overhead.

Nafai heard a sound of something hard scraping over rock. He looked back down at the rocks around him and saw what had made the noise. A half dozen of a larger, fiercer creature. The rats from the dreams the others had had. They were heavier and stronger-looking than the baboons had been, and Nafai well knew from the stories of other desert travelers that baboons were far stronger than a full-sized man. The teeth were fierce, but the hands—for they were hands, not claws—looked terrible indeed, especially because many of them held stones and seemed prepared to throw them.

Nafai thought of his pulse. How many of them can I kill before they hit me with a stone and knock me down? Two of them? Three? Better to die fighting than to let them take me without any cost at all.

Better? Why would it be better? Bad enough that one should die. What's to be gained by killing more, except that they'd feel more justified in having slain me.

So he set down his pulse on the ground in front of him, and clasped his hands across his knees, and waited.

They waited also. Their arms were still poised to throw. The angel still circled overhead, a silent witness except for occasional high-pitched squeals.

Then, suddenly, Nafai realized he had something in his hand. He opened his hands and saw that he was holding a fruit. He recognized it immediately as one of the fruits of the tree of life.

He lifted it to his lips and tasted it, and ah! It was as Father had said, as Nafai had tasted for just a moment before, the most exquisite sensation he could imagine feeling. Only this time there was no distraction, no confusion, no disharmony; he was at peace inside himself, and healed.

Without thinking, he took the fruit from his lips and offered it to the rat directly in front of him.

The rat looked down at his hand, then up at Nafai's face again, then down at the fruit.

Nafai thought of laying the fruit down and letting the rat pick it up himself, but then he realized that no, it would be wrong to let the fruit touch the ground, to let it be picked up like a rotting windfall. It should be taken from a hand. This fruit should always be taken from the tree itself, or from some-one's hand.

The rat sniffed, moved forward, sniffed again. And then it took the fruit out of Nafai's hand and took it to its lips and bit down. The fruit squirted, and some of the juice of it struck Nafai in the face, but he hardly noticed, except to lick his lip where it ran. For he couldn't take his eyes off the rat. It was frozen in place, unmoving, the juice of the fruit dribbling from the sides of its mouth. Have I poisoned it? thought Nafai. Have I killed it somehow with this fruit? I didn't mean to.

No, the rat had not been poisoned, merely stunned by it. Now it began making urgent sounds in its throat, and it scurried to its nearest companion, who took the fruit from its mouth with its own teeth. And so that one fruit passed around the circle, each one taking it into its mouth directly from the mouth of the one before, all the way around the circle until it came back to the first one. And that one came forward and offered its mouth to Nafai, the remnant of the fruit still there, still visible.

Nafai's face was not built to a point the way the rats' faces were, and so he had to reach out and take the fruit with his hand. But he put it at once in his own mouth, dreading what it would taste like now, but knowing he must do it. To his relief the flavor of the fruit was unchanged. If anything, it was sweeter now, for having been shared by these others.

He chewed, he swallowed. Only then did they also swallow whatever juice and bits of fruit remained in their mouths.

They came forward and laid at his feet the stones they had been holding to use as weapons. The pile was a pyramid in front of him. Fourteen stones. Then they filed away among the rocks.

At once the angel swooped back down, circled around him, chirping madly, flapping and flapping, until it landed heavily on his shoulders and enfolded him in its wings.

"I hope this means you're happy," said Nafai.

In answer the angel said nothing, but flew away itself.

Then Nafai stood and saw that he was not on the crest of a rocky peak at all, but was in a field, beside a tree, and near him was a river, and beside the river a path with an iron railing. He saw all that his father had seen, including the building on the other side.

And then, when he expected the dream to end—for he knew it was a dream—it changed. He saw himself, standing in the midst of a huge multitude of people and angels and rats, and they were all watching a bright light coming down out of the sky. They had been waiting, he understood. They had all been waiting, and now it was here. The Keeper of Earth.

Nafai wanted to get nearer, to see the face of the Keeper of Earth. But the light was too dazzling. He could see that it had four limbs, just from the shape of it, four limbs and a head, but beyond that the light simply blinded him as if the Keeper were a small star, a sun too bright to look into without burning your eyes.

Finally Nafai had to close his eyes, squint them shut to relieve them from the pain of staring into the sun. When he opened them, though, he knew he would be close enough, he knew he would see the face of the Keeper.

"Oo."

It was Yobar's face he was staring into.

"Oo yourself," whispered Nafai.

"Oo-oo."

"It's almost dark," said Nafai. "But you're pretty hungry, aren't you?"

Yobar sat back on his haunches expectantly.

"Let's see if I can find anything for you."

It wasn't hard, even in the dusky light, because the hares on this side of the valley hadn't grown scarce yet. When full night came, Yobar was still tearing at the corpse, devouring every scrap of it, breaking open the skull with a rock to get at the soft brains. Yobar's hands and face were covered with blood.

"If you have any wit at all," said Nafai, "you'll get home fast with what's left of this meat and all the blood on you so some female will make friends with you and let you play with her baby so you can make friends with *it* and become a full-fledged member of the troop."

It was unlikely that Yobar understood him, but then he didn't have to. He was already trying to hide the body of the hare from Nafai, preparatory to stealing it and running away. Nafai made his life easier by turning a little bit away so that Yobar would seize the opportunity and run. He heard the scampering of Yobar's feet and said silently to him, Buy what you can with this hare's blood, my friend. I've seen the face of the Keeper of Earth, and it is you.

Then, regretting at once the disrespectful thought, Nafai spoke silently to the Keeper of Earth—or to the Oversoul, or to nobody, he didn't know. Thank you for showing me, he said. Thank you for letting me see what Father saw. What all the others saw. Thank you for letting me be one of those who know.

Now, if someone could help me find my way home.

Whether it was the Oversoul helping him or simply his own memory and tracking ability, he found his way home by moonlight. Luet had been worried—so had Mother and Father, and others too. They had put off Shedemei's and Zdorab's wedding, because it would be wrong to do that on a night when Nafai might be in danger. Now that he was back, though, the wedding could go on, and nobody asked him where he had gone or what he had been doing, as if they knew it was something too strange or wonderful or awful to be discussed.

Only later that night, in bed with Luet, did he speak of it. First of feeding Yobar, and then of the dream.

"It sounds like everyone was satisfied tonight," said Luet.

"Even you?" he asked.

"You're home," she said, "and I'm content."

SIX

PULSES

They stayed in their camp in the Valley of Mebbekew, by the River of Elemak, longer than they intended. First they had to wait for the harvest. Then, despite the anti-vomiting herbs that Shedemei learned about from the Index, Luet was so weakened from pregnancy that Rasa refused to let them begin the journey and risk her life. By the time Luet's morning sickness had ended and she had regained some strength, all three pregnant women—Hushidh, Kokor, and Luet—were large enough in the belly that traveling would have been uncomfortable. Besides, they had been joined in their pregnancy by Sevet, Eiadh, Dol, and Lady Rasa herself. None of them were as sick as Luet had been, but neither were any of them much disposed to mount camels and ride all day and then pitch tents at night and strike them in the morning while subsisting on hard biscuit and jerky and dried melon.

So they ended up staying in their camp for more than a year, till all seven babies were born. Only two of them had sons. Volemak and Rasa named their boy Oykib, after Rasa's father, and Elemak and Eiadh named their firstborn son Protchnu, which meant *endurance*. Eiadh made mention of the fact that only her husband, Elemak, was as manly as Volemak, to put a son in her as Volemak had sired nothing but sons. By and large the others ignored her boasting and enjoyed their daughters.

Luet and Nafai named their little girl Chveya, because she had sewn them together into one soul. Hushidh's and Issib's daughter was the first birth of the new generation, and they named her simply Dza, because she was the answer to all the questions of their life. Kokor and Obring named their daughter Krasata, a name meaning *beauty* that had been rather in fashion in Basilica. Vas and Sevet named their daughter Vasnaminanya, partly because the name meant *memory,* but also because it was related to Vas's name; they called her Vasnya. And Mebbekew and Dol named their daughter Basilikya, after the city which they both still loved and dreamed of. Everyone knew that Meb meant his daughter's name to be a constant reproach to those who had dragged him from his proper home, so everyone picked up on the nickname Volemak thought of for her, and so called her Syelsika, meaning *country girl*. Of course this annoyed Meb, but he learned to stop protesting since it only caused the others to laugh at him.

Oykib and Protchnu, Chveya and Dza, Krasata, Vasnya, and Syelsika—on a cool morning more than a year after their parents had all come together in the Valley of Mebbekew, the babies were loosely wrapped in cool traveling clothes and laid in hammocks slung across their mothers' shoulders, so the babes could nurse during the day when they grew hungry. The women, except childless Shedemei, did none of the work of striking tents, though as the children grew they would soon be expected to resume their duties. And the men, strong now, tanned and hardened from a year's life and work in the desert, strutted a little before their wives, proud of what babies they had made together, full of their lofty responsibility to provide and care for wives and children.

All but Zdorab, of course, who was as quiet and unprepossessing as ever, with his wife still childless; the two seemed almost to disappear sometimes. They were the only members of the company unconnected to Rasa and Volemak by blood or marriage; they were the only childless ones; they were considerably older than any of the others of their generation except Elemak; no one would have said that they were *not* fully the equals of the rest of the company, but then, no one actually believed that they *were,* either.

As the company gathered to go, Luet, with Chveya asleep in her sling, carried an overripe melon on her shoulder down to where the baboon troop was pursuing its normal business. The baboons seemed agitated and jumpy, which was hardly surprising, considering the tumult up at the human camp. As Luet passed the perimeter of their feeding area, they kept glancing up at her, to see what she was doing. Some of the females approached, to see her baby—she had let them touch Chveya before, though of course she could never let them play with her the way they played with their *own* children; Chveya was far too fragile for their rough fondling.

It was a male, not a female, that Luet was looking for, and as soon as she moved away from the curious females, there he was—Yobar, the one who had been an outcast less than a year ago, and who now was best friends with the oldest daughter of the matriarch of the tribe; he had as much prestige as a male could get in this city of women. Luet brought the melon to where Yobar could see what she had. Then, turning slightly away so he wouldn't be too frightened, she cast it down on a rock and the melon burst open.

As she expected, Yobar jumped back, startled. When he saw that Luet was not afraid, however, he soon came closer to investigate. Now she could show him what she wanted him to see—the secret that they had so carefully kept from all the baboons during their year in this place. She reached down, picked up a fragment of rind with plenty of the meat of the fruit still clinging to it, and ate noisily.

The sound of her eating drew the others, but it was Yobar—

as she had expected—who followed her example and began to eat. He made no distinction between fruit and rind, of course, and seemed to enjoy both equally. When he was full, he jumped around, hooting and frolicking, until others—especially young males—began to venture forward to try the fruit.

Luet slowly stepped back, then turned and walked away.

She heard footsteps padding behind her. She glanced back; Yobar was following her. She had not expected this, but then Yobar had always surprised her. He was intelligent and curious indeed, among animals whose intelligence was only a little short of the human mind, and whose curiosity and eagerness to learn were sometimes greater.

"Come if you will, then," said Luet. She led him upstream to the garden, where the baboons had long been forbidden to go. The last of the third crop of melons was still on the vine, some ripe, some not yet. He hesitated at the edge of the garden, for the baboons had long since learned to respect that invisible boundary. She beckoned to him, though, and he carefully crossed the edge into the garden. She took him to a ripe melon. "Eat them when they look like this," she said. "When they *smell* like this." She held the melon out to him, still attached to the vine. He sniffed it, shook it, then thumped it on the ground. With enough thumping, he broke it. Then he took a bite and hooted happily at her.

"I'm not done yet," said Luet. "You have to pay attention through the whole lesson." She held out another melon, this one not ripe, and though she let Yobar sniff it, she wouldn't let him hold it. "No," she said. "Don't eat these. The seeds aren't mature, and if you eat them when they look like this, you won't have a crop next year." She set the unripe melon down behind her, and pointed to the broken ripe melon in pieces around Yobar's feet. "Eat the ripe ones. Shedemei says the seeds will pass right through your digestive system unharmed, and they'll sprout right in your turds and grow quite nicely. You can have melons forever, if you teach the others to eat only the ripe ones. If you teach them to *wait*."

Yobar looked at her steadily.

"You don't understand any of the words I'm saying," she said. "But that doesn't mean you don't understand the lesson, does it? You're a smart one. You'll figure it out. You'll teach the others before you move on to another troop, won't you? It's the only gift we can leave for you, our rent for using your valley this past year. Please take this from us, and use it well."

He hooted once.

She got up and walked away from him. The riding camels were ready for mounting now; they had been waiting for her. "I was just showing the garden to Yobar," she said. Of course Kokor rolled her eyes at that, but Luet hardly noticed—it was Nafai's smile, and Hushidh's nod, and Volemak's "Well done" that mattered.

On command, the camels lurched to their feet, burdened with tents and supplies, dryboxes and coldboxes full of seeds and embryos, and—above all—with not sixteen but twenty-three human beings now. As Elemak said only last night, the Oversoul had better lead them to their destination before the children get too big to ride with their mothers, or else it had better find them more camels along the way.

The first two days' travel took them northeast, along the same route they had taken from Basilica. It had been a year since they came that way, however, and almost nothing looked familiar—or at least nothing looked more familiar than anything else, since all grey-brown rocks and yellow-grey sand begin to look familiar after the first hour.

Mebbekew rode beside Elemak for a short way, late in the second afternoon. "We passed the place where you sentenced him to death, didn't we?"

Elemak was silent for a moment. Then: "No, we won't pass it at all."

"I thought I saw it."

"You didn't."

They rode in silence for a while more.

"Elemak," said Mebbekew.

"Yes?" He didn't sound as if he was enjoying the conversation.

"Who could stop us if we simply took our share of the tents, and three days' supplies, and headed north to Basilica?"

Sometimes it seemed to Elemak that Mebbekew's shortsightedness bordered on stupidity. "Apparently you've forgotten that we have no money. I can assure you that being poor in Basilica is even worse than being poor out here, because in Basilica the Oversoul won't give a lizard's tit for your survival."

"Oh, and we've been so well taken care of *here!*" said Meb scornfully.

"We were at a well-watered location for more than a year and not *once* did any travelers or bandits or eloping couples or families on holiday ever come near us."

"I know, we might as well have been on another planet. An uninhabited one! I can tell you, when Dolya was too pregnant to move, the baboon females were starting to look good to me."

Never had Mebbekew seemed more useless than now. "I'm not surprised," said Elemak.

Meb glared at him. "I was joking, pizdook."

"I wasn't," said Elemak.

"So you've sold your soul, is that it? You're Daddy's little boy now. Nafai senior."

Mebbekew's resentment of Nafai was only natural—since Nafai had shown him up so many times. But Elemak had long since decided to endure Nafai, at least as long as he stayed in his place, as long as he was *useful*. That's all Elemak really cared about now—whether a person contributed to the survival of the group. Of Elemak's wife and child. And it wouldn't hurt for Mebbekew to recall exactly how much *more* useful Nafai was than Meb himself. "We've lived a year together," said Elemak. "You've eaten meat that Nafai killed during every week of that year, and you still think he's nothing more than Father's favorite?"

"Oh, I know he's more than just that," said Mebbekew. "Everyone knows it. In fact, most of us realize that he's worth more than *you*."

Mebbekew must have seen something in Elemak's face, then, for he dropped back and stayed in line directly behind Elemak for some time.

Elemak knew that Meb's little insult was meant to enrage him—but Elemak was not going to play along. He understood what Mebbekew wanted: out of his marriage, away from the crying of his baby, and back to the city, with its baths and commodes, its cuisine and its art, and, above all, its endless supply of flatterable and uncomplicated women. And the truth was that if he went back, Mebbekew would probably do as well as ever in Basilica, with or without money; and Dol, too, would certainly find a good living there, being an almost-legendary child actress. For the two of them, Basilica would be a lot better than anything that lay ahead of them in the foreseeable future.

But that issue is closed, thought Elemak. It was closed when the Oversoul made such a fool of me. The message was clear—try to kill Nafai and you'll only be made to bumble and fumble around like a half-wit, unable even to tie a knot. And now it wouldn't be Nafai he'd have to overcome in order to change their destination, it would be Father. No, there was no escape for Elemak. And besides, Basilica had nothing for *him*. Unlike Meb, he wasn't content to hop from bed to bed and live off any woman who'd take him in. He needed to have stature in the city, he needed to know that when he spoke, men listened. Without money, there was little hope of *that*.

Besides, he loved Eiadh and was proud of little Proya, and he loved the desert life in a way that no one else, not even Volemak, could ever understand. And if he went back to Basilica, Eiadh would eventually not renew his marriage contract. He would again be in the unmanly position of having to look for a wife solely in order to maintain himself in the city. That would be unbearable—*this* was how men were meant to live, secure with their women, secure with their children. He had no desire to break up his family *now*. He had stopped dreaming of Basilica, or at least had stopped wishing for it, since the only kind of life worth living there was out of reach to him.

Only Meb and Dolya still had fantasies of returning. And, useless as they both were, it wouldn't hurt the company one bit to let them go.

So as Elemak and his father were choosing the site for that night's camp, he broached the subject. "You know that Meb and Dolya still want to go back to Basilica."

"They have so little imagination, I'm not surprised," said Volemak. "Some people only have one idea in their lives, and so they can hardly bear to let it go."

"You know that they're also nearly worthless to us."

"Not as worthless as Kokor," said Father.

"Yes, well, it's hard to compete with *her*."

"None of them are *completely* worthless," said Father. "They may not do their share of work, but we need their genes. We need their babies in our community."

"Our life would be much easier . . . a lot less conflict and annoyance . . . if—"

"No," said Volemak.

Elemak seethed. How dare Father not even let him finish his sentence.

"It's not by my choice," said Volemak. "I'd let anyone go back who wanted to, if it were up to me. But the Oversoul has chosen this company."

Elemak stopped paying attention almost as soon as Father mentioned the Oversoul. It always meant that the reasonable part of the discussion was over.

When they camped for the night, Elemak determined that during his watch, if Meb and Dolya decided to slip away, he'd make sure he didn't happen to notice them. It would be easy enough to find the way—the desert wasn't all that challenging through here, and they'd have the best chance of the whole journey to return to civilization. Which wasn't that good a chance, admittedly—there would be as great a risk of bandits as ever. Perhaps more, now that Moozh ruled in Basilica and would drive rough and uncivilized men from the city. Maybe the Oversoul would watch out for them and help them get back to Basilica—and maybe not. Whatever happened, Elemak wouldn't block their attempt, if they made one.

But they didn't. Elemak even stood a longer watch than usual, but they never slipped out of their tent, never tried to steal a camel or two. Elemak finally woke Vas for his watch and then went to bed, full of fresh contempt for Meb. If it had been *I* who wanted to leave the group and live somewhere else, I would have taken my wife and baby and *left*. But not Mebbekew. He takes *no* for an answer far too easily.

At midmorning on the third day of travel, they reached the point where, to return to Basilica, they would have traveled north. Elemak recognized the spot; so, of course, did Volemak. But no one else did; no one realized that when they continued eastward instead of turning straight north, they were closing their last hope of restoring something like their old life.

Elemak didn't feel at all sad about it. He wasn't like Mebbekew—his life had centered in the desert all along. He had only returned to Basilica in order to sell his goods and find a wife, though of course he always enjoyed the city and thought of it as home. It's just that the idea of *home* had never meant that much to him—he didn't get homesick or nostalgic or teary-eyed about it. Not till Eiadh gave birth and he held Proya in his arms and heard the boy's firm loud cry and saw his smile. And then home, to him, was the tent where Eiadh and Proya slept. He had no need of Basilica now. He was too strong in himself to hunger for a particular city the way Meb did.

But if this caravan was going to be Elemak's world for the next few years, he was determined to make sure his position in this small polity was as dominant and important as possible. In the valley, where Zdorab's garden brought in half the food and Nafai was as good at hunting as Elemak himself, there was no way for Elemak to fully emerge, secure in his position of leadership. Now, though, on camelback again, even Father deferred to Elemak's judgment on many, many issues, and while the Oversoul chose their general direction, it was Elemak who determined their exact path. He could look back over the company and find Eiadh, her eyes on him whenever she wasn't busy with nursing the baby. The journey was reminding her of how essential he was to the survival of the whole enterprise, and he loved the pride she took in that.

The Oversoul had told Father that if they found a good safe route and had plenty of supplies, sixty days of steady traveling would bring them to their destination. But of course, sixty days of traveling was out of the question. The babies could never endure that long a stretch of heat and dryness and instability. No, they would have to find another secure place and rest again. And perhaps another after that. And in each place, they would probably have to stay long enough to put in a crop and harvest it to feed them on the next leg of their journey. A year. A year in each place, perhaps three years to make a sixty-day journey. Yet through it all, it would be Elemak truly leading them, and by the end of it everyone should be turning to me for leadership, with Father reduced to nothing more than what he ought to be—a wise old counselor. But not the true leader, not anymore.

That will be me, by right. If I decide then that the Oversoul's destination is the place where I want to lead the group, then that's where I'll lead them, and they'll get there safely and in good time. If I decide otherwise, of course, then the Oversoul can go hang.

The Nividimu River wasn't a seasonal river—it rose from natural springs in the rugged Lyudy Mountains, which were high enough to catch snow in the winter. But the flow was never much, and when the river dropped steeply down the Krutohn Valley and reached the low, hot, dry desert, it sank into the sand and disappeared many kilometers before reaching the Scour Sea.

It was because of the Nividimu that the great north-south caravan trail climbed steeply up into the Lyudy Mountains and then followed the river down, almost to the point where it disappeared. It was the most dependable source of drinkable water between Basilica on the north and the Cities of Fire to the south. Perhaps a dozen caravans a year passed along the banks of the Nividimu, and so it was almost to be expected that the Index would instruct them to make camp for a week in the foothills of the Lyudy Mountains while a northbound caravan with a heavy military escort made its way up the valley and then down the twisting road out of the mountains.

The worst thing about the wait was that they couldn't make any fires. The military escort, the Index told them, was nervous and eager to find an enemy. Smoke would be taken as a sign of bandits, and the soldiers wouldn't wait to find out otherwise before slaughtering them all. So they ate the most miserable traveling rations and sat around getting annoyed with each other, waiting for the day that Volemak told them that the Index had decided they could leave.

It was on the second day, as Elemak and Vas were hunting together—for Vas had some talent as a tracker of animals—that they lost the first pulse. Vas probably shouldn't have been carrying one, but he asked for it, and it would have been too humiliating to forbid him to have one. Besides, there was always the chance that he'd surprise a dangerous beast of prey that had tracked the same quarry, and then he'd need the pulse to defend himself.

Vas was not usually clumsy. But as he crabwalked along a narrow ledge over a defile, he stumbled, and as he caught himself the pulse slipped out of his hand. It bounced on a rocky outcropping, and then sailed out into space and on into a canyon. Vas and Elemak never heard it strike bottom. "It could have been me," he kept saying, when he told the story that night.

Elemak didn't have the heart to tell him that it might have been better for everyone if it *had* been him. They only had four pulses, after all, and no way of getting more—eventually they would lose their ability to recharge themselves from sunlight, which was why Elemak was so careful about keeping two of them hidden away in a dark place. With one pulse gone, now one of the hidden ones had to come out and into use for hunting.

"Why were you hunting, anyway?" asked Volemak, who understood what the loss of the pulse might mean in the future. He directed his question at Elemak, which was proper, since it was Elemak's decision to take two pulses out into the desert that day.

Elemak answered as coldly as if he thought Volemak had no right to challenge his decision. "For meat," he said. "The wives can't nurse properly on hard biscuits and jerky."

"But since we can't cook the meat, what did you expect them to do, eat it raw?" asked Volemak.

"I thought I could sear the meat with the pulse," said Elemak. "It would be rare, but . . . "

"It would also be a waste of power that we can ill afford," said Volemak.

"We need the meat," said Elemak.

"Should I have jumped after the pulse?" asked Vas, nastily.

"Nobody wants *that,*" said Elemak scornfully. "This isn't about *you* anymore."

Hushidh watched the conversation in silence, as she usually did when there was conflict, seeing how the threads connecting them seemed to change. She knew that the lines she saw between people were not real, that they were simply a visual metaphor that her mind constructed for her—a sort of hallucinatory diagram. But their message about relationships and loyalties and hatreds and loves was real enough, as real as the rocks and sand and scrub around them.

Vas was the anomaly of the group and had been all along. No one hated him, no one resented him. But no one loved him, either. There was no great loyalty binding anyone to him—and none binding him to anybody else, either. Except the strange bond between him and Sevet, and the even stranger one between him and Obring. Sevet had little love or respect for her husband Vas—theirs had been a marriage in name only, for convenience, with no particular bond of loyalty between them, and no great love or friendship, either. But he seemed to feel something very powerful toward her, something that Hushidh did not understand, had never seen before. And his bond with Obring was almost the same, only a bit weaker. Which should not have been the case, since Vas had no reason to be closely tied to Obring. After all, hadn't Obring been the one who was caught in bed with Sevet the night that Kokor surprised them and almost killed her sister? Why should Vas feel a strong connection to Obring? Its strength—which Hushidh recognized by the thickness of the cord she saw connecting them—rivaled the strength of the strongest marriages in the company, like the one between Volemak and Rasa, or what Elemak felt toward Eiadh, or the growing bond between Hushidh herself and her beloved Issib, her devoted and sweet and brilliant and loving Issib, whose voice was the music underlying all her joy . . .

That, she knew, was not what Vas felt toward Sevet or Obring—and toward everyone else he seemed to feel almost nothing. Yet why Sevet and Obring, and no one else? Nothing connected *them* except their one-time adultery . . .

Was *that* the connection? Was it the adultery itself? Was Vas's powerful link with them an obsession with their betrayal of him? But that was absurd. He had known of Sevet's affairs all along; they had an easy marriage that way. And Hushidh would have recognized the connection between them if it had been hate or rage—she had seen plenty of *that* before.

Even now, when Vas should have been connected to everyone in the company by a thread of shame, of desire to make amends, to win approval, there was almost nothing. He didn't care. Indeed, he was almost satisfied.

"We could more easily have afforded the power to cook the meat," said Sevet, "back when we had all four pulses."

It astonished Hushidh that Vas's own wife would bring up Vas's culpability.

But it was no surprise when Kokor followed her sister and

pounced even more directly. "You might have watched your step in the first place, Vas," she said.

Vas turned and regarded Kokor with mild disdain. "Perhaps I should have learned about working carefully and efficiently by following *your* example."

Quarrels like this started far too easily and usually went on far too long. It didn't take a raveler like Hushidh to know where this argument would lead, if it was allowed to continue. "Drop it," said Volemak.

"I'm not going to take the blame for our having no cooked meat," said Vas mildly. "We still have three pulses and it's not my fault that we can't light fires."

Elemak put a hand on Vas's shoulder. "It's me that Father holds responsible, and rightly so. It was my misjudgment. There should never have been two pulses on the same hunting trip. When we blame *you* for our lack of meat, you'll know it."

"Yes, we'll start eating *you,*" said Obring.

It was funny enough that several people laughed, if only to release the tension; but Vas did not appreciate the joke's having come from Obring. Hushidh saw the odd connection between them flare and thicken, like a black hawser mooring Vas to Obring.

Hushidh watched, hoping that they might quarrel just long enough for her to understand what it was between them, but at that moment Shedemei spoke up. "There's no reason we can't eat the meat raw, if it's from a fresh kill and the animal was healthy," she said. "Searing the outside a little just before eating it would help kill any surface contamination without using much power. We have a good supply of antibiotics if someone *does* get sick, and even when we run out of *those,* we can make fairly adequate ones from available herbs if we need to."

"Raw meat," said Kokor in disgust.

"I don't know if I *can* eat it," said Eiadh.

"You just have to chew it more," said Shedemei. "Or cut it into finer pieces."

"It's the *taste* of it," said Eiadh.

"It's the *idea* of it," said Kokor, shuddering.

"It's only a psychological barrier," said Shedemei, "which you can easily overcome for the good of your babies."

"I don't know why someone without a baby should be telling the *rest* of us what's good for us," snapped Kokor.

Hushidh saw how Kokor's words stung Shedemei. It was one of Hushidh's most serious worries about their company, the way that Shedemei was becoming more and more isolated from the women. Hushidh talked about it with Luet rather often, and they had been doing their best to deal with it, but it wasn't easy, because much of the barrier was in Shedemei herself—she had persuaded herself that she didn't *want* children, but Hushidh knew from the way Shedemei focused so intently on all the babies in the group that unconsciously she judged her own value by the fact that she had no children. And when some shortsighted, unempathic little birdbrain like Kokor threw Shedemei's childlessness in her face, Hushidh could almost see Shedemei's connections with the rest of the group dropping away.

And the silence after Kokor's remark didn't help. Most of them were silent because that's how one responded to unspeakable social clumsiness—one gave it just a long enough silence to serve as a rebuke to the offensive one, and then one went on as if it had not been said. But Hushidh was sure that was not how *Shedya* interpreted the silence. After all, Shedya was not well versed in high manners, and she was also relentlessly aware of her childlessness, so to her the silence no doubt meant that everyone *agreed* with Kokor, but was too polite to say so. Just one more injury, one more scar on Shedemei's soul.

If it were not for the intense friendship between Shedemei and Zdorab, and the much slighter friendship that Luet and Hushidh had cultivated with Shedya, and Shedya's great love and respect for Rasa, the woman would have no positive connection with the rest of the company at all. It would be nothing but envy and resentment.

It was Luet who finally broke the silence. "If meat is what our babies need, then of course we'll eat it seared, or even raw. But I wonder—are we so close to the edge, nutritionally, that we can't go a *week* without meat?"

Elemak looked at her coldly. "You can treat *your* baby as you want. Ours will always suckle on milk that has been freshened with animal protein within three days."

"Oh, Elemak, do I *have* to eat it?" asked Eiadh.

"Yes," said Elemak.

"It'll be fine," said Nafai. "You'll never notice the difference."

They all turned to look at him. His remark was quite outrageous. "I think I can tell whether meat is raw or cooked, thank you," said Eiadh.

"We're all here because we're more or less susceptible to the Oversoul," said Nafai. "So I just asked if the Oversoul could make the meat taste acceptable to us. Make us *think* that there's nothing wrong with it. And it said that it could do that, if we didn't try to resist it. So if we don't dwell on the fact that we're eating raw meat, the Oversoul can influence us enough that we won't really be aware of the difference."

No one answered for a moment. Hushidh could see that Nafai's almost casual relationship with the Oversoul was quite unnerving to some of them—not least to Volemak himself, who only spoke to the Oversoul in solitude, or with the Index.

"You asked the Oversoul to *season our food?*" asked Issib.

"We know from experience that the Oversoul is good at making people stupid," said Nafai. "You went through it with me, Issya. So why not have the Oversoul make us just a little stupid about the taste of the meat?"

"I don't like the idea of the Oversoul messing with my mind," said Obring.

Meb looked at Obring and grinned. "Don't worry," he said. "I'm sure you can be adequately stupid without help."

The next day, when Nafai brought home a nolyen—a small deerlike creature, barely a half-meter from the shoulder to the ground—they cut it up and seared the meat and then ate it, rather gingerly, until they realized that either raw meat wasn't so bad or the Oversoul had done a good job of making them insensitive to the difference. They'd get by without fire whenever they had to.

But the Oversoul couldn't give them a new pulse to replace the lost one.

They lost two more pulses crossing the Nividimu. It was a stupid, unnecessary loss. The camels were reluctant to make the crossing, even though the ford was wide and shallow, and there was some jostling as they were herded across. Still, if all the loads had been competently and carefully tied in place, none of them would have come loose, none would have spilled their contents into the ice-cold water.

It took a few minutes before Elemak realized that this was the camel that carried two of the pulses; until then he had concentrated on getting the rest of the camels across before trying to retrieve the load. By the time he found the pulses, in a poke, wrapped in cloth, they had been immersed for a quarter of an hour. Pulses were durable, but they had not been meant for use under water. Their seals had been penetrated and the mechanism inside would corrode rapidly. He saved the pulses, of course, in the hope that perhaps they would *not* corrode, though he knew the chance of that was slim.

"Who packed this camel?" Elemak demanded.

No one seemed to recall having packed it.

"That's the problem," said Volemak. "The camel obviously packed itself, and it wasn't good with the knots."

The company laughed nervously. Elemak whirled on his father, prepared to castigate him for making light of a serious situation. When he met Volemak's gaze, however, he paused, for he could see that Volemak was taking things very seriously indeed. So Elemak nodded to his father and then sat down, to show that he was going to let Volemak handle it.

"Whoever loaded this camel knows his responsibility," said Volemak. "And finding out who it is will be very simple—I have only to ask the Index. But there will be no punishment, because there's nothing to be gained by it. If I ever feel a need, I will reveal who it was whose carelessness cost us our security, but in the meantime you are safe in your cowardly refusal to name yourself."

Still no one spoke up.

Volemak said no more, but instead nodded toward Elemak, who got up and held the last pulse in front of him. "This is the pulse we have used *most,*" he said. "Therefore this is the one whose charge is least durable, and yet it's all we have to bring us meat. It *could* last a couple of years—pulses have lasted that long before—but when this one is no longer workable, we have no other."

He walked to Nafai and held out the pulse to him. Nafai took it gingerly.

"You're the hunter," said Elemak. "You're the one who'll make best use of it. Just make sure you take care of it. Our lives and the lives of our children depend on how you fulfil this duty."

Nafai nodded his understanding.

Elemak turned to the others. "If anyone sees that the pulse is in any danger whatever, you must speak or act at once to protect it. But except for such a case, no one but Nafai is to touch the pulse for any reason. We'll no longer use it even to sear the meat—what meat we eat during dangerous passages, we'll eat raw. Now, let's get down this valley before we're discovered here."

By late afternoon they were at the place where caravans either went on south, into the inhabited valleys where the cities of Dovoda and Neeshtchy clung to life between the desert and the sea, or southeastward into the Razoryat Mountains, and then on down into the northern reaches of the Valley of Fires. Volemak led them up into Razoryat. But it occurred to more than one of them that if they went south into Dovoda or Neeshtchy, there would be more pulses they could buy, and decent food, for that matter. And above all, other faces, other voices. Hardly a one of them that didn't wish they could, at the very least, visit there.

But Volemak led them on up into the hills, where they camped that night without a fire, for fear it would be seen by some dweller in the distant cities.

It was slow travel, from then on, for the Index warned Volemak that there were three caravans coming north through the Valley of Fires, two of them from the Cities of Fire and another from the Cities of the Stars, even farther to the south. To most of them those were names out of legend, cities even older and more storied than Basilica. Tales of ancient heroes always seemed to begin, "Once upon a time in the Cities of the Stars," or "Here is how things were in the old days, in the Cities of Fire." They hoped, many of them: Perhaps that's where the Oversoul is taking us, to the great ancient cities of legend.

To avoid the caravans, however, they had to travel away from the road. In the desert that had been easy enough—the road was barely distinguishable from the rest of the desert, and it made little difference what path, precisely, one followed. But here it mattered a great deal, for the terrain was strange, and more difficult and confusing than in any other place in Harmony. They came down out of the mountains and saw at once that it was a greener place, with grass almost everywhere, and vines, and bushes, and even a few trees. It was also rocky and craggy, and the land was strangely stepped, as if someone had pushed together a thousand tables of different sizes and heights, so that every surface was flat, but no two surfaces met at a level. And between the grassy tables were cliffs, some only a meter or so high, but some towering a hundred meters, or five hundred.

And the strangeness grew even greater as they moved down into the Valley of Fires, for there were places where vents in the earth or cracks in a cliff gave off remarkable stenches. Most of them made faces and tried to breathe through their mouths, but Elemak and Volemak took the stinks very seriously indeed, often finding circuitous routes that avoided the vent where the gas was coming from. Only when Zdorab discovered that the Index could provide them with immediate spectroscopic analysis of the gas, at least during daylight, were they able to be sure which gases—and therefore which stinks—were safe to breathe.

Even more frightening—though Elemak assured them that it was much safer—were the smokeholes and the open flames. They would see them from miles away, either thick columns of smoke or bright flames, and they learned to bend their course toward them, especially after Shedemei assured them that they would certainly not explode. When they camped near the open flames, they used them to cook their meat and even bake fresh bread, though only Zdorab, Nafai, and Elemak were willing to do the actual cooking, since it involved running near enough to the flames to leave the meat and the loaves where there was enough heat to cook flesh—which, of course, meant that the heat could cook the cooks if they didn't get out fast enough. They would all help dress the meat that Nafai had killed, put it on griddles, and then cheer madly as Nafai, Zdorab, and Elemak, each in turn, ran toward the fire, set down a griddle of meat, and then ran back to cooler air. Fetching the meat was even harder, of course, since it took longer to pick up the hot griddles than to set down the cool ones, and sometimes when they came back their clothes were smoking.

"It's only our sweat steaming," Nafai insisted, when Luet announced she *preferred* to have her meat raw and keep her husband alive.

But there weren't *that* many fires that were usable, since they were not often located near sources of water, and as often as not they ate cold food.

It was a place of glorious beauty, the Valley of Fires, but there was also something frightening about it, to be confronted at every turn by evidence of the terrible forces that moved inside the planet they lived on—forces strong enough to lift solid rock hundreds of meters straight up in the air.

Glorious, frightening, and also inconvenient, they realized, when they came to a place where the route they had chosen funneled them into a cul-de-sac—a deep, hot lake, surrounded by five-hundred-meter cliffs on both sides. There was no getting across the lake, and no getting around it either. They would have to backtrack several days' journey, Volemak and Elemak decided, and choose another route even farther from the regular caravan roads, and much closer to the sea.

"Couldn't the Oversoul have seen *this?*" asked Mebbekew, rather caustically.

"The Index showed this lake," said Volemak. "That's why we came this way. What the Oversoul could not tell us was that there was no way around it on either side."

"Then the last three days of traveling are *wasted?*" Kokor whined.

"We've seen things that aren't even dreamed of in Basilica," Lady Rasa answered.

"Except in *nightmares,*" said Kokor.

"Some artists have been known to take sights like these and turn them into song," said Rasa. "Which reminds me—we've heard neither you nor Sevet sing this whole year and more, except when you sing to your babies. Nor Eiadh, for that matter—she never had a chance to try her career as my daughters did, but she has the sweetest voice."

Hushidh could have told her to save her breath—there would be no singing until something changed among the women. It was the old quarrel between Sevet and Kokor, of course. Sevet either could not sing anymore or chose not to, all as a result of the damage Kokor did by striking her on the larynx when she caught her in bed with Obring. And as long as Sevet wasn't singing, Kokor dared not sing—she feared Sevet's vengeance if she did. And Eiadh was hopelessly intimidated by the two older girls, who had been quite famous in Basilica, especially Sevet. Kokor had made it clear that if *she* couldn't sing, she didn't want to hear Eiadh's wretched little voice like a mockery of music. Which was unfair—Eiadh *did* have talent, and the very thinness of her voice might have been called bell-like purity if someone besides Kokor had been the critic. But whenever Eiadh did try to sing, Kokor made such a show of grimacing and *enduring* that Eiadh soon lost heart and never tried again. So there would be no songs in their company about the grandeur and majesty of the Valley of Fires.

There was another kind of poetry, though, and another kind of artist, and Hushidh and Luet were the audience as Shedemei rhapsodized about the forces of nature. "Two great landmasses, once a single continent but now divided," she said. "They pressed against each other like your two hands laid side by side on a table. But then they began to rotate in opposite directions, with the center right where your thumbs touch. Now they press toward each other at the fingertips, crushing into each other, even as they pull away from each other at the heels of the hands."

Shedemei was explaining this as she sat on the carpet in Luet's tent, holding both their babies sitting up on her knees, her arms around them, her hands in front of her, demonstrating. The babies seemed fascinated indeed—there was something in the color or intensity of Shedemei's voice that all the babies in the company were drawn to, for Hushidh saw how alert they all became when she spoke. Often Shedemei could quiet a fussy infant when the child's own mother could not—which meant that Kokor and Sevet never let Shedemei near their babies, out of jealousy at being shown up—and Dol was always dropping off her little Syelsika for Shedemei to tend, often leaving her until Dol's own breasts were so sore that she had no choice but to fetch her baby and nurse it.

Only Luet and Hushidh, it seemed, sought out Shedemei's company, and even *they* had to use their babies as an excuse—could you help us with our babies while we bathe? So it was that Shedya sat on the carpet in Luet's tent while the two sisters sponged the dirt of the several days' journey from each other's backs and washed each other's hair.

"The crushing at the fingertips raises the great mountains of the north," said Shedemei. "While the parting at the heels created the Scour Sea, and then the Sea of Smoke. The Valley of Fires is the upwelling at the center. Someday, when the tearing apart is done, Potokgavan will sink into the sea and the Valley of Fires will be an island in an ever-widening ocean. It will be the most glorious and isolated spot on all of Harmony, the place where the planet is most alive and dangerous and beautiful."

Chveya, Luet's daughter, made a gurgling sound in the back of her throat. Like a growl.

"That's right, Veyevniya," said Shedemei, using her own silly name for Chveya. "A place for wild animals like you."

"And what about the thumbs?" asked Hushidh. "What happens there?"

"The thumbs, the fulcrum, the center—that's Basilica," said Shedemei. "The stable heart of the world. There are other continents, but no place on any of them where the water is so hot and cold and deep or the land so old and unchangeable. Basilica is the place where Harmony is most at peace."

"Geologically speaking," said Hushidh.

"Humanity's little disturbances—what are they?" asked Shedemei. "The smallest unit of time that ever matters is the generation, not the minute, not the hour, not the day, not even the year. Those all come and go and are done in a moment. But the generation—that's where the true changes come, when a world is really alive."

"Is humanity dead, then, since we've gone forty million years without evolution?" asked Luet.

"Do you think these children aren't evolution in progress?" asked Shedemei. "Speciation comes at times of genetic stress, when a species—not a mere individual or even a tribe—is in danger of destruction. Then the vast variety of possibilities within the species is winnowed down to those few variations that offer particular advantages to survival. So a species seems to be unchanged for millions of years, only to have change come suddenly when the need arises. The truth is that the changes were present all along—they simply hadn't been isolated and exposed."

"You make it sound like a wonderful plan," said Luet.

"I know—that's how it's always taught among women, isn't it? The Oversoul's plan. The patterns of generation: coupling, conception, gestation, birth, nurturing, maturation, and then coupling again—all the plan of the Oversoul. But *we* know better, don't we? The machine in the sky is merely an expression of humanity's will—part of the reason why we have *not* undergone speciating stress in forty million years. A tool to keep us as widely varied as possible, without ever achieving power enough to destroy ourselves and our world, as we did on Earth. Isn't that what Nafai and Issib learned? Isn't that why we're here? Because this *isn't* a plan of the Oversoul, because the Oversoul is losing the power to keep humanity self-tamed. Yet I can't help but think that it might be a *good* thing to let the Oversoul wither and die. In the generations that came after that, in the terrible stresses that would come, maybe humanity would speciate again and develop something new." She leaned down to little Dza and poofed in her face, which always made Dza laugh. "Maybe *you* are the new thing that humanity is supposed to become," said Shedemei. "Isn't that right, Dazyitnikiya?"

"You *do* love children so," said Luet, with a wistful tone.

"I love *other people's* children," said Shedemei. "I can always give them back, and then have time for my work. For *you,* poor things, it never ends."

But Hushidh was not deceived. Not that Shedemei didn't mean what she said—far from it. Shedya was quite sincere in her decision that it was perfectly all right for her not to have children—that she actually preferred it that way. She meant it, or at least *meant* to mean it.

Hushidh was convinced, however, that the powerful bond between Shedemei and every baby in the camp was really the infants' unconscious response to Shedemei's irresistible hunger. She wanted babies. She wanted to be part of the vast passage of the generations through the world. And more than that—as Hushidh watched the love between her and Zdorab grow into one of the strongest friendships she had ever seen, Hushidh became more and more certain that Shedemei wanted to bear Zdorab's child, and it made Hushidh yearn more and more for that longing to come true.

She had even asked the Oversoul why it was that Shedemei didn't conceive, but the Oversoul had never answered—and Luet said that when *she* asked, she got the clear answer that what went on between Zdorab and Shedemei was none of her business.

Maybe it's none of our business, though Hushidh, but that doesn't mean we can't wish that Shedemei had all that she needs to make her happy. Didn't the Oversoul bring everyone into the company because *all* their genes were needful? Was it possible that the Oversoul had erred, and either Zdorab or Shedemei was sterile? Awfully clumsy of her, if that's what happened.

Even now, Shedemei was explaining how Zdorab was the one who had discovered the geological history of the Valley of Fires. "He plays the Index like a musical instrument. He found things in the past that even the Oversoul didn't know that she knew. Things that only the ancients who first settled here understood. They gave the memory to the Oversoul, but then programmed her so that she couldn't find those memories on her own. Zdorab found the back doors, though, the hidden passageways, the strange connections that led into so many, many secrets."

"I know," said Hushidh. "Issib marvels at him sometimes, even though Issya himself isn't bad at getting ideas out of the Index."

"Oh, indeed, I know that," said Shedemei. "Zdorab says all the time that Issib is the real explorer."

"And Issib says that's only because he has more time, being

useless at everything else," said Hushidh. "It's as if they both have to find reasons why the other is much better. I think they've become good friends."

"I know it," said Shedemei. "Issib is able to see how fine a man Zdorab really is."

"We all understand that," said Luet.

"Do you?" said Shedemei. "Sometimes it seems to me that everyone thinks of him as a sort of universal servant."

"We think of him as our cook because he's the best at it," said Hushidh. "And our librarian because he's the best at *that*."

"Ah, but only a few of us care about his archival skills; to most of the people in our company, his culinary skills are the only things they notice about him."

"And his gardening," said Luet.

Shedemei smiled. "You see? But he gets little respect for it."

"From some," said Hushidh. "But others respect him greatly."

"I know Nafai does," said Luet. "And I do."

"And I, and Issib—and Volemak, too, I know that," said Hushidh.

"And isn't that everybody that matters?" asked Luet.

"I tell him that," said Shedemei, "but he persists in playing the servant."

Hushidh could see that, for this moment at least, Shedemei was closer to opening her heart to someone than ever before on this journey. She hardly knew, though, how to encourage her to go on—should she prod with a question, or keep silence so as not to impede her?

She kept silence.

And so did Shedemei.

Until at last Shedemei sniffed loudly and put her nose down near Chveya's diaper. "Has our little kaka factory produced another load?" she asked. "*Now* is the time when my permanent aunthood pays off. Mama Luet, your baby needs you."

They laughed—because of course they knew that Shedemei was as likely to change a baby's diaper as not. This business of giving the baby back to the mother whenever taking care of it was a bother was only a joke.

No, not *only* a joke. It was also a wistful regret. Shedemei's reminder to herself that, like her husband Zdorab, she was not really one of the company of women. She had been on the verge, Hushidh knew it, of telling *something* that mattered... and then the moment had passed.

As Luet cleaned her baby, Shedemei watched, and Hushidh watched her watching. Near the end of her bath, Luet was wearing nothing but a light skirt, and the shape of her motherly body—heavy breasts, a belly still loose and full from the birthing not that many months ago—was sweetly framed as she knelt and bent over her baby. What does Shedemei see when she looks at Luet, whose figure was once as lean and boyish as Shedemei's is still? Does she wish for that transformation?

Apparently, though, Shedemei's own thoughts had taken a different turn. "Luet," she said, "when we were at that lake yesterday, did it remind you of the Lake of Women in Basilica?"

"Oh yes," said Luet.

"You were the waterseer there," said Shedemei. "Didn't you want to float out into the middle of it, and dream?"

Luet hesitated a moment. "There was no boat," she said. "And nothing to make one out of. And the water was too hot to float in it myself."

"Was it?" said Shedemei.

"Yes," said Luet. "Nafai checked for me. He passed through the Lake of Women too, you know."

"But didn't you wish that you could be—for just a little while—the person you were before?"

The longing in Shedemei's voice was so strong that Hushidh immediately understood. "But Luet *is* the same person," said Hushidh. "She's still the waterseer, even if she now spends her days on camelback and her nights in a tent and every hour with a baby fastened to her nipple."

"*Is* she the waterseer, then?" asked Shedemei. "She *was*—but *is* she? Or are we nothing more than what we're doing *now*?

Aren't we truly only what the people we live with *think* we are?"

"No," said Hushidh. "Or that would mean that in Basilica I was nothing *but* the raveler, and Luet was nothing *but* the waterseer, and you were nothing *but* a geneticist, and that was never true, either. There's always something above and behind and beneath the role that everyone sees us acting out. *They* may think that we *are* the script we act out, but *we* don't have to believe it."

"Who are we then?" asked Shedemei. "Who am *I*?"

"Always a scientist," said Luet, "because you're still doing science in your mind every hour you're awake."

"And our friend," said Hushidh.

"And the person in our company who understands best how things work," added Luet.

"And Zdorab's wife," said Hushidh. "That's the one that means the most to you, I think."

To their surprise and consternation, Shedemei's only answer was to lay down Dza on the carpet and lightly run from the tent. Hushidh caught only a glimpse of her face, but she was weeping. There was no doubt of that. She was weeping because Hushidh had said that being Zdorab's wife meant more to her than anything. It was what a woman might do if she doubted her husband's love. But how could she doubt? It was obvious that Zdorab's whole life was centered around her. There were no better *friends* in the company than Zodya and Shedya, everyone knew that—unless it was Luet and Hushidh, and they were sisters so it hardly counted.

What could possibly be wrong between Zdorab and Shedemei, that would cause such a strong woman to be so fragile on the subject? A mystery. Hushidh longed to ask the Oversoul, but knew she'd get the same answer as always—silence. Or else the answer Luet already got—mind your own business.

The best thing and the worst thing about turning back and taking another route south was that they could see the sea. In particular, they could see Dorova Bay, an eastern arm of the Scour Sea. And on clear nights—which all the nights were—they could see, on the far side of that bay, the lights of the city of Dorova.

It was not a city like Basilica, they all knew that. It was a scrubby edge-of-the-desert town filled with riffraff and profiteers, failures and thieves, violent and stupid men and women. They told each other that over and over, remembering tales of desert towns and how they weren't worth visiting even if they were the last town in the world.

Except that Dorova was the last town in the world—the last town in *their* world, anyway. The last they would ever see. It was the town they could have visited more than a week ago, when Volemak led them up into the mountains from the Nividimu and they left the last hope of civilization behind—or the last danger of it, for those who had that perspective.

Nafai saw how others looked at those lights, when they gathered at night, fireless, chilly, the bundled infants smacking and suckling away as they drank cold water and gnawed on jerky and hard biscuit and dried melon. How Obring got tears in his eyes—tears! And what was the city to him, anyway, except a place to get his hooy polished. Tears! And Sevet was no better, with her simple, steady gaze, that stony look on her face. She had a baby at her breast, and all she could think of was a city so small and filthy that she wouldn't have stepped into its streets two years ago. If they had offered her twenty times her normal fee to come and sing there, she would have sneered at the offer—and now she couldn't keep her eyes off of it.

But looking was *all* they could do, fortunately. They could see it, but they had no boat to cross the bay, and none of them could swim well enough to cross that many kilometers without a boat. Besides, they weren't at the beach, they were at least a kilometer above it, at the edge of a craggy, rugged incline that couldn't decide whether to be a cliff or a slope. There might be a way to get the camels down, but it wasn't likely, and even if they did, it would be several days' journey back along the beach, *with* the camels—and without them, there would be no water to drink and so they couldn't make it at all. No, nobody was going to be able to slip away from the group and make it to Dorova. The only way there was if the whole group went, and even then they would probably have to go back the way they came, which meant a week and a half at least, and probably one of the caravans from the south to contend with along the way. And it was all meaningless because Father would never go back.

And yet Nafai couldn't stop thinking about how *much* these people wanted that city.

How much *he* wanted it.

Yes, there was the trouble. That's what bothered him. *He* wanted the city, too. Not for any of the things *they* wanted, or at least the things he imagined that they wanted. Nafai had no desire for any wife but Luet; they were a family, and that wouldn't change no matter where they lived, he had decided that long ago. No, what Nafai wanted was a soft bed to lay Chveya in. A school to take her to. A house for Luet and Chveya and whatever children might come after. Neighbors and friends—friends that he might choose for himself, not this accidental collection of people most of whom he just didn't like that much. That's what those lights meant to him—and instead here he was on a grassy meadow that sloped deceptively downward toward the sea, so that if you just squinted a little you couldn't really tell you were a kilometer above sea level, you could pretend for a few moments that it was just a stroll across the meadow, and then a short ride on a boat across the bay, and then you'd be home, the journey would be over, you could bathe and then sleep in a bed and wake up to find breakfast cooking already, and you'd find your wife in your arms beside you, and then you'd hear the faint sound of your baby daughter waking, and you'd slip out of bed and go get her from her cradle and bring her in to your wife, who would sleepily draw her breast from inside her nightgown and put it into the mouth of the baby that now nestled in the crook of her arm on the bed, and you'd lie back down beside her and listen to the sucking and smacking of the baby as you also heard the birds singing outside the window and the noises of morning in the street not far away, the venders starting to cry out what they had to sell. Eggs. Berries. Cream. Sweet breads and cakes.

Oversoul, why couldn't you have left us alone? Why couldn't you have waited another generation? Forty million years, and you couldn't wait for Luet's and my great-grandchildren to have this great adventure? You couldn't have let Issib and me figure out how to build one of those marvelous ancient flying machines, so we could go to wherever you're taking us in just a few hours? Time, that's all we needed, really. Time to live before we lost our world.

Stop whining, said the Oversoul in Nafai's mind. Or maybe it wasn't the Oversoul. Maybe it was just Nafai's own sense that he had indulged himself too much already.

It was morning, just before dawn, at the spring the Index had told them was named Shazer, though why anyone should have bothered to name such an obscure place, and why the Oversoul had bothered to remember, Nafai could not begin to guess. Vas had had the last watch of the night, and then came and woke Nafai so they could hunt together. Three days since they last had meat, and this was a good campsite so they could take two days to hunt if need be. So Vas would catch sight of something, or find some fresh animal trace; Nafai would trail after him and, when the quarry was near, creep silently forward until the animal came in sight. Then Nafai would take the sacred pulse, aim so carefully, trying to guess which way the animal would move, and how far, and how fast, and then he would squeeze the trigger and the beam of light would burn a hole into the heart of the creature, sear it so that the wound would never bleed, except for a hot wet smoke that would stain the sand and rocks it fell on red and black.

Nafai was tired of it. But it was his duty, and so when Vas scratched softly on the cloth of the tent, near where he knew Nafai's head lay, Nafai awoke at once—if he had not already been awake, coasting on the verges of a dream—and got up and dressed without waking Luet or Chveya and took the pulse out of its box and joined Vas outside in the chilly darkness.

Vas nodded a greeting to him—they tried to avoid speaking, lest they wake babies unnecessarily—and then turned slowly, finally pointing toward the downhill slope. Not toward the city, but still toward the sea. Downward. Nafai normally thought it was a stupid plan to go downhill on the hunt, since it would mean carrying the game back uphill to get it to camp. But this time he *wanted* to go down. Even though he would never abandon their quest, even though he had no thought of betraying either Father or the Oversoul, nevertheless there was a part of him that longed for the sea, and for what lay across the sea, and so he nodded when Vas pointed toward the seaward slope of the meadow.

When they were well away from the camp, and over the brow of the hill, they stopped and peed, and then began the difficult descent into the tumble of rocks that led downward. All the slope ahead of them lay in shadow, since the dawn was coming up behind them. But Vas was the tracker, and Nafai had long since learned that he was both good at it and very proud of his prowess, so things went better if Nafai didn't try to second-guess him.

It wasn't an easy climb, though the darkness was easing with every moment that passed, for dawn seemed to light the sky from horizon to horizon far more quickly here than it ever had in Basilica. Was it the latitude? The dry desert air? Whatever the cause, he could see, but what he saw was a confusion of cliffs and crags, ledges and outcroppings that would challenge the nimblest of animals. What kind of creature do you hope to find, Vas? What kind of animal could live here?

But these were just Nafai's normal doubts—fearing the worst even as he knew that there was plenty of vegetation here, and there'd be no difficulty finding game. It would just be hard to get it home. Which was another reason why Elemak had always sent a hunter and tracker together, either Nafai and Vas or, back when there was more than one pulse, Elemak as hunter and Obring as tracker. When they were successful, the team would come home with each man carrying half a beast over his shoulders. It happened more often with Nafai and Vas, however, in part because Nafai was the best shot, and in part because Obring could never really keep his mind on tracking well enough to do a good job, so that Elemak ended up having to divide his concentration to do both jobs.

Vas, though, could concentrate very well, seeing things that no one else had noticed. Vas could follow the same prey relentlessly for hours and hours. Like a fighting dog that gripped with its teeth and never let go. It was part of the reason why Nafai succeeded so much more often—because Vas would bring him to the prey. The rest of the success, however, was Nafai's own. Nobody could approach so near to the prey in silence; nobody's aim was as steady and true. They were a good team, and yet in all their lives they had never imagined that they'd be good at hunting. It would never have crossed their minds.

Soon enough, Vas found something—a small mark. Nafai had long since given up trying to see all the things that Vas saw—to him it didn't look like an animal sign, but then it often didn't. Nafai just followed along, keeping his eyes open for predators that might decide that human beings were either a threat or a meal. The animal's trail led farther and farther down the slope, so far that by midmorning Nafai could see a clear and easy route that would lead down to the beach. For reasons he wasn't proud of, he wanted to go down that path and at least put his feet in the water of Dorova Bay. But Vas was not going that way—he was leading them across the face of an increasingly steep and dangerous cliff.

Why would an animal have chosen *this* route? Nafai wondered. What kind of animal is it? But of course he said nothing; it was a point of pride, to maintain perfect silence throughout the hunt.

Just as they reached the most dangerous part of the passage, where they would have to traverse a smooth surface of rock with no ledge at all, only friction to keep them from falling down fifty meters or more, Vas stopped and pointed, indicating that the prey was on the other side of the traverse. That was bad news. It would mean that Nafai would have to make the passage with his pulse out and ready to fire—that, in fact, he would have to aim and fire from that very slope.

But after all this tracking, they couldn't give up and start over just because it was momentarily difficult.

Vas pressed himself against the cliff wall, and Nafai passed behind him, then drew the pulse out of the sling he carried it in and moved ahead onto the difficult traverse.

At that moment the thought came into his head: Don't go on. Vas is planning to kill you.

This is stupid, thought Nafai. It's one thing to be afraid of the traverse—I'm only human. But if Vas wanted to kill me he had only to shrug when I was passing behind him on the ledge just now.

Don't take another step.

And leave the family without meat, because I got a sudden attack of jitters? Not a chance.

Nafai swallowed his fear and moved across the face. He arched his body out a little, so that there would be the greatest possible pressure and therefore the greatest possible friction on the soles of his climbing boots. Even so, he could feel that there was too much give—this was very dangerous indeed, and shooting from this point would be almost impossible.

He reached the point where he could at last see all of the area that had been hidden before, and now he stopped and looked for the animal. He couldn't see it. This sometimes happened—especially because they hunted in silence. Vas would lead him to an animal with good natural camouflage, and when Nafai got within range the animal would see or smell him and freeze, becoming almost completely invisible. Sometimes it took a long time before the animal moved and Nafai could see him. This was going to be one of those waiting games. Nafai hated it that he would have to do his waiting on this traverse, but he was perfectly visible now, and if he moved any closer the animal would bolt and they would have to start over.

He gingerly shifted his hands so that all his weight was on his feet and the hand *without* the pulse, then brought the pulse to where he could easily aim at any point on the face of the mountain before him. Was the animal in those shrubs? Perhaps behind a rock, ready to emerge at any moment?

Holding the same pose in that awkward place was hard. Nafai was strong, and used to holding still for long periods of time—but this posture was one he had never had to hold before. He could feel sweat dripping down his forehead. If it got in his eye it would sting mercilessly, mixed as it was with dust from his face. Yet there was no way he could move to wipe it away without spooking the animal.

An animal I haven't even seen.

Forget the animal. Just get off the face of this rock.

No, I'm stronger than that. I need to get the food for the family—I won't go back and say we'll have no meat today because I was afraid to wait in stillness on a rock.

He could hear Vas moving behind him, traversing the rock. That was stupid—why was Vas doing that?

To kill me.

Why couldn't he shake that idea? No, Vas was coming because he could tell that Nafai hadn't seen the animal yet, and he wanted to point it out. But how would he do *that?* Nafai couldn't turn to look at him, and Vas couldn't pass him to get into his field of view.

Oh, no. Vas was going to *talk* to him.

"It's too dangerous," said Vas. "You're going to slip."

And just as he said it, the friction holding Nafai's right foot in place suddenly gave way. His foot slipped inward and down, and now with the abrupt movement his left foot couldn't hold and he began to slide. It must have been very quick but it felt like forever; he tried to dig in with his hand, with the butt of the pulse, but they both just rubbed along the rock, doing almost nothing even to slow his fall. And then the rock grew steeper and he wasn't sliding, he was falling, falling, and he knew he was going to die.

"Nafai!" screamed Vas. "Nafai!

Luet was at the stream, washing clothes, when suddenly there came a clear thought into her mind: ⟨He's not dead.⟩

Not dead? Who's not dead? Why should he be dead?

⟨Nafai is not dead. He'll come home.⟩

She knew at once that it was the Oversoul speaking to her. Reassuring her. But she was not reassured. Or rather, she *was* reassured to know that Nafai was all right. But now she had to know, *demanded* to know what had happened.

⟨He fell.⟩

How did he fall?

⟨His foot slipped on the face of the rock.⟩

Nafai is sure-footed. *Why* did his foot slip? What is it that you're not telling me?

⟨I was watching Vas very carefully with Sevet and Obring. Watching all the time. He has murder in his heart.⟩

Did Vas have something to do with Nafai's fall?

⟨Not until they were traversing the rock did I see the plan in his mind. He had already destroyed the first three pulses. I knew he meant to destroy the last one, but I wasn't concerned because there are alternatives. I never saw it in his mind, not until the last moment, that the simplest way to destroy the last pulse was to lead Nafai to a dangerous place and then push his foot so he would fall.⟩

You never saw a plan like that in his mind?

⟨All the way down the mountain he was thinking of a route to the sea. How to get down to the bay so he could walk to Dorova. That's all that was in his mind as he led Nafai after quarry that didn't exist. Vas has remarkable powers of concentration. He thought of nothing but the path to the sea, until the very last moment.⟩

Didn't you warn Nafai?

⟨He heard me, but he didn't realize it was my voice he was

hearing. He thought it was his own fear, and he fought it down.⟩

So Vas is a murderer.

⟨Vas is what he is. He will do anything to get his vengeance on Obring and Sevet for their betrayal of him back in Basilica.⟩

But he seemed so calm about it.

⟨He can be cold.⟩

What now? What now, Oversoul?

⟨I will watch.⟩

That's what you've been doing all along, and yet you never gave any of us a glimpse of what you saw. You knew what Vas was planning. Hushidh even saw those powerful bonds between him and Sevet and Obring and you never told her what they *were*.

⟨This is how I was programmed. To watch. Not to interfere unless and until the danger would damage my purpose. If I stopped every bad person from doing bad things, who would be free? How would humans still be human, then? So I let them plan their plans, and I watch. Often they change their minds, freely, without my interference.⟩

Couldn't you have made Vas stupid and forgetful long enough to stop this?

⟨I told you. Vas has a very strong ability to concentrate.⟩

What now? What now?

⟨I will watch.⟩

Have you told Volemak?

⟨I told *you*.⟩

Should *I* tell anyone?

⟨Vas will deny it. Nafai doesn't even realize that he was the victim of a would-be murderer. I told you because I don't trust my own ability now to predict what Vas will do.⟩

And what can *I* do?

⟨You're the human. You're the one who's able to think of things that exceed your programming.⟩

No, I don't believe you. I don't believe that you don't have a plan.

⟨If I have a plan, it includes you making your own decisions about what to do.⟩

Hushidh. I have to tell my sister.

⟨If I have a plan, it includes you making your own decisions.⟩

Does that mean I *mustn't* consult with Hushidh, because then my decision wouldn't be my own? Or does it mean that consulting with Hushidh is one of the decisions I need to make on my own?

⟨If I have a plan, it is for you to make your own decisions about your own decisions about your own decisions.⟩

And then she felt that she was alone again; the Oversoul was not talking to her.

The clothes lay in the grass beside the stream, except for the one gown of Chveya's that she had been washing; that one she still held in the stream, her hands freezing cold now because through all this conversation with the Oversoul she had not moved.

I must talk to Hushidh, and so that's the first decision I will make. I'll talk to Hushidh *and* Issib.

But first I'll finish washing these clothes. That way no one will know anything is wrong. I think that's the right thing to do, to keep anyone from knowing that something's wrong, at least for now.

After all, Nafai is all right. Or at least Nafai is not dead. But Vas *is* a murderer in his heart. And Obring and Sevet are in danger from him. Not to mention Nafai, if Vas even suspects that Nafai knows what Vas tried to do to him. Not to mention *me,* if Vas realizes that I also know.

How could the Oversoul have let things get to such a point? Isn't she responsible for all of this? Doesn't she know that she has brought terrible people along with us on this journey? How could she make us travel and camp for so many months, for a *year* and more, for many years ahead, with a *murderer?*

Because she hoped that he would decide not to murder after all, of course. Because she has to allow humans to be human, even now. Especially now.

But not when it comes to killing my husband. That is going too far, Oversoul. You took too great a chance. If he had died I would never have forgiven you. I would refuse to serve you anymore.

No answer came from the Oversoul. Instead it came from her own heart: An individual's death can come at any time. It isn't the task of the Oversoul to prevent it. The Oversoul's task is to prevent the death of a world.

Nafai lay stunned in the grass. It was a ledge invisible from above because of the way the cliff bowed out. He had fallen only five or six meters, after sliding down the face of the rock for a while. It was enough to knock the breath out of him; enough that he blacked out. But he was uninjured, except for a sore hip where he landed.

If he had not fetched up on the ledge, he would have plummeted another hundred meters or more and surely died.

I can't believe I lived through this. I should never have tried to kill the animal from that position. It was stupid. I was right to be afraid. I should have listened to my fears and if we lost that animal, fine, because we can always find another beast to follow and kill. What we can't find again is another father for Chveya, another husband for Luet, another hunter who isn't needed for other tasks.

Or another pulse.

He looked around and realized that the pulse wasn't on the ledge. Wasn't anywhere that he could see. He must have let go of it as he fell, and it must have bounced. Where was it?

He crept to the lip of the ledge and looked over. Oh, yes, straight down, except for a few small outcroppings—if the pulse struck them, then it would have bounced and kept on falling. There was nowhere that the pulse could have fetched up and stopped except at the bottom of the cliff. If that's where it was, Nafai couldn't possibly see it from here—it would be lost in the bushes. Or were those treetops?

"Nafai!" It was Vas, calling for him.

"I'm here!" Nafai cried.

"Thank God!" cried Vas. "Are you injured?"

"No," said Nafai. "But I'm on a ledge. I think I can get off to the south. I'm about ten meters below you. Can you move south too? I may need your help. There's nothing below me but a deadly fall, and I don't see any obvious way to get up to where you are."

"Do you have the pulse?" asked Vas.

Of course he had to ask about the pulse. Nafai blushed with shame. "No, I must have dropped it as I fell," he said. "It's got to be at the bottom of the cliff, unless you can see it somewhere up there."

"It's not here—you had it with you as you fell."

"Then it's at the bottom. Move south with me," said Nafai.

He found, though, that it was easier to talk about moving along the face of the cliff than it was to do it. The fall might not have injured him seriously, but the terror of it had done something to him, oh yes—he could barely bring himself to get to his feet, for fear of the edge, for fear of the fall.

I didn't fall because I lost my balance, thought Nafai. I fell because friction simply wasn't strong enough to hold me in that dangerous place. This ledge isn't like that. I can stand securely here.

So he stood, his back to the cliff, breathing deeply, telling himself to move, to sidle south along the ledge, around the corner, because there might be a way to get up. Yet the more he told himself this, the more his eyes focused on the empty space beyond the edge of the cliff, not a meter from his feet. If I lean just a little, I'll fall. If I fell forward now, I'd plunge over the side.

No, he told himself. I can't think that way, or I'll never be good for anything again. I've taken ledges like this a hundred times. They're nothing. They're easy. And it would help if I faced the cliff instead of facing the empty space leading down to the sea.

He turned and stepped carefully along the ledge, pressing

himself rather closer to the cliff than he would have in former times. But his confidence increased with every step he took.

When he rounded the bend in the cliff, he saw that the ledge ended—but now it was only two meters from this ledge to the next one up, and from there it was an easy climb back to where he and Vas had come down less than an hour ago. "Vas!" he called. He continued until he stood directly under the place where the ledge above was nearest. He could almost reach far enough onto the ledge to lift himself by his own arms, but there was nothing to hold on to, and the edge was crumbly and unreliable. It would be safer if Vas helped him. "Vas, here I am! I need you!"

But he heard nothing from Vas. And then he remembered the thought that had come into his mind as he was starting the dangerous traverse: Don't go on. Vas is planning to kill you.

Is it possible that that was a warning from the Oversoul?

Absurd.

But Nafai didn't wait for Vas to answer. Instead he reached his arms as far as they could go onto the ledge above, then dug his fingers into the loose grassy soil. It slipped and came away, but by scrabbling constantly, grabbing more and more, he was able to get enough of a purchase that he could get his shoulders above the edge of the cliff, and then it was a relatively easy matter to swing a leg up onto the ledge and pull himself to safety. He rolled onto his back and lay there, panting in relief. He could hardly believe that he had done such a dangerous thing so soon after falling—if he had slipped at any time while clambering up onto this ledge, he would have had a hard time catching himself on the ledge below. He was risking death—but he had done it.

Vas came now. "Ah," he said. "You're already up. Look—this way. Right back to where we were."

"I've got to find the pulse."

"It's bound to be broken and useless," said Vas. "It wasn't built for a fall like that."

"I can't go back and tell them that I don't have the pulse," said Nafai. "That I *lost* it. It's down there, and even if it's in forty pieces, I'll bring those pieces home."

"It's better to tell them you broke it than to tell them you lost it?" asked Vas.

"Yes," said Nafai. "It's better to show them the pieces than have them always wonder whether, if I had only looked, I might have found it. Don't you understand that this is our families' *meat* supply we're talking about?"

"Oh, I understand," said Vas. "And now that you put it that way, of course I see we must search for it. Look, we can come down this way—it's an easy enough path."

"I know," said Nafai. "Right down to the sea."

"Do you think so?" asked Vas.

"Down that way, and jogging to the left—see?"

"Oh, that *would* probably work."

It made Nafai faintly ashamed, that *he* had noticed the route to the sea, while Vas had not even thought of it.

Instead of going down to the sea, however, they scrambled down to the brush where the pulse must have fallen. They didn't have to search long before they found it—split in half, right down the middle. Several small internal components were also scattered here and there in the bushes, and without doubt there were others that they didn't find. There would be no repairing this pulse.

Still, Nafai put the pieces, large and small, into the sling he had made for carrying the pulse, and tied it closed. Then he and Vas began the long climb up the mountain. Nafai suggested that Vas should lead, since he would do a better job of remembering the way, and Vas agreed at once. Nafai didn't give the slightest hint that he didn't dare let Vas walk behind him, where he couldn't see what he was doing.

Oversoul, was that warning from you?

He didn't get any answer from the Oversoul, or at least not a direct answer to his question. What he got instead was the clear thought that he should talk to Luet when he got back to camp. And since that was what he would have done anyway, especially after an experience like this, being so close to death, he assumed that it was his own thought, and the Oversoul had not spoken to him at all.

SEVEN

THE BOW

The loss of the pulse was such a blow that neither Volemak nor Elemak made any effort to keep the situation calm—not until it was already almost out of control. There lay the pieces of the pulse, spread out on a cloth; nearby were the two water-damaged pulses that Elemak had saved. Zdorab sat by them, the Index in his lap, reading out the numbers of the broken parts. Almost everyone else stood—few were calm enough to sit—waiting, watching, pacing, grumbling as he tried to find out if one whole pulse could be salvaged from the parts.

"It's no use," said Zdorab. "Even if we had all the parts, the Index says that we don't have the tools that would be needed, and no way of making them without spending fifty years achieving the appropriate level of technology."

"What a brilliant plan the Oversoul had," said Elemak. "Keep all of humanity at a low level of technology—so low that even though we can manufacture pulses, we don't understand how they work and can't repair them if they break."

"It wasn't the Oversoul's plan," said Issib.

"Does it matter?" said Mebbekew. "We're going to die out here now."

Dol burst into tears, and for once they sounded real.

"I'm sorry," said Nafai.

"Yes, well, how glad we all are that you're remorseful," said Elemak. "What were you doing in a dangerous place like that anyway? You had the sole surviving pulse, and that's what you do with it?"

"That's where the animal was," said Nafai.

"If your quarry had leapt from the cliff, would you have followed?" asked Volemak.

Nafai was devastated that Father had joined in with Elemak's tongue-lashing. And Elemak himself was far from finished. "Let me put it to you plainly, my dear little brother: If you could have chosen whether you or the pulse would land on the ledge instead of bouncing down to destruction, it would have been more convenient to everybody if you had arranged for it to be the pulse!"

The unfairness of it was almost unbearable. "I'm not the one who lost the first three."

"But when we lost the first three, we still had a pulse left, so it wasn't quite as serious," said Father. "You knew it was the last pulse, and still took such a chance."

"Enough!" said Rasa. "We all agree, including Nafai, that it was a horrible mistake to put the pulse at risk. But now the pulse is gone, it can't be repaired, and here we are in this strange place with no way to kill meat. Perhaps one of you has thought of what we're going to *do* now, besides heaping blame on Nafai's shoulders."

Thank you, Mother, said Nafai silently.

"Isn't it obvious?" said Vas. "The expedition is over."

"No, it isn't obvious," Volemak answered sharply. "The Oversoul's purpose is nothing less than saving Harmony from the same destruction that came to Earth forty million years ago. Are we going to give that up because we lost a weapon?"

"It's not the weapon," said Eiadh. "It's the meat. We need to find meat."

"And it isn't just a matter of having a balanced diet," added Shedemei. "Even if we made camp right here and planted crops immediately—and it's not the season for it, so we couldn't anyway—but even if we did, we'd have no harvest of basic protein crops until long after we suffered from serious malnutrition."

"What do you mean by *serious* malnutrition?" asked Volemak.

"Some deaths by starvation, primarily among the children," said Shedemei.

"That's awful!" wailed Kokor. "You've practically killed my baby!"

Her cry set off a chorus of whining. In the din, Nafai silently spoke to the Oversoul: *Is* there some other way?

⟨Do you have a suggestion?⟩

Nafai tried to think of a hunting weapon that could be made from materials at hand. He remembered that the Gorayni soldiers had been armed with spears, with bows and arrows. Would either of those do for hunting, or were they only useful in war?

The thought came into his head: ⟨Anything that will kill a man will probably kill any other animal. To hunt with a spear requires a group of hunters to drive the prey—otherwise it's rare to get close enough for the kill, even with an atlatl to extend your throw.⟩

Then what about the bow and arrow?

⟨A good bow has a range four times that of the pulse. But they're very hard to make.⟩

What about a second-rate bow, with a range only about the *same* as a pulse? Could you teach me how to make one of *those?*

⟨Yes.⟩

And do you think I could find prey with it, or does it take too long to learn the skill?

⟨It takes as long as it takes.⟩

That was probably as good an answer as he was likely to get from the Oversoul, and it wasn't a bad answer at that. There was a hope, at least.

When Nafai's attention returned to the others, they had apparently goaded Volemak beyond his patience. "Do you think *I* planned all this?" he asked. "Do you think *I* asked the Oversoul to lead us to this hideous place, to have babies in the desert and wander aimlessly through wilderness without enough to eat? Do you think *I* wouldn't rather be in a house? With a bed?"

Nafai could see that Volemak had surprised everyone by joining his own complaints to theirs. But it hardly reassured them—some looked frightened indeed, to have their pillar of strength show a crack. And Elemak's face barely concealed his contempt for Father. It was not Volemak's proudest moment, Nafai could see that—and it was so unnecessary. If he had only asked the Oversoul the questions Nafai had asked, he would have been reassured. There *was* a way.

Vas spoke up again. "I tell you, all of this is completely unnecessary. Nafai and I found a fairly easy way down the mountain. We may not be able to bring the camels, but then, if we're simply walking around the bay to get to Dorova, all we need to carry is a day's provisions and water."

"Abandon the camels?" said Elemak. "The tents?"

"The coldboxes and dryboxes?" asked Shedemei.

"Some of you stay here then," said Mebbekew, "and lead the camels around the long way. Without the women and babies it won't take more than a week, and in the meantime the rest of us will be in the city. Give us a couple of months and we'll be back in Basilica. Or wherever the rest of you decide to go."

There was a murmur of assent.

"No," said Nafai. "This isn't about *us,* this is about Harmony, about the Oversoul."

"Nobody asked if I wanted to volunteer for this noble cause," said Obring, "and I for one am sick of hearing about it."

"The city's right over there," said Sevet. "We could be there so quickly."

"Fools," said Elemak. "Just because you can see the city, just because you can see the beach you'd walk along to reach it, that doesn't mean you could walk it easily. In a single day? Laughable. You've got stronger in the past year, yes, but none of you are in fit condition to walk that far carrying a baby, let alone the liters of water you'd need, and the food. Walking in sand is hard work, and slow, and the more heavily burdened you are the more slowly you go, which means that you have to carry *more* provisions to last you through the longer journey, which means you'll be more heavily burdened and travel even more sluggishly."

"Then we're trapped here till we *die*?" wailed Kokor.

"Oh, shut up," said Sevet.

"We're not trapped here," said Nafai, "and we don't have to abandon the expedition. Before there were ever pulses, human beings were able to kill meat. There are other weapons."

"What, will you strangle them?" asked Mebbekew. "Or use that wire of Gaballufix's, to cut off their heads?"

Nafai steeled himself to resist his own anger at Mebbekew's taunting. "A bow. Arrows. The Oversoul knows how they're made."

"Then let the Oversoul make them," said Obring. "That doesn't mean that any of us know how to *use* them."

"For once Obring is right," said Elemak. "It takes years of training to become a good bowman. Why do you think I brought pulses? Bows are better—they have a longer range, they never run out of power, and they do less damage to the meat. But I don't know how to use one, let alone make one."

"Neither do I," said Nafai. "But the Oversoul can teach me."

"In a month, perhaps," said Elemak. "But we don't have a month."

"In a day," said Nafai. "Give me until sundown tomorrow. If I haven't brought back meat, then I'll agree with Vas and Meb that we have to go to Dorova, at least for a while."

"If we go to Dorova, it's the end of this foolish expedition," said Meb. "I'll never get back on a camel for any reason except to go *home*."

Several agreed with him.

"Give me a day, and I'll agree with you," said Nafai. "We're not running out of provisions yet, and this is a good place to wait. A day."

"A waste of time," said Elemak. "You can't possibly do it."

"Then what harm will it do to let me prove it to you? But I say I *can* do it, with the Oversoul to help me. The knowledge is all there in its memory. And the game is easy to find here."

"I'll track for you," said Vas.

"No!" said Luet. Nafai looked at her, startled—she had said nothing till now. "Nafai will do this alone. He and the Oversoul. That's how it has to be." Then she looked up at him, steadily and intently.

She knows something, thought Nafai. Then he remembered again the thoughts that came to him on the mountain this morning—that Vas had been trying to kill him. That Vas caused his fall. Did the Oversoul speak clearly to her? Were my fears justified? Is that why she'd rather send me out alone?

"So you'll leave in the morning?" asked Volemak.

"No," said Nafai. "Today. I hope to make a bow today, so I can have tomorrow for the hunt. After all, my first few targets may get away."

"This is stupid," said Meb. "What does Nafai think he is, one of the Heroes of Pyiretsiss?"

"I'm not going to let this expedition fail!" shouted Nafai. "That's who I am. And if I won't let a broken pulse stop us, you can bet all the snot in your nose that I won't let *you* get in the way."

Meb looked at him and laughed. "You've got a bet, Nyef, my sweet little brother. All the snot in my nose says you'll fail."

"Done."

"Except we haven't specified what *you* give *me* when you fail."

"It doesn't matter," said Nafai. "I won't fail."

"But if you do . . . then you're my personal servant."

Meb's words were greeted with derision by many around the circle. "Snot against servitude," said Eiadh contemptuously. "Just what I'd expect of *you,* Meb."

"He doesn't have to take the bet," said Meb.

"Set a time limit on it," said Nafai. "Say—a month."

"A year. A year in which you do whatever I command."

"This is sickening," said Volemak. "I forbid it."

"You already agreed to it, Nafai," said Mebbekew. "If you back out of it now, you'll stand before us all as an oathbreaker."

"When I lay the meat down at your feet, Meb, you'll decide then what I am, and it won't be on oathbreaker, that's certain."

And so it was agreed. They'd wait until sundown tomorrow for Nafai to return.

He left them, hurried to the kitchen tent, and gathered what he'd need—biscuit and dried melon and jerky. Then he headed for the spring to refill his flagon. With his knife at his side, he'd need no more.

Luet met him there, as he knelt beside the pool, immersing the flagon to fill it.

"Where's Chveya?" he asked.

"With Shuya," she answered. "I needed to talk to you. Instead we had that . . . meeting."

"And I needed to talk to you, too," he said. "But things got out of hand, and now there's no time."

"I hope there's time for you to take *this,*" she said.

In her hand was a spool of twine.

"I hear that bows don't work without a string," she said. "And the Oversoul said that this kind would be best."

"You asked?"

"She seemed to think you were about to rush off without it, and that you'd regret the lack of it by and by."

"I would have, yes." He took it, put it in his pouch. Then he bent to her and kissed her. "You always look out for me."

"When I can," she said. "Nafai, while you were gone, the Oversoul spoke to me. Very clearly."

"Yes?"

"Was Vas near you when you fell?"

"He was."

"Near enough that he could have caused it? By, for instance, pushing your foot?"

Nafai instantly recalled that terrible moment on the face of the rock, when his right foot first slipped. It had slid inward, toward his left foot. If it had just been friction giving way, wouldn't the foot have slid straight down?

"Yes," said Nafai. "The Oversoul tried to warn me, but . . . "

"But you thought it was your own fear and ignored it."

Nafai nodded. She knew how the Oversoul's voice felt—like your own thoughts, like your own fears.

"You men," she said. "Always afraid of being afraid. Don't you know that fear is the most fundamental tool that evolution uses to keep a species alive? Yet you ignore it as if you hoped to die."

"Yes, well, I can't help what testosterone does to me. You'd enjoy being married to me a lot less if I didn't have any."

She smiled. But the smile didn't last long. "Something else the Oversoul told me," said Luet. "Vas is planning . . . "

But at that moment Obring and Kokor sauntered over. "Having second thoughts, little brother?" asked Kokor.

"My thoughts often come in threes and fours," said Nafai. "Not one at a time, like yours."

"I just wanted to wish you well," said Kokor. "I really hope you bring home some scruffy little hare for us to eat. Because if you *don't* then *we'll* have to go to a *city* and eat *cooked* food, and that would be just awful, don't you think?"

"Somehow I think your heart isn't in your kind words," said Nafai.

"If I thought you had a chance of succeeding," said Obring, "I'd break your arm."

"If a man like you could break my arm," said Nafai, "I really *wouldn't* have a chance."

"Please," said Luet. "Don't we have trouble enough?"

"Sweet little peacemaker," said Kokor. "Not much for looks, are you, but maybe you'll grow old gracefully."

Nafai couldn't help it. Kokor's insults were so childish, so much like what passed for cleverness among schoolchildren, that he had to laugh.

Kokor didn't like it. "Laugh all you want," said Kokor. "But I can sing my way back to wealth, and Mother still has a household in Basilica that I can inherit. What does your *father* have for *you?* And what kind of household will your little orphan wife establish for you in Basilica?"

Luet stepped forward and faced Kokor; Nafai noticed for the first time that they were almost the same height, which meant Luet had been growing this past year. She really *is* still a child, he thought.

"Koya," said Luet. "You forget whom you're speaking to. You may think that Nafai is just your younger brother. In the future, though, I hope you'll remember that he is the husband of the waterseer."

Kokor answered with defiance. "And what does that matter *here?*"

"It doesn't matter at all . . . *here.* But if we were to return to Basilica, dear Koya, I wonder how far your career will go if you're known to be the enemy of the waterseer."

Kokor blanched. "You wouldn't."

"No," said Luet, "I wouldn't. I never used my influence that way. And besides—we're not going back to Basilica."

Nafai had never seen Luet act so imperious before. He was enough of a Basilican to feel somewhat overawed at the title of waterseer; it was easy to forget sometimes that the woman he took to bed every night was the same woman whose dreams, whose words, were whispered house to house in Basilica. Once she had come to him at great risk, leaving the city in the middle of the night to wake him and warn him of danger to his father—and on that night she did not show any sign that she was aware of her lofty role in the city. Once she had taken him, when he was being chased by Gaballufix's men, and led him down into the waters of the Lake of Women, where no man was allowed to go and return alive—and even then, as she faced down those who would have killed him, she had not taken this tone, but rather had spoken calmly, quietly.

And then it dawned on Nafai—Luet wasn't putting on this air of haughty majesty because it was any part of *her.* She was acting this way because this is how *Kokor* would have acted, if she had even the tinest shred of power. Luet was speaking to Nafai's half-sister in language that she could understand. And the message was received. Kokor plucked at Obring's sleeve and the two of them left.

"You're very good at that," said Nafai. "I can't wait to hear you use that voice on Chveya, the first time she sasses you."

"I intend to raise Chveya to be the kind of woman with whom that voice would never need to be used."

"I didn't even know you *had* that voice."

Luet smiled. "Neither did I." She kissed him again.

"You were telling me something about Vas."

"Something Hushidh saw but didn't understand; the Oversoul explained it to me. Vas hasn't forgotten that Sevet betrayed him with Obring and brought public humiliation to him."

"No?"

"The Oversoul says he plans to murder them."

Nafai hooted once in derision. "Vas? He was the picture of calm. Mother said that she'd never seen anybody take a bad situation so well."

"He saves up his revenge for later, I guess," said Luet. "We have plenty of evidence now to suggest that Vas isn't quite as calm and cooperative as he seems."

"No," said Nafai, "he's not, is he? Meb and Dol, Obring and Kokor, they whine and moan about wanting to go back to the city. But not Vas. He takes it silently, seems to go along, and then sets out to destroy the pulses so we *have* to go back."

"You've got to admit, it was a clever plan."

"And if he happens to kill me in the process, well, that's the way it goes. It makes me think—if Gaballufix had been as subtle as Vas, he would be king of Basilica by now."

"No, Nafai. He'd be dead."

"Why?"

"Because the Oversoul would have told you to kill him in order to get the Index."

Nafai looked at her, uncomprehending. "*You* throw this up to me?"

She shook her head firmly. "I remind you of it so you don't forget how strong *you* are. You are more ruthless *and* more clever than Vas, when you know you're serving the Oversoul's plan. Now go, Nafai. You have a few hours of daylight left. You *will* succeed."

With the touch of her hand on his cheek still alive in the memory of his skin, with her voice still in his ear, with her trust and honor still hot inside his heart, he did indeed feel like one of the Heroes of Pyiretsiss. Most particularly like Velikodushnu, who ate the living heart of the god Zaveest, so that the people of Pyiretsiss could live in peace instead of constantly conspiring to get the advantage over each other and tear down those who succeeded. The illustration in the version of the tale that Nafai had read showed Velikodushnu with his head jammed into the gaping chest cavity of the god, even as Zaveest flayed the hero's back with his long fingernails. It was one of the most powerful images of his childhood, that picture of a man who ignored his own inextinguishable agony in order to consume the evil that was destroying his people.

That's what a hero was, to Nafai, what a *good man* was, and if he could only think of Gaballufix as Zaveest, then it was good and right to have killed him.

But that idea only helped him for a moment; then, once again, the horror of having murdered Gaballufix as he lay drunk and helpless on the street returned to him. And he realized that perhaps that memory, that guilt, that shame, that horror—

perhaps that was his own version of having his back flayed open by Zaveest even as he consumed the heart of the most vicious of the gods.

Never mind. Put it back where it belongs, in memory, not in the forefront of thought. I am the man who killed Gaballufix, yes, but I'm also the man who must make a bow, kill an animal, and bring it home by nightfall tomorrow or the Oversoul will have to begin again.

Obring ducked through the door of Vas's and Sevet's tent. It was the first time he had been with Sevet with any kind of privacy since Kokor caught the two of them bouncing away back in Basilica. Not that it was *really* privacy, with Vas there. But in a way the fact that he sanctioned this meeting meant that, perhaps, the long freeze-out was over.

"Thanks for stopping by," said Vas.

There was enough irony in Vas's tone that Obring realized he must have done something wrong, and Vas was reproving him. Oh—maybe he had taken too long getting here. "You said to come without Kokor, and I can't always just walk away. She always asks where I'm going, you know. And then watches to make sure I go there."

From the curl of Sevet's lip, Obring knew that she was enjoying the idea of him in such bondage to Kokor. Though if anyone should understand his predicament, Sevet should—wasn't she, too, in Vas's relentless custody? Or perhaps not—Vas wasn't vindictive like Kokor. Vas didn't even get angry that night more than a year ago. So maybe Sevet hadn't been suffering the way Obring had.

Looking at Sevet, though, Obring could hardly remember why he had been so eager to have her. Her body had certainly collapsed since the old days. No doubt having a baby had done part of it—the thick abdomen, the too-full breasts—but it was in her face, too, a kind of jowliness, a grimness around the eyes. She was not a beautiful woman. But then, it wasn't really her body that Obring had loved, was it? It was partly her fame, as one of the leading singers in Basilica, and partly—admit it to yourself, Obring, old man—that she was Koya's sister. Even then, Obring had wanted to stick it to his pretty, sexy, contemptuous wife and prove to her that he could get a better woman than her if he wanted to. No doubt, however, he had proven nothing of the kind, for Sevet almost certainly slept with him for similar reasons—if he had *not* been Kokor's husband, Sevet wouldn't have wasted the saliva to spit on him. They were both out to hurt Kokor, and they had succeeded, and they had been paying for it ever since.

Yet now here they were, together at Vas's invitation, and it seemed like things might be improving now, that Obring might actually be *included* in something in this miserable company so dominated by Volemak's and Rasa's children.

"I think it's time we put an end to this whole stupid expedition, don't you?" said Vas.

Obring laughed bitterly. "That's been tried before, and then Nafai pulled his little magic tricks."

"Some of us have only been biding our time," said Vas. "But this is the last chance—the last reasonable one, anyway. Dorova is in plain sight. We don't need Elemak to guide us there. Yesterday I found a route down the mountain. It isn't easy, but we can do it."

"We?"

"You and Sevet and me."

Obring looked over at where their baby, Vasnya, lay sleeping. "Carrying a baby? In the middle of the night?"

"There's a moon and I know the way," said Vas. "And we're not bringing the baby."

"Not bringing the—"

"Don't get stupid on me, Obring—give it a little thought. Our purpose isn't to get away from the group, our purpose is to get the whole group to give up the expedition. We aren't doing this for ourselves, we're doing it for *them,* to save them from themselves—from the Oversoul's absurd plans. We're going to Dorova so they *have* to follow us. We couldn't take babies with us, because they'd slow us down and they might suffer from the journey. So we leave them behind. Then they have to bring Vasnya to me and Sevet, and they have to bring Kokor and Krassya to *you*. Only *they* take the long way round, so the babies are safe."

"That makes . . . a kind of sense," said Obring.

"How kind of you to say so," said Vas.

"So if Nafai comes back without meat, we leave that night?"

"Are you such a fool you believe they'll keep their agreement?" asked Vas. "No, they'll find some other excuse to go on—putting our children at risk, taking us farther and farther from our last hope of a decent life. No, Briya, my friend, we wait for nothing. We force their hand before Nafai and the Oversoul have a chance to pull another trick."

"So . . . when do we leave? After supper?"

"They'd notice it and follow us and stop us immediately," said Vas. "So tonight I'll volunteer for late watch and you volunteer for last watch. A while into my watch, I'll get Sevet up and then scratch the tent for you. Kokor will think you're merely getting up to take your watch and she'll go right back to sleep. There's a good moon tonight—we'll be hours on our way before anybody else wakes up."

Obring nodded. "Sounds good." Then he looked at Sevet. Her expression was as impenetrable as ever. He wanted to get past that mask, just a little, and so he said, "But won't your teats get sore, leaving the baby behind when you're nursing?"

"Hushidh produces enough milk for four babies," said Sevet. "It's what she was born for."

Her words were hardly tender, but at least she had spoken. "Count me in," said Obring.

Then he had a second thought. A doubt about Vas's motive. "But why *me?*"

"Because you're not one of *them,*" he said. "You don't care about the Oversoul, you hate this life, and you're not caught up in some foolish notion of family loyalty. Who else could I get? If Sevet and I did this alone, they might decide to keep our baby and go on. We needed somebody else with us, to split another family, and who was there besides you? The only other unconnected people are Zdorab and Shedemei, who don't have a baby so they do us no good at all, and Hushidh and Luet, and they're thicker with the Oversoul than anybody else. Oh, and Dol, of course, but she's so besotted with Mebbekew, God knows why, and such a lazy coward anyway, that she wouldn't come with us and we wouldn't want her if she would. That leaves *you,* Obring. And believe me, I'm asking you only because you're a little less repugnant to me than Dolya."

Now *that* was a motive that Obring could believe. "I'm in, then," he said.

Shedemei waited until she saw Zdorab head for Volemak's tent. He would be borrowing the Index, of course—with no cooking allowed these days, he had more free time for study. So she excused herself from the group washing clothes, asking Hushidh to pick up Zdorab's and her laundry from the shrubs when it was dry. When Zdorab came through the door of the tent, the Index carefully tucked under his arm, Shedemei was waiting for him.

"Did you want to be alone?" Zdorab asked.

"I wanted to talk to *you,*" said Shedemei.

Zdorab sat down, then set the Index aside so she wouldn't think he was impatient to use it—though of course she knew that he was.

"Dorova is our last chance," said Shedemei. "To return to civilization."

Zdorab nodded—not agreement, only a sign that he understood.

"Zodya, we don't belong here," she said. "We're not part of this. It's a life of endless servitude for you, a life in which all my work is wasted. We've done it for a year—we've served well. The reason for your oath to Nafai was to keep you from giving the alarm in Basilica back when it would have meant soldiers capturing him if you returned to the city. Well, that's hardly likely to happen *now,* don't you think?"

"I don't stay here because of my oath, Shedya."

"I know," she said, and then, despite herself, her tears came.

"Do you think I don't see how you suffer here?" he said. "We thought that having the outward form of marriage would be enough for you, but it isn't. You want to belong, and you can't do that as long as you don't have a child."

It made her furious, to hear him analyze her that way—clearly he had been watching and deciding what her "problem" was, and he was wrong. Or at least he was only half right. "It isn't about *belonging,*" she said angrily. "It's about *life.* I'm nobody here—I'm not a scientist, I'm not a mother, I'm not even a good *servant* like you, I can't plumb the depths of the Index because its voice isn't as clear to me—I find myself echoing *your* wisdom when I talk to others because nobody can even *understand* the things *I* know—and when I see the others with their babies I want one of my own, I'm *hungry* for one, not so I can be like *them* but because I want to be part of the net of life, I want to pass my genes on, to see a child grow with a face half-mine. Can't you understand that? I'm not reproductively handicapped like you, I'm cut off from my own biological identity because I'm trapped here in this company and if I don't get out I'll die and I will have made *no difference in the world.*"

Silence was thick in the air in their tent, when she was done with her impassioned speech. What is he thinking? What does he think of me? I've hurt him, I know—I've told him that I hate being married to him, which is not true really, because he is my true friend—who else in all my life have I been able to pour out my heart to, until him?

"I shouldn't have spoken," she said in a whisper. "But I saw the lights of the city, and I thought—we could both return to a world that values us."

"*That* world didn't value me any more than this one," said Zdorab. "And you forget—how can I ever leave the Index?"

Didn't he understand what she was proposing? "Take it," she said. "We can take the Index and hurry around the bay. We have no children to slow us down. They can't catch us. With the Index you will have knowledge to sell as surely as I have—we can buy our way out of Dorova and back to the wide world in the north before they can get this caravan back north to chase us. *They* don't *need* the Index—don't you see how Luet and Nafai and Volemak and Hushidh all talk to the Oversoul without the help of the Index?"

"They don't *really* need it, and so we aren't *really* thieves for taking it," said Zdorab.

"Yes of course we're really thieves," said Shedemei. "But thieves who steal from those who don't need what they're taking can live with their crime a little more easily than thieves who take bread from the mouths of the poor."

"I don't know that it's the magnitude of the crime that decides whether the criminal can live with it," said Zdorab. "I think it's the natural goodness of the person who commits the crime. Murderers often live with their murders more easily than honest men live with a small lie."

"And you're so honest . . . "

"Yes, I am," said Zdorab. "And so are you."

"We're both living a lie every day we spend with this company." It was a terrible thing to say, and yet she was so desperate for change, for *something* to change, that she hurled at him everything that came to mind.

"Are we? Is it a very big lie?" Zdorab seemed not so much hurt as . . . thoughtful. Pondering. "Hushidh mentioned to me the other day that you and I are among the very closest bondings in this caravan. We talk about everything. We have immense respect for each other. We *love* each other—that's what she saw, and I believe her. It *is* true, isn't it?"

"Yes," whispered Shedemei.

"So what is the lie? The lie is that I'm your partner in reproduction. That's all. And if that lie became the truth, and there were a child in your belly, you would be whole, wouldn't you? The lie would no longer tear at your heart, because you would *be* what now you only seem—a wife—and you could become a part of that net of life."

She studied his face, trying to find mockery in it, but there was none. "*Can* you?"

"I don't know. I was never interested enough to try, and even if I had been, I would have had no willing partner. But—if I can find some small satisfactions from my own imagining, by myself, then why couldn't I—give a gift of love to my dearest friend? Not because *I* desire it, but because *she* desires it so much?"

"Out of pity," she said.

"Out of love," he said. "More love than these other men who jump their wives every night out of a desire no deeper than the scratching of an itch, or the voiding of a bladder."

What he was offering—to father a child on her—was something she had never considered as a possibility. Wasn't his condition his destiny?

"Doesn't love show its face," he went on, "when it satisfies the need of the loved one, for that loved one's sake alone? Which of these husbands can claim *that*?"

"But isn't a woman's body—repulsive to you?"

"To some, perhaps. Most of us, though, are simply... indifferent. The way ordinary men are toward other men. But I can tell you things to do that can awaken desire; I can perhaps imagine other partners out of my past, if you will forgive me for such... disloyalty... in the cause of giving you a child."

"But Zdorab. I don't want you to give *me* a child," she said. She was uncertain how to say this, since the idea had only just come to her, but the words came out clearly enough. "I want *us* to have a child."

"Yes," he said. "That's what I mean, too. I'll be a father to our child—I won't have to pretend to do *that*. My condition is not, strictly speaking, hereditary. If we have a son, he'll not necessarily be... like me."

"Ah, Zodya," she said, "don't you know that in so many ways I want our sons to be *just* like you?"

"Sons?" he said. "Don't try to net your fish before you reach the sea, my dear Shedya. We don't know if we can do this even once, let alone often enough to conceive a single child. It may be so awful for both of us that we never try again."

"But you *will* try the once?"

"I will try until we succeed, or until you tell me to stop trying." He leaned toward her and kissed her cheek. "The hardest thing for me may well be this: That in my heart, I think of you as my dearest sister. Coupling with you might feel like incest."

"Oh, do try not to feel *that* way," she said. "The only problems we'll have with that are when a child of Luet's falls in love with a child of Hushidh's—double first cousins! You and I are genetically remote."

"And yet so close to each other," he said. "Help me do this for you. If we can do it, it will bring us so much joy. And running away, stealing from our friends, parting from each other, defying the Oversoul—what joy could that ever bring? This is the best way, Shedya. Stay with me."

Nafai found the wood easily enough—the Oversoul did have a fair idea of what kinds of vegetation grew where in this area, and of course knew perfectly well which woods were chosen by the bowmakers of different cities and cultures. What the Oversoul could *not* do was give Nafai any skill with his hands. Not that Nafai was unusually clumsy. It was just that he had never worked with wood, or with knives, really, except for gutting and flaying game. He spoiled two potential bows, and now it was coming on evening and he hadn't even begun to make arrows, the bow was causing him such grief.

You can't acquire in an hour a skill that others take a lifetime to develop.

Was it the Oversoul speaking in his mind, when this thought came? Or it was the voice of despair?

Nafai sat on a flat rock, despondent. He had his third piece of bow-wood across his knees, his knife in hand, freshly whetted and sharp. But he knew little more now about working with wood than he did at the start—all he had was a catalog of ways that knives could slip and ruin wood, or that wood could split in the wrong places or at the wrong angle. He had not been more frustrated since the time when the Oversoul put Father's dream into his mind and it nearly drove him mad.

Thinking back to that time made him shudder. But then, thinking about it, he realized that it might also be a way to . . .

"Oversoul," he whispered. "There are master bowmakers in this world. Right now, this very moment, there is a bowmaker whittling a piece of wood to shape it properly."

⟨None with tools as primitive as yours,⟩ said the Oversoul in his mind.

"Then find one and fill him with the idea of whittling one with a simple knife. Then put his thoughts, his movements into my mind. Let me have the feeling of it."

⟨It will drive you mad.⟩

"Find a bowmaker in your memory, one who *always* worked this way—there must have been one, in forty million years, one who loved the feel of the knife, who could whittle a bow *without thinking.*"

⟨Ah . . . without thinking . . . pure habit, pure reflex . . . ⟩

"Father was concentrating so hard on everything in his dream—that's why I couldn't bear to have his memories in my mind. But a bowmaker whose hands work without thought. Put those skills in me. Let me know how it feels, so that I also have those reflexes."

⟨I've never done such a thing. It wasn't what I was designed to do. It might still make you mad.⟩

"It might also make a bow," said Nafai. "And if I fail at this, the expedition is over."

⟨I'll try. Give me time. It takes time to find one man, in all the years of human life on Harmony, who worked so mindlessly . . . ⟩

So Nafai waited. A minute, two minutes. And then a strange feeling came over him. A tingling, not in his arms, really, but in the *idea* of his arms that constantly dwelt inside his mind. A need to move the muscles, to work. It's happening, thought Nafai, the muscle memory, the nerve memory, and I must learn how to receive it, how to let this body of mine be guided by someone else's hands and fingers, wrists and arms.

He shifted the knife in his hand until it felt comfortable. And then he began to wipe the knife across the surface of the wood, not even letting the blade bite, just feeling the face of the sapling. And then, at last, he knew—or rather felt—when the wood invited the blade to dip into its surface, to peel away the thin bark. He pulled the knife through the wood like a fish moving through the sea, feeling the resistance of the wood and learning from it, finding the hard places, the weak places, and working around them, easing up where too much pressure would split the wood, biting hard where the wood cried out for discipline from the blade.

The sun was down, the moon just rising when he finished. But the bow was smooth and beautiful.

Green wood, so it won't hold its spring long.

How did I know that? thought Nafai, and then laughed at himself. How had he known any of this?

We can choose the saplings that we need and make green-wood bows from them at first, but also save others, season them, so that the bows we make later will last. There are plenty of stands of wood on our way south that will do for our needs. We won't even have to wait here for bow-wood gathering.

Carefully he looped and knotted one end of the twine Luet had given him, and tightened it around the narrow waist of the string-nock he had cut in one end of the bow. Then he drew the twine along the length of the bow to the other end, looped it around the other string-nock, and tightened it down. Far enough that there would be constant tension on the string, so that when he released an arrow the string would not wobble, but would return to perfect straightness, so the arrow would fly true. It felt right, as if he had done it a thousand times, and he easily and skillfully tied the loop in the twine, cut off the long excess, and then strung it into place.

"If I think about it," he whispered to the Oversoul, "then I can't do it."

⟨Because it's reflex⟩ came the answer in his mind. ⟨It's deeper than thought.⟩

"But will I remember it? Can I teach it to others?"

⟨You'll remember some of it. You'll make mistakes but it will come back to you, because it's now deep in *your* mind, too. You may not be able to explain well what you do, but they can watch you and learn that way.⟩

The bow was ready. He unstrung it again and then began work on the arrows. The Oversoul had led him to a place where many birds nested—he found no shortage of feathers there. And the short straight arrow shafts came from the tough woody reeds growing around a pool. And the arrowheads from obsidian crumbling out of the side of a hill. He gathered them all, having no idea of how to work with them; yet now the knowledge poured out of his fingers without ever reaching his conscious mind. By dawn he would have his arrows, his bow, perhaps in time enough for him to get a few hours of sleep. After that it would be daylight, and his real test: to track and follow his prey, and kill it, and bring it home.

And if I do, what then? I will be the hero, striding back into camp, triumphant, with the blood of the kill on my hands, on my clothing. I will be the one who brought meat when no one else could have. I will be the one who made it possible for the expedition to go on. I will be Velikodushnu, I will be the savior of my family and my friends, everyone will know that when even my father shrank from the journey I was the one who found a way to continue, so that when we go forth among the stars and human feet again step on the soil of Earth, it will have been *my* triumph, because I made this bow, these arrows, and brought meat home to the wives . . .

Then, in the midst of his imagined triumph, another thought:

I will be the one held responsible from then on if anything goes wrong. I will be the one blamed for every misfortune on the journey. It will be *my* expedition, and even Father will look to me for leadership. On that day Father will be irretrievably weakened. Who will lead then? Until now, the answer would have been clear: Elemak. Who could rival him? Who would follow anybody else, except the handful who will do whatever the Oversoul asks? But now, if I return as the hero, I will be in a position to rival Elemak. Not in a position to overwhelm him, though. Only to rival him. Only strong enough to tear the company apart. It would lead to bitterness no matter who won; it might lead to bloodshed. It must not happen now, if the expedition is to succeed.

So I can't return as a hero. I must find a way to bring back the meat we need to live, to feed the babies—and yet still leave Father's leadership unweakened.

As he thought and thought, his fingers and hands continued at their work, expertly finding the straightest reeds and nocking them for the bowstring, slicing them in deft spirals for the feathers, and splitting and lashing the other end to hold the tiny obsidian arrowheads.

Zdorab lay beside Shedemei, sweating and exhausted. The sheer physical exertion of it had almost defeated him. How could something that brought the two of them so little pleasure be so important to her—and, in its own way, to him? Yet they had accomplished it, despite his body's initial disinterest. He remembered something that an old lover of his had once said—that when it came down to it, human males could mate with any creature that held still long enough and didn't bite very hard. Perhaps so . . .

He had been hoping, though, in the back of his mind, that when he finally mated with a woman there would be some place in his brain, some gland in his body that would awaken and say, Ah, so *this* is how it's done. Then the days of his isolation would be over, and his body would know its proper place in the scheme of nature. But the truth was that nature had no scheme. Only a series of accidents. A species "worked" if enough of its members reproduced faithfully and often enough to keep it going; so what if some insignificant percentage—*my* percentage, Zdorab thought bitterly—ends up being reproductively irrelevant. Nature wasn't a child's birthday party; nature didn't care about including everybody. Zdorab's body would be cycled back through the wheels and gears of life, whether or not his genes happened to reproduce themselves along the way.

And yet. And yet. Even though his body had had no particular joy from Shedemei's (and certainly hers had finally become exhausted from the effort to please *his),* yet there was joy in it on another level. Because the gift had been given. Sheer friction and stimulation of nerves had won in the end, sparking the reflex that deposited a million hopeful half-humans-to-be into the matrix that would keep them alive for the day or two of their race toward their other half, the all-mother, the Infinite Egg. What did *they* care whether Zdorab had lusted after Shedemei or merely acted out of duty while desperately trying to fantasize another lover of a reproductively irrelevant sex? Their life was lived on another plane—and it was on exactly that plane that the great net of life that Shedemei so worshipped was woven together.

I have finally been caught in that net, for reasons that no gene could plan for; I was greased at birth, to slip away from the net forever, but I have been caught anyway, I have *chosen* to be caught, and who is to say that mine is not the better fatherhood, because I acted out of pure love, and not out of some inborn instinct that captured me. Indeed, I acted *against* my instinct. There's something in that. A hero of copulation, a *real* cocksman, if the others only knew. Anybody can pilot his boat to shore in a fair wind; I have come to shore by tacking in contrary winds, by rowing against an ebbing tide.

So let the little suckers make it to the egg. Shedemei said it was a good time for them to have their competition for survival.

Let one of them, a strong and sturdy one, reach his microscopic goal and pierce that cell wall and join his helical deoxyribonucleic acid to hers and make a baby on our very first try, so I don't have to go through all of this again.

But if I have to, I will. For Shedemei.

He reached out and found her hand and clasped it in his. She did not awaken, but still her hand closed ever so slightly, gently enclosing his.

Luet could hardly sleep. She couldn't stop thinking about Nafai, worrying about him. In vain did the Oversoul assure her: He's doing well, all will be well. It was long after dark, long after Chveya slept from her last suckling of the night, before Luet drifted off to sleep.

It was no restful sleep, either. She kept dreaming of Nafai sidling along rocky ledges, creeping up the face of sheer cliffs with sometimes a bow in one hand, sometimes a pulse, only in her dream the cliff would grow steeper and steeper until finally it bent backward and Nafai was clinging like an insect to the underside of the cliff and finally he would lose his grip and drop away . . .

And she would come half-awake, realize it had been a dream, and impatiently turn her sweaty pillow and try to sleep again.

Until a dream came that was not of Nafai dying. Instead he was in a room that shone with silver, with chromium, with platinum, with ice. In her dream he lay down upon a block of ice and the heat of his body melted into it, and he sank and sank until he was completely inside the ice and it closed over him and froze. What is this dream? she thought. And then she thought, If I know that this is a dream, does that mean that I'm awake? And if I'm awake, why doesn't the dream stop?

It did not stop. Instead she saw that, instead of being trapped in the ice, Nafai was sinking all the way through it. Now the shape of his back and buttocks, his calves and heels, his elbows and fingertips and the back of his head began to bow downward at the bottom of the ice block, and she thought—what holds this ice in the middle of the air like this? Why didn't it also hold Nafai? His body bulged farther and farther downward, and then he dropped through, falling the meter or so to the shining floor. His eyes opened, as if he had been asleep during his passage through the ice. He rolled out from under the block, out of the shadow of it, and as soon as he stood up in the light, she could see that his body was no longer what it had been. Now, where the lights struck him, his skin shone brightly, as if it had been coated with the finest possible layer of the same metal the walls were made of. Like armor. Like a new skin. It sparkled so . . . and then she realized that it was not reflecting light at all, but rather it was giving off its own light. Whatever he was wearing now drew its power from his body, and when he thought of any part of himself, to move a limb, or even just to look at it, it fairly sparked with light.

Look at him, thought Luet. He has become a god, not just a hero. He shines like the Oversoul. His is the body of the Oversoul.

But that's nonsense. The Oversoul is a computer, and needs no body of flesh and bone. Far from it—caught in a human body it would lose its vast memory, its light-fast speed.

Nevertheless, Nafai's body sparkled with light as he moved, and she knew that it was the Oversoul's body he was wearing, though it made no sense to her at all.

In the dream she saw him come to her, and embrace her, and when she was joined to him, she could feel that the sparkling armor that he wore grew to include her, so that she also shone with light. It made her skin feel so alive, as if every nerve had been connected to the molecule-thin metal coating that surrounded her like sweat. And she realized—every point that sparks is where a nerve connects to this layer of light. She pulled away from Nafai, and the new skin stayed with her, even though she had not passed through the ice that gave it to him. It is his skin I'm wearing now, she thought; and yet she also thought: I too am wearing the body of the Oversoul, and am alive now for the first time.

What does this dream mean?

But since she was asking the question in a dream, she got only a dream answer: She saw the dream Nafai and her dream-self make love, with such passion that she forgot it was a dream and lost herself in the ecstasy of it. And when their coupling was done, she saw the belly of her dreamself grow, and then a baby emerged from her groin and slid shining into Nafai's arms, for the babe, too, was coated with the new skin, alive with light. Ah, the child was beautiful, so beautiful.

⟨Wake up.⟩

She heard it like a voice, it was so clear and strong.

⟨Wake up.⟩

She sat bolt upright, trying to see who had spoken to her, to recognize the voice that lingered in her memory.

⟨Get up.⟩

It was not a voice at all. It was the Oversoul. But why was the Oversoul interrupting her dream, when surely the Oversoul had *sent* the dream in the first place?

⟨Get up, Waterseer, rise up in silence, and walk in the moonlight to the place where Vas plans to kill his wife and his rival. On the ledge that saved Nafai's life you must wait for them.⟩

But I'm not strong enough to stop him, if murder is in his heart.

⟨Being there will be enough. But you *must* be there, and you must go now, for he is on watch now, and thinks that he and Sevet are the only ones awake . . . he will soon be scratching on Obring's tent, and then it will be too late, you'll not make it to the mountain unobserved.⟩

Luet passed through the door of her tent, so sleepy that she still felt as if she were in a dream.

Why must I go down the mountain? she asked, confused. Why not just tell Obring and Sevet what Vas plans for them?

⟨Because if they believe you, Vas will be destroyed as a member of this company. And if they don't believe you, Vas will be your enemy and you will never be safe again. Trust me. Do this my way, and all will live, all will live.⟩

Are you sure of this?

⟨Of course.⟩

You're no better at telling the future than anybody else. How sure are you?

⟨The odds of success are, perhaps, sixty percent.⟩

Oh, wonderful. What about the forty percent chance of failure?

⟨You are such an intelligent woman, you'll improvise, you'll make it work.⟩

I wish I had as much faith in you as you seem to have in me.

⟨The only reason you don't is because you don't know me as well as I know you.⟩

You can read my thoughts, dear Oversoul, but you can never know me, because there is no part of you that can feel the way I feel, or think the way I think.

⟨Do you imagine I don't know that, boastful human? Must you taunt me for it? Go down the mountain. Carefully, carefully. The path is visible by moonlight, but treacherous. Obring is awake now; you have made it just in time. Now stay ahead of them, far enough that they can't hear you, far enough that they can't see.⟩

Elemak had noticed when Sevet and Obring both took extra flagons from the stores. He knew at once what it meant—that there was a plan to make a run for Dorova. At the same time, though, he could not believe that *those* two would ever have come up with a plan together—they never spoke to each other privately, if only because Kokor made sure they had no opportunity. No, there was someone else involved, someone who was better at this sort of deception, so that Elemak hadn't noticed his or her theft of an extra flagon.

And then, just before night, Vas had volunteered for the hated late watch, the second-to-last one before morning. Obring had taken the last watch already. It didn't take a genius to realize that they intended to leave on Vas's watch. Fools. Did they think they could make it down the mountain and across the waterless sand of the beach around the bay on two flagons of fresh water each? Not carrying babies they couldn't.

They aren't going to take their babies.

The thought was so outrageous that Elemak almost didn't believe it. But then he realized that it must be true. His loathing for Obring redoubled. But Vas . . . it was hard to believe that Vas would do such a thing. The man doted on his daughter. He had even named her for himself—would he leave her, heartlessly?

No. No, he has no intention of leaving her. Obring would leave his baby, yes. Obring would leave Kokor, for that matter—he chafed constantly in his marriage. But Vas would not leave his baby. He has another motive now. And it does not include escaping to the city with Sevet and Obring. On the contrary. His plan is to tell us that Sevet and Obring left for the city after he was asleep from his watch, and he followed them down the mountain, hoping to stop them, but instead he found their dead bodies, fallen from a cliff . . .

How do I know all this? wondered Elemak. Why is this all so clear to me? And yet he could not doubt it.

So he gave himself the middle watch, and at the end of it, after he had wakened Vas and returned to his tent, Elemak did not let himself sleep, though he lay still with his eyes closed, breathing in a heavy imitation of sleep, in case Vas came to check on him. But no, Vas did not come. Did not come, and did not go to Obring's tent. The watch dragged on and on, and finally against his will Elemak *did* sleep. Perhaps only for a moment. But he must have slept because he awoke with a start, his heart pounding with alarm. Something . . . some sound. He sat upright in the darkness, listening. Beside him he could hear Edhya's breathing, and Proya's; it was hard to hear anything else beyond that. As quietly as possible he arose, went to the door of his tent, stepped outside. Vas was not on watch, and neither was anyone else.

Quietly, quietly he went to Vas's tent. Gone, and Sevet, too—but baby Vasnaminanya was still there. Elemak's heart filled with rage at the monstrosity of it. Whatever Vas was planning—either to abandon his daughter or kill the child's mother—it was unspeakable.

I will find him, thought Elemak, and when I do he will pay for this. I knew there were fools on this journey, fools and dolts and weaklings, but I never knew there was someone so cruel-hearted. I never knew that Vas was capable of this. I never knew Vas at all, I think. And I never will, because as soon as I find him he'll be dead.

It was so easy, leading them down the mountain. Their trust in him was complete. It was the payoff for his year of pretending not to mind that they had betrayed him. If he had ever shown even a spark of anger, beyond a certain coldness toward Obring, there was no chance the man would have trusted him enough to come along like a hog to the slaughter. But Obring *did* trust him, and Sevet too, in her sullen way.

The path itself had some difficulty—more than once he had to help them through a tricky place. But in the moonlight they often couldn't see how very dangerous a passage it was, and whenever it was hard, he would stay and help them. So carefully taking Sevet's hand and guiding her down a slope, or between two rocks. Whispering: "Do you see the limb you must hold on to, Obring?" And Obring's answer, "Yes," or a nod, I see it, I can handle it, Vas, because I'm a *man*. What a laugh. What a joke on Obring, who is so pathetically proud to be included in this great plan. How I will weep when we come down to carry the bodies back up the mountain. How the others will cry for me as I hold my little daughter in my arms, crooning to her about her lost mother, and how she is an orphan now. An orphan—but one named for her father. And I will raise her so no trace of her traitorous mother remains in her. She will be a woman of honor, who would never betray a good man who would have forgiven her *anything* but to give her body to her own sister's husband, that contemptible, slimy little social climber. You let him empty his little tin cup into you, Sevet, my dear, and so I will have done with you.

"Here's the place where Nafai and I tried to cross over," he whispered to them. "See how we had to traverse that bare rock, shining in the moonlight?"

Obring nodded.

"But the ledge that saved his life is the real path," said Vas. "There's one hard place—a drop of two meters—but then it's a smooth passage along the face of the cliff, and then we reach the easy part, right down to the beach."

They followed him past the place where he had silently watched Nafai's struggle. When it was clear that Nafai was going to make it after all, then he had called out and come to help him. Now he would help them down onto the ledge. Only he would not climb down to join them. Instead he would kick Obring in the head and send him over the side. Sevet would understand then. Sevet would know why he had brought her here. And she would, at long last, beg him for forgiveness. She would plead with him for understanding, she would weep, she would sob for him. And his answer would be to pick up the heaviest stones he could find and throw them down on her, until she had to run along the ledge. He would drive her to the narrow place and still he would throw stones until finally she stumbled or was knocked off balance. She would fall then, and scream, and he would hear the sound and treasure it in his heart forever.

Then, of course, he would climb down the true path to the bottom, and find their broken bodies where the pulse had been. If one of them happened somehow to still be alive, he would have no trouble breaking a neck or two—it wouldn't be surprising to anyone, to find their necks broken in the fall. But he doubted they'd live. It was quite a long fall. The pulse had been completely shattered. That annoying little pizdoon Nafai would have been just as broken up if he hadn't found that invisible ledge to land on. Ah, well, Nafai was only an annoyance—Vas didn't care much whether he lived or died, as long as the pulses were all destroyed so they would have to head back to civilization. And now, before they *did* turn back, was his chance to have his revenge and yet no one would suspect him. "I think they must have heard me following them, because they were going much too fast, especially for nighttime travel. And then I saw they were heading for that ledge. I knew how dangerous it was, I called out to them, but they didn't understand, I guess, that I was warning them away. Or maybe they didn't care. God help me, but I loved her! The mother of my child!" I'll even shed a tear for them, and they'll believe me. What choice will they have? Everyone knows that I long since forgave and forgot their adultery.

I'm not a very demanding man. I don't expect perfection from others. I get along and do my part. But when someone treats me like a worm, as if I didn't exist, as if I didn't *matter,* then I don't forget, no, I never forget, I never forgive, I simply bide my time and then they see: I *do* matter, and despising me was the gravest error of their lives. That's what Sevet will be thinking as the stones strike her and she has no place to flee to except the open air as she falls to her death: If only I had been true to him, I would live to raise my daughter.

"Here," he said. "Here's the place where we have to drop down to that lower ledge."

Sevet was clearly frightened, and Obring put on a mask of bravado that showed his fear as clearly as if he had simply wet himself and whimpered. Which he would do soon enough. "No problem," he said.

"Sevet first," said Vas.

"Why me?" she said.

"Because the two of us can lower you down more safely," said Vas. And mostly because then I can kick Obring in the head as soon as I lower *him,* and you'll already be trapped on the ledge where you can see everything but do nothing.

It was going to work. Sevet squatted at the lip of the ledge, preparing to turn and go over the side. And then there came that other voice, that unexpected, terrible voice.

"The Oversoul forbids you to go down, Sevet."

They all turned, and there she stood, shining in the moonlight, her white gown flapping a little in the wind, which was stronger where she stood.

How did she know? thought Vas. How did she know to come here? I thought the Oversoul would consent to this—simple justice! If the Oversoul had not wanted him to do this, to make Obring and Sevet pay for their crime, then why didn't he stop him before? Why *now,* when he was so close? No, he wouldn't let her stop him at all. It was too late. There would be *three* bodies at the bottom of the cliff, not two. And instead of climbing back up the mountain, he would take three flagons of water and head for Dorova. He would get there and leave again long before any accusations could overtake him. And in Seggidugu or Potokgavan, wherever he ended up, he would deny everything. There *were* no witnesses, and none of these people would have standing anyway. He would lose his daughter—but that would be fit and fair punishment for killing Luet. It would all be even. He would owe no debt of vengeance to the universe, and the universe would owe no debt of vengeance to him. All would be balanced and settled and right.

"You know me, Sevet," said Luet. "I speak to you as the waterseer. If you go down that ledge you'll never see your child again, and there is no greater crime in the eyes of the Oversoul than for a mother to abandon her child."

"As *your* mother did to you and Hushidh?" said Vas. "Spare us your lies about crimes in the eyes of the Oversoul. The Oversoul is a computer set by some distant ancestor to keep his eyes on us, and nothing more—your own husband says so, doesn't he? My wife is not superstitious enough to believe you."

No, no, he shouldn't have said so much. He should have *acted.* He should have taken three steps and shoved the frail-bodied girl off the edge. She couldn't possibly resist him. Then, having seen him do murder, the others would be all the quicker to obey and be on their way—to safety, to the city, they *think.* To argue with her was stupid. He was being stupid.

"The Oversoul chose the three of you to be part of her company," said Luet. "I tell you now that if you go over that edge, you will not live to see daylight, not one of you."

"Prophecy?" said Vas. "I didn't know that was one of your many gifts." Kill her now! he screamed inside, and yet his own body didn't heed him.

"The Oversoul tells me that Nafai has made his bow and arrows, and they fly straight and true. This expedition will continue, and you will continue with it," she said. "If you go back now, your daughters will never know that you once abandoned them. The Oversoul will fulfil her promises to you—that you will inherit a land of plenty, and your children will be a great nation."

"When were any of those promises for *me,*" said Obring. "For Volemak's sons, yes, but not for *me.* For me it's nothing but taking orders and getting yelled at because I don't do everything the way King Elemak wants me to."

"Stop whining," said Vas. "Don't you see that she's trying to ensnare us all?"

"The Oversoul sent me here to save your lives," said Luet.

"That's a lie," said Vas. "And you know it's a lie. My life has not been in danger for a single moment."

"I tell you that if you had succeeded in your plan, Vas, your life would not have lasted five more minutes."

"And how would this miracle have happened?" asked Vas.

That was when Elemak's voice came from behind him, and he knew that he had lost everything.

"I would have killed you myself," said Elemak. "With my bare hands."

Vas whirled on him, furious and, for once, unable to contain his rage. Why *should* he contain it? He was as good as dead now, with Elemak here—so why not speak his contempt openly? "Would you!" he cried. "Do you think you're a match for me! You've never been a match for me! I've thwarted you at every turn! And you never guessed, you never *suspected*. You fool, strutting and bragging about how only you know how to lead our caravan—who was it who did what you couldn't do, and turned us back?"

"Turned us back? It wasn't *you* that . . . " But then Elemak paused, and Vas could see understanding come to his eyes. *Now* Elya knew who had destroyed the pulses. "Yes," said Elemak. "Like the coward and sneak you are, you endangered us all, you put *my* wife and *my* son at risk, and we didn't catch you because it never occurred to any of us that anyone in our company could be so slimy and vile as to deliberately—"

"Enough," said Luet. "Say no more, or there'll be accusations that must be dealt with openly, which can still be handled in silence."

Vas understood at once. Luet didn't want Elemak to say outright that Vas had destroyed the pulses, not in front of Obring and Sevet, or there'd have to be a punishment. And she didn't want him punished. She didn't want him killed. Luet was the waterseer; she spoke for the Oversoul; and that meant that the Oversoul wanted him alive.

⟨That's right.⟩

The thought was as clear as a voice inside his head.

⟨I want you alive. I want Luet alive. I want Sevet and Obring alive. Do not force me to choose which of you will die.⟩

"Come back up the mountain," said Elemak. "All three of you."

"I don't want to go back," said Obring. "There's nothing for me here. The city's where I belong."

"Yes," said Elemak, "in a city your weakness and laziness and cowardice and stupidity can be concealed behind fine clothing and a few jests and people will think you're a man. But don't worry—there's plenty of time for that. When Nafai fails and we return to the city—"

"But *she* says that he's made his bow," said Obring.

Elemak looked over at Luet and seemed to see the confirmation in her eyes. "Making a bow is not the same thing as knowing how to use it," he said. "If he brings home meat, then I'll know the Oversoul is truly with him, and more powerful than I ever thought. But it won't happen, Waterseer. Your husband will do his best, but he'll fail, not because he wasn't good enough but because it can't be done. And when he fails, we'll turn north and return to the city. There's no need for you to have done this."

Vas listened and understood the real message. Whether or not Elemak actually believed Nafai would fail, he was speaking in such a way that Sevet and Obring would think that nothing more had been going on here than an attempted escape to the city. He did not intend to tell them that Vas had been meaning to kill them.

Or perhaps he didn't know. Perhaps Luet didn't know. Perhaps when she spoke of the three of them dying if they went down onto the ledge, she meant that Elemak would kill them to prevent their escape. Perhaps it was all still a secret.

"Go back up the way you came," said Elemak. "Agree to that, and there'll be no punishment. We still have time enough before morning that no one beyond the five of us will need to know what happened."

"Yes," said Obring. "I will, I'm sorry, thank you."

He is so *weak,* though Vas.

Obring passed Elemak and began to scramble back up the path. Sevet silently followed him.

"Go on ahead, Luet," said Elemak. "You've done good work here tonight. I won't bother asking the waterseer how she knew to be here before them. I'll only say that if you hadn't delayed them, there would have been killing here tonight."

Were the others out of earshot? Vas wondered. Or was Elemak still thinking only of his *own* killing—that he would have caught them and punished them for trying to escape?

Luet passed them by, and followed the others up the mountain. Vas and Elemak were alone.

"What was the plan?" asked Elemak. "To push them as you lowered them down onto the ledge?"

So he knew.

"If you had harmed either one of them, I would have torn you apart."

"Would you?" asked Vas.

Elemak's hand snaked out and took him by the throat, jamming him back against the rock wall behind him. Vas clutched at Elemak's arm, then at his hand, trying to pry the fingers away. He couldn't breathe, and it *hurt,* Elemak wasn't just pretending, wasn't just demonstrating his power, he meant to kill him, and Vas filled with panic. Just as he was about to claw at Elemak's eyes—anything to get him to let go—Elemak's other hand seized Vas's crotch and squeezed. The pain was indescribable, and yet he couldn't scream or even gasp because his throat was closed. He gagged and retched, and some of his stomach bile *did* manage to force its way past the constriction in his throat; he could taste it in his mouth. This is death, he thought.

Elemak gave a final squeeze, both to Vas's throat and to his testicles, as if to prove that he hadn't been using his full strength all along, and then released him.

Vas gasped and whimpered. The pain in his crotch was, if anything, worse, a throbbing ache, and his throat also ached as he sucked in air.

"I didn't do this in front of the others," said Elemak, "because I want you to be useful. I don't want you to be broken or humiliated in front of the others. But I want you to remember this. When you start plotting your next murder, remember that Luet is watching you, and the Oversoul is watching you, and, more to the point, *I'm* watching you. I won't give you a millimeter of slack from now on, Vasya, my friend. If I see any hint that you're planning any more sabotage or any more subtle little murders, I won't wait to see how things turn out, I'll simply come to you in the middle of the night and break your neck. You know I can do it. You know you can't stop me. As long as I live, you will take no vengeance against Sevet or Obring. *Or* me. I won't ask for your oath, because your word is piss from your mouth. I simply expect to be obeyed, because you're a sneaky coward who is terrified of pain, and you will never, never stand against me again because you will remember how you feel right now, at this moment."

Vas heard all this and knew that Elemak was right, he would never stand against him, because he could never bear to feel the fear and pain he had just gone through, was still going through.

But I *will* hate you, Elemak. And someday. Someday. When you're old and feeble and helpless, I will put things back in balance. I'll kill Sevet and Obring and you won't be able to stop me. You won't even know that I did it. And then one day I'll come to you and say, I did it in spite of you. And you'll rage at me and I'll only laugh, because you'll be helpless then and in your helplessness I will make you feel what you made *me* feel, the pain of it, the fear, the *panic* as you can't breathe even enough to scream out your agony—oh, you'll feel it. And as you lie there dying, I'll tell you the rest of my vengeance—that I will kill all your children, too, and your wife, and everything and everyone you love, and you can't stop me. Then you'll die, and only then will I be satisfied, knowing that your death was the most terrible death that can be imagined.

But there's no hurry, Elemak. I will dream of this every night. I will never forget. *You* will forget. Until the day that I make you remember, however many years it is before that day comes.

When Vas was able to walk, Elemak dragged him to his feet and shoved him up the trail leading to the camp.

At dawn, everyone was back in place, and no one but the participants knew of the scene that had played itself out in the moonlight, halfway down the mountain.

The sun was scarcely up when Nafai strode across the meadow toward the camp. Luet was awake—though barely so—nursing Chveya as Zdorab passed around biscuits smeared with sugary preserves for breakfast. She looked up and there he was, coming toward them, the first sunlight catching in his hair. She thought of how he had looked in her strange dream, sparking and sparkling with the light of his invisible metal armor. What did that mean? she wondered. And then she thought, What does it matter what it meant?

"Why are you back!" cried Issib, who was holding Dazya on his lap on his chair while Hushidh was off peeing or whatever.

In answer, Nafai held up the bow in one hand, five arrows in the other.

She leapt to her feet and ran to him, still holding the baby—though Chveya soon lost her grip on Luet's breast and began to protest at all this bouncing when she was trying to eat. The baby was fussing rather loudly, but Luet paid no attention to her as she kissed her husband, clung to him with her free hand.

"You have the bow," she said.

"What is a bow?" he asked. "The Oversoul taught me how to make it—it took no skill of mine. But what *you* accomplished . . ."

"You know, then?"

"The Oversoul showed me in a dream—I woke when it ended and came back at once."

"So you know that we're saying nothing about it."

"Yes," he said. "Except to each other. Except for me to tell you that you are a magnificent woman, the strongest, bravest person that I know."

She loved to hear those words from him, even though she knew they weren't true—that she had not been brave at all, but terrified that Vas would kill her right along with the others. That she had been so relieved when Elemak came that she almost wept. Soon enough she'd tell him all of that. But for now she loved to hear his words of love and honor, and to feel his arm around her as they walked together back to camp.

"I see you have the bow, but no meat," said Issib, when they got nearer.

"So you've given up?" asked Mebbekew, hopefully.

"I have until sundown," said Nafai.

"Then why are you here?" asked Elemak.

Everyone had come out of the tents now, and were gathered, watching.

"I came because having the bow is nothing—the Oversoul could have taught any of us how to do that. What I need now is for Father to tell me where to go to find game."

Volemak was surprised. "And how should I know that, Nyef? I'm not a hunter."

"I have to know where to find game that is so tame that I can creep up on it very close," said Nafai. "And where it's so plentiful that I can find more when I miss my first attempts."

"Take Vas with you, then, to track," said Volemak.

"No," said Elemak quickly. "No, Nafai is right. Neither Vas nor Obring will go with him this morning as trackers."

Luet knew perfectly well why Elemak insisted on *that*—but it still left Volemak nonplussed. "Then let Elemak tell you where to go to find game like that."

"Elemak doesn't know this country any better than I do," said Nafai.

"And I don't know it at all," said Volemak.

"Nevertheless," said Nafai, "I will only hunt where you tell me to. This is too important to leave it up to chance. Everything depends on this, Father. Tell me where to hunt, or I'll have no hope."

Volemak stood in silence, looking at his son. Luet didn't really understand why Nafai was doing this—he had never needed Volemak to tell him where to search for game before. And yet she sensed that it was very important—that for some reason the success of the expedition hinged on its being Volemak who decided where the hunt would take place.

"I will ask the Index," said Volemak.

"Thank you, Father," said Nafai. He followed his father into his tent.

Luet looked around the company as they waited. What do they make of this? Her eyes met Elemak's. He smiled a tight little smile. She smiled back, not understanding what it was *he* thought was going on.

It was Hushidh who clarified it for her. "Your husband is the clever one," she whispered.

Luet turned in surprise—she hadn't noticed Hushidh coming to her.

"When he came back with the bow and arrows, it weakened Volemak. It weakened him yesterday, in fact, when it was Nafai who insisted on trying to continue. All the bonds that held this company together weakened then. I could see it when I got up this morning—fracture. Chaos verging. And something worse, between Vas and Elemak—a terrible hatred that I don't understand. But Nafai has now handed the authority back to his father. He could have snatched it for himself and torn us all apart, but he didn't—he gave it back, and already I can see us settling back into old patterns."

"Sometimes, Shuya, I wish I had *your* gift instead of mine."

"Mine is more comfortable and practical sometimes," said Hushidh. "But you are the waterseer."

Since Chveya was tugging away on Luet's breast, slurping obscenely, as if passionately eager to get all she could before Luet took off running somewhere again, it was hard for Luet to take her noble calling all that seriously. She answered Hushidh with a laugh. Her laugh was heard by those who could not have heard their hushed conversation; many turned to look at her. What could possibly be amusing, they seemed to be wondering, on a morning like this, where our whole future is being decided?

Nafai and Volemak emerged from the tent. Volemak's air of puzzlement was gone. He was firmly in command now; he embraced his son, pointed toward the southeast, and said, "You'll find game there, Nafai. Come back soon enough and I'll allow the meat to be cooked. Let the Dorovyets wonder why there's a new column of smoke coming from across the bay! By the time they can come and investigate, we'll be on our way south again."

Luet knew that many heard those confident words with more despair than hope—but their longing for the city was a weakness in them, nothing to be proud of, not a desire to be indulged. Vas's sabotage might have turned them back, but that would have made all their lives meaningless, at least compared to what they were going to accomplish when Nafai succeeded.

If he succeeded.

Elemak spoke to Nafai then. "Are you a good shot with that thing?" he asked.

"I don't know," said Nafai. "I haven't tried it yet. It was too dark last night. I do know *this*—I can't shoot far. I don't have strong enough muscles in the right places yet, for drawing a bow." He grinned. "I'm going to have to find some animal that's very stupid, very slow, or deaf, blind, and upwind of me."

No one laughed. Instead they all stood and watched him stride away, heading unwaveringly in the exact direction his father had pointed.

From then on it was a tense morning in the camp. Not the tension of quarrels barely contained—they had experienced *that* often enough—but the tension of waiting. For there was nothing to do but care for the babies and wonder whether Nafai would, against all probability, bring back meat with his bow and arrows.

The only exception to the general air of glum nervousness was Shedemei and Zdorab. Not that they were *happy,* really—they were as quiet as ever, going about their business. But Luet could not help but notice that they seemed more—what, *aware* of each other today. They kept *looking* at each other, with some barely contained secret.

It didn't dawn on Luet until late in the morning, when Shedemei was holding naked Chveya while Luet washed the second gown and diaper that her daughter had managed to soil that morning. Shedemei couldn't stop giggling right along with

Chveya while they played, and as Luet wondered about Shedemei's unaccustomed lightness of spirit, she realized: Shedemei must be pregnant. At long last, after everyone had concluded that she was sterile, Shedya was going to have a baby.

And, being Luet, she did not hesitate to ask the question outright—after all, they were alone, and no woman kept a secret from the waterseer, if she wanted to know it.

"No," said Shedemei, startled. "I mean—I might be, but how could I know so soon?"

It was only then that it occurred to Luet for the first time: Shedemei had not been pregnant till now because she and Zdorab had never coupled. They must have married for convenience, so they could share a tent. They had been *friends* all this time, and they were so *aware* of each other, Shedemei was so *happy* today because last night they must have made their marriage real for the first time.

"Congratulations anyway," said Luet.

Shedemei blushed and looked down at the baby, tickling her a little.

"And maybe it *will* be soon. Some women conceive immediately. *I* did, I think."

"Don't tell anyone else," said Shedemei.

"Hushidh will know that something has changed," said Luet.

"Her then, but no one else."

"I promise," said Luet.

But there was something in Shedemei's smile then that told her that while she knew *part* of the secret, perhaps, there was more that was yet untold. Never mind, Luet said silently. I'm not one of those who has to know everything. What goes on between you and Zdorab is none of my affair, except as you make it plain to me. But whatever happened, I know this: It has made you happier today. More hopeful than I've seen you in this whole journey.

Or perhaps it is *I* who am more hopeful than ever before, because we weathered such a terrible crisis this morning. And, best of all, because Elemak was on the side of the Oversoul.

So what if Vas is a sneak and a murderer in his heart? So what if Obring and Sevet would leave their babies? If Elemak was no longer the enemy of the Oversoul, then all would be well indeed.

Nafai came home before noon. No one saw him coming because no one was looking for him so early. Suddenly he was there at the edge of the tents.

"Zdorab!" he called.

Zdorab emerged from Volemak's tent, where he and Issib had been working with the Index together. "Nafai," he said. "I guess this means you're back."

Nafai held out the skinless carcass of a hare in one hand and an equally naked and bloody yozh in the other. "Neither one's very much by itself, I suppose, but since Father said we could make stew if I got back early enough, I say start up a fire, Zodya! We have fat-riddled animal protein to put in our bellies tonight!"

Not everyone was overjoyed to know that the expedition would go on—but they were all glad of the cooked meat, the spicy stew, and the end of the uncertainty. Volemak was positively jovial as he presided over the meal that night. Luet wondered at that—wouldn't it have been easier for him, now, to let the mantle of authority slip away, to pass it to one of his sons? But no. Heavy as the burden of authority might be, it was far lighter than the unbearable weight of losing it.

She noticed as they sat and ate together that Nafai stank from his exertions of the day. It wasn't exactly an unfamiliar odor—no one could maintain Basilican standards of hygiene here—but it was unpleasant. "You smell," she whispered to him, while the others listened to Mebbekew chanting out a bawdy old poem he had learned in his theatrical days.

"I admit it, I need a bath," said Nafai.

"I'll give you one tonight," said Luet.

"I was hoping you'd say that," he answered. "I see you give them to Veya and I get so jealous."

"You were magnificent today," she said.

"Just a little whittling while the Oversoul pumped knowledge into my head. And then killing animals too stupid to run away."

"Yes, all of that—magnificent. And more. What you did with your father."

"It was the right way to do it," he said. "Nothing more than that. Not like what *you* did. In fact, it's *you* that deserves to be pampered and babied tonight."

"I know it," she said. "But I have to bathe you *first*. It's no fun being babied by someone who smells so bad it makes you choke."

In answer, he embraced her, burying her nose in his armpit. She tickled him to break free.

Rasa, looking across the fire at them, thought: Such children. So young, so playful. I'm so glad that they can still be that way. Someday, when real adult responsibilities settle on them, they'll lose that. It will be replaced by a slower, quieter kind of play. But for now, they can cast away care and remember how good it is to be alive. In the desert or the city, in a house or a tent, that's what happiness means, isn't it?

EIGHT

PLENTY

The next morning they loaded the camels and moved southeast. No one said anything about it, but everyone understood that they were moving to put some distance between them and Dorova Bay. It was still no easy task finding a way through the Valley of Fires, and several times they had to backtrack, though now Elemak usually rode ahead, often with Vas, in order to scout a path that led somewhere useful. Volemak would tell him in the morning what the Index advised, and Elemak would then mark a trail that led to the easiest ascents and descents from plateau to plateau.

After a few days, they found another spring of drinkable water, which they named Strelay, because they would use their time there to make arrows. Nafai went out first and found examples of all the kinds of tree that the Oversoul knew would make good bows; soon they had gathered several dozen saplings. Some of them they made into bows at once, for practice and for their immediate hunting needs; the rest they would carry with them, allowing them to season into wood that would hold its spring. They also made hundreds of arrows, and practiced shooting at targets, men and women alike, because, as Elemak said, "There may come a time when our lives depend on the archery of our wives."

Those who had been good shots with a pulse were as good with the bow, after some practice, but the real challenge was developing the strength to pull far enough and steadily enough to hit more distant targets. There wasn't a one of them without aching arms and backs and shoulders for the first week; Kokor, Dol, and Rasa gave up early and never tried again. Sevet and Hushidh, however, developed into rather good archers, as long as they used smaller bows than the men.

It was Issib who thought of dyeing the arrow shafts a bright unnatural color so spent arrows would be easier to retrieve.

Then they moved on again, from fountain to fire, practicing archery as they went. They began to be proud of the strength in their arms. The competition in archery among the men became rather fierce; the women noticed but mentioned only among themselves that the men cared about no targets but the ones placed far enough away that Sevet's and Hushidh's smaller bows could not accurately reach them. "Let them have their game," said Hushidh. "It would be too humiliating for any of them to be beaten by a woman."

Without meaning to, they were soon running parallel to the caravan route, and rather close—they were back to raw meat for a while. Then one morning Volemak came out of his tent, holding the Index, and saying, "The Oversoul says we must now head west into the mountains until we come to the sea."

"Let me guess," said Obring. "We won't be able to see a city there."

No one answered him. Nor did anyone else mention their last venture near the Scour Sea.

"Why are we heading west now?" asked Elemak. "We've gone barely half the length of the Valley of Fires—the caravan trail doesn't come to the sea again until it reaches the Sea of Fire, due south of here. All we're doing is going far out of our way to the west."

"There are rivers to the west," said Volemak.

"No there aren't," said Elemak. "If there were, the caravanners through here would have found them and used them. There'd be cities there."

"Nevertheless," said Volemak, "we're going west. The Oversoul says that we'll need to make a long camp again—to plant crops, to harvest them."

"Why?" asked Mebbekew. "We're making good progress. The babies are all thriving well. Why another camp?"

"Because Shedemei is pregnant, of course," said Volemak, "and getting sicker with each passing day."

They all looked at Shedemei in surprise. She blushed—and looked no less surprised than the others. "I only began to suspect it myself this morning," she said. "How can the Oversoul know what I'm only guessing at?"

Volemak shrugged. "He knows what he knows."

"Pretty poor timing, Shedya," said Elemak. "All the other women are holding off on pregnancy because they're nursing, but now we have to wait for you."

For once Zdorab spoke up sharply. "Some things can't be *timed* precisely, Elya, so don't lay blame where there was no volition."

Elemak looked at him steadily. "I never do," he said. But then he dropped the matter and set out to the west, blazing a trail for the caravan.

Their route led up into real mountains—volcanic ones, with some relatively recent lava flows that had not yet been broken into soil. Issib used the Index to come up with information about the area—there were at least fifty active and dormant volcanos in this range of mountains fronting on the Scour Sea. "The last eruption was only last year," he said, "but much farther to the south."

"Which may be the reason the Oversoul is sending us to the sea this far north," said Volemak.

Hard as the climb was, coming down the other side of the mountain range was harder—it was steeper and more heavily overgrown. Indeed, it was almost a jungle high on the slopes of the mountain.

"The winter winds come off the sea," said Issib, "and there are squalls almost every day in summer, too. The mountains catch the clouds, force them up into the colder atmosphere, and bring down whatever moisture is in them. So it's a rain forest here in the mountains. It won't be as wet down by the sea." They were becoming used to Issib being the one who explored the Index; during days of travel, he was the only one with no other duties, and he carried the Index with him, one hand constantly on it, exploring. Zdorab had shown him so many tricks and back doors that he was almost as deft now as the librarian himself. And no one disparaged the value of the information Issib provided, because it was all he *could* provide.

They were in the middle of a tricky passage down a tangled ravine when they felt an earthquake—rather a violent one, which threw two of the camels off their feet and set the others to stamping and turning in confusion.

"Out of the ravine!" cried Issib at once.

"Out? How?" answered Volemak.

"Any way we can!" shouted Issib. "The Index says that this earthquake jarred loose a lake high up in the mountains—anything in the ravine is going to be swept away!"

It was a particularly bad time for an emergency—Elemak and Vas were far ahead, blazing a trail, and Nafai and Obring were hunting higher up in the mountain. But Volemak had been journeying far longer than Elemak, and had resources of his own. He quickly sized up the walls of the ravine and chose a route up through a jumble of rocks into a side canyon that might lead to the top. "I'll lead the way," he said, "because I'm the one who knows best what camels can do. Luet, you bring the women and children along—Meb, you and Zdorab herd the pack animals after us. Supplies first, cold- and dryboxes last. Issib, you stay within earshot of them, and stay in touch with the Index. Tell them when there's no more time. When they have to abandon the rest of the camels and save themselves. They *must* save themselves, as must you, Issya—more important than anything else. Do you understand?"

He was asking everyone, and everyone nodded, wide-eyed, terrified.

"Elemak is in the ravine," said Eiadh. "Someone has to warn him."

"Elya is fit to hear the voice of the Oversoul himself," said Volemak. "The water is coming faster than anyone can ride to catch up with him. Save his baby and his wife, Edhya. Now come *on*." He turned his camel and began the ascent.

Camels were not made for climbing. Their sedentary pace was maddening. But steadily they climbed. The earth shook again, and again—but the aftershocks were not as violent as the first had been. Volemak and the women made it to the top. Volemak had a fleeting thought of going back down to help, but Luet reminded him that in several places the path was not wide enough for two camels to pass—far from helping, he'd slow down the evacuation.

All the camels were above the floor of the ravine when Issib cried out, "Now! For your lives!" As soon as he saw that Meb and Zdorab both had heard, he turned his own camel and pushed his way in among the pack beasts. However, he could not control his animal forcefully enough to make headway faster than the rest. As Meb overtook him, he reached out and took the reins from Issib's feeble grasp, then began to drag Issib's camel faster and faster. Soon, though, they reached a narrow place where the two camels couldn't pass side by side, especially because of the bulk of Issib's chair. Without hesitation—without even waiting for his camel to kneel to let him dismount—Meb slid off to the ground, let go of his own camel's reins, and dragged on the reins of Issib's mount, hurrying it through the gap.

Moments later, Zdorab came through the same narrow place, then came up beside them. "The Index!" he shouted.

Issib, who couldn't lift it, pointed to the bag on his lap. "It's looped to the pommel!" he shouted.

Zdorab maneuvered his animal close; Meb held Issib's camel steady. Deftly Zdorab reached out, unlooped the bag, and then, brandishing it high like a trophy, rode on ahead.

"Leave me now!" Issib shouted at Meb.

Meb ignored him and continued to drag his camel upward, passing the slower pack animals.

Soon they came to a place where Zdorab, Luet, Hushidh, Shedemei, Sevet, and Eiadh waited on foot. Mebbekew realized that he must be near the top now—Zdorab must have left the Index with Volemak, and Rasa and the other women must be keeping the infants on high ground. "Take Issib!" shouted Meb, handing the reins to Zdorab. Then Meb rushed back down the canyon to the next pack beast. He thrust the reins of the animal in Luet's hands. "Drag him up!" he cried. To each woman in turn he gave the reins of a pack animal. They could hear the water now, a roaring sound; they could feel the rumbling in the earth. "Faster!" he cried.

There were just enough of them to take the reins of all the pack animals. Only Meb's own mount, now last in line, was untended. She was clearly frightened by the noise of the water, by the shaking of the earth, and didn't stay close behind. Meb called to her, "Glupost! Come on! Hurry, Glupost!" But he kept tugging on the reins of the last pack animal, knowing that the coldboxes it carried would be more important, in the long run, than his own mount.

"Let go, Meb!" cried Zdorab. "Here it comes!"

They could see the wall of water from where they were, that's how high it was—higher, in fact, than the top of the ravine, so that they instinctively ran even higher up the slope they were standing on. Those at the top were never in danger of being swept away, though, for the water stayed lower than they were.

However, the water that was snagged into the side canyon they had climbed through shot up into it with such force that it rose higher than the main body of water in the ravine. It slammed into the last two camels and then into Meb, lifting them all off their feet and heaving them the rest of the way up the side canyon. Meb could hear women screaming—was that Dol, howling out Meb's name?—and then he felt the water subsiding almost as fast as it had risen, sucking him downward. For a moment he thought of letting go of the reins and saving himself; then he realized that the pack camel had braced itself and was now more secure on the ground than Meb himself. So he clung to the reins and was not swept away. But as he hung there, pressed against the side of the camel that he had saved, and which was now saving him, he saw his mount Glupost get dragged off her feet and sucked down into the maelstrom in the ravine.

In moments, he felt many hands on him, prying the reins from his fingers, leading him, sopping wet and trembling, up to where the others waited. Volemak embraced him, weeping. "I thought I had lost you, my son, my son."

"What about Elya?" wailed Eiadh. "How could he save himself from that?"

"Not to mention Vas," said Rasa softly.

Several people looked at Sevet, whose face was hard and set.

"Not everyone shows fear the same way," murmured Luet, putting an end to any hard judgments anyone might be inclined to make about the difference between Eiadh's and Sevet's reaction. Luet knew well that Sevet had little reason to care much whether Vas lived or died—though she wondered how much Sevet herself actually knew.

What was most in Luet's heart was the fact that Nafai was also not with them. He and Obring were almost certainly on high ground, and safe. But they would no doubt be deeply worried.

Tell him that we're safe, she said silently to the Oversoul. And tell *me*—is Elemak alive? And Vas?

Alive, came the answer in her mind.

She said so.

The others looked at her, half in relief, half in doubt. "Alive," she said again. "That's all the Oversoul told me. Isn't it enough?"

The water subsided, the level dropping rapidly. Volemak and Zdorab walked down the side canyon together. They found it a tangle of half-uprooted trees and bushes—not even the boulders were where they had been.

But the side canyon was nothing compared to the ravine itself. There was nothing left. A quarter hour ago it had been lush with vegetation—so lush that it was hard to make way through it, and they had often had to lead the camels through the stream itself in order to pass some of the tangles of vegetation. Now the walls of the ravine, from top to bottom, had not a single plant clinging to them. The soil itself had been scoured away, so that bare rock was exposed. And on the floor of the ravine, there were only a few heavy boulders and the sediments left behind by the water as it dropped.

"Look how the floor of the ravine is bare rock near the edges," said Volemak. "But deep sediment in the middle, near the water."

It was true: already the stream that remained—larger than the original one—was cutting a channel a meter deep through the thick mud. The new banks of the stream would collapse here and there, a few meters of mud slipping down into the water. It would take some time before the floor of the ravine stabilized.

"It'll be green as ever within six weeks," said Zdorab. "And in five years you'd never know this happened."

"What do you think?" asked Volemak. "If we stay to the edges, is it safe to use this as a highway down to the sea?"

"The reason we were using the ravine in the first place was because Elemak said the top was not passable—it keeps getting cut by deep canyons or blocked by steep hills."

"So we keep to the edges," said Volemak. "And we hope."

It took a while at the top of the ravine to check the camels' loads and be sure nothing had come loose during the scramble to safety. "It's better than we could have hoped, that we lost only the one camel," said Volemak.

Zdorab led his own mount forward, and held out the reins to Meb.

"No," said Meb.

"Please," said Zdorab. "Every step I take on foot will be my way of giving honor to my brave friend."

"Take it," whispered Volemak.

Meb took the reins from Zdorab. "Thank you," he said. "But there were *no* cowards here today."

Zdorab embraced him quickly, then went back to help Shedemei get the women with babies onto their camels.

It turned out that neither Zdorab nor Meb nor Volemak did much riding the rest of that day. They spent their time on foot, patrolling the length of the caravan, making sure the camels never strayed toward the thick and treacherous mud in the middle of the ravine. They had visions of a camel sinking immediately over its head. The footing was wet, slimy, and treacherous, but by keeping the pace slow, they soon reached the mouth of the ravine, where it empted into a wide river.

There had obviously been much damage here, too, for the opposite side of the river valley was a mess of mud and boulders, with many trees knocked down and much bare soil and rock exposed. And the rest of the way down the river they could see that both banks had been torn apart. Ironically, though, because the force of the flood had been less intense here than in the ravine, their passage through the debris it left behind would be far harder.

"This way!"

It was Elemak, with Vas behind him. The two of them were on foot, but they could see that their camels were not far behind. They were on higher ground. It would be a steep but not very difficult climb to reach them.

"We have a path here through the high ground!" called Elemak.

In a few minutes they were gathered at the beginning of

Elemak's path through the forest. As husbands and wives embraced, Issib noticed that the forest here was considerably less dense than it had been higher up the mountain. "We must be near sea level now," he said.

"The river makes a sharp bend to the west over there," said Vas, one arm around Sevet, his baby held against his shoulder. "And from there you can see the Scour Sea. Between this river and the one to the south it's open grassland, mostly, a few trees here and there. Higher ground, thank the Oversoul. We felt the earthquakes, but when they passed we didn't think anything of them, except to worry that it might have been worse up where you were. Then suddenly Elya insisted we needed to go to the higher ground and look over the area, and just as we got there we heard this roaring noise and the river went crazy. We had images of seeing all the camels floating by, with all of you still riding on top of them."

"Issib was warned through the Index," said Volemak.

"It's a good thing we *weren't* all together," said Issib. "Four more camels, and we would have lost them. As it was, Meb lost his mount—because he was saving pack animals, I might add."

"We can wait for the stories until we're at our camp for the night," said Elemak. "We can reach the place between rivers before nightfall. There's little moon, so we want to have the tents up before dark."

That night they stayed up late around the fire, partly because they were waiting for dinner to cook, partly because they were too keyed-up to sleep, and partly because they kept hoping that Nafai and Obring would find the camp that night. That was when the stories were told. And as Hushidh bade Luet goodnight in the tent where she would be sleeping alone with her baby, she said, "I wish you could see as I see, Luet. That flood did what nothing else could have managed—the bonds between us all are so much stronger. And Meb . . . the honor that flows to him now . . ."

"A nice change," said Luet.

"I just hope he doesn't strut too much about it," said Hushidh, "or he'll waste it all."

"Maybe he's growing up," said Luet.

"Or maybe he just needed the right circumstance to discover the best in himself. He didn't hesitate, Issya says. Just dismounted and risked his own life dragging Issib to safety."

"And Zdorab took the Index, and then led us back down . . ."

"I know, I'm not saying Meb was the only one. But you know how it is with Zdorab. That gesture he made, giving his mount to Meb. It was a generous thing to do, and it helped bind the group together—but it also had the effect of erasing the memory of Zdorab's own role in saving us. Our minds were all on Mebbekew."

"Well, maybe that's how Zodya wants it," said Luet.

"But *we* won't forget," said Hushidh.

"Hardly," said Luet. "Now go to bed. The babies won't care how little sleep we got tonight—they'll be starving on schedule in the morning."

It was only a few hours after dawn when Nafai and Obring returned. They had been far from the flood, of course, but they had also been on the wrong side of it, so that coming home they had to find a place to cross either the ravine itself or the river. They ended up dragging the camels across the river upstream of the ravine, making a long detour around the worst of the destruction, and then crossing the river in shallow marshes and sand bars near the sea—at low tide. "The camels are getting less and less happy about crossing water," said Nafai.

"But we brought back two deers," said Obring happily.

With everyone reunited, Volemak made a little speech establishing this place as their campsite. "The river to the north we will name Oykib, for the firstborn boy of this expedition, and the river to the south is Protchnu, for the firstborn boy of the next generation."

Rasa was outraged. "Why not name them Dza and Chveya, for the first two *children* born on our journey?"

Volemak looked at her steadily without answering.

"Then we had better leave this place before the boys are old enough to know how you have honored them solely because they have penises."

"If we had had only two girls, and two rivers, Father would have named the rivers for *them,*" said Issib, trying to make peace.

They knew it wasn't true, of course. For several weeks after they got there, Rasa insisted on calling them the North River and the South River; Volemak was just as adamant in calling them the River Oykib and the River Protchnu. But since it was the men who did more traveling, and therefore crossed the rivers more often, and fished in them, and had to tell each other about places and events up and down the rivers' lengths, it was the names Oykib and Protchnu that stayed. Whether anyone else noticed or not, however, Luet saw that Rasa never used Volemak's names for the rivers, and grew silent and cold whenever others spoke their names.

Only once did Nafai and Luet discuss the matter. Nafai was singularly unsympathetic. "Rasa didn't mind when women decided everything in Basilica, and men weren't even allowed to *look* at the lakes."

"That was a holy place for women. The only place like it in the world."

"What does it matter?" said Nafai. "It's just a couple of names for a couple of rivers. When we leave here, no one else will ever remember what we named them."

"So why not North River and South River?"

"It's only a problem because Mother made it a problem," said Nafai. "Now let's *not* make it a problem between *us.*"

"I just want to know why *you* go along with it!"

Nafai sighed. "Think, for just a moment, what it would mean if I had called them the North and South rivers. What it would have meant to Father. And to the other men. Then it really *would* have been divisive. I don't need anything more to separate me from the others."

Luet chewed on that idea for a while.

"All right," she said. "I can see that."

And then, after she had thought a little more, she said, "But you didn't see anything wrong with naming the rivers after the boys until Mother pointed it out, did you?"

He didn't answer.

"In fact, you really don't see anything wrong with it now, do you?"

"I love you," said Nafai.

"That's not an answer," she said.

"I think it is," he said.

"And what if I never give you a son?" she said.

"Then I will keep making love to you until we have a hundred daughters," said Nafai.

"In your *dreams,*" she said nastily.

"In *yours,* you mean," he said.

She made the deliberate decision not to stay angry with him for this, and as they made love she was as willing and passionate as ever. But afterward, when he was asleep, it worried her. What would it mean to them for the men to make their company as male-dominated as Basilica had been female-dominated?

Why must we do this? she wondered. We had a chance to make our society different from the rest of the world. Balanced and fair, even-handed, *right*. And yet even Nafai and Issib seem content to unbalance it. Is the rivalry between men and women such that one must always be in ascendancy at the expense of the other? Is it built into our genes? Must the community always be ruled by one sex or the other?

Maybe so, she thought. Maybe we're like the baboons. When we're stable and civilized, the women decide things, establish the households, the connections between them, create the neighborhoods and the friendships. But when we're nomadic, living lives on the edge of survival, the men rule, and brook no interference from the women. Perhaps that's what civilization *means*—is the dominance of the female over the male. And wherever that lapses, we call the result *uncivilized, barbarian . . . manly*.

* * *

They spent a year between the rivers, waiting for Shedemei's baby to be born. It was a son; they named him Padarok—*gift*—and called him Rokya. They might have moved on then, after the first year, but by the time little Rokya was born, three of the other women had conceived—including Rasa and Luet, who were the most fragile during pregnancy. So they stayed for a second harvest, and a few months more, until all the women but Sevet had completed their pregnancy and borne a child. So there were thirty of them that began the next stage of the journey, and the first generation of children were walking and most of them beginning to talk before they were on their way.

It had been a good two years. Instead of desert farming, they had lush, rain-watered fields on good soil. Their crops were more varied; the hunting was better; and even the camels thrived, giving birth to fifteen new beasts of burden. Making saddles was harder—none of them had ever learned the skill—but they found a way to put two toddlers on each of the four most docile animals, which always traveled in train with the women's camels. When the children first tried out the saddles, some of them were terrified—camels ride so high above the ground—but soon enough they were used to it, and even enjoyed it.

The journey was easy through the savanna along the seacoast; they ate up the kilometers as they never had before, even on the smooth desert west and south of Basilica. In three days they reached a well-watered bay that the men were already familiar with, having hunted and fished there during the past two years. But in the morning, Volemak dismayed them all by telling them that their course now lay, not south as they had all expected, but west.

West! Into the sea!

Volemak pointed at the rocky island that rose out of the sea not two kilometers away. "Beyond it is another island, a huge island. We have as long a journey on that island as we have had since we left the Valley of Mebbekew."

At low tide, Nafai and Elemak tried fording the strait between the mainland and the island. They could do it, with only a short swim in the middle. But the camels balked, and so they ended up building rafts. "I've done it before," said Elemak. "Never for a saltwater crossing, of course, but the water here is placid enough."

So they felled trees and floated the logs in the bay, binding them together with ropes made of the fibers of marsh reeds. It took a week to make the rafts, and two days to take the camels across—one at a time—and then the cargo, and then, last of all, the women and children. They camped on the shore where they had landed, as the men poled the rafts around the island to the southwestern tip, where again they would need the rafts to ferry everyone and everything to the large island. In another week the company had traversed the small island and crossed to the large one; they pushed the rafts into the water and watched them float away.

The northern tip of the large island was mountainous and heavily forested. But gradually the mountains gave way to hills, and then to broad savannas. They could stand at the crest of the low rolling plain and see the Scour Sea to the west and the Sea of Fire to the east, the island was so narrow here. And the farther south they went, the more they understood how the Sea of Fire earned its name. Volcanos rose out of the sea, and in the distance they could see the smoke of a minor eruption from time to time. "This island was part of the mainland until five million years ago," Issib explained to them. "Until then, the Valley of Fires came right down onto this island, south of us—and the fires still continue in the sea that has filled the space between the two parts of the valley."

Growing up in Basilica, most of them had never understood the forces of nature—Basilica was such an unchanging place, with so much pride in its ancienthood. Here, even though the timespans were measured in the millions of years, they could clearly see the enormous power of the planet, and the virtual irrelevancy of the human lives on its surface.

"And yet we're *not* irrelevant," said Issib. "Because we are the ones who see the changes, and know them, and understand that they *are* changes, that once things were different. Everything else in the universe, every living and non-living thing, lives in the infinite now, which never changes, which always is exactly as it is. Only *we* know the passage of time, that one thing causes another and that we are changed by the past and will change the future."

The island widened, and the ground became more rugged. They all recognized it as being the same kind of terrain as the Valley of Fires—the continuation of that valley that Issib had predicted. But it was quieter—they never found a place where gases from inside the earth burned on the surface—and the water was more likely to be pure. It was also drier and drier the farther south they went, though they were rising up into mountain country.

"These mountains have a name," Issib told them, from the Index. "Dalatoi. People lived here before the island split away from the mainland. In fact, the greatest and most ancient of the Cities of Fire was here."

"Skudnooy?" asked Luet, remembering the story of the city of misers who withdrew from the world and supposedly held most of the gold of Harmony in hidden vaults beneath their hidden city.

"No, Raspyatny," said Issib. And they all remembered the stories of the city of stone and moss, where streams flowed through every room in a city the size of a mountain, so high that the upper rooms would freeze, and those who lived there had to burn fires to melt the rivers so that the lower rooms would have water all year.

"Will we see it?" they asked.

"What's left of it," said Issib. "It was abandoned ten million years ago, but it *was* made out of stone. The ancient road we're following led there."

Only then did they realize that they were indeed following an ancient road. There was no trace of pavement, and the road

was sometimes cut by ravines or eroded away. But they kept returning to the path of least resistance, and now and then they could see that hills had been cut into to make a place for the road to go, and the occasional valley had been partly filled in with stone which had not yet worn down to nothing. "If there had been more rain here," said Issib, "there'd be nothing left. But the island has moved south so that this land is now in the latitudes of the Great Southern Desert, and so the air is drier and there's less erosion. Some of the works of humankind leave traces, even after all this time."

"Someone must have used this road in the past ten million years," said Elemak.

"No," said Issib. "No human being has set foot on this island since it fully split off from the mainland."

"How can you know that!" Mebbekew scoffed.

"Because the Oversoul has kept humans from coming here. No one even remembers that this island exists. That's how the Oversoul wanted it. To keep things safe and ready . . . for us, I guess."

They saw Raspyatny for a whole day before they reached it. At first it simply looked like an oddly textured mountain, but the closer they got, the more they realized that what they were seeing were windows carved into the stone. It was a high mountain, too, so that the city carved into the face of it must be vast.

They camped northeast of the city, where a small stream flowed. They followed the stream and found that it flowed right out of the city itself. Inside, it made cascades and the walls near it were thick with moss; it was much colder than the desert air outside.

They took turns exploring, in large groups, leaving some in charge of the children and animals while the others clambered through the remnants of the city. Away from the stream, the city had not been so badly eroded inside, though nowhere was the interior as well preserved as the outer wall. They realized why, when they found a few traces of an aqueduct system that had, just as the legend said, carried water into every room of the city. What surprised them, though, was the lack of internal corridors. Rooms simply led into each other. "How did they have any privacy?" asked Hushidh. "How did they ever have any time to themselves, if every room was an avenue for people to walk right through?"

No one had an answer.

"More than two hundred thousand people lived here, in the old days," said Issib. "Back when this whole area was farther north, and much better watered—all the land outside was farmed, for kilometers to the north, and yet their enemies could never attack them successfully because they kept ten years' worth of food inside these walls, and they never lacked for water. Their enemies could burn their fields and besiege them, but then they'd starve long before anyone in Raspyatny ever felt the slightest want. Only nature itself could depopulate this place."

"Why wasn't all of this destroyed in the earthquakes of the Valley of Fires?" asked Nafai.

"We haven't seen the eastern slope. The Index says that half the city was wiped out in two great earthquakes when the rift first opened and the sea poured through."

"It would have been glorious to see a flood like *that*," said Zdorab. "From a safe place, of course."

"The whole eastern side of the city collapsed," said Issib. "Now it's just a mountainside. But this side stayed. Ten million years. You never know. Of course, the streams are eroding it away from the inside, making the outside more and more of a hollow shell. Eventually it'll cave in. Maybe all at once. One part will break, and that'll put too much stress on what is left, and the whole thing will come down like a sandcastle on the beach."

"We have seen one of the cities of the heroes," said Luet.

"And the stories were true," said Obring. "Which leads me to wonder whether the city of Skudnooy might be around here somewhere, too."

"The Index says not," said Issib. "I asked."

"Too bad," said Obring. "All that gold!"

"Oh, right," said Elemak. "And where would you sell it? Or did you think you'd eat it? Or wear it?"

"Oh, I'm not allowed even to *dream* of tremendous wealth, is that it?" said Obring defiantly. "Only practical dreams allowed?"

Elemak shrugged and let the matter drop.

After leaving the vicinity of Raspyatny—and it took them another whole day to pass around the western side of the city, which really seemed to have covered the whole face of the mountain—they made their way through a high pass, which once again seemed to have been made almost uniform in width in order to accommodate a heavily trafficked road. "Once this was the highway between the Cities of Fire and the Cities of the Stars," said Issib. "Now it leads only to desert."

They came out of the pass and a vast, dry savanna spread out below them; they could see that the island narrowed here, with the Sea of Stars to the east and, far to the west, the blue shimmer of the southern reaches of the Scour Sea. As they descended, they lost sight of the western sea; instead, at the urging of the Oversoul, they hugged the eastern shore, because more rain fell there, and they could fish in the sea.

It was a hard passage—dry, so that three times they had to dig wells, and hot, with the tropical sun beating down on them. But this was exactly the sort of terrain that Elemak and Volemak had both learned to deal with from their youth, and they made good time. Ten days after they came down from the pass through the Dalatoi Mountains, the Oversoul had them strike south when the coastline turned southeast, and as they climbed through gently rolling hills, the grass grew thicker, and here and there more trees dotted the landscape. They passed through low and well-weathered mountains, down through a river valley, up over more hills, and then down through the most beautiful land they had ever seen.

Stands of forest were evenly balanced with broad meadows; bees hummed over fields of wildflowers, promising honey easily found. There were streams with clear water, all leading to a wide, meandering river. Shedemei dismounted from her camel and probed into the soil. "It isn't like desert grassland," she said. "Not just roots. There's true topsoil here. We can farm these meadows without destroying them."

For the first time in their journey, Elemak didn't bother riding ahead to confer with Volemak about a campsite. There was no place that they passed through where they could *not* have stopped and spent the night.

"This land could hold the population of Seggidugu and they could all live in wealth," said Elemak. "Don't you think so, Father?"

"And we're the only humans here," he answered. "The Oversoul prepared this place for us. Ten million years, it waited here for us."

"Then we stay here? This is where we were coming?"

"We stay here for now," said Volemak. "For several years at least. The Oversoul isn't ready yet to take us out into the stars, back to Earth. So for now this is our home."

"How *many* years?" asked Elemak.

"Long enough that we should build houses of wood, and let our poor old tents become awnings and curtains," said Volemak. "There'll be no more journeying by land or sea from this place. Only when we rise up into the stars will we leave here. So let us call this place Dostatok, because it has plenty for our needs. The river we will name Rasa, because it is strong and full of life and it will never cease to supply us with all we need."

Rasa nodded her head gently to acknowledge the honor of the naming; as she did, she had the tiniest smile, which Luet, at least, recognized as a sign that Rasa knew her husband was trying to be conciliatory in his naming.

They made their settlement on a low promontory overlooking the mouth of the River Rasa, where it poured into the Southern Ocean—for that was how far south they had come, leaving the Scour Sea and the Sea of Stars behind them. Within a month they all had houses of wood, with thatched roofs, and in this latitude they had a growing season almost all the year, so it hardly mattered when they planted; there were some rains almost every day, and heavy storms swept over quickly, doing no damage.

The animals were so tame they had no fear of man; they soon domesticated the wild goats, which clearly were descended from the same animals that were herded in the hills near Basilica—camel's milk at last became a liquid that only baby camels had to drink, and the term "camel's cheese" became a euphemism for what well-fed babies left in their diapers. In the next six years, more babies were born, until there were thirty-five young ones, ranging in age from nearly eight years to several newborns. They farmed their fields together, and shared equally from the produce; from time to time the men would leave and hunt together, bringing home meat for drying and salting and skins for tanning. Rasa, Issib, and Shedemei undertook the education of the children by starting a school.

Not that their lives were one unrelenting tale of joy and peace. There were quarrels—for an entire year Kokor would not speak to Sevet over some trivial slight; there was another quarrel between Meb and Obring that led to Obring building a house farther from the rest of the group. There were resentments—some felt that others weren't working hard enough; some felt that their kind of work was of greater value than the labor of others. And there was a constant undercurrent of tension between the women, who looked to Rasa for leadership, and the men, who seemed to assume that no decision was final unless Volemak or Elemak had approved it. But they weathered all these crises, all these tensions, finding some balance of leadership between Volemak's loyalty to the purposes of the Oversoul, Rasa's clear-sighted compassion, and Elemak's hardheaded assessments of what they needed to survive. Any unhappiness that they might harbor in their hearts was kept in check, buried under the hard work that marked the rhythms of their lives, and then dissolved in the moments when joy was bountiful and love unstinted.

Life was good enough over the years that there was not a one of them who did not wish, when they thought of it at all, that the Oversoul would forget that they were there, and leave them in peace and happiness in Dostatok.

NINE
PERIMETER

When Chveya was seven years old she had understood perfectly how the world worked. Now she was eight, and there were some questions.

Like all the children of Dostatok, she grew up understanding the pure and simple relationships among families. For instance, Dazya and her younger brothers and sisters belonged to Hushidh and Issib. Krassya and Nokya and their younger brothers and sisters belonged to Kokor and Obring. Vasnya and her brother and sister belonged to Sevet and Vas. And so on, each set of children belonging to a mother and father.

The only oddity in this clear picture of the universe, at least until Chveya was eight, had been Grandfather and Grandmother, Volemak and Rasa, who not only had two children of their own—the brothers Okya and Yaya, who might as well be twins because, as Vasnya had said once, they had but one brain between them—but also were, in some vague way, the parents of all the other parents. She knew this because, in odd moments, she had heard adults call Grandmother not only "Lady Rasa" or "Grandmother" but also "Mother," and she heard her own father and Proya's father Elemak and Skiya's father Mebbekew call Grandfather "Father" more often than not.

In Chveya's mind this meant that Volemak and Rasa were the First Parents, having given rise to all of humanity. Now, she knew in the forepart of her mind that this was not accurate, for Shedemei had made it plain in school that there were millions of other humans living in faraway places, and clearly Grandfather and Grandmother had not given life to all of *them*. But those places were legendary. They were never seen. The whole world was the safe and beautiful land of Dostatok, and in that place there was no one, or so it seemed, who had not come from the marriage of Volemak and Rasa.

To Chveya, in fact, the world of the adults was remote enough to satisfy any need she had for strangeness; she had no need to wonder about mythical lands like Basilica and Potokgavan and Gorayni and Earth and Harmony, some of which were planets and some of which were cities and some of which were nations, though Chveya had never grasped the rules for which term went with each name. No, Chveya's world was dominated by the continual power struggle between Dazya and Proya for ascendancy among the children.

Dazya was Oldest Child, which conferred on her enormous authority which she cheerfully misused by exploiting the younger children whenever possible, converting it to personal service and "favors" which were received without gratitude. If any of the younger ones failed to obey, she would freeze them out of all games simply by letting it be known that if "that child" were part of a game or contest, she would not participate. Dazya's attitude toward the girls more near her own age was much the same, though it was more subtle—she didn't insist on humiliating personal services, but she *did* expect that when she decided things would be done a certain way, all the other girls would go along, and anyone who resisted was politely ostracized. Since Chveya was Second Child, and only three days younger, she saw no reason to accept a subservient role. The result was that she had a lot of time to herself, for Dazya would brook no equals, and none of the other girls had the spine to stand up to her.

At the same time that Dazya had forged her kingdom among the younger children and the older girls, Proya—Elemak's eldest son, and Second Boy—had made himself prince among princes. He was the only person who could ridicule Dazya and laugh at her rules, and all the older boys would follow him. Dazya would, of course, immediately ostracize the older boys, but this meant nothing to them since the games they wanted to join and the approval they craved were Proya's. The worst humiliation to Dazya was that her own brother Xodhya would join with Proya and use Proya's power as a shield for his own independence from his older sister's rule. Chveya's own younger brother Zhyat, and sometimes even Motya, a year younger than Zhyat and not really one of the older boys, joined with Proya regularly, but she didn't mind at all, for that meant even more humiliation for Dazya.

Of course, at times of struggle Chveya would join with the older girls in alternately sneering at and snubbing the rebel boys, but in her heart Chveya longed to be part of Proya's kingdom. *They* were the ones who played rough and wonderful games involving hunting and death. She would even act the deer if they would only invite her to play, letting them hunt her and shoot at her with their blunt-tipped arrows, if only she could be part of them instead of being miserably trapped in Dazya's demesne. But when she hinted at this desire to her brother Zhyat, he made a great show of gagging and retching and she gave up the idea.

Her greatest envy was reserved for Okya and Yaya, the two sons of Grandmother and Grandfather. Okya was First Boy and Yaya was Fourth Boy. They could easily have dislodged Proya from his position of seniority among the boys, especially because the two brothers did everything together and could have thrashed all the other boys into submission. But they never bothered, only joining in Proya's games when they felt like it, and giving no concern at all to who was in charge. For they fancied themselves to be adults, not children at all. "*We* are of the same generation as your parents," Yaya had once said to her, quite haughtily. Chveya had thereupon pointed out that Yaya was considerably shorter than her and still had a teeny-weeny hooy like a hare, which caused the other children to laugh in spite of their awe for Yaya. Yaya, for his part, only looked at her with withering disdain and walked away. But Chveya noticed that he also stopped peeing in front of the other children.

When Chveya was brutally honest with herself, she had to admit that the reason she was so often completely isolated from the other children was because she simply could not keep her mouth shut. If she saw someone being a bully or unfair or selfish, she said so. Never mind that she also spoke up when somebody was noble or good or kind—praise was quickly forgotten, while offenses were treasured forever. Thus Chveya had no real friends among the other children—they were all too busy making sweet with Dazya or Proya to give real friendship to Chveya, except Okya and Yaya, of course, who were even more aloof and involved with each other in their supposed adultness.

It was when Chveya turned eight years old and saw how little heed anyone but her own parents paid to her birthday, after the enormous fuss made over Dazya's birthday, that she entirely despaired of ever being a person of significance in the world. Wasn't it bad enough that Dazya lorded it over everybody so outrageously as it was—why did the adults have to make a festival out of Dazya's birthday? Father explained, of course, that the festival wasn't about Dza herself, but rather because her birthday marked the beginning of their whole generation of children—but what did it matter if the adults thought of it that way or not? The fact remained that with this festival they had affirmed Dazya's iron rule over the other children, and in fact had even given her a temporary ascendancy over Proya himself, and Okya and Yaya had sulked through the whole party when they were snubbed and lumped in among the children, which they felt was wrong since they were *not* part of the younger generation. How could the adults so heedlessly and destructively have intervened in the children's hierarchy? It was as if the adults did not think of the children's lives as *real*.

It was then that Chveya reached her profound insight that the adult world and the children's world were probably identical in the way they worked, except that the children were perpetually subservient to the adults. It began in a conversation with her mother as she combed Chveya's hair after her bath. "The younger boys are, the more disgusting they are," Chveya said, thinking of her second brother Motya, who had just discovered how much tumult he could cause by picking his nose and wiping it on his sisters' clothing, a practice which Chveya had no intention of tolerating, whether he did it to her or to little Zuya, who couldn't defend herself.

"That's not necessarily true," said Mother. "They simply find different *ways* of being disgusting when they get older."

Mother said it offhandedly, like a joke, but to Chveya it was a grand illuminating moment. She tried to picture Krassya's father, Obring, for instance, picking his nose and wiping it on Mother, and knew that it could never happen. But perhaps there were other disgusting things, adult things, that Obring might do. I must watch him and find out, thought Chveya.

She didn't question that it was Obring she should watch—she had often seen the way Mother grew impatient when Obring spoke in council meetings. She had no respect for him, and neither did Father, though he hid it better. So if any adult male might exemplify disgusting behavior, it would certainly be Obring.

From now on, Chveya would focus all her attention on the adults around her, watching to see who was the Dazya of the mothers and who was the Proya of the fathers. In the process, she began to understand things that she had never understood before. The world was not as clear and simple a place as she had thought till now.

The most shocking revelation came on the day she discussed marriage with her parents. It had recently dawned on her that eventually the children would all grow up and pair off with each other and have babies and start the whole cycle all over again—this because of some vile remark by Toya about what Proya really wanted to do to Dazya. Toya had meant it to be an obscene horror, but Chveya realized that, far from being a horror, it was probably a prophecy. Wouldn't Proya and Dazya be the perfect pair? Proya would be just like Elemak, and Dazya would probably smile at Proya with complete devotion the way Eiadh did with Elemak. Or would Dazya be like her mother Hushidh, so much stronger than her husband Issib that she even carried him around and bathed him like a baby? Or would Proya and Dazya continue their struggle for supremacy all through their lives, trying to turn their own babies against each other?

That thought led Chveya to wonder which of the boys *she* would marry. Would it be one of the boys of the first year, her own age? That would mean either Proya or Okya, and the thought of either one repelled her. Then what about boys of the second year? Dazya's little brother Xodhya, Proya's little brother Nadya, or the "adult" Yaya—what a proud selection! And the children of the third year were the same age as her revolting brother Motya—how could she *dream* of marrying someone *that* young?

So she broached the subject with her parents as they were eating breakfast on a morning when Father was not going hunting, so they could eat together. "Will I have to marry Xodhya, do you think?" she asked—for she had decided that Xodhya was the least disgusting of all the alternatives.

"Definitely not," said Mother, without a moment's hesitation.

"In fact," said Father, "we would forbid it."

"Well, *who* then? Okya? Yaya?"

"Almost as bad," said Father. "What is this, are you planning to start a family anytime soon?"

"Of course she's thinking about it, Nyef," said Mother. "Girls think about such things at this age."

"Well, then, she might keep in mind that she isn't going to marry a full uncle and *certainly* not a full double first cousin."

These words meant absolutely nothing to Chveya, but they hinted at dark mysteries. What unspeakable thing had Xodhya done to become a "full double first cousin"? So she asked.

"It's not what *he* did," said Mother. "It's just that his mother, Hushidh, is my full sister—we both have the same mother and the same father. And Zaxodh's father, Issib, is your father's full brother—they both have the same mother and father, who happen to be Grandmother and Grandfather. That means that you have *all* your ancestors in common—it's the closest blood relation among all the children, and marriage between you is out of the question."

"If we can possibly avoid it," added Father.

"We can avoid *that* one, anyway," said Mother. "And I feel almost as strongly about Oykib and Yasai, because they are *also* sons of both Rasa and Volemak."

Chveya took all this in with outward calm, but inwardly she was in turmoil. Hushidh and Mother were full sisters, but *not* daughters of Grandmother and Grandfather! And Father and Issib were full brothers, as were Oykib and Yasai, and this fullness of their brotherhood was because they all *were* sons of Grandmother and Grandfather. Yet the very use of the word *full* implied that there were some here who were *not* full brothers, and therefore *not* sons of both Volemak and Rasa. How could that be?

"What's wrong?" asked Father.

"I just . . . who is it that I *can* marry?"

"Isn't it a little early . . . " began Father.

Mother intervened. "The boys who disgust you today will look far more interesting to you as you get older. Take that on faith, my dear Veya, because you won't believe *that* particular prophecy until it comes true. But when that wonderful day comes . . . "

"Dreadful day, you mean," muttered Father.

" . . . you can certainly cast your gaze on Padarok, for instance, because he's not related to anybody at all except his baby sister Dabrota and his parents, Zdorab and Shedemei."

That was the first time Chveya realized that Zdorab and Shedemei weren't kin to the others, but *now* she remembered that she had long disliked Padarok because he always referred to Grandmother and Grandfather as Rasa and Volemak, which seemed disrespectful; but it was *not* disrespectful at all, because they really *weren't* his grandmother or grandfather. Did everybody else understand this all along?

"And," added Father, "because there's only one Rokya to service the nubile young girls of Dostatok . . . "

"Nyef!" said Mother sharply.

". . . you'll have no choice but to also—how did you say it, my dear Waterseer?—oh yes, *cast your gaze* upon Protchnu or Nadezhny, because their mother, Eiadh, is no kin of anybody else here, and their father, Elemak, is only my half-brother. Likewise with Umene, whose father, Vas, is not kin of ours, and whose mother, Sevet, is only my half-sister."

Never mind about Proya and Nadya and Umya. "How can Sevet be only half your sister?" Chveya asked. "Is that because you have so many brothers that she can't be a whole sister to you?"

"Oh, this is a nightmare," said Mother. "Did it have to be this morning?"

Father, however, went ahead and explained about how Volemak had been married to two other women in Basilica, who gave birth to Elemak and Mebbekew, and then had married Rasa long enough to have Issib; and then Lady Rasa "didn't renew" the marriage and instead married a man named Gaballufix, who was also Elemak's half-brother because *his* mother had been one of Volemak's earlier wives, and it was with Gaballufix that Lady Rasa had given birth to Sevet and Kokor, and then she didn't renew *him* and returned to marry Volemak permanently and then they had Nafai and, more recently, Okya and Yaya.

"Did you understand that?"

Chveya could only give a stupefied nod. Her entire world had been turned upside down. Not just by the confusion of who was really kin to whom after all, but by the whole idea that the same people didn't have to stay married all their lives—that somebody's mother and father might end up being married to completely different people and have children who thought of only one of them as Mother and the other one as a complete stranger! It was terrifying, and that night she had a terrible dream in which giant rats came into their house and carried off Father in his sleep, and when Mother woke up she didn't even notice he was gone, she simply brought in little Proya—only full-sized now, because this was a dream—and said, "This is your new father, till the rats take *him*."

She woke up sobbing.

"What was the dream?" asked Mother, as she comforted her. "Tell me, Veya, why do you cry?"

So she told her.

Mother carried her into Father's and her room and woke Father and made Chveya tell *him* the dream, too. He didn't even seem interested in the most horrible thing, which was Proya coming into their house and taking his place. All he wanted to know about were the giant rats. He made her describe them again and again, even though she couldn't think of anything to say about them except that they were rats and they were very large and they seemed to be chuckling to each other about how clever they were as they carried Father away.

"Still," said Father, "it's the first time in the new generation. And not from the Oversoul, but from the Keeper."

"It might mean nothing," said Mother. "Maybe she heard of one of the other dreams."

But when they asked her whether she had heard stories of giant rats before this dream, Chveya had no idea of what they were talking about. The only rats she had heard about were the ones that were constantly trying to steal food from the barns. Did other people dream of giant rats, too? Adults were so strange—they thought nothing of families being torn apart and children having half-brothers and half-sisters and other monstrosities like that, but a dream of a giant rat, now, *that* was important to them. Father even said, "If you ever dream of giant rats again—or other strange animals—you must tell us at once. It can be very important."

It was only as Luet was covering her up again in bed that Chveya was able to ask about the question that was gnawing at *her*. "Mother, if you ever don't renew Father, who will be our new father then?"

Instantly a look of understanding and compassion came to Mother's face. "Oh, Veya, my dear little seamstress, is *that* what's worrying you? We left laws like that behind when we left Basilica. Marriages are forever here. Till we die. So Father will always be the father in our family, and I will always be the mother, and that's it. You can count on that."

Much reassured, Chveya settled down to sleep. She thought several thoughts as she was drifting off: How awful it must have been, to live in Basilica and never know who would be married to your parents from year to year—you might as well live in a house where the floor might be the ceiling tomorrow. And then: I am the first of the new generation to have a dream of giant rats, and somehow that is very wonderful so I must be very proud of myself and if I'd known that I would have dreamed about giant rats before. And then: Rokya is the boy who is no kin to anybody, and so he's the very best one to marry, and so I shall marry him and *that* will show Dazya who's the best.

Nafai and Luet got little sleep that night. Each had keyed in on a different aspect of Chveya's dream. To Luet, what mattered was that one of the children had finally shown some of the ability that the Oversoul had been selecting for. She knew it was vain of her, but she felt it appropriate that the firstborn of the waterseer should be the first to have a meaningful dream. She could hardly bear to wait until she could first take her daughter into the water of the river to see if she could learn to deliberately fall into the kind of sleep that brought true dreams, the way Luet had schooled herself to do.

To Nafai, on the other hand, what mattered was that after so long a silence, someone had received some kind of message at all. And the message, however vague it was, however tied to childish puzzlements, was nevertheless from the Keeper of Earth, which somehow made it more important than if it had come from the Oversoul.

After all, they had conversation with the Oversoul all the time, through the Index. The Index only allowed them access to the Oversoul's memory, however. It did not let them plumb the Oversoul's plans, to find out through the Index exactly what the Oversoul expected them to do this year or the next. For that they waited, as they had always waited, for the Oversoul to initiate things through dreams or a voice in their own minds. All these years in Dostatok, and the Oversoul had sent no dream, no voice, and the only message the Index had for them, beyond their own research into memory, was: Stay and wait.

But the Keeper of Earth was not tied to any plan or schedule of the Oversoul; it sent its dreams through the lightyears from Earth itself. It was impossible to guess what the Keeper's purpose was—the dreams it sent seemed to get tangled up in the concerns of the person having the dream, just as happened with Chveya's dream of the rats. Yet there were themes that kept recurring—hadn't Hushidh dreamed of rats also as enemies, attacking her family? This seemed to hint that somehow these large rats were going to be a problem to them on Earth—though there were also the dreams that showed the rats and angels of Earth linked with humans as friends and equals. It was so hard to make sense of all of it—but one thing was certain. The dreams from the Keeper of Earth had not stopped coming, and so perhaps something would happen soon, perhaps the next stage of their journey would begin.

For Nafai was growing impatient. Like all the others, he loved the way they lived at Dostatok, yet he could not forget that this was not the object of their journey. There was an unfinished task ahead of them, a journey through space to the planet where humankind originated, the return of humans for the first time after forty million years, and Nafai longed to go. Life in Dostatok was sweet, but it was also far too closed and neat. Things seemed to have *ended* here, and Nafai didn't like the feeling that somehow the future had been tied off, that there would be no more changes other than the predictable changes of growing older.

Oversoul, said Nafai silently, now that the Keeper of Earth has awakened again, will you also awaken? Will you also set us on the next stage of our journey?

Nafai was keenly aware of how different were his and Luet's responses to Chveya's dream. He was at once disdainful and envious of Luet's attitude. Disdainful, for she seemed to have let Dostatok become her whole world—what she cared most about was the children, and how this meant that they might also become visionaries, and most specifically how wonderful it was that their Chveya was the first to dream true dreams. How could this matter compared to the news that the Keeper of Earth was stirring again? And yet he envied her for very connectedness with their present life in Dostatok—he could not help but think that she was far happier than he, because her world *did* center around the children, the family, the community. I live in a larger world, but have little connection with it; she lives in a smaller one, but is able to change it and be changed by it far more than I.

I can't become as she is, nor can she become like me. Individual people have always been more important to her than to me. It's my weakness, that I don't have her awareness of other people's feelings. Perhaps, had I been as observant, as empathic as she, I would not have inadvertently said and done the things that made my older brothers hate me so much, and then our whole path through life might have been different, Elya and I might have been friends all along. Instead, even now when Elemak gives me respect as a hunter and listens to me in council, there is still no closeness between us, and Elemak is wary of me, watching for signs that I seek to displace him. Luet, on the other hand, seems to cause no envy among the other women. As Waterseer, she could just as easily be seen as a rival to Mother's dominance over the women as Elemak is the rival to Father's leadership, and I am the rival to Elemak, but instead there is no sense of competition at all. They are one. Why couldn't Elemak and I have been one, and Elemak and Father?

Perhaps there is something lacking in men, so that we can never join together and make one soul out of many. If so then it is a terrible loss. I look at Luet and see how close she is to the other women, even the ones she doesn't like all that well; I see how close she and the other women are to the children; and then I see how distant I am from the other men, and I feel so lonely.

With those thoughts Nafai finally slept, but only a few hours before dawn, and when he got out of bed he found Luet just as weary from undersleeping, stirring the morning porridge virtually in her sleep. "And there's no school today," Luet said, "so we have all the children and there's no hope of a nap."

"Let them play outside," said Nafai, "except the twins of course, and we can probably leave them with Shuya and then we can sleep."

"Or we could take turns ourselves, instead of imposing on them," said Luet.

"Take turns?" said Nafai. "How dull."

"I want to *sleep,*" said Luet. "Why is it that men are never so tired that they stop thinking about *that?*"

"Men who stop thinking about *that,* as you so sweetly call it, are either eunuchs or dead."

"We need to tell your parents about Chveya's dream," said Luet.

"We need to tell *everybody.*"

"I don't think so," said Luet. "It would cause too much jealousy."

"Oh, who but you will care about which child was first to have true dreams?" But he knew as he said it that *all* the parents would care, and that she was right about needing to avoid jealousy.

She made a face at him. "*You* are so completely above envy, O noble one, that it makes me envious."

"I'm sorry," he said.

"And besides," she said, "it wouldn't be good for Chveya if a big fuss were made about this. Look what happened to Dza when we made her birthday into a festival—she's really quite a bully with the other children, and it worries Shuya, and that public fuss only made her worse."

"There are times when I see her making the other children run meaningless errands for her that I want to slap her silly," said Nafai.

"But Lady Rasa says—"

"That children must be free to establish their own society, and deal with tyranny in their own way, I know," said Nafai. "But I can't help but wonder if she's right. After all, hers was an educational theory that thrived only in the womb of Basilica. Couldn't we see our own conflicts early on in our journeying as a result of exactly her attitude?"

"No, we couldn't," said Luet. "Particularly because the people who caused the *most* trouble were the ones who spent the *least* time being educated by Lady Rasa. Namely Elemak and Mebbekew, who left her school as soon as they came of age to decide for themselves, and Vas and Obring, who were never students of hers."

"Not so, my dear reductionist, since Zdorab is the best of us and *he* never studied with her, while Kokor and Sevet, her own daughters, are just as bad as the worst of the others."

"You only *prove* my point, since *they* went to Dhelembuvex's school and not your mother's at all. Zdorab is an exception to everything anyway."

At that point the twins, Serp and Spel, toddled into the kitchen, and frank adult conversation was over.

By the time they both got free enough to take a nap, the day's activities had wakened them so thoroughly that they didn't want to sleep. So they headed for Volemak's and Rasa's house to confer about the dream.

On the way they passed a group of older boys competing with their slings. They stopped and watched for a while, mostly to see how their own two older boys, Zhatva and Motiga, were doing. The boys saw them watching, of course, and immediately set out to impress their parents—but it wasn't their prowess with the sling and stones that most interested Luet and Nafai, it was how they were with the other boys. Motiga, of course, was an incessant tease—he was keenly aware of being younger than the other boys and his silly pranks and clowning were his strategy for trying to ingratiate his way into the inner circle. Zhatva, however, being older, was there by right, and what worried his parents was how pliant he was—how he seemed to worship Proya, a strutting cock-of-the-walk who didn't deserve so much of Zhatva's respect.

A typical moment—Xodhya got hit in the arm by Motya's careless swinging of his loaded sling. His eyes immediately filled with tears, and Proya taunted him. "You'll never be a man, Xodhya! You'll always just be coming near!" That was a play on his name, of course, and a rather clever one—but also cruel, and it did nothing but add to Xodhya's misery. Then, without any of the boys being particularly aware of it, Xodhya turned in his misery to Zhyat, who offhandedly threw his arm around Xodhya's shoulder as he barked at his little brother Motya, "Be careful with your sling, monkey brains!"

It was a simple, instinctive thing, but Luet and Nafai smiled at each other when they saw it. Not only did Zhatva offer physical comfort to Xodhya, without a hint of condescension, but also he drew attention away from Xodhya's pain and incipient tears and threw the blame where it rightly belonged, on Motya's carelessness. It was done easily and gracefully, without giving the slightest challenge to Proya's authority among the boys.

"When will Zhyat see that *he's* the one the other boys turn to when they're in trouble?" asked Nafai.

"Maybe he fills that role so well because he *doesn't* know that he's filling it."

"I envy him," said Nafai. "If only I could have done that."

"Oh? And why couldn't you?"

"You know *me,* Luet. I would have been yelling at Protchnu that it wasn't fair for him to tease Xodhya because it was Motya's fault and if it had happened to Protchnu he'd be crying too."

"All true, of course."

"All true, but it would have made Protchnu my enemy," said Nafai. He hardly needed to point out the consequence of *that*. Hadn't Luet lived through it with him often enough?

"All that matters to me is that our Zhatva has the love of the other boys, and he deserves it," said Luet.

"If only Motya could learn from him."

"Motya's still a baby," said Luet, "and we don't know what he'll be except that it'll be something loud and noticeable and underfoot. The one that I wish could learn from Zhatva is Chveya."

"Yes, well, each child is different," said Nafai. He turned and led Luet away from the stone-slinging and on toward Father and Mother's house. But he well understood Luet's wish: Chveya's loneliness and isolation from the other children was such a worry to them both—she was the only complete misfit among all the older children, and they didn't understand why, because she did nothing to antagonize the others, really. She simply didn't have a place in their childish hierarchies. Or perhaps she had one, but refused to take it. How ironic, thought Nafai—we worry because Zhatva fits in *too* well in a subservient role, and then we worry because Chveya refuses to accept a subservient role. Maybe what we really want is for our children to be the dominant ones! Maybe I'm trying to see my own ambitions fulfilled in them, and that would be wrong, so I should be content with what they are.

Luet must have been thinking along the same lines, because she said, out of the silence between them, "They're both finding their own paths through the thickets of human society, and well enough. All we can really do is observe and comfort and, now and then, give a hint."

Or turn bossy little Queen Dza upside down and shake her until her arrogance falls out. But no, that would only cause a quarrel between families—and the last family that they would ever quarrel with would be Shuya's and Issya's.

Volemak and Rasa listened with interest to their tale of Chveya's dream. "I've wondered, from time to time, when the Oversoul would act again," said Father, "but I'll confess that I haven't been asking, because it's been so good here that I didn't want to do anything to hasten our departure."

"Not that anything we might do *could* hasten our departure," said Mother. "After all, the Oversoul has her own schedule to keep, and it has little to do with us. She never cared whether we spent these years at that first miserable desert valley, or that much better place between the North and South rivers, or here, which is quite possibly the most perfect spot on Harmony. All she cared about was getting us together and ready for when she needs us. For all we know, it's the children she plans to take on the voyage to Earth, and not us at all. And that would suit me well enough, though I'd really prefer it if she took the great-grandchildren, long after we're all dead, so we'll never have to see them go and break our hearts missing the voyagers."

"It's how we all feel sometimes," said Luet.

Nafai held his tongue.

It didn't matter. Father saw right through him. "All but Nafai. He's ready for a change. You're a cripple, Nyef. You can't stand happiness for very long—it's conflict and uncertainty that bring you to life."

"I don't like conflict, Father," protested Nafai.

"You may not *like* it, but you thrive on it," said Volemak. "It's not an insult, son, it's just a fact."

"The question is," said Rasa, "do we *do* anything because of Chveya's dream?"

"No," said Luet hastily. "Not a thing. We just wanted you to know."

"Still," said Father, "what if some of the other children are having dreams from the Keeper but haven't told anybody about them? Perhaps we should alert all the parents to listen to their children's dream tales."

"Put the word out like that," said Rasa, "and you know that Kokor and Dol will start coaching their daughters on what dreams they ought to have, and get nasty with them if they don't come up with good giant rat dreams."

They all laughed, but they knew it was true.

"So we'll do nothing for now," said Father. "Just wait and see. The Oversoul will act when it's time for him to act, and till then we'll work hard when there's work to be done, and in the meantime try to raise perfect children who never quarrel."

"Oh, is that the standard of success?" asked Luet, teasingly. "The ones who never quarrel are the good ones?"

Rasa laughed wryly. "If that's the case, the only good children are the ones who have no spine at all."

"Which means no descendent of yours, my love," said Father.

The visit ended; they returned home and went on with the day's work. But Nafai was not content to wait and see. It troubled him that there had been so few visions, and that now the only one to receive anything from the Keeper was Chveya, and her the loneliest child, and too young to make real sense of her own dream.

Why *was* the Oversoul delaying so long? It had been in quite a hurry to get them out of Basilica nine years ago. They had given up everything they had ever expected their lives to bring them, and plunged into the desert. Yes, things had turned out rather well in the end, but it *wasn't* the end, was it? There were more than a hundred lightyears ahead of them, the part of their journey they had completed so far was nothing, and there was no sign of resuming it.

Answer me!

But there was no answer.

* * *

It took another dream to stir Nafai to action. It was Luet this time; Nafai woke from a sound sleep to find her whimpering, moaning, then crying out. He shook her awake, speaking soothingly to her so she would be calmed as she emerged from her dream. "A nightmare," he said. "You're having a nightmare."

"The Oversoul," she said. "She's lost. She's lost."

"Luet, wake up. You're having a dream."

"I *am* awake now," she said. "I'm trying to tell you the dream."

"You dreamed about the Oversoul?"

"I saw myself in the dream. Only young—Chveya's age. The way I used to see myself in dreams."

It occurred to Nafai that it hadn't been all *that* long since Luet *was* Chveya's age. She had been a child when he met and married her, barely in her teens. So when she saw herself as a child, how different could it be from how she saw herself now? "So you saw yourself as a child," said Nafai.

"No—I saw a person who *looked* like me, but I thought, This is the waterseer. And then I thought, No, this is the Oversoul, wearing the face and body of the waterseer. Which is what many women believed about me, you know."

"Yes, I know that," said Nafai.

"And then I knew that I was seeing the Oversoul, only she was wearing my face. And she was searching, desperately. Searching for something, and she kept thinking she had found it, only then she looked in her hands and she didn't have it. And then I realized that what she was chasing, around and around, was a giant rat, and then as she caught it and embraced it, it turned into an angel and flew away. Only she hadn't noticed the transformation and so she thought the rat had slipped away. I think the reason we're waiting here is that the Oversoul is confused about something. Searching for something."

But Nafai's thoughts had hung up on the fact that there were rats and angels in her dream. "This is a dream from the Keeper?" asked Nafai. "But how could the Keeper have known a hundred years ago that the Oversoul would be having trouble *now?*"

"It's only our *guess* that the dreams we've had from the Keeper are traveling at lightspeed," said Luet. "Perhaps the Keeper knows more than we're giving her credit for."

It grated on Nafai's nerves when the women who knew about the Keeper at all simply assumed that it would be a female, as they imagined the Oversoul to be. Somehow it seemed all right with the Oversoul, but faintly arrogant with the Keeper. Perhaps just because Nafai knew the Oversoul was a computer, but had no idea what the Keeper of Earth might be. If it really *was* a god, or something like a god, he resented the thought that it *had* to be female.

"Perhaps the Keeper is watching us and knows us very well, and is trying to wake us up—and through us wake up the Oversoul."

"The Oversoul isn't asleep," said Nafai. "We talk to it all the time through the Index."

"I tell you what I saw in my dream," said Luet.

"Then in the morning let's go and talk to Issib and Zdorab and see what they can get out of the Index about it."

"Now," said Luet. "Let's go now."

"Wake them in the middle of the night? They have children, that would be irresponsible."

"In the middle of the night there won't be interruptions," said Luet. "And it's almost dawn."

It was true; the first light was brightening the sky outside their parchment-glazed window.

Zdorab woke instantly, coming to open the door even before Nafai and Luet reached it. Shedemei appeared in a moment, and after a few whispered words she left to go summon Issib and Hushidh. They gathered then at the house where the Index was kept. Luet told them all her dream, and Zdorab and Issib at once began searching through the Index, trying to find answers.

Luet grew impatient first, as they waited in silence. "I'm useless here for now," she said. "And the children will want me."

"Me too," said Hushidh, and Shedemei reluctantly left with them, each returning to her house. Nafai knew that when it came to searching the Index, he wasn't much use, either—it was Issib and Zdorab who had made exploration of the Oversoul's memory their life's work, and he couldn't compete with them. He knew that the women would resent his tacit assumption that he could stay and Luet needed to leave . . . but he also knew that it was true. The children's routines revolved around Luet, who was always there, while Nafai was so often gone on hunting expeditions that his presence or absence barely made a difference in their lives. Not that they didn't *care* whether he was there or not—they cared a great deal—but it didn't change the normal events of their day.

So Nafai stayed in the Index House as Zodya and Issya asked it questions. He heard their murmuring, and now and then one would ask him a question, but he was truly useless to them.

He reached out his hand across the table and rested the back of his fingers against the Index. "You're looping, aren't you," he said.

"Yes," said the Index. "I realized that as soon as Luet had her dream from the Keeper. Issib and Zdorab are already working to find the loop."

"It must be in your primitive routines," said Nafai, "because you could find it and program your way out of it if it were your own self-programming."

"Yes," said the Index again. "Zdorab assumed that at once, and that's where we're exploring."

"It must be a loop where you think you've found something only you haven't really," said Nafai, remembering the dream.

"Yes," said the Index. It couldn't be sounding impatient, could it? "Issib insisted on that from the start, so we're trying to find something that I can't detect myself. It's very hard to search my memory to find what I haven't detected."

Nafai realized that all his thoughts were doing nothing but following far behind Zdorab and Issib, and so he sighed and took his hand away from the Index, sat back in the chair, and waited. He loathed being a spectator at important events. It's what Elemak has so often said about me, Nafai told himself nastily. I have to make myself the hero of every story I take part in. What was it he said that time? That someday if he didn't stop me I'd find a way to be the protagonist of Elemak's own autobiography. Thus I fancy myself to be vital to the process of discovering what has the Oversoul going in circles, wasting its time, wasting our time . . .

Wasting our time? This is a *waste* of time, to live in peace and plenty with my wife and children? May I waste the rest of my life, then.

Like a hunt, around in circles, the poor Oversoul is tying itself up in knots, covering the same ground without realizing it.

And as he thought this, Nafai envisioned the path he took on his most recent hunt as if he were above the ground, looking down at it like a map, seeing his own path drawn out among the trees, watching as he went in twisting, interlocking circles, but never quite passed the same tree from the same direction so he never guessed it *except* by seeing the map.

That's what the Oversoul needs to do—see its own tracks.

He reached out and touched the Index and said so to the Oversoul.

"Yes," said the Index—still maddeningly unreproachful. "Zdorab already suggested that I look through my recent history to find repetitive behavior. But I don't track my own behavior. Only human behavior. I have no autobiography stored here, except insofar as my actions impinge on humanity. And apparently whatever I'm doing that has me in a loop has no direct effect on humanity—or is so primitive that I'm unaware of it. Either way, I can't retrace my own steps."

Stymied again, Nafai didn't take his hand away. It might be too disturbing to the others, to keep touching the Index and then removing his hand.

Disturbing? No. He simply didn't want the embarrassment

of having them know that *again* his would-be contribution was futile.

He was still sleepy. Luet's dream had woken him too early, and sitting here now, with nothing to do, he began to doze. He laid his head down on the table, resting on his other arm; still his fingers touched the Index.

He went back to that image of himself seen from above, a map being traced behind him as he hunted in circles through the woods. Maybe I really do that, he thought, drifting on the edge of sleep. Maybe I really move in circles.

"No you don't," said the Index. "Except when the animal you're tracking moved that way."

I might, said Nafai silently. I might drift around and around in large circles, casting for the tracks of some beast, never realizing that I'm seeing my own tracks. Maybe sometimes I hunt myself. Maybe I find my own tracks and think, what an exceptionally large beast, this will feed us for a week, and then I track myself and track myself and never catch up until one day I come upon my own body, lying there exhausted and starving, *dying* so that in my madness I now imagine myself detached from my body and . . .

I was dozing, he said silently.

"Here's the map of all your journeys," said the Index. "You'll see that you never make circles, except when tracking a beast."

Nafai saw in his mind a clear map of the land all around Dostatok, clear up to the mountains and beyond, showing all his journeys.

I've really covered this territory, haven't I, said Nafai silently.

But even as he said it, he saw it wasn't true. There was an area where none of his hunts had ever taken him. A sort of wedge right up among the mountains, tending toward the desert side of them, where none of his paths went.

Do you have a map of the others' hunting trips? asked Nafai.

Almost at once, a map that he "knew" was Elemak's hunts was superimposed on his own, and then a map of Vas's and

Obring's hunts, and the group hunts. They interlocked until they formed a tight net all around Dostatok.

Except for that wedge in the mountains.

What's in that place in the mountains, where none of our paths meet?

"What are you talking about?" asked the Index.

The gap in the maps. The place where no one has been.

"There *is* no gap," said the Index.

Nafai focused on the spot, giving it all its attention. There! he shouted inside his mind.

"You speak to me as if you were pointing, and I can see you giving great attention to something, yet there is no point on the map that you're singling out above any other."

Could there be something here that is hidden even from yourself?

"Nothing on Harmony is hidden from me."

Why did you bring us to Dostatok?

"Because I've prepared this place for you to wait until I'm ready."

Ready for what?

"For you to carry me on the voyage to Earth."

And why should we have come *here* to wait?

"Because this is the nearest place where you could sustain your lives until I'm ready."

The nearest place to what?

"To yourselves. To where you are."

This was getting circular again, Nafai could see. He tried a different tack. When will you be ready for us to carry you to Earth? Nafai asked.

"When I call you forth," said the Index.

Call us forth from where, to where?

"From Dostatok," said the Index.

To where?

"To Earth," said the Index.

To Nafai it was clear—the empty place on the map, which

the Index could not see, was also the place where they would gather to leave for Earth—again, a place that the Index could not name.

"I can name any place on Harmony," said the Index. "I can report to you any name that any human has ever given to any spot on this planet."

Then tell me the name of *this* place? asked Nafai, again focusing on the gap in the hunting maps.

"Point to a place and I'll tell you."

On a whim, Nafai mentally drew a circle all around the gap in the paths.

"Vusadka," said the Index.

Vusadka, thought Nafai. An ancient-sounding name. But not dissimilar to the word for a single step just outside a door. He asked the Index: What does Vusadka mean?

"It's the name of this place."

How long has it had this name? asked Nafai.

"It was called this by the people of Raspyatny."

And where did they learn this name?

"It was well known among the Cities of the Stars and the Cities of Fire."

What is the oldest reference to this name?

"What name?" asked the Index.

The Oversoul could not have forgotten already. So he must have run into the block in its memory again. Nafai asked: When is the oldest reference to this name in the Cities of Fire?

"Twenty million years ago," said the Index.

Is there an older reference in the Cities of the Stars?

"Of course—they're much older, too. Thirty-nine million years ago."

Did Vusadka have a meaning in the language they spoke then?

"The languages of Harmony are all related," said the Index.

Again it was being non-responsive. Nafai tried another circling approach that might bring him the information he needed:

What is the word in the language of the Cities of the Stars thirty-nine million years ago that most closely resembles Vusadka without *being* Vusadka?

"Vuissashivat'h," answered the Index.

And what did that word mean, to them?

"To disembark."

From what?

"From a boat," said the Index.

But why would this place in the mountains be given a name that is related to a verb meaning to disembark from a boat? Was there once a shoreline that touched here?

"These are very ancient mountains—before the rift that created the Valley of Fires, these mountains were already old."

So there was never a shoreline that touched this land of Vusadka?

"Never," said the Index. "Not since humans disembarked from their starships on the world of Harmony."

Because it used the modern word *disembark* in reference to the original starships, Nafai knew at once that the Oversoul had done its best to confirm what he already had surmised: that Vusadka was the very place where the starships had landed forty million years ago, and therefore the very place where, if there were any possibility of a starship still existing, it would most likely be.

And another thought: *You* are there, aren't you, Oversoul? Where the starships landed, that's where *you* are. All your memories, all your processors, all are centered on this very place.

"What place?" asked the Index.

Nafai stood up, fully awake now. The scraping of his stool across the wooden floor brought the others out of their reveries. "I'm going to find the Oversoul," Nafai said to them.

"Yes," said Issib. "The Oversoul showed us its conversation with you."

"Very deftly done," said Zdorab. "I would never have thought of starting with the map of the hunting trips."

Nafai almost didn't tell them that he hadn't done that deliberately; it felt good to be thought clever. But he realized that if he let them continue to think this about him, it would be a kind of lie. "I was just dozing," said Nafai. "The hunting trip thing was just a mad idea on the edges of a dream. The Oversoul knew that it could not know that it knew, and it recognized that through the map it could communicate with me, that's all. It had to fool itself into telling me."

Issib laughed. "All right, then, Nyef," he said. "We'll agree that you really aren't very bright at all."

"That's right," said Nafai. "All I did was hear it when the Oversoul found an oblique way to call me past barriers in its own mind. Tell the others that I've gone hunting, if anyone asks. But to Luet and your wives, of course, you can tell the truth—I'm off searching for the Oversoul. Both statements are true."

Zdorab nodded wisely. "We've had peace here all these years," he said, "because this was a good land and there was room for us all and plenty to share. No one will be glad to think of uprooting ourselves again. Some will be less glad than others—it's just as well to postpone telling them until we actually know something."

Issib grimaced. "I can imagine a *real* battle over this one. I almost wish we hadn't had so long a time of happiness here. This will divide the community and I can't begin to guess what damage might be done before it's through."

Nafai shook his head. "It doesn't have to be that way," he said. "The Oversoul brought all of us on this journey. The Keeper of Earth is calling to all of us as well."

"All are called," said Zdorab, "but who will come?"

"At this moment," said Nafai, "I will *go*."

"Remember to take a bow and arrows, then," said Issib. "Just in case you find supper for us on the way." He didn't say: So that our story of your having gone hunting will be believed.

It was a good idea in any event, so Nafai stopped by his house to get the bow and arrows.

"And if you hadn't needed those," said Luet, "you wouldn't

have stopped by and bid me farewell or explained anything at all, would you?" She sounded quite annoyed.

"Of course I would," said Nafai.

"No," she said. "You probably already asked the other two to let me know where you had gone."

Nafai shrugged. "Either way, I made sure you'd know."

"And yet it was *my* dream, and Chveya's," she said.

"Because *you* had the dreams, *you* own the outcome of it?" he asked, getting just as annoyed as she was.

"No, Nyef," she said, sighing impatiently. "Because I had the dream today, I should have been your partner in this. Your fair and equal partner. Instead you treat me like a child."

"I didn't ask them to tell *Chveya,* did I? So I hardly treated you like a child, I think."

"Can't you just admit you acted like a baboon, Nafai?" asked Luet. "Can't you just say that you treated me as if only men mattered in our community, as if women were nothing, and you're *sorry* you treated me that way?"

"I didn't act like a baboon," said Nafai. "I acted like a human male. When I act like a human male it doesn't make me any less *human,* it just makes me less *female.* Don't you ever tell me again that because I don't act like a woman wants me to act, that makes me an animal."

Nafai was surprised by the anger in his own voice.

"So it comes to this in our own house, too," said Luet softly.

"Only because you brought it to this," said Nafai. "Don't ever call me an animal again."

"Then don't act like one," said Luet. "Being civilized means transcending your own animal nature. Not indulging it, not glorying in it. *That's* how you remind me of a male baboon—because you can't be civilized as long as you treat women like something to be bullied. You can only be civilized when you treat us like friends."

Nafai stood there in the doorway, burning inside with the unfairness of what she was saying. Not because she wasn't speaking the truth, but because she was wrong to apply it to *him* this way. "I *did* treat you as my friend, and as my wife," said Nafai. "I assumed that you loved me enough that we weren't competing to see who *owns* the dreams."

"I wasn't angry because you appropriated the results of my dream," said Luet.

"Oh?"

"I was hurt because you didn't share the results of *your* dream with *me*. I didn't jump up from bed and go tell Hushidh and Shedemei my dream, and then ask them to tell you about it later."

Only when she put it that way did he understand why she was so upset. "Oh," he said. "I'm sorry."

She was still angry, and his apology was too little too late. "Go," said Luet. "Go and find the Oversoul. Go and find the ruins of the ancient starships in the ancient landing place. Go and be the sole hero of our expedition. When I go to sleep tonight, I'll expect to find you starring in my own dreams. I hope you have a tiny role in mind for *me* to play. Perhaps holding your coat."

Almost Nafai let her words hurl him out the door. She had as much as repeated Elemak's insult to him—and she *knew* how much Elemak's words had hurt him because he had confided it to her long ago. It was cruel and unfair of her to say it now. She of all people should have known that it wasn't his desire to be a hero that impelled him now, it was his passion to find out what would happen next, to *make* the next thing happen. She, if she loved him, should have understood. So he almost left right then, letting her bitter words travel with him all the way up into the mountains.

Instead he strode into the children's room. They were still asleep, except for Chveya, who perhaps had been wakened by their low-key but intense quarreling. Nafai kissed each one, Chveya last. "I'm going to find the place where the best dreams come from," he whispered, so as not to wake the other children.

"Save room in all the dreams for me," she whispered back.

He kissed her again and then returned to the kitchen, which was the main room of the house, where Luet was stirring the porridge in the pot by the fire.

"Thank you for finding room for me in your dreams," he said to her. "You're always welcome in mine, too." Then he kissed her, and to his relief she kissed him back. They had resolved nothing except to reaffirm that even when they were angry at each other, they still loved each other. That was enough to send him on his way content instead of brooding.

He would need to have his heart at peace, because it was obvious that the Oversoul was protecting the hidden place without even knowing that it was doing so. At least, so he surmised, for *something* must have turned them all aside whenever they were hunting, keeping them from going to Vusadka, and it was certainly the Oversoul's talent for making people forget ideas it didn't want them to act on. Yet the Oversoul hadn't been able to see that place itself, or even see that it could not see it. This certainly meant that the Oversoul's own deflection routines must have been turned against the Oversoul itself, so it wasn't likely that the Oversoul would be able to turn them off and let Nafai pass. On the contrary—Nafai would have to fight his way through, as he and Issib had fought their way past the Oversoul's barriers back in Basilica so long ago, fighting to think thoughts that the Oversoul had forbidden. Only now it wasn't just ideas that he had to struggle to think of. It was a place where he had to struggle to go. A place that even the Oversoul couldn't see.

"I must overcome you," he whispered to the Oversoul, as he walked across the meadows north of the houses. "I must get past your barriers."

⟨What barriers?⟩

This was going to be so hard. It made Nafai tired just to think of it. And there'd be no clever trick to get around it, either. He would just have to bull his way through by brute force of will. If he could. If he was strong enough.

* * *

It was dusk, and Nafai was near despair. After a day's travel just to get here, he had spent this whole day doing the same useless things, over and over. He would stand outside the forbidden zone and ask the Oversoul to show him the map of all the paths taken by all the hunters, and easily see which direction he needed to travel in order to reach Vusadka. He would even scratch an arrow or write the direction in the dirt with a stick. And then, after setting boldly forth, he would soon find himself back outside the "hidden" area, a hundred meters from where he had written the direction. If he had written "northeast," he would find himself due west of the writing; if his arrow pointed toward the east, he would find himself south of it. He simply couldn't get past the barrier.

He railed against the Oversoul, but the answers he got showed the Oversoul to be oblivious to what was going on. "I want to go southeast from this spot," he would say. "Help me." And then he would find himself far to the north and the Oversoul would say, in his mind, You didn't listen to me. I told you to go southwest, and you didn't listen.

Now the sun was down and the sky was darkening fast. He hated the idea of returning to Dostatok tomorrow, a complete failure.

⟨I don't understand what you're trying to do.⟩

"I'm trying to find you," said Nafai.

⟨But here I am.⟩

"I know where you are. But I can't get to you."

⟨I'm not stopping you.⟩

It was true, Nafai knew it. The Oversoul might not even be doing this. If the Oversoul could be given the power to block human minds, to turn humans away from actions they were planning, then couldn't the first humans on Harmony have set up another set of defenses to protect this place? Defenses not under the Oversoul's control—indeed, defenses that warded away the Oversoul itself?

Show me all the paths I've taken today, said Nafai silently. Make me see them here on the ground.

He saw them—faint shimmerings, which coalesced into threads on the ground. He saw how they began, time after time, heading straight toward the center of the circle around Vusadka. Then they stopped cold, every one of them, and began again not very far to the north or south, obliquely coasting along the borderline.

That really struck him—how precise the border was. He must be penetrating no more than a meter or so inside it before he was turned away. In fact, he could draw a line on the ground marking the exact border of the Oversoul's vision. And because he could, he did. He used the last half-hour of light to mark the border with a stick, scratching a line or digging a shallow trench several hundred meters.

As he marked the border of his futility, he could hear the hooting of baboons in the near distance, calling sleepily to each other as they headed for their sleeping cliffs. It was only when he was done, when full darkness had descended and the baboons were quiet again, that he realized that while some of their calls had begun outside the border, clearly they all ended up within it.

Of course. The border is impervious to humans, but other animals have not been altered to be susceptible to this kind of fending. So the baboons cross the boundary with impunity.

If only I were a baboon.

He could almost hear Issib say, quietly, "And you're sure that you're not?"

He found a grassy place on highish ground and curled up to sleep. It was a clear night, with little chance of rain, and though it cooled off more here than it did back near Dostatok—he was near the desert, and the air was noticeably drier—he would be comfortable tonight.

Comfortable, but it would still be hard to sleep.

He dreamed, of course, but couldn't be sure if the dream had meaning or was simply the result of his sleeping lightly and so remembering more of the normal dreams of the night. But in one of the dreams, at least, he saw himself with Yobar.

In the dream Yobar was leading him through a maze of rock. When they came to a tiny hole in the rocks, Yobar ducked down easily and climbed through. But Nafai stood there looking at the hole, thinking, I'm not small enough to fit through there. Of course, this was not true—Nafai could see it, even in the dream, the hole was not that small. Yet he couldn't seem to think of squatting down and squirming through. He kept looking for a way to get through while standing upright.

Yobar came back through the hole and touched him by the hand. And when he did, Nafai suddenly shrank down and became a baboon. Then he had no trouble at all getting through the hole. Once he was on the other side, he turned back to human size immediately. And when he turned around to look at the tiny hole, it had changed—it was now as tall as an adult human, and he could pass through standing up.

In the morning, that was the dream that showed the most promise of being worthwhile. He lay, shivering now and then in the predawn breeze, trying to think of some way to use some insight from the dream. Clearly the dream was reflecting his knowledge that the baboons could pass easily through the barrier, while he, a human, could not. Clearly if he turned into a baboon he could cross the barrier too. But that was exactly what he had wished for the night before, and wishing wasn't likely to make anything useful happen.

In the dream, thought Nafai, the hole seemed to be too small for me to get through. But I *could* have got through it easily at any time, because it was really as tall as a man. The barrier was only in my mind—which is true of this barrier as well. The more firmly I try to cross the barrier, the more firmly I'm rejected. Well, maybe it's the *intention* to cross the boundary that pushes me away.

No, that's foolish. The barrier must surely have been designed to fend away even people who were completely unaware of the boundary. Wandering hunters, explorers, settlers, merchants—whoever might inadvertently head toward Vusadka—the barrier would turn them away.

But then, it would take only the mildest of suggestions to turn away someone who had no firm intention of heading toward Vusadka—they wouldn't even notice they were being turned. After all, did any of us ever notice that we were avoiding that area on all our hunting trips during all these years in Dostatok? So those original paths didn't define a sharp, clear border the way that I'm defining it *now*. And our paths didn't turn all that sharply . . . we just lost track of our prey, or for some other reason turned gradually away. So the *force* the barrier uses must increase with my firm intention to cross it. And if I somehow were able just to *wander* through here, the barrier's strength might be much weaker.

Yet how can I casually and accidentally wander where I know full well that I *must* go?

With that thought, his plan came to him full-blown; yet he also hardly dared to think it clearly, lest it trigger the barrier and fail before he tried it. Instead, he began to focus on a whole new intention. He must hunt now, and bring prey to feed the children. He himself was certainly hungry, and if he was hungry then the young ones must be famished. Only the young ones he thought of feeding were the young baboons. He remembered the baboons of the Valley of Mebbekew and felt himself responsible for bringing them meat—as Yobar had scavenged food, to please the females and strengthen the young.

So he set out in any direction that morning, not particularly orienting himself toward Vusadka, and searched until he found the pellets of a hare. Then he stalked his prey until, within the hour, he was able to put an arrow through it.

It wasn't dead, of course—arrows rarely killed immediately, and he usually finished the animal off with his knife. But this time he left it alive, terrified and whimpering; he drew the arrow from its haunch and carried it by the ears. The sounds it made were exactly what he needed—the baboons would be much more interested in a living but injured animal. He had to find the baboons.

It wasn't hard—baboons fear few animals, and defend themselves from *those* by being alert and giving good warning to each other. So they made no effort to be quiet. Nafai found them foraging in a long valley that stretched from west to east, with a stream flowing down the middle. They looked up when they saw him. There was no panic—he was still a safe distance away—and they looked at the hare with great curiosity.

Nafai moved closer. Now they became alert—the males stood on their foreknuckles and complained a little about his approach. And Nafai felt a great reluctance to come nearer to them.

But I *must* come nearer, to give them meat.

So he took a few more steps toward them, holding the hare out in front of him. He wasn't sure how they'd take this offering, of course. They might take it as proof that he was a killer, or perhaps as a suggestion that he already *had* his prey and so they were safe. But some of them had to be thinking of the hare as meat that they could eat. Baboons weren't the world's best hunters, but they loved meat, and this bleating hare had to look like a good meal to them.

He approached slowly, feeling more reluctance with every step. Yet he also saw that more and more of them—especially the juvenile males—were looking from him to the hare. He helped them think more of the meat by averting his own gaze whenever they looked at him—he knew it would only challenge and frighten them if he made eye contact.

They backed away from him, but not far. As he had expected, their natural tendency was to retreat toward their sleeping cliffs. He followed them. He kept thinking. This is not a good idea. They don't need this meat. But he shouted down the thoughts, trying to focus on one thing: These mothers need the protein, their babies need to have it from their milk. I've got to get this meat to them.

You can't, this is stupid, you should drop the hare and then retreat.

But if I do, then the hare will go to the strongest males and not to the females at all. Somehow I've got to get this nearer to *them,* so it can benefit the young ones. That's my *job,* as the hunter for this tribe, to bring them food. I've got to feed them. I can't let anything stop me from reaching them.

How long did it take him? It was so hard to keep his mind on what he was doing. Several times he felt as though he had just wakened, though he knew he had not been asleep, and then he shook himself and pushed on, relentlessly heading toward the females, who increasingly arrayed themselves toward the sleeping cliffs.

I have to get behind them, closer to the sleeping cliffs than they are, he thought. I've got to get on the side where the females are.

He began to sidle northward, but he never let his attention waver from the females. And, around noon, he finally found himself where he wanted to be—between the baboons and their sleeping cliffs. The hare had finally fallen silent—but the baboons wouldn't be bothered by the fact that it had already died, since it was alive when it arrived, and besides, they weren't all *that* fussy, if the meat was warm. So Nafai tossed the hare toward them, aiming for the center of the group of females.

Pandemonium broke out, but things went about as Nafai had planned. Some of the juvenile males made a play for the hare, but the older males stood their ground against Nafai himself, for he seemed, at least momentarily, to be a threat. Thus the hare was back among the females, who easily brushed away the juveniles. The hare hadn't been dead after all—it squealed again as the dominant females tore into it, devouring whatever they could get their teeth into. The fact that baboons didn't bother with killing their prey before eating it had bothered Nafai when he first lived in close proximity to baboons back in the desert, but he was used to it now, and was delighted that his plan had worked and the females had got to the meat first.

As the males began to realize that they were missing out on the treat, they grew more and more agitated, and at last Nafai began to back away, closer and closer to the sleeping cliffs;

when he was finally far enough away, the males charged into the group, scattering females and pummeling each other in their struggle for scraps of hare. Some of them did indeed come away with big pieces, but Nafai knew that the females had got more than their usual share of the meat. That made him feel good.

Now, though, it would be best for him to get as far from the baboons as possible. A *long* way away, up this valley. In fact, it wouldn't hurt if he found more prey up here, to bring back to them.

Gradually, though, as he headed farther and farther away from the baboons, he realized that his reluctance was getting easier and easier to fight off. Daringly, he let himself remember his real purpose in coming here. At once his reluctance to proceed returned—it became almost a panic inside him—but he did not lose control of himself. As he had hoped, the barrier was strongest at the borderline. He could overcome *this* level of interference—it was more like what he had felt back in Basilica, when he and Issib were first trying to push past the Oversoul's barriers and think about forbidden things.

Or maybe I'm feeling easier about it because the barrier has *already* pushed me away toward the border—maybe without realizing it I've been defeated.

"Am I outside or inside?" he whispered to the Oversoul.

No answer came at all.

He felt a thrill of fear. The Oversoul couldn't see this area itself—what if, when he crossed the border, he simply *disappeared* from the Oversoul's sight?

Then it occurred to him that this could be precisely why the force of the resistance might be weaker now. Maybe, without the Oversoul realizing it, this barrier had combined its own strength with the Oversoul's power—at the border. But in here, where the Oversoul itself could not penetrate, the barrier had only its own aversive power to draw on, and that's why it was defeatable.

It made sense to Nafai, and so he continued to head eastward, toward the center of Vusadka.

Or had he been heading north? For suddenly, as he crested a hill, he saw a completely barren landscape before him. Not fifty yards away, it was as if someone had built an invisible wall. On one side was the verdance of the land of Dostatok, and on the other side was stark desert—the driest, most lifeless desert Nafai had ever seen. Not a bird, not a lizard, not a weed, *nothing* with life in it was beyond the line.

It was too artificial. It had to be a sign of another kind of barrier, another borderline, one that excluded all living things. Perhaps it was a barrier that *killed* anything that crossed it. Was Nafai expected to cross this?

"Is there a gateway somewhere?" he asked the Oversoul.

No answer came.

Carefully he approached the barrier. When he was near enough, he reached out a hand toward it.

Invisible it might be, but it was tangible—he could press his hand against it, and feel it sliding under his hand, as if it were faintly slimy and constantly in motion. In a way, though, the very tangibility of it was reassuring—if it kept living things out by blocking their passage, then perhaps it didn't have any mechanism for killing them.

Can I cross? If humans *can't* cross this boundary, then why bother to have the mental barrier so far back? True, it might be simply a way of preventing humans from seeing this clear borderline and making a famous legend out of it, attracting undue attention to this place. But it was just as possible, as far as Nafai knew, that the barrier of aversion was designed to keep humans away because a determined human being *could* cross this physical barrier. One barrier for humans, farther out; and another barrier for animals. It made sense.

Of course, there was no guarantee that just because something made sense to Nafai it would therefore have any relation to reality. For a moment he even thought of returning to Dostatok and telling them what he had discovered so far, so they could explore the Index and find out if there was some clever way to cross the barrier.

As far as Nafai knew, however, the very thought of returning to Dostatok might be a sign of the barrier working within his mind, trying to get him to find excuses to go away. And maybe the barrier had some kind of intelligence and was able to learn, in which case it might never be fooled again by his device of concentrating on his urgent need to feed the baboons rather than his *real* purpose of getting past the barrier. No, alone as he was, it was up to him to make a decision.

It will kill you.

What was that, the Oversoul talking in his mind? Or the barrier? Or just his own fear? Whatever the source, he knew that the fear was not irrational. Beyond that barrier nothing was alive—there must be a reason for that. Why should he imagine that he would be the exception, the one living thing that could cross? After all, when the barrier was built in the first place there must have been plants on both sides of the barrier, and even if it were impassable, life should have continued on both sides. Perhaps forty million years of evolution would have made the flora and fauna of the two sides quite different from each other, but life should have flourished, shouldn't it? Mere isolation couldn't kill off all life with such brutal thoroughness.

It will kill you.

Maybe it will, thought Nafai defiantly. Maybe I'll die. But the Oversoul brought us here for a purpose—to get us to Earth. Even though the Oversoul couldn't think directly of Vusadka, or at least could not speak of it to humans, nevertheless Vusadka had to be the reason the Oversoul had brought them *here,* so close to it. So, one way or another, we have to get past this barrier.

Only *we* are not here. Only *I* am here. And it's quite possible that no one will ever be here again, if I don't succeed this time. If I fail, then that's fine, we'll try *then* to seek another way in. And if I succeed in crossing the barrier and then find that something beyond it kills me before I can get back, well, the others will at least know, from the fact that I never return, that they have to be more careful about getting into this place.

Never return.

He thought of his children—quiet, brilliant Chveya; Zhatva, wise and compassionate; mischievous Motiga; bright-spirited Izuchaya; and the little twins, Serp and Spel. Can I leave them fatherless?

I can if I must. I can because they'll have Luet as their mother, and Shuya and Issya to help her, and Father and Mother too. I can leave them if I must because that would be better than returning to them, having failed to fulfil the purpose of our lives for no reason better than fear of my own death.

He pressed against the barrier. It seemed not to give at all under his hand. The harder he pressed, the more it seemed to slide around under his hand. Yet with all that illusion of sliding, his hand did not actually slip to the right or the left, up or down. In fact, the friction seemed almost perfect—while pressing inward he *couldn't* slide his hand across the surface, even though it felt like the surface was madly sliding in every direction under his hand.

He stepped back, picked up a rock, and lobbed it at the barrier. It hit the invisible wall, stuck for a moment, and then gradually slid downward.

This thing isn't a wall at all, realized Nafai, not if it can grab the stone and then let it slide down. Could it even *sense* what the thing is that struck it, and respond differently for stones than for, say, birds?

Nafai picked up a clod of turf. He saw with satisfaction that there were several grubs and an earthworm in it. He heaved it at the barrier.

Again it stuck for a moment and then began to slide downward. But not at the same rate. The dirt went first, cleanly separated from the roots. Then all the vegetable matter slid down, leaving only the grubs and the earthworm on the face of the barrier. At last they, too, slid down.

This barrier is able to sort out what strikes it, thought Nafai.

It is able to tell the difference between living and dead, between animal and vegetable. Why not between human and nonhuman?

Nafai looked down at his own clothing. What would the barrier make of *that*? He had no idea how the barrier sensed the nature of the things that struck it. Perhaps it could tell before he touched it that he was human. But there was also the chance that the clothing would disguise him a little. Of course, he had no idea whether that would be good or bad.

Again he picked up a rock, but this time he didn't lob it, he threw it as hard as he could. Again it stuck on the barrier.

No, this time it stuck *in* the barrier. Nafai could see by pressing his hands to the barrier on either side of the stone, as it slid downward, that the stone had actually embedded itself in the barrier.

Nafai took his sling from his belt, laid a stone in the pocket, swung it vigorously, and hurled it at the barrier.

It stuck, and for a moment Nafai thought that it was going to behave like the other items.

Instead, the rock clung for a moment and then dropped down *inside* the barrier.

It had crossed! It had had enough momentum and it had passed through. The barrier had slowed it so much that it *almost* didn't make it, but it had kept just enough momentum to make it through. The only trouble was that Nafai had no idea how to hurl himself at the barrier with anything like the force that the stone had had. Even if he could, the force of striking it might kill him.

Maybe the barrier has different rules for humans. Maybe, if I try hard enough, it will *let* me through.

Oh, yes, of *course* it will, Nafai, you fool. The whole barrier system was set up to exclude humans, so of *course* it will let you pass through.

Nafai leaned back against the barrier to think. To his surprise, after a couple of moments the barrier began to slide him down toward the ground. Or rather, it slid his *clothing* toward the ground, taking him with it. It had done nothing of the kind to his hands. When he touched the wall with bare skin, it had let him stay in place and did not move him at all.

With difficulty he pulled himself away from the invisible wall. It *clung* to his clothing as it had held the rocks, the dirt, the grass, the grubs and the worm. There *are* different rules for humans, he realized. This wall *does* know the difference between me and my clothing.

Impulsively he stripped off his tunic, baring his arms. Then he swung his arm as fast as he could, hurling his fist into the barrier. It stung like hitting a brick wall—but it passed through.

It passed through! His fist was on the other side of the barrier, just like the stone that had passed. And where his arm stuck through the barrier he couldn't feel anything unusual at all. He could unflex his fist on the other side and wiggle his fingers, and though the air was perhaps a bit cooler there, there was no pain, no distortion, no obvious problem at all.

Can I follow my hand through the wall?

He pushed forward, and was able to slowly push his arm in right to the shoulder. But when his chest reached the barrier, he was blocked; when he twisted for a better angle, his head also came up against the barrier and stopped.

What if I'm stuck here forever—half in and half out?

In alarm he pulled away, and his arm came out easily enough. He could feel some resistance, but nothing painful, and nothing pressed against his skin to hold him. In a few moments he was free.

He touched the arm and hand that had been on the other side and couldn't find anything wrong with them. Whatever kept life from thriving on the other side hadn't killed him *yet*—if it was a poison, it wasn't immediate, and it certainly wasn't the barrier itself.

He reviewed the rules he had learned for crossing the wall. It had to be bare skin. He had to strike it with some force. And if he wanted his whole body through, he'd have to strike the barrier with his whole body at once.

He stripped off his clothing, folding it neatly and laying it on top of his bow and arrows. Then he piled some rocks on top of them so they wouldn't blow away. Silently he hoped that he would indeed need these clothes again.

For a moment he contemplated leaping face first against the wall, but didn't like the idea—striking it with his fist had felt like hitting a wall, after all, and he didn't relish doing that with his face *or* his groin. Not that it would feel wonderful to do it backfirst either, but it was the lesser of two evils.

He walked a ways along the edge of the barrier until he came to a place where there was a fairly steep hill. He walked to the top and then, after a few deep breaths and a whispered farewell to his family, he ran headlong down the hill. Within moments his running was completely out of control, except that when he neared the wall he planted a foot and flung his body in a wild spin designed to lay him flat against the barrier.

Flat was not what he achieved at all. Instead his buttocks passed through first, and then, as he slowed, his thighs and his body up to the shoulders. His arms and head remained outside the barrier, even as his feet fell through and struck the stony ground on the other side. His heels hurt, but he hardly cared about that, because here he stood, his body inside, his arms and head outside.

I've got to get back outside, he thought, and try it again.

Too late. In the last moments before he stopped moving at all, his shoulders had passed inside. He was stuck again as he had been before, unable to bring his body along to follow his arms. The key difference this time was that his head was outside the barrier, and his chin and ears seemed to be reluctant to follow him inside. Worse, he couldn't even bring his arms all the way inside, because he needed the full weight of his body to pull them through, and with his chin hung up on the barrier he couldn't do it.

This has got to be the stupidest way anyone ever found to die, thought Nafai.

Remember your geometry, he told himself. Remember *anatomy*. My chin may be at too sharp an angle from my neck for me to pull it through, but at the top of my head there's a smooth, continuous curve. If I can just jut my chin forward and pull my head back... assuming that I don't rip my ears off in the process... but those can flex, can't they?

Slowly, laboriously, he tilted his head back and felt himself pulling through. I can do it, he thought. And then my arms will be easy enough.

His head came through all at once, at the end, his face fully inside the barrier. Only his arms continued to protrude through to the outside.

He meant to pull his arms through at once, after resting for just a moment, but as he rested, panting from the exertion, he realized that his need to breathe only increased, and was growing desperate. He was suffocating somehow, even as he drew great draughts of strange-smelling air into his lungs.

Strange-smelling air, dry and cool, and he wasn't getting any oxygen. Even as the panic of suffocation rose within him, his rational mind realized what he should have known all along: The reason that nothing lived behind the barrier was that there was no oxygen in here. It was a place designed to eliminate all decay—and most decay, the rapidest of it, was linked to the presence of oxygen, or oxygen and hydrogen joined to form water. There could be no life, and therefore not even microbes to eat away at surfaces; no water to condense or freeze or flow; no oxidation of metals. And if the atmosphere also failed to support anaerobic life-forms, there'd be little within the barrier to cause decay except sunlight, cosmic radiation, and atomic decay. The barrier had been set up to preserve everything within it, so it could last for forty million years.

This sudden comprehension of the purpose of the barrier was no comfort. For his rational mind was not particularly in control right now. No sooner had he realized that he could not breathe than his hands, still sticking through the barrier, began clutching for air, trying to pull him back through the barrier. But he was in exactly the same situation he had been in before, on the outside, when only an arm was through the wall. He could push his arms deeper into the barrier, but when his face and chest reached the wall, he could go no farther. His hands could touch the breathable air on the other side, but that was all.

Made savage by fear, he beat his head against the barrier, but there simply wasn't leverage—even with panic driving his muscles—to get force enough to push his face through to the breathable air. He really was going to die. Yet he still struck his head against the barrier, again, again, harder.

Perhaps with the last blow he stunned himself; perhaps he was simply weakening from lack of oxygen, or merely losing his balance. Whatever happened, he fell backward, the resistance of the barrier slowing his fall as his arms slipped inside through the invisible wall.

This is fine, thought Nafai. If I can just get to where the slope goes the other way, I can run down toward the barrier and get through again, only this time face first. Even as he thought of this cheerful plan, he knew it wouldn't work. He had spent too long already trying to get through the barrier right here—he had used up too much oxygen inside his own body, and there was no way he had enough left to climb another hill and make another downward run before he blacked out.

His hands came free and he fell backward onto the stony ground.

He must have struck very hard, for to him it sounded like the loudest, longest thunderclap he had ever heard. And then wind tore across his body, picking him up, rolling him, twisting him.

As he gasped in the wind, he could feel that somehow, miraculously, his breathing was *working* again. He was getting oxygen. He was also getting bruised as the wind tossed him here and there. On the stones. On the grass.

On the grass.

The wind had died down to a gusty breeze—he opened his eyes. He had been flung every which way, perhaps fifty yards. It took him a while to orient himself. But, lying on grass, he knew he was outside the barrier. Was the wind another defense mechanism, then, hurling intruders through the wall? Certainly his body was scraped and bruised enough to bear that interpretation. He could still see a few dust devils whirling in the distance, far within the dead land.

He got up and walked to the barrier. He reached out for it, but it wasn't there. The barrier was gone.

That was the cause of the wind. Atmospheres that had not mixed in forty million years had suddenly combined again, and the pressure must not have been equal on both sides of the barrier. It was like a balloon popping, and he had been tossed about like a scrap of the balloon's skin.

Why had the barrier disappeared?

Because a human passed through it completely. Because if the barrier had not come down, you would have died.

To Nafai it seemed like the voice of the Oversoul inside his head.

⟨Yes, I'm here, you know me.⟩

"I destroyed the barrier?"

⟨No, I did. As soon as you passed all the way through, the perimeter systems informed me that a human being had penetrated. All at once I became aware of parts of myself that had been hidden from me for forty million years. I could see all the barriers, knew at once all their history and understood their purpose and how to control them. If you had been some exceptionally determined intruder who didn't belong here, I would have told the perimeter systems to let you die; they would have immediately been hidden from me again. That has happened twice before, in all these years. But you were the very one I meant to bring here, and so the purpose of the barrier was finished. I ordered its collapse, bringing oxygen to you and, therefore, to the rest of this place.⟩

"I appreciate that decision," said Nafai.

⟨It means that decay has reentered this place. Not that it has been wholly excluded. The barrier excluded most harmful radiation, but not all. There *has* been damage. Nothing here was meant to last *this* long. But now that I can find myself instead of running into the perimeter system blocks, maybe I can figure out why I was looping.

⟨Or Issib and Zdorab can figure it out—they're at the Index even now, and the moment you passed through the perimeter, the blocks went down for them, too. I've shown them everything you did, and they're now searching through the new areas of memory opened to all of us.⟩

"Then I made it," said Nafai. "I did it. I'm done."

⟨Don't be a fool. You got through the barrier. The work is only just beginning. Come to me, Nafai.⟩

"To *you?*"

⟨To where I *am*. I have found myself at last, though I had never been able to think of searching for myself until now. Come to me—beyond those hills.⟩

Nafai searched for his clothes and found them scattered—winds that could blow his body around had easily snatched his clothing out from under the stones. What he needed most were shoes, of course, to make the trek across the stony ground. But he wanted the other clothes, too—eventually he'd have to come home.

⟨I have clothing waiting for you there. Come to me.⟩

"Yes, well, I'm coming," said Nafai. "But let me get my shoes on whether you think I need them or not." He also pulled on his breeches, and pulled his tunic over his head as he walked. And the bow—he searched a moment for his bow, and didn't give up until he found a piece of it and realized that it had broken in the wind. He was lucky that none of his bones had done likewise.

At last he headed out in the direction that the Oversoul showed him inside his mind. It took perhaps a half hour of walking—and he wasn't quick, either, his body was so bruised and sore. Finally, though, he crested the last hill and looked down into a perfect bowl-shaped depression in the earth, perhaps two kilometers across. In the center of it, six immense towers rose up out of the ground.

The recognition in his mind was instantaneous: the starships.

He knew the information came from the Oversoul, along with many facts about them. What he was seeing was really protective shells over the tops of the ships, and even then, only about a quarter of each ship rose above the ground. The rest was underground, protected and thoroughly linked into the systems of Vusadka. He knew without having to think about it that the rest of Vusadka was also underground, a vast city of electronics, almost all of it devoted to maintaining the Oversoul itself. All that was visible of the Oversoul were the bowl-shaped devices that pointed at the sky, communicating with the satellites that were its eyes and ears, its hands and fingers in the world.

⟨For all these years, I have forgotten how to see myself, have forgotten where I was and what I looked like. I remember only enough to set certain tasks in motion, and to bring you near here to Dostatok. When the tasks failed, when I began looping, I was helpless to help myself because I couldn't find where to search for the cause. Now Zdorab and Issib and I have seen the place. There has been damage to my memory—forty million years of atomic decay and cosmic radiation has scarred me. The redundancy of my systems has compensated for most of it, but not for damage within primitive systems that I couldn't even examine because they were hidden from me. I have lost the ability to control my robots. They were not meant to last this long, even in a place without oxygen. My robots were reporting to me that they had completed all safety checks on the systems inside the barrier, but when I tried to open the perimeter the system refused because the safety checks had not been completed. So I initiated the safety checks again, and the robots again reported that all was complete, and on and on. And I couldn't discover the loop because all of this was at the level of reflex to me—like the beating of your heart is to you. No, even less obvious. More like the production of hormones by the glands inside your body.⟩

"What would have happened if you could have broken out of the loop?" asked Nafai.

⟨If I could have found myself, I would have recognized the problem and brought you here at once.⟩

"You mean you could have shut down the barrier?"

⟨I wouldn't have needed to. Shutting it down was within your power all along. That's what the Index was for.⟩

"The Index!"

⟨If you had brought the Index with you, you would have met no resistance at any point. No mental aversion, and when you touched the Index to the physical barrier it would have gradually dissolved itself—avoiding the winds, which were not helpful, since they stirred dust into the air.⟩

"But you never told us the Index could do that."

⟨I didn't know it myself. I *couldn't* know it. All I knew was that whoever was coming to the starships would have to have the Index. Then, when the safety checks were completed, the perimeter system would have opened everything up to me and I would have understood what was needed and could have told you what you needed to do.⟩

"So my nearly suffocating myself to death and then getting bruised up in the windstorm wasn't a stupid waste of perfectly good panic."

⟨Forcing your way in here was the only way I would ever have broken out of my loop. I have read the memory of the perimeter system and I am delighted at the way you used the baboons to draw you through.⟩

"Didn't you show me that in my dream? That I needed to follow a baboon through the barrier?"

⟨Dream? Oh, I remember now, you dreamed. No, that wasn't from me.⟩

"From the Keeper, then?"

⟨Why must you look for an outside source? Don't you think your own unconscious mind is capable of giving you a true dream now and then? Aren't you willing to admit to yourself that perhaps it was your own mind that solved this problem?⟩

Nafai couldn't keep himself from laughing in delight. "I did it, then!"

⟨You did it. But you aren't done. *Come* to me, Nafai. I have work for you to do, and tools for you to do it with.⟩

Nafai strode down the hill into the valley of Vusadka. The place of disembarkation. The place where human feet had first touched the soil of Harmony, and where those first settlers had placed the computer that would protect their children from self-destruction for so many years that to them it must have seemed the protection would be forever.

But it would not be forever. It was dying already. And now Nafai was walking among the towers of the starships, the first human being to tread in their footsteps since they built this place. Whatever the Oversoul meant for him to do now, he would do it, and when it was done, human beings would return again to Earth.

TEN
SHIPMASTER

Volemak and Rasa called the community together the moment Zdorab and Issib finished reporting what they had learned from the Index. It had been a long time since a meeting had been called without Elemak knowing in advance what it was about. It worried him. At some level it *frightened* him, but since he could not live with the idea of fear, he interpreted it as anger. He was *angry* that a meeting was called without his knowledge, without Father having sought his advice in advance. It suggested to him that the meeting was Rasa's, somehow—that the women were making some play for power and had deliberately cut him out of the process. Someday the old hag will push too hard, thought Elemak, and *then* she'll find out what power and strength really are—and that she doesn't have any.

This was the filter of interpretation through which Elemak received the morning's news. Chveya and Luet had dreamed . . . ah, yes, the *women* trying to assert their spiritual leadership, the waterseer and her no-doubt-well-coached daughter angling for the old dominance Luet had back in Basilica. And then Nafai, Issib, and Zdorab had searched the Index for information, and Nafai—of course, it had to be Luet's *husband,* the Oversoul's favorite boy—had found a secret place that none of them had visited in all their hunts. Such nonsense! Elemak had covered every kilometer of the surrounding country in his hunts and explorations—there *was* no hidden place.

So Nafai had taken off on a hunt for a non-existent place, and only this morning had figured out a way past all the barriers. Once a human being made it inside, the barrier came down, and now Nafai was walking among the ancient starships, while in the meantime Issib and Zdorab were able to find things through the Index that no one had guessed at before. "This is the landing place," Father explained. "We are living now at the site of the First City, the oldest human settlement on Harmony. Older than the Cities of the Stars. Older than Basilica."

"There was no city here when we came," said Obring.

"But this *place,*" said Father. "We have brought the human race full circle. And even now, Nafai is walking where the ancient fathers and mothers of us all first set their feet upon the soil of Harmony."

Romantic bushwa, thought Elemak. Nafai could be napping in the noonday sun right now for all anybody here knows. The Index was just a way for the weaklings of their company to assert control over the strong ones.

"You know what this means, of course," said Father.

"It means," said Elemak, "that because of what people who have nothing better to do have supposedly learned from a metal ball, our lives are going to be disrupted *again.*"

Father looked at him in surprise. "Disrupted?" he asked. "What do you think we came here *for,* except to prepare for a journey to Earth? The Oversoul itself was caught up in a feedback loop, that's all, and Nyef finally broke through and set it free. The disruption is *over* now, Elya."

"Don't pretend that you don't know what I mean," said Elemak. "We have plenty here. A good life. In many ways a better life than we would have had in Basilica, hard as that is for Obring to believe. We have families now—wives and children—and our lives are good. We work hard, but we're happy, and there's room for our children and our children's children here for a thousand years and more. We have no enemies, we have no dangers beyond the normal mishaps of being alive. And you're telling me that *this* is the disruption, while wasting our time trying to get into *space* is our normal course? Please, don't insult our intelligence."

Elemak could sense easily enough who was with him in this. As he painted the true picture of what this all would mean, he could see Meb and Vas and Obring nodding grimly, and their wives would go along easily enough. Furthermore, he could see that he had put some doubt in the minds of some of the others. Zdorab and Shedemei especially had thoughtful expressions, and even Luet had glanced around at her children when Elemak spoke of how good their lives were, how they faced no danger, how they could have a good future here in Dostatok.

"I don't know what Nafai found, or if he found anything at all," Elemak went on. "I honestly don't care. Nyef is a good hunter and a bright fellow, but he's hardly suited to lead us into some hideous danger using forty-million-year-old starships. My family and I are not going to let my little brother make us waste our time in the foolish pursuit of an impossible project. Nyef's murder of Gaballufix forced us all to leave Basilica as fugitives—but I've forgiven him for that. I certainly *won't* forgive him if he disrupts our lives again."

Elemak kept his expression calm, but inwardly it was all he could do to keep from smiling as he watched Luet's feeble attempt to absolve her husband of guilt for Gaballufix's murder. Her words didn't matter—Elemak knew he had done the job thoroughly with the first blow. Nafai was discredited even before he returned. It was his fault we left the city; we forgive him for that; but nothing he says is going to change the way we live here. Elemak had provided the reasonable justification for total resistance to this latest maneuver by the women and their little male puppet. The proof of his success was the fact that neither Father nor Mother—nor anyone else, except Luet—was mounting any kind of defense, and *she* had been sidetracked onto the issue of why Nafai killed Gaballufix. The idea of starships and hidden lands was dead.

Until Oykib walked out into the middle of the meeting area. "Shame on you all," he said. "Shame on you!"

They fell silent, except Rasa. "Okya, dear, this is an adult conversation."

"Shame on *you,* too. Have you all forgotten that we came here because of the Oversoul? Have you all forgotten that the reason we have such a perfect place to live is that the Oversoul prepared it for us? Have you forgotten that the only reason there weren't already ten cities here was because the Oversoul kept other people away—except us? You, Elemak, could *you* have found this place? Would *you* have known to lead the family across the water and down the island to here?"

"What do you know of this, little boy?" said Elemak scornfully, trying to wrench control back from this *child.*

"No, you wouldn't," said Oykib. "None of you knew *anything* and none of us would *have* anything if the Oversoul hadn't chosen us all and brought us here. I wasn't even born when a lot of this happened, and I was a baby through most of the rest, so why do *I* remember, when you older ones—my older and wiser brothers and sisters, my *parents*—seem to have forgotten?"

His high piping voice grated on Elemak's nerves. What was going on here? He knew how to neutralize all the adults—he hadn't counted on having to deal with Father's and Rasa's new spawn as well. "Sit down, child," said Elemak. "You're out of your depth."

"We're *all* out of our depth," said Luet. "But only Oykib seems to have remembered how to swim."

"No doubt you coached him on what to say," said Elemak.

"Oh, yes, exactly," said Luet. "As if any of us knew in advance what *you* would say. Though we should have. I thought these matters were all settled long ago, but we should have known that you would never cease to be ambitious."

"Me!" shouted Elemak, leaping to his feet. "*I'm* not the one who staged this phony visit to an invisible city, which we know about only because of supposed reports from a metal ball that only *you* can interpret!"

"If you would lay your hand on the Index," said Father, "the Index would gladly speak to you."

"There's nothing I want to hear from a computer," said Elemak. "I tell you again, I will not put my family's lives and happiness at risk because of supposed instructions from an invisible computer that these *women* persist in worshipping as a god!"

Father rose to his feet. "I see that you are disposed to doubt," he said. "Perhaps it was a mistake to share the good news with everyone. Perhaps we should have waited until Nafai came back, and we could all go to the place he found, and see what he has seen. But I thought that there should be no secrets among us, and so I insisted that we tell the story now, so no one could say later that they were not informed."

"A little late to try the honesty approach, isn't it, Father?" asked Mebbekew. "You said yourself that when Nafai left day before yesterday, he was searching for this hidden place and he *thought* it was probably where the first humans disembarked from their starships. Yet you didn't think of telling us all *then,* did you?"

Father glanced at Rasa, and Elemak felt completely confirmed in his suspicions. The old man was dancing to the old lady's tune. She had insisted it be kept secret before, and had probably counseled him against telling now, knowing her.

Nevertheless, it was time for Elemak's next move—he had to seize the high ground, now that Oykib had undercut his previous position. "Let's not be unfair," said Elemak. "We've only heard *about* Nafai. We don't have to decide anything or *do* anything yet. Let's wait until he gets home, and see how we feel then." Elemak turned to Oykib, who still stood in the middle of the group. "As for you, I'm proud that my next-to-last brother has such fire in him. You're going to be a real man, Oykib, and when you grow old enough to understand the issues instead of blindly following what others tell you, your voice will be well listened to in council, I can assure you."

Oykib's face reddened—with embarrassment, not anger. He was young enough to have heard only the clear praise and completely missed the subtle insult. Thus I wipe *you* out, too, Okya, dear brother, without your even realizing it.

"I say this meeting is over," said Elemak. "We'll meet again when Nafai comes back, except, of course, for the little conspiratorial meetings in the Index House where all this was cooked up in the first place. I have no doubt that *those* meetings will continue unabated." And with those words he put a sinister meaning into any kind of conversation that Rasa's party entered into, thus deeply weakening *them*.

These poor people—they thought they were so clever, until they actually came up against somebody who understood how power worked. And because it was Elemak who dismissed the meeting, and in effect announced the next one, he had gone a long way toward stripping Father of his leadership in Dostatok. The only test now was whether the meeting actually broke up with Elemak's departure. If he walked away, but the meeting went on substantially intact, then Elemak would have a much tougher time establishing leadership—in fact, he would have lost ground today.

But he needn't have worried. Meb arose almost at once and, with Dol and their children in tow, followed him away from the meeting; Vas and Obring and their wives also got up, and then Zdorab and Shedemei. The meeting was over—and it was over because Elemak had said it was over.

Round one for me, thought Elemak, and I'll be surprised if that isn't the whole match. Poor Nafai. Whatever you're doing out in the woods, you're going to come home and find all your plots and plans in disarray. Did you think you could really face me down from a distance and *win*?

There was no writing anywhere, no signs, no instructions.

⟨No one needs instructions here. I am with you always in this place, showing you what you need to know.⟩

"And they were content with this?" asked Nafai. "All of them?" His voice was so loud in the silence of this place, as he scuffed along the dustless catwalks and corridors, making his way downward, downward into the earth.

⟨They knew me. They had made me, had programmed me. They knew what I could do. They thought of me as—their library, their all-purpose instruction manual, their second memory. In those days I knew only what they had taught me. Now I have forty million years of experience with human beings, and have reached my own conclusions. In those days I was much more dependent on *them*—I reflected back to them their own picture of the world.⟩

"And their picture—was it wrong?"

⟨They did not understand how much of their behavior was animal, not intellectual. They thought that they had overcome the beast in them, and that with my help all their descendants would drive out the beast in a few generations—or a few hundred, anyway. Their vision was long, but no human being can have *that* long a vision. Eventually the numbers, the dimensions of time, become meaningless.⟩

"But they built well," said Nafai.

⟨Well but not perfectly. I have suffered forty million years of cosmic and nuclear radiation that has torn apart much of my memory. I have vast redundancy, and so in my data storage there has been no meaningful loss. Even in my programming, I have monitored all changes and corrected them. What I could not monitor was the area hidden from myself. So when the programs there decayed, I could not know it and could not compensate for it. I couldn't copy those areas and restore them when any one copy decayed.⟩

"So they didn't plan well at all," said Nafai, "since those programs were at your very core."

⟨You mustn't judge them harshly. It never occurred to them that it would take even a million years for their children's children to learn peace and be worthy to enter this place and learn all about advanced technologies. How could they guess that century after century, millennium after millennium, the humans of Harmony would never learn peace, would never cease trying to rule over one another by force or deception? I was never meant to keep this place closed off for even a million years, let alone forty million. So they built well indeed—the flaws and failures in my secret core were not fatal, were they? After all, you're here, aren't you?⟩

Nafai remembered his terror when he had had no air to breathe, and wasn't sure that they hadn't cut it all a little fine.

"Where are *you?*" asked Nafai.

⟨All around you.⟩

Nafai looked, and saw nothing in particular.

⟨The sensors there, in the ceiling—those are how I see you right now, and hear you, besides my ways of seeing through your eyes, and hearing your words before you say them. Behind all these walls are bank after bank of static memory—all of that is my self. The machinery pumping air through these underground passages—they are also me.⟩

"Then why did you need me at all?" asked Nafai.

⟨You are the one who broke me out of my loop and opened up my vision to include my own heart, and you ask me that?⟩

"Why do you need me *now?*"

⟨I also need you—all of you—because the Keeper has sent you dreams. The Keeper wants you, and so I will bring you.⟩

"Why do you need *me?*" he asked, clarifying the question even further.

⟨Because my robots were all controlled by a place in my memory that has become completely untrustworthy. I have shut them down because they were reporting falsely to me. No one ship of these six has a fully uncorrupted memory. I need you